The Lucky Country

Rose M Cullen

In memory of my father, Michael Cullen, whose life,
more colourful than any fiction, inspired this tale.

There's something here a man can't cheat.

BEN DOWN AND THE OLD TIME

Old time, before, whole world sleeping. Everything quiet, nothing move, nothing grow. Animals sleep under the earth. People sleeping under the earth. F J Holdens and telephones sleep. Desperate Dan and Sputnik sleep.

One day the big rainbow snake she wake up and she push up, up to the top and her push everything away, even them Boeing airplanes. And then she move her great body round, twist and turn, make tracks all over the country. She move one side, other side, make hills and valleys and she force her way into the rocks and her track make deep gorge.

After, she tired, she coil up in cave and she dreaming. When she wake up, she call to the frogs, them sleeping under the earth. They coming with big bellies all full of water. Rainbow snake tickle 'em and frogs they laughing, make noise like thunder. They laugh and laugh, the water's coming out their mouths. Big water. Fill all the tracks the rainbow snake made. All the water is gone from their stomachs. The frogs they lost their voices, when a sound come back it is, CRAKK, CRAKK! CRAKK, CRAKK! And that's how rivers and lakes and waterholes and billabongs were made. Then the grass 'n trees grow and the earth fill with all the life we see today.

When he was little, Binni tickle Maali's stomach when I tell him that one. She laugh and laugh.

And Binni say, 'Where's the water?'

And Maali say, 'Hey, I'm not a frog!

And Binni he say, 'But you got big round tummy mummy, same like frog!'

And Maali say, 'That's baby, her name Mindui.'

But when Mindui born she already gone with the ancestor spirits and from the belly of Maali there's only coming tears.

PART ONE

Killpool Hill

FIELD OF GOLD

There was nothing like that wheat. The buyer that came to appraise it, a man from Cork, said that it was wheat so good they'd use it for seed.

'And you a first-time farmer, Mr Glendon, it's like you were born to it.'

'I'd go every summer to my cousins near Mountmellick.' Patrick responded not wishing to give the impression that he was a complete ignoramus.

'That's a grand crop.' The buyer said in that sing song way they have down in Cork.

It was a day when the sun shone and a light breeze ruffled the blonde hair of the wheat. It was so gorgeous Patrick wanted to dive right in and muss himself up in it. But pleased as the buyer was with the crop Patrick didn't want to let his guard slip. The man could try and fleece him with the price.

'When are you planning to harvest her?'

'I was thinking tomorrow I'd make a start.'

The buyer made a show of ruminating, reminding Patrick of nothing so much as his cow Jenny chewing the cud and looking at you in that way that said she wouldn't be budged.

'Or maybe after the weekend.'

'A few more days of the like of this sun would be a grand thing right enough. You must be the envy of all your neighbours. I see O'Shaughnessy over on the hill beyond watching us this long time and wishing he hadn't so many fields in hay.'

'Wheat like this is hard work,' Patrick reminded nodding up towards his neighbour, 'and there are those less disposed to the effort.'

'Or the risk, the way you've given all over to it.' The buyer nodded, 'These old farmers, they're needing youngsters like you to put the bejasus up them.' And the man allowed himself the sliver of a grin. 'I like your spirit Mr Glendon. What say we take it all?'

'I'd say that was very fine.'

The man extended his hand.

Patrick kept his in his pockets. 'Depending on the price.'

They haggled in the friendly way of men who know that the sale is already agreed and can play with a figure or two here and there.

'You drive a hard bargain.' The buyer shook his head and clicked his teeth as he made the final concession.

Patrick allowed himself a smile knowing full well it was a fair and middling price.

They shook hands and the deal was done.

That evening you would have taken Patrick Glendon for the happiest man alive as he whirled Maeve around the kitchen, their two young children yapping with excitement at their heels.

'Won't you be glad you married me now, Maeve McMahon?!' Laughter gurgling in his throat and his heart beating with pride.

THE GYPSY CARAVAN

Nieve's special place at Killpool Hill Farm was the gypsy caravan. You had to go right around a field golden with wheat. On the far side, through some trees, where once she had surprised a fox with glittering dark eyes, there was a track and this is where the gypsy caravan was. It had been abandoned. All Nieve knew about Gypsies was from a song that her friend Carmel Marie sang,

My mother said I never should
Play with the Gypsies in the wood

The caravan was all rotted and full of squirming beetles and had only one broken wheel on its side with the weeds growing up through it. But you could still see flowers painted around the door, green and red and white. Inside smelled damp and fusty and there was an old rusty pot with a hole in the bottom and all kinds of rubbish. Straightaway Nieve had decided to tidy it up and turn it into her hidey hole. The only person she let come in was Carmel Marie, who was one year older and lived next door.

And my father said that if I did
He'd rap my head with the teapot-lid!

Nieve heard a tractor trundling up the lane with a putt-putt-bang-bang but paid it no attention. Her thoughts were consumed with The Micky Mouse Club. She would need to learn a song if she was to become a mouseketeer. Her mother was always singing as she padded around the big flag-stoned kitchen, *I just blew in from the Windy City, the Windy City is mighty pretty but it ain't got what we got, no*

11

siree. That's as much as her mammie ever sang, it was about a cowgirl called Clammity Jane. Nieve wanted to be a cowgirl when she grew up. Her da said she could be one right there in Wicklow. He would lift her up on to the back of Jenny when they brought the two cows in from the field.

'Giddy up there, girl!' her da would say and give Jenny a slap on the bottom and she would do a little run, with Nieve bouncing about on top holding tight to the rope, scared and excited all at the same time.

'… the Windy City is mighty pretty but it ain't got what we got—'

Another voice cut in, '—I'm a telling you boys, I ain't a swapping half of Deadwood for the whole of Illinois!'

Nieve was startled to see Raymond poking his head in at the door and grinning at her. Raymond was one of Carmel Marie's big brothers. Carmel Marie had six brothers. Her mother cried with happiness when she was born because she would have a daughter to help in the house and buy ribbons for. But Mr O'Shaughnessy was not so happy because he was a seventh son and the seventh son of a seventh son was some sort of magic. Raymond was number three and Carmel Marie's favourite brother because he read stories from his comic and jigged her on his knee.

'So, this is your little den, is it?' Raymond said and Nieve bristled knowing that her friend must have told him about their secret place.

'Ye have it nice.' Raymond flicked his quiff and nodded to the old crate, a tea towel begged from her mother for a table cloth.

'Is Carmel Marie with you?' Nieve asked.

'She's away into town after a communion dress.'

Carmel Marie was always going on about her First Holy Communion.

'Ye's are all on ye're ownsome; no one to play wit ye's?'

'I'm all right on my own.'

'Ah, but you'd prefer to have someone to play wit, wouldn't ye?' Raymond stepped inside, blocking out the sunshine. One of the boards of the floor began to crack under the

12

weight of his wellie boot. 'Jaze, this old place is falling apart.'

Nieve wanted to shout at him to get out, he was too big.

'How about we's have a little game?'

'What game?' Nieve asked, worried it might be a game that she didn't know the rules.

'Oh, I don't know ... you could be the doctor and I could be your patient.'

Nieve frowned, Carmel Marie must have told him that this was their favourite game and that she was always the doctor because she had two doctor uncles and one of them had saved John John's life when he had appendicitis. Nieve felt annoyed, she didn't think she would tell her anything ever again because of her big blabbermouth.

'G'wan Nieve, I'll lie down and you can examine me, how would that be?' Raymond stretched himself out on the creaking boards, chuckling like it was a big joke, and Nieve wondered if maybe he was laughing at her. 'Ah, come on, get your stethoscope out and give me a good going over, I've got a terrible pain down below.' He was nodding encouragement, smiling and serious at the same time. 'Oh, Jaze doctor it's killin' me!' He groaned and rolled about a bit clutching his stomach. Nieve had to admit that he was much better at being a patient than Carmel Marie.

She reached behind for her tin, a big round one with an old-fashioned picture of a soldier in a red uniform and a woman who carried an umbrella. Inside the tin were all the found things which Nieve had collected. She pulled out the piece of tube which was ideal for being a doctor.

Raymond widened his eyes with worry, 'Be careful what you do with that thing now doc.'

He unbuttoned the few buttons that were left on his shirt and straightaway Nieve could see he didn't have a vest on.

'The pain is right here.' He rubbed his tummy. 'In fact, doctor I think it's moved down a bit now.' He fiddled with his buckle. 'You'll need to get a proper look.'

Nieve could see that the thick leather belt was holding his trousers up because they were too big for him. Carmel Marie

13

said she was the only one in the family that didn't have 'hand-me-downs', being the only girl.

'Do you know what a cock is Doctor Nieve?'

Nieve nodded, Sultan Ahmed in the chicken coop. Nieve smiled as she drew to mind her mother, the chickens would rush towards her thrusting their fierce little beaks and her mammie would squeal with terror and fling the bucket of grains in one go and quickly shut the wire gate behind her again. Nieve laughed out loud thinking about it.

'Jaze you're a one. But it'll be our secret now, d'ye hear me?

Nieve was puzzled, wondering what exactly the secret was.

'C'mon now and put your hand down here doc, I've a terrible ache.'

It was then that the big stones fell out of the sky. One minute it was bright as bright and then it was dark as dark. For a few seconds there was just a pitter patter on the roof and then it was banging and crashing above them louder than any drum Nieve had ever heard.

'What the feck?' Raymond said, and shot up, nearly tripping over Nieve as he rushed to the doorway yanking his belt through the buckle.

'Feck, feck and double feck!'

Nieve tried to squeeze her head around the side of him to see what was causing the commotion.

All around the caravan, in the ditch and on the lane, she could see that it was covered in little white stones with more bouncing off the ground as big as marbles. Raymond pushed back as they were hitting him.

'Jasus, Mary and Joseph!'

Nieve had never seen anything like it before. 'What is it?'

'Hail, is what it is, feckin hailstones the size of gobstoppers!'

You could hardly hear yourself for the racket on the roof so they continued to watch in stunned silence as the onslaught continued. It seemed to Nieve that everything would be battered to the ground and never be able to get up again.

As suddenly as the hail started it stopped and moments later the sun was even brighter than before and the stones sparkled and glittered and Nieve thought it was the most beautiful sight that she had ever seen.

Raymond jumped up on the tractor. 'Come on y'old bastard!' He shouted. At last it spluttered and shuddered and then chugged up the lane. Raymond hadn't even turned to say goodbye, Nieve felt a twinge of resentment.

Then she saw that the stones were melting and a drip fell on her nose from the caravan roof. And suddenly she felt a happiness tingling all through her because she knew another line of her song and she would always remember it because of the hailstones.

'I'm a telling you boys, I ain't a swapping half of Deadwood for the whole of Illynoise!'

THE HARD LIFE

The devastation was total. Field after field. Hailstones beating his eyes shut as he ran wildly through their barrage. Piercing him like a latter-day St. Sebastian. Then, blinking in the shattering return of sunlight Patrick looked around in horror. It was as if a clumsy oaf of a giant had danced all over his land. Everywhere the sheaves lay flattened, broken and massacred. Picking through the sodden wheat he found a handful that might be called dry. For desperate moments he wondered whether they might rescue the best of it, but how? Harvest it by hand? Even as he held the precious seeds in his palm, he could feel the scream which was vibrating through his body.

'Why God? Why God ...' he was still muttering when, cap in hand, Joe appeared beside him.

'Mr Glendon ... you better put this on.' He was proffering an old leather jacket. 'You could catch your death with that wind rising up off the sea.'

'Why? Why?'

Joe shook his head. 'Sure, who would know the rhyme or reason, only God.'

'I'm ruined Joe.' Patrick whispered.

That evening Patrick sat in the deep shadows of the hammock swing gently rocking back and forth, Maeve's small white hand clenched tight in his with the effort to keep his reddening tears at bay

'I just blew in ...' Nieve danced across the lawn.

Patrick's eyes pricked.

'... ain't got what we got ...'

Patrick bit his lip.

'... the whole of Illynoise! Dah Illy noise!' Nieve twirled

16

and grinned, a drowning sun bathing her in an orange glow, flaxen hair on fire.

Patrick's eyesight blurred as swaying before him he saw his field of golden wheat.

UPSIDE DOWN

Nieve lay on her back staring up at the sky. A frond of grass tickled her ear. The grass was long but no one would be cutting it now. She felt dizzy as she watched the thin wisps of cloud scudding across her eyeline. She could imagine the earth as a spinning ball and felt the movement beneath her, reeling and wondering if the earth stopped spinning what would happen, would everyone just drop off and float around in space? She clutched at the thick grass on either side. Nothing felt stable anymore that much she knew; everything was spinning around and around and it was hard to keep your feet on the ground.

That was the very thing her mammie said, 'Why couldn't you just keep your feet on the ground instead of always racing ahead.'

'Rewards come to those who take risks.'

Her mother slammed the tea pot on the table. 'And what happens when you fail?'

'Maybe it's a blessing in disguise.'

'You call it a blessing to be ruined with two small children and another one on the way!' Her mammie started to tremble. 'Where will we go? Back to Dublin? Will your brother take you back into the family business?'

'I'm not going back anywhere with my tail between my legs. We're off to The Lucky Country.'

'What are you talking about, Patrick?' Her mother frowned as though her da were being loopy.

'Australia is what I'm talking about!'

Australia, the word shot through Nieve like a shockwave and now she kept turning it over and over in her mind, Aus-tra-lia, tumbling through kangaroos and koala bears, Aus-tra-lia rolling over gum trees and boomerangs that don't come

18

back. The other side of the world.

If you dug a hole and kept digging then one day you would come out in Australia. On the beach her cousin Sean started to dig a hole and at the end of the day it was above his head but there was still no sign of Australia. The tide had turned with remarkable speed and every so often a crashing wave would carry all the way up spilling over the edge of the hole, so they decided on a swimming pool instead and ran with buckets whooping into the sea to fill her up. As she lay on the lawn feeling the blades of grass prickle her bare legs and arms Nieve wondered whether if you were to dig all the way to Australia your head or your feet would pop out first.

THE VAN

The van from Pierson's Shipping Co. had been and gone taking all the possessions they would keep; far too many to Patrick's mind. Maeve's brother Kevin had arrived in his Mercedes saloon the week before and collected herself and the children.

'Well this is a fresh start Pat, we're all agreed on that.'

Patrick never liked being called 'Pat', it felt diminutive coming from Kevin, he almost expected to get a 'pat' on the back along with the familiarity.

'And what are your plans when you get to Sydney?'

Patrick didn't have any plans. He felt annoyed. Kevin was the kind of man who liked everything in order, just like his own life; school, college, surgeon, marriage to childhood sweetheart, four children, big house in Ballyboden.

'They say there's plenty of opportunities.'

'Well, you're a hard worker, we all know that.' And sure enough, Kevin gave him a pat on the back.

That morning Joe had been to collect his final wages, cap in hand, his little terrier Flan at his heels. 'If it isn't too much trouble Mr Glendon ...'

'You've earned it Joe,' Patrick assured him counting out the crisp pound notes. 'I'm only sorry ...'

'Right enough ...' Joe shook his head as one in mourning, for surely that's what they were about. 'There was never the like of that wheat ...'

The two men stood in silence.

Joe scuffed his boot against a discarded tyre. 'That O'Shaughnessy's a lucky bastard.'

Thieving bastard, Patrick could have added. For that was what galled him more than anything, the price he had been forced to agree, to shake hands on as O'Shaughnessy eyed him with his sly winking grin. After all the hard work, every morning up with the lark, to hand it all over to that squinty-eyed robber and the big lumps of sons he had. All Patrick's dreaming and scheming to come to nothing, less than nothing, to get less than he'd paid and ploughed in himself, it was enough to stick in any man's throat, and he wondered whether he'd ever get rid of the sour taste.

'Has he offered you a job?'

Joe shook his head, 'I wouldn't work for the likes of him for all the tea in China, Mr Glendon. I've a sister down in Tinahely and sure ...'

'There's always work for a good man such as yourself.'

They edged into the shelter of the barn as a squall of wind blew a flurry of leaves and spitting rain across the yard, Flan sniffing into the corners, tail wagging.

'I hear Australia's a great place for wheat.'

'And sheep; But my farming days are behind me now.'

'Tis a pity, you've a feel for the land more than many that's born to it.'

'You need more than that though, don't you Joe? She's a hard mistress.'

'Right enough ...' Joe slapped his thin scrap of a cap back on his head, 'I'd better be on my way, Mr Glendon, God be wit you and yours.'

Patrick nodded, 'And yerself.'

Joe shouldered his pack and gave a short sharp whistle; Flan flew out after him.

Patrick watched the final tip of Joe's forelock before he disappeared over the cattle grilles and it was then that he felt truly alone for the first time since the debacle. A gut-wrenching wave of despair passed over him, his knees shaking under him and big tears welling up, brimming and spilling over even as he tried to gulp them down. He wiped them away roughly and shook his head, shook out his whole body like a wet rag. This was no time to be maudlin he admonished himself as he ran a hand over the tractor engine still with the gleam of newness about it. Part of the deal, all the animals and the machinery thrown in with the price. No point resenting that it wasn't himself starting out with such a sweet deal. Debts had to be paid and that was the end of it. He was a free man now, in the clear. Enough for the passage to Australia with a bit to get them started and, by god, he would grasp that country with both hands and he would make his way.

The more he thought of Australia the more the smallness of Ireland irritated him. A feudal backwater was what it was.

The anger surged up in him to recall the day Father Flynn arrived at the door in his brand-new Hillman Imp. Maeve fussed over him with the best tea set and he scoffed the cake she had baked for their tea and insisted on her calling Patrick in from the field for a *wee word*. And what was the *wee word* but to remark that the dues to the church were late; an oversight necessitating a visit, implying an inconvenience no doubt.

For Father Flynn to stand in his own front parlour and tantamount to demand *the usual quarter* with a crumb of cake still in the crease of his quivering chins made Patrick's blood boil. The greed of the church and this priest's smug and self-righteous air.

The colour rising in his cheeks Patrick went to the bureau and withdrawn a sheaf of notes, extracted a couple and held them up to Father Flynn. 'Will this do you?'

'If it is all you can spare at the moment, I've rather caught you on the hop, I know.' Father Flynn remarked with a patronising sniff, 'By the way it's customary to place the contributions in an envelope.'

Patrick threw the money down on the sideboard, 'Take it or leave it and it's the last you'll ever get from me.'

The priest bristled at the affront, chins wobbling over his dog collar as his mouth worked open and shut. At last he picked up the notes and slipped them into his inner pocket. 'God sees all.' he intoned pompously as he lumbered off.

On Sunday Patrick found an excuse not to go to Mass. But of course, it was only those he loved who were hurt in his absence. Father Flynn pointedly read out the generous offerings to Holy Mother Church from the local landowners and left Patrick's paltry contribution to the last. Maeve's cheeks had flamed as the parishioners shifted in their seats and strained to cast sneaking glances in her direction. The whisper of gossip followed her out of the very gates of St. Fintan's and by the time she returned home to Killpool Hill she was livid.

'How can I show my face at Mass again?'

'Don't.' Patrick flared back. 'It's a lot of nonsense stories for children anyway.'

'You may have lost your faith, Patrick Glendon, but I certainly haven't.' She stomped off in a huff.

'What stories da?' Nieve piped in, curious as ever.

He swept her up into his arms and gave her one of his giant bear hugs, which made her squeal. 'I'll tell you stories Nieve, stories will make your hairs stand on end!' and he growled the giant bear growl and she laughed and squirmed out of his arms like a silvery fish and ran off to hide in one of her secret places.

God sees all. The words rang again in Patrick's ears. Involuntarily he looked skyward half expecting to catch the glint of a narrowed eye. He was brought back down to earth by the sound of the old Rover grinding up the drive. Desmond sat up front with the old man and one of the other boys was in the back, Gerry or Raymond, he wasn't sure which.

With an effort, O'Shaughnessy hoisted himself out and cast a proprietorial eye around the yard, the barns, the outbuildings and the old dilapidated Georgian house, which Patrick had dreamed of restoring to former glory. Desmond sprang out of the passenger side, careful all the same not to knock the top of his ridiculous quiff. He clapped his hands and rubbed them together doing nothing to hide his glee.

Patrick felt reluctant to step forward and greet them but knew he must. 'Good day to you.'

O'Shaughnessy grunted a greeting in response.

'Grand day, Mr Glendon.' grinned Desmond, 'That bit of rain's passed.'

'I've the keys here, will show you round.' Patrick walked

23

past them wanting to get the business over with.

Inside, Desmond was poking his head in cupboards and testing the furniture. 'It's a draughty old place but we could make it cosy right enough.' He said almost shyly.

'Des here is after getting himself engaged.' O'Shaughnessy offered by way of explanation. The other boy sniggered and Desmond made a play of a left hook towards him.

As they were going up the stairs Desmond stooped and picked up a plastic toy cowboy. 'One of yours left behind?'

'Keep it.' Patrick offered and then a sudden image of Nieve running down the stairs yelling 'Hi Ho Silver!' flashed through his mind and he had to stop himself from asking for the return of the little cowboy figure.

'Yourself and Nancy may have use for it soon enough.' The boy directed to his brother and dodged another cuffing.

Outside a great orange sun was sinking with a faint mist lending an eerie autumnal sheen to the turning trees. They'd finished the tour of the outbuildings. The boy was to stay and milk the two cows. Old Jenny stamped and objected as Desmond made a quick examination of her mouth, Minnie was skittish and wild eyed like she knew something was afoot, Patrick patted her rump in a gesture of comfort.

'Well, you'd all the big ideas, Mr Glendon. Isn't it the pity they've come to this pass?'

Patrick held his tongue.

'We'll be sticking to the old ways wont we boys?' O'Shaughnessy concluded with satisfaction.

'I'll be away so.' Patrick headed towards his car. He would be on the night ferry on the morrow and then all of this could be put behind him.

The boy, Raymond it was, saluted, 'Be sure to give my best to young Nieve, Mr Glendon, she's a character, so she is.' And there was something in his tone that made Patrick feel a momentary unease he couldn't quite put his finger on.

Patrick forced himself not to look back as he rattled over the grilles, out past the rusting gate and the wooden sign which he had made and painted himself, Killpool Hill, until he turned at last into the darkening lane.

BEN DOWN BUILDS A HUMPY

This camp Billangilil a dump. One standing pipe. One long drop for shitting. This mob no good. Fencers working on dingo netting, they drinking mob. Too much whiskey. The women they no good, same like men. The kids wild like dogs. They give up the Tribal Law, now they have no Law.

Maali want to build own humpy, away from this camp. These humpies no good, boards and tin sheets, too hot. Better new one. We been fighting. Maali don't want to come near wadjelas. She want to live in the old ways, far away.

'Where that be?' I say, 'On the moon?'

I think she too much dreaming. Too late now, this white fella world here now. We been losing old ways. Been moving all over country. Now this time we stay. Mission school here, Binni he's clever fella. He can go school, learn new way.

Boss Anderson come talk to me 'bout the job. He find me putting up wurlie in this clearing. I been showing Binni how it's done. Put the opening to the East, catch the sunrise. Boss Anderson want to know what I'm doing. I tell him this is where we going to camp, good shade, and away from the other mob.

'You're going to live in that?!' 'im shock.

I tell him I gonna build better humpy.

'That's the camp back there, Ben.' He says. 'You've got accommodation.' His eyes narrow. 'I can't have your lot sticking up shacks wherever you like, you'd be all over my property.'

I shuffle 'bout. Maali watching me close.

'We camping here Boss. That's the way it got to be. Won't be no trouble.'

Boss Anderson he looks at me, he one top-notch bastard,

25

'You want this job or not?'

'Yes Boss.'

'I should tell you to sling your hook, Ben Down.'

'Yes Boss.'

'Don't go cutting any of these trees. And I want this place just as you've found it when you leave, which might be sooner than you think.'

'Yes Boss.'

'You better be a good worker, is all I can say.' Then he's look at Maali and he say he wants her to do cooking 'n cleaning up at the Big House. I say she's not going up the Big House.

'You know she won't get no rations then?'

I can see he real mad and I don't want tell him Maali won't work for no wadjelas.

'We'll be fine Boss.'

26

UNDER THE BRIDGE

The immigration official looked up from examining Patrick's passport and gave him the once over. Patrick shuffled his feet, not sure why he was feeling so nervous, perhaps it was just that anyone in officialdom made him feel uneasy. The ship had been full of memories for him of his own short career as a cadet officer at sea.

'That's an interesting profession you've put down here, Mr Glendon. Does Australia have need of a 'Gentleman' do you think?'

'I'd have hoped a Gentleman would be welcome anywhere.' Patrick tried not to sound too confrontational.

'Never heard of a 'gentleman Paddy' before, mostly we get them straight from the bog, thick as two short planks and full of grog—bad as the abos some of them.' The man stared aggressively at Patrick.

Patrick felt his cheek twitch. 'Indeed?'

'But I can see that you're cut of a different cloth Mr Glendon, you're a real Gentleman isn't that right?'

'I'd like to think so, yes.'

'And what does a bloke have to do to be a Gentleman?'

Patrick hesitated, not sure if this man had the power to actually turn him away at the last, make him walk right back up the gangway to work his passage home.

'He just is.' He said at last, firmly.

The man's eyes narrowed. Then he held out the passport. 'Welcome to Australia mate.'

The December heat was a killer. Even with the window wide open and the ancient fan whirring round with a regular clunk Patrick was wiping the sweat from his brow every two minutes. He tossed and turned for most of the night unable to sleep and now was trying to lie as still as he could to minimise the combined discomfort of the heat and the sagging mattress. The first couple of frenetic days he spent finding this cheap but decent enough hotel after the first had him eaten alive with the fleas. Then the dispiriting hunt for a job. Five days in and still no prospects. That was the other cause of the sleepless nights.

He had met with a cousin of Niall's in a pub on the previous evening. After a mix up over pints and schooners accompanied by guffaws from the regulars, he settled on a midi of the thin light beer and taken it outside to enjoy the breeze off the water. You had to admit that Sydney was a fine city, draped around the elegant shoulders of the harbour. He felt his spirits calming at last as he admired the yachts gliding across the ruffle of waves and fancied that one day it would be himself out there with Maeve's hand on the tiller whilst he expertly tacked about, both of them tanned and bleached blonde. God, but he missed her.

A shadow cut across his view, a short thin strip of a man, shirt and tie loosened at the collar, jacket slung over his shoulder and carrying a well-worn briefcase.

'Patrick Glendon?'

Patrick rose awkwardly to his feet, extending his hand.

'Austin Farrell. So ye're just arrived off the boat?'

Patrick nodded, noting that the Dublin accent was still discernable.

'An old school pal of Niall's?'

'We were at The Dominicans.'

'Janey, I'd say that was grim. Himself was only in short pants when I saw him last, I've been out here since the end of the war.'

'Can I get you a drink?'

'Whatever you're having.' Patrick turned to go inside with Austin's voice following. 'And a Whiskey Chaser, sure why not?'

Austin was an Insurance Agent for a Sydney based company covering most of New South Wales which meant he spent a lot of time on the road. For much of the evening he bemoaned the long hours to make any decent commission.

'Sydney's civilized enough but twenty miles in any direction and they're barbarians, Red Necks the lot of them.'

After several rounds of drinks, most of which Patrick paid for, it became clear the man was a drunk and wasn't in any position to help. Patrick was on his own. That was the way it should be anyway; he didn't need a leg up from anyone. Still, he had imagined that it would be easier than it had proved to pick up a decent job in the Land of Opportunity. There was the rub, jobs were to be had, but of the menial sort. And with half a dozen Poms, Ities and Balts going for every decent opening along with the Aussies themselves his luck hadn't been in.

His options seemed to be narrowing in front of his eyes. So much for the expensive boarding school education. He had hated every minute of his time there and not just because the war was on and even in neutral Ireland there was shortage and cold-water showers. It didn't help that he was in the wake of two of his brothers, John, with his scholarly achievements, had gone on to the law and Frank was captain of the rugby team when he arrived but far too busy with ambitions to lift the inter-schools' trophy to be any protection against the bully boys.

Patrick ran away, slipped off as a gaggle of boys crossed the yard after the morning Latin. Climbed the sopping ivy over the wall, scuffing his new shoes in the process and walked what seemed interminable miles along muddy roads until eventually he had been able to hitch a lift in a pig lorry, not a moment too soon as the first globules of rain spattered the windscreen.

'Wont yer da have yer hide?' The driver asked with a yellow toothed grin as he was fumbling on the dashboard for yet another Sweet Afton.

Patrick gulped and looked out the window at the rain lashed winter fields, a queasy feeling in the pit of his stomach. He imagined his parents would understand, see at once that he had been sorely mistreated. Bring him in to sit beside the fire with a steaming cup of hot chocolate brought up by Eileen, the skivvy. Now he wondered. He glanced over at the thick-necked driver with his rough stubble, the ciggie hanging off his bottom lip and could see him as a man who would tan the hide off any son who gave him gyp. But his own father had never raised a hand. No.

His mother would fuss over him when she saw the bruises on his shins where he'd been kicked by Quinn, and the strap marks across his hands from the belting he'd received from Brother Anthony because he let out a yelp in consequence and been charged with fooling in class. He could still see Quinn's grinning face as he was called up to the front of the class and asked to stretch out his hand. His first time and he had been unprepared for the searing pain, it was all he could do to keep the gasp of shock in check. Knowing what was to come with the second strike he squeezed his eyes tight shut against the sting. And then his other hand received the same punishment with the tears pricking behind his eyes and the injustice flaming his cheeks. Patrick was certain the strap marks were still visible on his palms; his parents would surely see them.

The darkening fields gave way to the familiar grey houses of the city and the street lights blinked on one after another. The driver dropped him at O'Connell Street on his way to the docks and wished him good luck with a wry shake of the head. The rain abated and, in its place, a damp curling mist drifted off the Liffey and seeped up onto the pavement where Patrick stood by the bridge trying to get his bearings. Already the dim orange glow of the street lamps shimmered in the puddles of the gutters. He had no money for a bus. By the time that he walked the length of the Rathmines Road to Palmerston Park he was chilled to the bone, his school blazer no shield to the clawing talons of a bitter wind.

Outside the large red brick house, he hesitated. A soft light could be seen through a gap in the curtains. With only his sister Brigid at home his parents would be having a light supper. His father would pour a single glass of stout for medicinal purposes, and they would be listening to the wireless. All the talk was of the German Chancellor and whether or not there would be a war and speculation on which side of things De Valera would fetch up. Patrick had heard his father discussing the matter with John on one occasion, John fiddling with his spectacles and nodding seriously now that he was started in a law practice. His father said that Hitler had done a great deal of good for Germany, stabilised the economy and created wealth and there was a lesson or two to be learned.

As he shivered by the gate Patrick debated with himself, should he walk up the steps and ring at the front door or slip round the back to the kitchen? He began to wish that he could short circuit it all and be tucked up in his bed with a hot water bottle under instructions to rest and sleep late. Before he could stop himself, a tear was trickling down his cheek, and he was trembling in every limb. He sniffed and wiped his face across his cuff but the tears refused to stop and a ribbon of snot rolled onto his upper lip. Upstairs a curtain twitched and a slim shaft of light caught him in its beam. He flinched and stepped back.

Moments later the front door opened and his father was standing on the porch, 'Patrick is that you?'

'Yes father.' He mumbled between his shivering sobs.

The Dominicans had phoned.

Tight lipped his father led him into the drawing room, passing his mother who looked at him sadly and shook her head before she turned away towards the back parlour without a word. He could sense rather than see Brigid peering down the stairwell with beady eyed interest.

His father stood by the mantelpiece and began to empty and clean out his pipe. His back was still turned against Patrick when he came at last to speak. 'I'd been given to understand that you were making good progress.' His father sifted the tobacco from his pouch, expertly extracting the desired amount, and then began to plug his pipe afresh.

'Papa ...'

'You have something to say Patrick?' His father turned to

31

face him with a look of such palpable hurt that Patrick felt his very spirit collapsing. A log in the fire cracked and fizzed in the silence which weighed heavily between them.

'We are to return tonight.' his father said. 'You will apologise to Brother Bartholomew for the anxiety which you have caused. If you are punished you will accept it with good grace and offer it up to Our Lord. We leave at once, it's a long drive. I expect that you are hungry but a night without supper will do no harm and may make you more appreciative of the many advantages which you have.'

On the journey they prayed. His father leading them through the decades of the Rosary. Our Father. Hail Mary. Glory Be. The rhythm of the prayers in time with the scraping back and forth of the windscreen wipers. Patrick almost longed for reproaches, for heat and fury, anything but the air of wounded disappointment. At the gates of the college they were met by Brother Anthony with his sharp inquisitorial features. His father shook hands and drove away at once.

'Well, well young master Glendon, you're for it now.' Brother Anthony declared with relish.

Patrick felt the whack of leather then and if that wasn't bad enough his brother Frank cuffed his ears for being a sissy. A boy called Niall with unruly red hair and freckles saved him. Niall fended off the bullies not with fists but with his clowning and with his inexhaustible fund of corny jokes he soothed the loneliness with laughter.

Patrick wiped the sweat from his brow. A dawn light was beginning to seep through the blinds. He would get up and shower before the early morning bottleneck of men with their thin grey towels and blunt razors. A chap had suggested that there might be work in the warehouse at a biscuit factory over on the North Side. Patrick would go along and take whatever might be going, it would be a start.

BEN DOWN AND THE DEATH OF YAGAN

Maali don't like me drinkin' grog. Say it's grog that done for the black fella. She think it did for her mother. Let that bunji-man in her humpy. A miner, name Murphy, mined her all right, three kids by him and then he buggers off and all them kids got taken away to missions and her mother only left with the grog. It's an old story. Her mother died last year, our people never live much past forty. Live hard, die young. But sometime a bloke feel like a beer and what Maali don't know isn't gonna harm her.

I get sent into Darinup with the station manager to pick up seed. I do the lifting, he's an old fella got a crook back. Don't talk much but that day he look me strange and say, 'They think the Final Solution can't come again, but those people just find another way.'

I don't know what he talking 'bout but I say, 'Sure you're right mate.'

We do the pickup and the old man says he's got his own business and I got an hour. There's a hotel with a dog window for us blacks. After all the hot work, I'm ready. A couple of other black fellas are hanging out by the window, an old fella and a kulamandi just lost work at the Davidson farm 'n he been drowning his sorrows. He grunt and roll this big blue marble over and over in his hand catching the sunlight.

The old fella's telling story. He's Binjareb, talking about fighting alongside Yagan, how he and Yagan was great warriors and killed lot of the other mob. Puff himself up like a cockatoo, fix me with his watery eyes. Show me a hole in his leg. 'Big battle that one.' He say. And me, I been tapping my fingers on the sill waiting to be served. I know that bastard runs this dump, he deliberately showing me his fat

33

arse.

'Yagan come again we show them that mob.'

'Sure will old fella.' I say; but Yagan he been killed back in eighteen hundred something. By the time I got my grog I ready to kill for it myself. A mangy old dog wanders round. He sniffs up my leg and then slumps down in the shade panting in the noonday. He look me, like not to run him off. I must be going soft.

'Them yella fellas, them's a bad mob.' The old man shakes his grizzled head. This one ...' he points to a scar running down one cheek, 'I got from that mob.' He grin his gummy one tooth grin at me. 'But I done for that fella, got him good.' I look at his face he not that old, just look old, grog done that.

A cop car drive in a big cloud of red dust and it that bastard Sgt. Brooke behind the wheel and he's a mean bastard and no mistake. Got a young gunji with him, a big bugger, all shiny and keen.

Brooke leans out the window, 'Any of yous mob from the Davidson place?'

I drink my beer and keep my mouth shut.

'Them yella fellas took one of my mates, shot him right in head.' The old fella talking into his cheap whiskey. 'Bad mob.' He shouts.

Brooke nods over to the young gunji who jumps out the car. He a big un, this bloke, he six foot more. Hands on his hips, looks that young black fella.

'You know an abo name of Danny Yamatji?'

The kulamandi don't look up.

'Funny, 'cause you look just like the description we got from Mr Davidson. Got any papers on you?'

Young fella shake his head and the gunji suck 'im teeth. 'Gonna have to ask you to come down the station.'

'You know them yella fellas? I fight 'em, me and Yagan, big war.'

'Come on, get up.'

'In jungle, big war that one was.'

Gunji bend down to young fella. 'You heard me.'

'Ain't done nuthin.' Kulamandi grunt.

'Come on you lazy bastard, get up, we don't have all day to be pissing about with you lot.'

The old fella is swaying over to the gunji pointing to the hole in his leg. '... they done this that mob.'

'Blimey, you stink old man!' Gunji 'im step back, look like he be sick.

'What I done?' Young fella got angry look on him and me thinkin' it's not good.

'That you're a thievin' no good abo. Now get up Danny and let's get on with it.'

'Done nuthin.'

Constable call back over 'im shoulder, 'It's him all right Sarg.'

Brooke get out of the car, he big man too, big belly. He spit. 'Bring him in then.'

Me, I drink up, quick like. It time to go.

'And you can stop right there.' Brooke don't look at me. He don't have to.

'Sarg, I got to get back work, boss waiting for me.' I try.

'You shoulda thought of that before you got yourself Drunk and Disorderly.' He's turn to me now, them little eyes.

'Sarg, only had one beer.'

Old fella, he waving some old papers. Look like he got a dog license, must been fighting against the Japs.

'Take 'em all in Len.'

No, don't argue with Sgt. Brooke. That Danny Yamatji shoulda known but he put up his fists at Len, saying Davidson the thievin' bastard didn't give him the pay he owed. Some farmers like that, fire a bloke for nothin then don't pay him right. Then Danny hit that gunji on the chin. Big trouble. I know he goin' behind bars now. But young fella been hit Len on head. Real hard. They mad, got 'im now in them cuffs, silly fella.

Old man waving license, like it mean something. He fight that war and they give 'im piece of paper.

I been throw in cell with old fella, stinking hole but been in them places before. I worry Maali, her gonna go crazy. Old

35

fella curl up on the bench, him snoring. Pissed his pants in patrol car. Walala. I near laugh out loud.

Couple hours later Len come up at the cell door, 'Come on, you're out of here, Ben.'

I don't hang about.

'You're one lucky bastard.'

Out front old Van der Berj at the desk talking with Sgt. Brooke.

'I don't want to see you back here again boy.' Brooke look at me with him piggy eyes.

'No Sarg.'

Behind the desk I see old photograph. It big, hollow boab tree, got bars. Under it say, *Police Lock Up, Western Australia*. In old time, lock up for blackfellas.

Sun gone down and we're back. Mr Van der Berj tell to boss Anderson that coppers locking me up was mistake. But Anderson look me hard. Say he dock my wages for time been lost. He mean bugger 'im.

Binni come running to me when I get back to Billangilil, 'You get me something in town dad?'

In my pocket and I pull out a big blue marble, turn it round in my hand then throw it to Binni.

'Walala, she's a beaut!' Binni grin and rus back to show Maali. She waiting for me outside humpy and she not grinning.

Week later, I hear Danny Yamatji been found dead. Well, that's what been written in papers, back page of The Bodenham Herald. Hung himself in his cell.

LETTERS HOME: ATLANTIC OCEAN

May 1962

Dear mammie,

Hoping this finds all of you well.

The sea is calm at last after days of rocking and rolling off Biscay. As you know the Southern Cross is all One Class, I believe it is very bad down below in stormy weather so it is fortunate to be on the upper deck. Still, the children have been sea sick from the moment we set sail and I've been up and down most nights with them and baby crying poor mite.

Yesterday morning we slept late with exhaustion and we missed our breakfast. One of the stewards noticed our absence and the upshot is that the Captain, no less, has organised a nurse to help each morning, and she has arranged that breakfast and cereal and juice are brought to the cabin—she's a godsend and from Galway. Shaw Savill Lines are a very good company and all the staff have been wonderful. There are all sorts of activities, deck games, quoits and so on and of course now we are entering warmer climes Nieve and John Niece will enjoy the paddling pool.

We arrive in The Canaries tomorrow and I can post this letter then. The children are very excited and asking if there are lots of little yellow birds flying around. They are thinking of Granny Glendon's little Joey, though he's in a cage of course. It was very kind of her to make the journey to Southampton. Of course, Kevin was tremendous with everything. Patrick's sister Brigid and her husband joined us from Cheltenham. I think they were overwhelmed at the thought that we might never meet again, but I cannot be thinking like that as you well know. Mrs Glendon gave Nieve a beautiful gold cross, very fine and delicate, with her

37

name carved on the back and for John Mrs. a silver St. Christopher medal, and to me she presented an antique brooch which had belonged to her mother, made of an unusually dark green Connemara marble; it's not the sort of thing that I would wear myself but it was terribly generous. Brigid wished us *bon voyage* but couldn't resist a catty remark about Patrick, hoping he isn't taking us half way round the world on a wild goose chase – she'd never have said it to his face, I'm sure.

I have made a friend, Mrs Una Holmes, who is on her way home to Durban. She says we are making a great mistake and that we should settle in South Africa where you can live very well and have servants galore. I have to say that before I got the help from Maureen, I was on the point of agreeing with her. But I'm sure Patrick has made the right decision and the children tell everyone that they are going to have a kangaroo and a koala bear for pets.

Una is amazed that I am traveling on my own with three such young children, but I've explained that Patrick needed to go out last year to set things up and I was expecting with little Patsy and couldn't really set off until she was a good four months old. The other day Una wanted to know what Patrick was like. The ship was heaving about and I had eyes in the back of my head with John John running around the deck and I looked at him and then at her and I said if he were to fall overboard right now and Patrick was here he would dive straight in after him without a moment's thought – even though he can't swim. She nodded and then said, but of course the sensible thing would be to throw a life belt first!

I showed her the photograph I keep in my purse; Patrick wasn't long back from Canada then and his hair was bleached with just the glint of red, the photo is in black and white so she couldn't see that—but Una did think he reminded her of Burt Lancaster.

I haven't had a chance to wear the purple voile cocktail dress yet—after all my worrying about getting it finished in time, but Maureen has promised to look after the children one evening and Una is insisting that I join her for the cabaret night. She's very poised and confident in her manner but even she says that a woman without her husband is like a social leper!

By the way, the fold up pram which you gave us has been a tremendous help and of course everyone makes a great fuss of Patsy when I take her out on deck.

I feel like the Big Adventure is really about to start and after all our bitter disappointments last year perhaps it was all part of God's Plan all along.

Your very loving daughter,

Maeve

P.S. The Ten Pound Poms are what the Australians call the British who go over on assisted passage, it costs ten pounds one way for the adults and under eighteen are free. There were thousands at the railway station and I wondered how we would all fit but then the ship is very big. It was a great send off, very moving.

THE MAGICIAN

Knick knack paddy whack give a dog a bone
this old man came rolling home!

John John was doing rolling all around the deck making himself nice and dizzy with the song and one minute seeing the sea and then not seeing the sea, seeing the sea, deck, not seeing the sea, seeing the sea, deck –

'John John! Would you watch where you're going!'

A pair of shiny, shiny black shoes, the biggest shoes John John had ever seen, shiny black. 'Ohhh ...' he stared.

'John John, come here now at once!'

His eyes ranged up green baggy trousers, then a dress – a dress? Going up and up and up, a lady giant? 'Ohhh …!'

'I do apologise, I'm so sorry. John John come out of the way and let the gentleman pass.'

'Heh, heh, no problem auntie.'

A loud voice, like a drum knocking around John John's head, boom, boom. A giant, definitely. Green dress but no boobies? And then black. Black face, black eyes, 'Ohhh!'

'You gonna teach me that song, little man? Heh, heh.'

A wide grinning mouth. John John stared. A hand came towards him, grabbed his ear, he felt his ear being twisted, hurting. 'Ouch!

'Excuse me ...!' Mammie rushed over.

'Well, what we got here?' The big hand opened up.

A sweetie, a yellow sweetie. John John stared at the sweetie and then brimming over with excitement stared at the big black man, sure that he must be a magician.

'For you, little man.'

'What do you say? Say thank you John John.'

'Thank you.' John John took the sweetie and stepped back.

'Heh, heh, heh.' The giant magician raised his hand to his round hat and raised it in salute. Would it be a rabbit or maybe a lion that he was hiding in there. No animals and no hair, none, just shiny shiny black.

'Good morning to you, auntie.'

'Good morning.' His mammie said.

The magician disappeared with his dress flapping like a big cloak in the breeze. John John looked down at the yellow sweetie in his hand. 'Mmm.'

'Give that to me.'

'Mammie?'

'You don't know where it's been.'

John John watched in horror as his mammie threw the magic sweetie into the sea. But it was swallowed up by a monster who was on its way to eat the ship and the big monster went, Boom! Boom! And was killed.

Nieve lay reading in the top bunk bed. John John wanted to be in the top bunk, but he was not old enough, 'I am never old enough!' he countered angrily. In revenge, he kicks the top bunk whenever Nieve is in it until she gets mad with him. 'I should be in the top bunk!' is his excuse.

Nieve was mad because she didn't see the magician. She had been with her new best friend, Doreen, who speaks funny because she is a Brummie. John John was surprised to learn that they in turn were called Paddies. John John often thought that he would like to be called Paddy like his da but instead he had been named John John. 'So good we named you twice!' his da would say. He was called after his *Seanathair* McMahon and his grandfather Glendon because they were both called John so he had been christened John John.

He wondered if he would see the magician again? He rubbed his ear and hoped that if the magician did find a sweetie again that it would not be in his ear and that mammie would not be watching. Kick, kick.

'Mammie, will you tell John John not to kick me.'

41

'John, John ...'

Patsy was crying, her gummy mouth open wide. He had seen where a little tooth was beginning to poke through.

'Mammie why did the big black man call you 'auntie'?'

'Auntie?' Nieve leaned down over the side of the bunk and John John thought she looked like a funny monster because her head was upside down.

'Ha, ha, ha!' He felt all buzzy with excitement because Nieve was mad and because she did not know that their mammie was the black man's auntie.

'I don't know – but I'm certainly not his auntie. Look, into your jim jams right now the pair of you. And John John, no shoes in the bed!'

'But then why did he say you were his auntie?'

'I don't know, I don't know – now get those shoes off this minute or I'll have to smack you with the hairbrush.'

'I'm only asking.' Kick, kick.

'Mammie ...!' Nieve disappeared up top.

'Whisht the pair of you.'

'If I see him again, I will ask if he is a relative that we didn't know.'

'Shhh, Patsy, Patsy, Patsy, shhh.'

'Mammie, where do the black people come from?'

'Africa.'

'Is that where the man comes from?'

'I think so.'

'Can we go to Africa?'

'We're going to Africa right now.'

John John sat up; his ears pricked. 'Right now?'

'We're sailing right beside it and we are going to stop at a place called Cape Town and then a place called Durban.'

'Are all the people in Africa black people?'

'No.'

'Oh. What colour are they? Red? Yellow? Ha, Ha! Green? Ha, ha, ha!' John John rolled back onto the bed.

'In America there are Red Indians.' Nieve said in her know all voice.

John John glowered, 'I know that, I don't need you to tell

me that, I know that!' Kick, kick.

'There are white people in Africa.' His mammie said.

'Oh.' John John stopped kicking.

'Mrs Holmes lives in Africa.'

Nieve appeared again over the side of the top bunk. Thwack! *The Book of Irish Folk Tales* hit John John on the side of his head.

'Ow! Ow! Ow!'

'Right that's enough! Nieve come down here right now.'

'He started it.'

'Now!'

'He keeps kicking me! It's not fair!'

Sulkily Nieve climbed down the ladder. John John hurled the fairy tales back at her, but without aim the book just glanced her arm. 'Mammie, look what John John just did!'

Patsy wailed. The tooth must be coming through the skin right now, John John guessed.

'Mammie!' He shouted as loud as he could. He turned around to look at his mammie and saw that she was jigging Patsy up and down but that it was not Patsy who was crying.

'Mammie, what's the matter?' Nieve stood beside her.

John John jumped out of the bottom bunk and looked at his mother. Big silent tears rolled down her cheeks.

'What's the matter, mammie?' Nieve asked again and put her arms around their mother's shoulder.

John John awkwardly stroked his mammie's knee, 'Don't cry mammie.' He had never seen his mother crying like this, it made him feel wobbly inside like he might cry too.

Patsy did a big burp then, looking at him with her big startled eyes and he laughed and then he laughed again because Patsy grinned her gummy grin. Then his mammie was still crying but she was also laughing as well. And then Nieve started laughing but she was crying as well. His mother put an arm around John John and hugged him close and then she turned and gave Nieve a kiss and suddenly all of them were kissing and hugging and laughing and crying, except John John didn't cry, he was a boy.

LETTERS HOME: DURBAN

May 1962

Dear Kevin

I'm at my wits end with worry. Please, please don't tell mammie and daddy. I've had a bit of a shock. We've arrived in Durban after some rough seas around Cape Town, and I went along to the poste restante to find a letter from Patrick. He has lost the job at Arnotts. Some dispute with the management and after he had seemed to be doing so well with the promotion before we set sail. So, I don't know what to expect when we arrive in Sydney.

I am sure that I am worrying unnecessarily but getting it off my chest is a help.

Your loving sister

Maeve

P.S. To top it all there is an outbreak of measles on board so the children are under quarantine and have not been able to go ashore.

DADDY'S GIRL

Nieve ran ahead down the gangplank with her mother shouting at her to hold her horses but it was too late they were galloping away with her already. All she could think was that today she would see her da and everything in her world would right itself, all the topsy turvy, upside-downedness, all the queer strangeness of their lives would fall away. She leaped onto the dockside, hardly registering that she was setting foot on her new homeland after all the weeks at sea. She felt dizzy and momentarily seasick. Her heart was thumping with all the hoohah and the thrill of the arrival at this city of water and boats glittering under a blue sky.

The big ship had entered the harbour with great blasts of the horn which thrummed through all the decks of the ship and seemed to echo inside her. Whistles blew, sailors raced along the decks. Men shouted. The ship was a buzz. People scurrying everywhere, rushing to get a place at the railings. Little sailing yachts and dinghies surrounded the ship just like the flock of seagulls swirling overhead, the people on board waving and shouting greetings. Her mammie yelling at them all to stay together. And as they drew near to the Overseas Passengers Terminal right under the shadow of the arching bridge a man let them squeeze through so that they too could see the crowds lined up on the docks waving flags and cards with peoples' names on. Nieve, waving and waving until her arm hurt, because somewhere in that great teeming crowd was her da and he would surely see her.

Nieve felt the land swell and heave underfoot and herself swaying, about to topple over, and then she was in his arms. The great bear hug, the growling in her ear. Her own squirming delight.

'Da! Da! Da!'

'Jaze Nieve but you're getting heavy! Let me look at you.' He placed her back down on the quay and gave her the once over. 'Wouldn't I hardly recognise you? Look at the height of you. And the colour in your cheeks with all that sun and sea air, anyone would take you for a seasoned sailor.' And indeed, her mammie had dressed herself and John John in the little blue and white sailor outfits which made other passengers coo and pinch their cheeks, so that they flinched when anyone came near them.

Nieve looked up at her da and appraised him equally. He was tanned like a film star, his hair a golden red crown, his blue eyes as tempting to dive into as the blue of the ship's swimming pool. She felt that she would burst with the happiness and hoped that everyone could see.

And then John John was rushing into her da's arms for his bear hug and growling back like a young cub and her da was mussing up John John's hair and asking if he taken good care of all the women.

And her mammie had tears in her eyes, tears of joy Nieve was relieved to note, and they were kissing and hugging, her mammie swept up and swung around until she protested with laughter. Protested that her da was forgetting that he hadn't said hello to the newcomer.

Her da stopped and looked over at the pram which had the hood up to protect Patsy from the sun.

In the stillness of that moment they could hear Patsy gurgling, one of her funny, bubbling, spitty gurgles. Her da reached in and lifted out the baby coddled in her all-in-one suit with her head covered in a soft fluff of hair and Nieve saw that her da fell in love with Patsy from that moment, that her big eyes gobbled up his heart.

'You're mine.' he said. 'You're daddy's girl.'

THE TENNIS HOP

The children were finally settled, cranky and tired after the excitement of the day. Standing on opposite sides of the double bed Patrick suddenly found that the long months of separation had created a shy strangeness to each other. For so many lonely nights he had dreamed of this moment. Imagined that they would whisper endearments into each other's ears whilst their kisses would grow more passionate and his vision would melt into their two bodies entwined beneath the sheets. Here she was in the flesh, a living breathing reality and he felt hesitant to approach. He made an excuse; he might have forgotten to lock the back door. Sure enough when he returned, Maeve was in the bed and already feigning sleep. He pulled on his crisp new pajamas and slipped in beside her. '

'Goodnight Macushla.' he whispered as he switched off the bedside lamp.

Lying there in the dark he reassured himself that all would be well. Maeve had traveled across the world to be with him and she was his wife. He had won her. She thought him a crazy fool when he proposed on the night they first met but he had known immediately; that sudden flash which the French call a *coup de foudre*. Painful in its searing sensation of certainty. This was the woman he must have, would love and want for all his life.

A Tennis Hop of all places. His brother Peter had inveigled him to drive that evening. Then suggested, on a whim, that they drop by Fitzwilliam for an aperitif before they went on to a drinking club. Patrick had just returned from Canada but the atmosphere at home was suffocating. A shock to see the deterioration in his father since The Stroke, the lopsided face and the stilted conversation, his father struggling to pronounce his words, to speak. It was pitiable and Patrick couldn't bear to be a witness.

At the tennis club, Peter immediately met old friends and was swept on to the dance floor by a pert young woman with a tight perm. Patrick tapped out a cigarette. A couple of the girls were eyeing him. Without being unduly vain he knew he presented a striking figure, the deep blue of his eyes set off by the tan from his time at sea. His jacket didn't fit as well as it once had, he had grown broader in the shoulder, but this emphasised his muscular physique.

He had no time for dancing, so he wouldn't be whisking any of them onto the floor. He blew smoke rings above his head and watched the curling wisps join the halo of smoke hovering overhead. A bored lethargy crept over him and he wondered why he had returned from Montreal at all. But he knew why. His father was dying. Nobody spoke of it but they all knew it.

Peter had assumed the day to day running of the factory. Patrick doubted he was up to it. There was something soft and ineffectual about him, a man who enjoyed the easy life, the comforts of good company, drinking and eating and pleasing. He was not a decision maker or a risk taker. He was not a leader or an inspiration. He was not their father. None of them were. Although each of his brothers had won their father's approval in some way, John, the lawyer and budding politician, Frank a sporting hero, James the priest doing God's work in darkest Africa, Peter set to follow into the family business. But Patrick the youngest, what had he ever done to gain his father's approbation? All he had ever done was to run away, away from school, away from home, away to sea. Frank was making a career of the sea, captain of his own merchantman, but Patrick knew deep down that the sea was not for him, it had served as a refuge, a way to get himself as far away from the disappointment in his father's eyes as possible. He assured himself that he would return when he had made something of himself, and could say, *look father, look at my great works, look at me and be proud that I am your son.*

Well he was home with nothing to show for the four long years of his absence. Worse, the father who might have smiled on him and said, *well done my son, in you I am well pleased* was no more, was a shell and a misshapen one at that. Patrick was adrift. Without aim or purpose.

That was when he saw her. The girl in the pearly white dress. His breath held in abeyance and everything else fell away. There was only her. The movement of her lithe body, the tilt of her head, a crease of amusement in her smile. Something vulnerable yet strong in her profile, which he would later come to know was an impression lent by the slight crookedness of her nose where it had been broken by a brother careless with a cricket bat.

Patrick's cigarette burnt down to the filter, he stubbed it out and watched as another chap cut in. This older man was an accomplished dancer, smooth and confident. The girl completely at ease in his arms. Patrick felt a surge of rage. He hated the man with his slicked black hair, the sheen of his tailored suit, his obvious poise and charm. Patrick felt a fool, a dull clot. How could he ever impress such a girl?

'What'll you have to drink, Paddy.' It was his brother at his shoulder.

At that moment the girl swept by, Patrick's eyes followed her every movement.

'I think your little brother has other things on his mind at this precise moment.' The pert young woman grabbed Peter's arm and let loose a shrill laugh.

'Who is she?'

'Princess Margaret Rose.' The girl made a motion of snootiness with a flick of her head. 'And you've as much chance.' She tugged at Peter's arm. 'Mine's a martini, dry, since you're asking.'

'One for the road.' His brother continued pointedly.

'Oh, you're not leaving us so soon? You want to stay, don't you?' And a sharp little nose was poked in front of Patrick along with a knowing wink. 'Stay a little longer the pair of you and I'll tell you all about Maeve McMahon. I'm Dympna by the way, since your brother hasn't taken the trouble to

49

introduce us, an oversight I'm sure.'

'Maeve McMahon?' Even her name had a sweet taste.

'You've heard of the McMahons? Everyone knows all those handsome brothers, all spoken for I'm afraid, us Dublin girls are desperate.' The shrill laugh again.

'And Maeve, is she spoken for?' Patrick dared to ask.

'My feet are killing me in these stilettos.' Dympna led Patrick towards a couple of free chairs by the wall. 'Sit there now, it'll give you the best view.' She teased.

Another time Patrick might have been irked by her familiar, impertinent tone but he needed to know everything he could possibly glean about this woman he already knew he loved, with a passion the force of which surprised and overwhelmed him.

'Word is that the chap she's with now, Jean Pierre or is it Jean Marie? French Lebanese, is very wealthy. Anyway, there may be wedding bells. He's very thick with her father, in the same line of course, textiles. But it's not a done deal.'

Patrick nodded vaguely; his eyes trained on the couple as they sashayed around the floor.

'So, you can live in hopes.' Dympna continued. 'Though you don't strike me as the marrying kind I have to say. Heard you were a bit of a rover. Is that right? The love them and leave them type?'

'Like me. Love them and leave them.' Peter had the drinks.

'Oh, Peter you are terrible!'

'And leave we must. Come on Paddy drink up.'

Despite the protestations from Dympna and Patrick's reluctance Peter hurried them away. 'That Dympna, she'd have me in her clutches given half a chance.' He'd laughed and slapped Patrick on the back. 'Come on, let's go and meet some real party girls.'

On the drive across the city, as his brother chattered on, Patrick felt the knot in his stomach tighten. He must see Maeve again. See her there and then. Somehow, let her know that it was him she must love. Because no one else would love her as he would love her. It would be the greatest mistake of her life if she were to marry anyone else. There was not a moment to be lost. If he did not act, he himself would be lost. He pressed on the horn, again and again.'

'Jeez, what has your goat?' Peter eyed him sardonically.

'I'll drop you at Brophy's and give you the money for a cab later.'

Peter drew out his cigarettes and knocked a couple from the pack, offering one to Patrick. He lit the cigarettes. 'She's a heart breaker, you don't want to go having your heart broken Paddy. A man is better off being the one that's pursued— although we all think the game is the other way.'

Patrick listened as his brother continued in the same vein but the words washed over him or rather, they failed to impress, he even felt vaguely superior. What did Peter know about love, about passion? Peter was incapable of such depth of feeling. Patrick could imagine that Peter would settle for a girl just like Dympna; Dympna and bridge parties and golf and cosy domesticity and the occasional easy-going flirtation with a secretary.

On the route back to Fitzwilliam he drove as though the devil were on his tail, cutting through changing traffic lights, overtaking on St. Stephen's Green his nerves jangling as he passed a Gardai patrol car. He prayed that the foreigner would not have whisked Maeve away to a late supper at a dining club or a moonlit walk by the Liffey. Such images threw him into a frenzy of anxiety. And she did not even know that he existed.

His heart was thumping ten to the dozen as he re-entered the heaving dance hall and tried to make his way to the edge of the floor. It was almost a shock to find himself face to face with Maeve.

'Sorry, did I bump you?' She was turning, smiling.

'No, no, no ...'

She tilted her head in a charming manner, about to turn away again.

'If it's not too much of an imposition, may I ask you to dance.' He blurted and felt foolish and school-boyish.

She paused. 'No.' she responded.

He felt his heart about to fail.

'It's not an imposition at all.'

The dancers whirled passed in a furious quickstep. Patrick felt a lurch of horror as he guided Maeve towards the floor, desperately trying to conjure his dim memories of the dancing lessons to which his mother had sent them all.

'You look terrified.' she laughed gaily.

'I think I am.' He admitted. 'My dancing is a little rusty – to be honest it was never well oiled in the first place.'

'Would you rather wait for something slower?'

'Perhaps I could offer you a drink?'

'Thank you, but I already have one.'

He followed her glance to the end of the bar where Jean Marie was engrossed in conversation with another man.

'It's awfully stuffy in here isn't it? Perhaps you could take me outside for a breath of fresh air if that isn't too much of an imposition?'

'No. Yes. Of course.'

'I don't even know your name.'

'Patrick. Patrick Glendon.'

He led her through the throng, his body attempting to shield her from the jostling revelers.

'Glendon. Do you have a brother John? A lawyer?'

'Yes, that would be him; he's wanting to stand for the Dail.'

'Married to Felicity?'

Patrick nodded.

'She's a darling. He's well ... he's a little ...'

'Pompous?' He suggested.

'Yes, just a little.' And her eyes twinkled. 'But you're not pompous, are you?'

They emerged into the clear night, a starry canvas overhead. It was early September and the evening held the scent of roses. Maeve shivered and wrapped her arms about.

Patrick scrambled out of his jacket and draped it over her shoulders. 'Here take this.'

'You're very gallant, kind sir. But won't you be cold now?'

'No. No. I'm really quite warm.' He hesitated wondering if he could ever find the words to say the right thing, the thing that would make her understand. 'In fact, I feel as though I'm on fire.'

'Oh, you haven't got a fever, have you? Only, I've just recovered from a summer cold and I'd be a touch miffed Patrick if I caught another one.'

'No nothing like that.'

'You look very healthy I have to say, have you been sunning yourself abroad?'

'Canada.'

She wanted to know all about his travels. Laughed at his stories. The time that he bought a fur coat in Newfoundland stowed it away in his locker only to find it eaten alive after they'd crossed the Equator. The time won a monkey in a game of cards on the Ivory Coast and then been forced to donate it to a zoo after it stole the First Officer's cap and clamboured up the rigging.

They wandered alongside the manicured lawns of the tennis courts and in the gloom stumbled on another couple in a passionate clinch. The girl flushed and straightened her crumpled frock. The man glared at Patrick. Somewhere in the distance a clock struck midnight.

'Oh dear, is it that late. This is where I turn into a pumpkin.' Maeve sighed. 'Jean Marie will be wondering where I am.'

'Are you engaged?'

'No. Why do you ask?'

'Would you like to be?' Patrick felt his whole body tense.

'I haven't thought of it.'

'Marry me.'

She laughed and trapped the laughter in her throat midway as she caught the intensity of his gaze. 'Seriously?'

'I've never been more serious about anything. Say yes.'

'We don't even know each other.' She smiled warmly then. 'You're very sweet. Thank you for asking. Believe it or not, you're my first proposal.'

He saw the glowing tip of a cigarette approaching.

'I need to see you again.' Patrick pressed.

'Maeve, ma petite, I was beginning to worry ...' Jean Marie held out her wrap.

'You shouldn't have.' She responded, slipping off the jacket, patting it down and holding it out to Patrick. 'I've been very well taken care of by Mr Glendon.'

Jean Maire bowed slightly, 'Merci monsieur.'

'Goodnight Patrick. We were all going to meet at Fairyhouse next weekend. Will you still be in Dublin?'

'I'll be there, you can bet on it.'

'Oh, my bets will all be on the odds on favourite.'

'Goodnight' He walked off swiftly no longer able to bear the sight of the proprietary hand which rested so casually on Maeve's shoulder. He sensed in that moment that if the other man were to stand in his way, he might kill him with his bare hands and think nothing of it.

Patsy cried in the night. Patrick felt himself swimming out of a dream. Maeve was already out of the bed, alert with the antennae of motherhood. By the time he joined her to stand over the cot Patsy had been settled again.

'She's teething, poor mite.'

Patrick squeezed Maeve's shoulder. 'She's beautiful, like her mother.'

'Hmm, I'm sure I picked up a few grey hairs on the crossing.'

'They'd suit you even if you had.' He drew her into a hug and kissed the top of her head. 'My poor darling, you must be exhausted. Three of them. All on your own. But you're here now. I'll look after you, all of you. It'll be all right. Everything will be all right.'

As he soothed her, he felt her relaxing into him, letting the tension go. And he hugged her tighter wanting to communicate his determination to make her glad to have chosen him.

LETTERS HOME: SYDNEY

June 1962

Dear Mammie,

Well, we are all arrived safe at last! Docking at the Sydney Harbour Bridge was really quite spectacular.

Patrick has found a perfect little bungalow in Newport. To one side we have the beach, which the children are in ecstasies about and even though it is quite chilly they have been busy building sand castles. On the other is a large inlet, The Pittwater, with lovely walks through the trees and boats bobbing about in the water. Very picturesque. I have already been out snapping with the new camera from Kevin, as you will see from the enclosed. I particularly like the photograph of Nieve and John John in their tartan trousers searching the mail box – hint, hint!

Patrick bought a brand-new washing machine as a welcoming present for me—Thank God he's more practical than romantic! There was a beautiful doll for Nieve, which I'm afraid she hasn't shown much interest in being the little tomboy that she is, and a toy boomerang for John John which he is delighted with but hasn't yet succeeded in getting to come back! Patrick can't take his eyes off Patsy; he even helps with the bottle feeding but needless to say he's not so enthusiastic when it comes to the other end!

The house has a covered porch which will be another room once the weather improves. The garden is mainly lawn but with all sorts of strange new plants and shrubs. One I know is called a 'bottle brush' because that is exactly what it looks like. If there are any that might grow in your garden, I will send you the seeds. And I have a Hill's Hoist rotary line! They really are the latest thing, like a giant umbrella you can fold down—not much chance of that with Patsy in nappies.

People do seem to have a good standard of living and an outdoors sort of life. Well, you know I have never been the sporty type but I think that I shall enjoy the walks and the swimming – though I shall be sticking to the pools, they have all manner of terrible sea creatures and around the house we have been warned to watch out for the funnel web spiders which are deadly!

The accent is very harsh, I am forever misunderstanding people and of course they don't seem to understand me at all. But Australians are friendly and welcoming. Next door we have Hal and Bonnie, from Scotland, who have three sons, the youngest only a couple of years older than Nieve and yesterday he invited her to see his tree house and of course now she wants one of her own, but for the moment Patrick is far too busy!

The big news is that Patrick has his own business! A petrol station franchise. The poor darling has to work all the hours that God sends but he is tremendously enthusiastic and I feel certain that he will be able to make a go of it. Must dash now, Patsy is yelling for her next feed!

Your loving daughter Maeve

PS The petrol station is one of the Golden Fleece chain, so I tease Patrick that he is Jason and we are all his argonauts.

BEN DOWN AND THE WOMAN IN THE MOON

Desperate Dan make me laugh, all he think 'bout is cow pie. He big 'n strong but he is bloody stupid. Maali say I should get Lord Snooty out *The Dandy* and do something useful.

'Like what?'

'Binni ...'

Maali always going on like she come from where crow fly backward—but she from mission down Moore River, what she know 'bout old ways? Me, I was born 'n grow up in ashes.

Binni look me, eyes big, 'What will you learn me today, dad?'

I throw the comic down and look them both. But I know I gonna get no peace.

Binni come runnin', jumping over termite mounds, try to catch me but I don't stop. I pick up big stick, wave it around, call out—making big noise. Binni coming behind making noises same like, I know he pick up stick same. He thinking it ceremony. 'Stead me just bein' stupid.

I got stick—now I have idea. I start tapping on some young gums. Binni stop and look. Me tapping and listening. Tapping and listening. Then me look Binni for 'im do same. Binni go and tap a young tree. He look me.

'That one too big.' I say. He look me confuse like. I grinin'.

I tap next one. Binni's ears stand up, this one different sound. Young tree. I tap all way up, maybe five foot. I nod.

'This one.'

I get knife and cut 'im down, careful like old murran taught me.

'Okay, now look inside.'

Binni put his eye right up, look and make funny face. 'There's nothing in there, dad'

'Yeah, that's right. You know why?'

Binni shake 'im head.

'White ants done this, eat it all out. That stick you got there, clean it out, make smooth like baby bum.'

I roll a ciggie, Binni doin' good job, he real serious. Make me happy, father and son. He not my boy, but same like.

'What's it for dad?'

'Wait now.' I say, 'n lick ciggie paper.

We walk back to long grass and sit down. We take off the bark.

I say, 'Quick, go get you paint—Maali no see.'

I get wax.

We mix the brown and red. I tell Binni where 'im paint red first. Black ring near bottom and top. Then white paint I make long tall dancing man. Binni help make white dots round him. It's hot day so dry bloody quick.

'What you think, Binni?'

'I think it's a didge.' He got big grin.

'You maybe right, clever fella.'

I put bees' wax round the end for mouth.

'Black fella name Yi-da-ki, You say Yidaki, mum she like that.'

I put the didge to my mouth. My cheeks fill up with wind. Then blow, Yi-da-ki, Yi-da-ki. Then sniffing smell of country. It like something blow with wind, come from ancestors. From when Creators first sound these sound, brung world into bein'. Thing like that.

'Can I have a go?'

'Sure.'

Binni puff up his cheeks and let out big raspberry.

'Ha, look easy, huh? Okay, I show you. Give me your hand.'

I show him how to put thumb straight, then first finger bend so it 'about half way, bit angle, rest of fingers make cup. Me fit lips inside, make big buzzin' noise. 'Make loud you can.'

58

I look Binni.

Binni try and he big eyes light up noise he make 'im hand.

'Now you practice anytime.'

I show him make different sounds, just with hand. Like dog barking, kookaburra laughin'. I make noise and he say animal. We laugh when he get it right and we laugh when he get wrong. And Binni try, he blowin' hard and I laugh, say, 'What animal this one? Never heard this animal!'

'Righteo, now time for didge.'

Binni try hard. He hold didge different now, special, sacred like. Say anythin' he like.

'Hey, you play good. Next time I show you breath right.'

Got good fire going for the evening, sun is orange in the west. I nod Binni. He bring out didge.

'Look mum, it's a Yidaki.'

'You made that?'

Binni look at me.

'He did. Found the right gum. We cut it down. He clean it up, paint it. It's good one. That one big noise, blow Black Cockatoo right out the bush.'

For little fella Binni got lotta wind and he gonna play real good with didge. Got right feelin'.

Maali is all smiling.

Moon come up big in sky. I nod. Remember story murran tell me.

'One woman picking flowers to make self beautiful …'

Binni stop. I look Binni for 'im carry on play didge. 'In same place was Byamee throwin' his kerl—'

'What's that?' Maali ask.

'Boomerang.'

Maali nods, she like new name, kerl.

'One time kerl come back near this woman, not to Byamee. The woman pick it up and keep it.

Byamee say, *Bring my magic kerl back to me woman!*

She just shake her head.

Why do you not give me my kerl? he shout at her.

Because you don't throw good, the kerl don't come back to you, it come to me, and now I keep it.'

Maali big grin. She like this story.

'What happened then dad?' Binni say.

'Byamee become angry he put a curse on the woman. Sent her up into the sky and turn her into moon, look like a kerl in night sky. Every night she grow fatter and fatter until she become a big fat round moon. Then she get old and go back to nothing left. But always that woman come back, time again.'

Binni let the didge go down low then up, up high.

We look up in the night sky, it dark, now she coming up over gum trees. The kerl, the moon, she getting fat again.

'You done good Binni.' I say.

Binni he yawn and curl up on the ground holding didge like it his new friend. His eyes drop. Sleep now.

'She always coming back, just like kerl.' Maali say and she happy.

'Shouldn't been argue with Byamee, her still been picking flowers.' I grin.

'Byamee just mad at her 'cause that woman see he not so clever fella.'

'Good woman, she never tell man he not clever. She pick up kerl and give it back, like maybe something wrong with kerl. Nothing wrong with man throwing.'

'Maybe I'd rather be a big fat moon.' say Maali.

THE CUBBY HOUSE

Nieve was hanging upside down from the low branch. If she stretched her fingers, she could touch the ground. She wondered what Carmel Marie was doing? She would probably be asleep, because her mammie had told her that when it was day in Australia it was night in Ireland, and when it was today in Australia it was yesterday back there and whilst she had been on her winter holiday, Carmel Marie was on her summer holyers. Her father had been the one to buy their farm. The gypsy caravan would be her playhouse and Raymond might play doctors with her now. Or, Carmel Marie might have a new best friend.

Nieve wondered when she would have a new best friend. She was starting at her new school the following day. It would be her third school. In Dublin she hadn't made any friends because they all knew that she was going to Australia and they knew it wasn't worth it and they called her a *culchie* because she had lived on a farm. Nieve hoped that this new school in Sydney would be better, but when she thought about meeting her new teacher and classmates, she got the collywobbles.

Malcolm was sort of a new friend. He lived next door and wore glasses and was nine years old. He had brothers but they were already at big school so they never played with him anymore. He didn't seem to have any friends. Nieve liked going over because of Mrs Bonnie's cakes and the cubby house in the tree. But she wasn't sure that she liked Malcolm, even though he knew a lot about animals, ones that Nieve didn't even know they had in Australia like crocodiles. Fresh water and sea water crocodiles he had informed her with relish. And sharks of course which would bite your leg off even when you were just paddling. They'd caught one recently, Malcolm said, and cut it open and a man's hand was still waving inside.

They would sit in the tree house to watch birds and that was one of the few times that Malcolm would be quiet so that the birds would come in close. Australia was like a great big zoo, full of strange and colourful creatures. Nieve had never seen birds like the ones here, the white cockatoos with their yellow crests screeching and squawking, the cheeky Willy Wagtails and the gawky Ibis with their long, curved beaks always pecking for food. Twice Malcolm pointed out a King Parrot, each time saying *Ooh aar Jim me lad. Pieces of Eight! Pieces of Eight!* Which sounded like nonsense to Nieve and confirmed her suspicions that Malcolm might be a little bit loopy.

At dusk Nieve would hear the bats up in the date palm, sounding like cats having their tails pulled. Malcolm told her with delight that they urinated in the trees to mark their territory. In the mornings the woop whoop of the Kookaburra might wake you up and was better she thought than the piercing cock-a-doodle-doo of old Sultan Ahmed back at Killpool Hill farm.

There was a lot to learn in this new country. People looked the same and spoke English but they were hard to understand. To become a dinkum Aussie was like having to learn another lingo. Nieve listened carefully to the way Malcolm pronounced things and asked what some of the strange words were. Like you said snaggers instead of sausages and sweeties were lollies and avo for afternoon and daggy was for something that was not nice looking and bluey was someone with red hair, which was a bit odd, and then he taught her naughtier words like norks for women's boobies. Fortunately for Nieve, Malcolm liked talking. He talked all the time.

Malcolm said the really important thing for her to learn was how to say 'G'day.' They spent one whole avo saying 'G'day' to each other and when one of them said it they couldn't stop laughing. Malcolm's mother came out with glasses of lemonade and slices of cake and said, 'G'day

Niv.' in her way that sounded as if she was asking a question and she and Malcolm rolled around the lawn nearly choking on their laughter.

'I don't know what you twos are finding so funny, I only said 'g'day?''

That set them off for another two minutes. Mrs Bonnie shook her head and went back indoors.

They were lined up in rows. Nieve directed to join the end of the line for her class. She could see Malcolm two rows along but he ignored her. One of the older boys was pulling on a rope by a pole and at last the Australian Flag unfurled.

There were three other children at the front, they held up tin fifes to their puckered lips, took a deep breath and began to play and all the children began to sing,

God Save Our Gracious Queen,
Long Live our noble Queen ...

Nieve knew it was about the Queen of England but wondered why they were singing about her in Australia?

The teacher, Mrs Wilson, was young and kind and because Nieve wasn't the only new girl the other children weren't all looking at her. In fact, they hardly seemed to notice her at all because the other girls starting in the class were identical twins; everything about them was identical, including their hair parting and ribbons and the new shoes.

One day Mrs Wilson brought out a box of badges and told the class to ask their parents for the money to buy one. They were little tin badges and on them was a photo of a smiling aboriginal child with a boomerang underneath; above was written *Help educate aboriginal children.* The money was to run the mission schools, Mrs Wilson said.

In Ireland the children were asked by the nuns to bring in tins of beans or peaches to send to the starving children in

Africa. When she knew that the Southern Cross was going to stop in South Africa Nieve had been excited because she imagined that she might give some of her sweeties to the starving children of Africa. But she got the measles and John John got it too and they were in the ship's hospital with all the other children. She had the bed next to Doreen, thank goodness, and played Snap and Happy Families all day long. Still, she would have liked to have met the black babies. Australia had their own little black children; they were aborigines but everyone called them abos or women were called jins. She asked Malcolm if he knew any.

He looked at her as if she was mad, 'No way. Crikey, don't you know you can get diseased just looking at 'em. Dad says they're all bludgers and keep out of their way.'

Nieve felt disappointed, she wasn't quite sure why. A couple of days later their da took the family on a trip to the Botanical Gardens and they passed a huddle of three black men who were drinking from brown paper bags. The men were ragged and filthy, their hair matted and sticking out and one of them didn't even have any shoes on. A police officer tried to move them away and the one with no shoes got angry and then one of the others shouted and hurled his brown paper bag into the air and it smashed on the pavement in front of Nieve narrowly missing her with a spray of broken glass and liquid. She screamed before she could stop herself. They were all startled and her da pulled herself and John John quickly by the hand and her mammie rushed ahead with the pram.

Nieve had been frightened, they were not at all like the pictures in her book about Australia which showed a grinning curly haired aboriginal throwing a boomerang.

LE BEAU MONDE

The ease of familiarity brought Maeve close again and the lovemaking followed. Maeve had always been poised and somehow decorous, receptive but lacking in the fire and passion which surged through Patrick and for which he would then feel almost ashamed. Aroused, his thoughts sometimes seemed improper even lewd, thoughts which he tried to separate from the woman he cherished as his wife and the mother of his children.

One night as they made love under the cover of darkness and his desire throbbed urgently through his body Patrick found himself not thinking of Maeve at all but conjuring erotic images of a girl he had known in the years when he was a junior officer at sea, Mirrielle.

On arrival in Montreal the crew had gone to a favourite haunt near the Pont Victoria. As the night wore on and copious amounts of alcohol suffused Patrick with tender feelings for his brother man, a well-dressed Argentine approached him offering an enormous sum of money to join an expedition smuggling arms across the Platte for the anti-Peronists. Patrick had been swept along by the prospect.

'Leave the boy alone, Jorges, he's been reading too much Hemingway for his own good.' Greene the First Mate squeezed into a seat and wagged a finger at Patrick. 'Your predecessor, young Mick, took up Jorges' offer last year and is presently languishing in the Villa Devoto as a guest of Juan Peron, and that, I can assure you, is no holiday camp.'

Jorges shrugged, 'Miguel was caught, but you, amigo,' he nodded to Patrick, 'I think you are a clever man.'

'Clever enough to say no to hair brained schemes amigo!'

Greene laughed and yanked Patrick by the arm. 'Come along Lucky Jim we're off to Franny's Place and you'll have better sport there I can assure you.'

Patrick's experience of prostitutes was scant. A boyhood initiation with gap-toothed Sally and the memory of her ripe vocabulary still brought a blush to his cheeks. Then the fumbled encounter in a Rotterdam alleyway which cost him a stolen wallet. All sorry, guilt ridden affairs. The women, even the younger ones, far from exciting his desire had left him feeling both pity and disgust, pity for them and disgust with himself.

Franny's Place was a Private Club, off Boulevard St. Laurent, with a small dance-floor and a jazz set. A certain code of conduct was expected. Patrick could see immediately that the girls were of a different order. Any breaches were enforced by Franny's right hand, a thick set man who seldom spoke and little needed to.

Mirielle had a good figure, neat hips, a tight little waist and a cleavage which she knew how to accentuate. Her full pouting lips distracted from her rather aquiline nose and narrow dark eyes.

Alone in the dimly lit satin draped bedchamber he felt the stirrings of real desire. Mirielle moved with an almost insolent, graceful arrogance as she slipped from her silky dress and posed naked, uninhibited. She teased him as he fumbled shyly with the buttons of his uniform. Head hammering with cheap champagne an anger stirred in him. He wanted to show her that he was someone to be respected. He wanted to beat into her with the hardening force between his legs. Her eyes twinkled, mischievous. He sensed that she could read his every thought. She grinned as he pulled her onto the bed.

'You must learn to control it Patrick.' Her voice was husky in his ear. 'Can you control it?' She bit his ear lobe. Hard.

Patrick yelped with surprise, 'Jaze! You little bitch!'

As he cradled the stinging tender lobe, she nudged him onto his back and climbed astride his chest.

'Now you are a boy but one day, ah oui, you look a little

like Burt Lancasteur. He must be a very good lover, don't you think? He has le physique, but with elegance like a cat.'

Patrick found his eyes drawn to her perfect breasts, small but somehow rounded and full and he wanted to reach out and trace their contours with his fingers, with his tongue, to suck the crimson nipples into his mouth.

She twined her fingers into the dark hair growing up to his throat. 'But you are more like a dog, a young stupid dog.'

Her laughter tinkled above him. She bit into her full lower lip and he could feel that she was slowly grinding her sex across his stomach. 'You must learn to play too Patrick, or we will not have a good time.'

Her gaze fixed him with her challenge. For a moment he hesitated, uncertain and then he found that he was nodding and everything was all right and he was grinning like a loon and he felt that she could do whatever she liked with him and he found that this was a relief.

Patrick badgered Greene to find out more about Mirrielle.

'Do you think she really has a choice?' Patrick quizzed.

Greene shrugged. 'No one's forcing her. Franny keeps a clean house, takes care of those girls. Business is business. Take my advice Paddy and don't go getting any other ideas about Mirrielle.'

They were on the return north from Buenos Aires and Patrick's attention strayed to the young fellow Irishman running up and down the length of the deck. The Captain had swung by the police chief in Buenos Aires, spun some yarn about a fight on board and young Mick jumping ship up the coast from La Bocca. He was a naughty boy, but could the ship have him back. Grudgingly the authorities released him. Mick was still prison gaunt but putting on weight again. He would joke that Cookie's slop was *cordon bleu* in comparison to the muck he had been surviving on courtesy of Juan Peron. Mick was all bravado and boasts of what he'd do with the money he'd collect back in Montreal; having been caught only after the goods were delivered and

67

Peron's bully boys unable to pin anything on him. It was all a great joke, great craic and Patrick would grin along with the rest of them even as he caught the gleam of fear lurking in Mick's eye.

Late into the evenings Mick taught Patrick to play poker. Five Card Draw to start with, Texas Hold'em, Omaha High, Stud. After the war in Paris when cigarettes were still the main currency of Europe, Mick had won ten thousand in one game, a fortune. He had blown it all on bartering for presents for his family back in Mullingar, 'Ungrateful bastards!'

Patrick was smart enough not to allow cigarettes or money into it so they played for matchsticks but Mick always played to win. And win he did. Patrick wondered whether it was all luck and skill or sleight of hand and marked cards, but if there was a trick to it, he couldn't see it.

One night, in the small hours, Patrick heard Mick in the bunk above tossing and turning more than usual. They were at the Equator, nights thick and humid, the stillness of the sea ghostly in the moonlight which reflected through the open porthole. Patrick's naked skin blistered with sweat.

'Are you awake Paddy?'

Patrick did not reply, he couldn't have told you why.

'By God you're a lucky man if you can sleep in this …'

Moments passed and then the sound of a long-drawn sigh.

'I killed a man, Paddy.'

Patrick held his breath and the hum of the engines and the soft slop of the sea was all that could be heard. After a while Patrick wondered if he had imagined Mick's declaration. Mick started to rummage in the bunk above. There was the strike of a match and the sudden pungent whiff of sulphur. Smoke drifted down and Patrick felt his own urgent desire to take a long drag on a cigarette. No chance of that.

'We'd just snuck across the Plate, up-river from Montevideo. Some sort of guard, came from nowhere he did. I knifed him. It was him or us. Can't get his feckin' eyes out of my dreams! Jasus, what a feckin' joke.'

Mick slid down over the side of the bunk and dropped to the floor. The cigarette was stubbed violently in the ashtray, sparks flying. Patrick could just see him from the corner of his eye, naked in the moonlight.

There was a bitter frost in the air as they docked in Montreal. Stevedores stamped their feet against the cold and pulled their woolen hats low over their ears. Patrick watched his breath fume and coil in the half light of dawn as he secured the gangplank. Mick was at his side before the last latch, duffle bag slung over his shoulder.

'Isn't it a grand day!'

'Well for some.'

'I'll have a bottle of champers waiting for you.'

Patrick nodded. 'Good luck Mick.'

'Oh, I don't need luck, Paddy. I'm a Man of Destiny.'

And he was half way down the gangplank before Patrick thought to call after him, 'What Destiny?'

Mick waved without looking back.

Destiny? Did he himself have a destiny? It didn't much feel like it. It felt like he was treading water waiting for something to happen. Then he thought of Mirrielle and his impatience to see her again and he was just glad that he was young and vital with all his life before him.

Patrick examined himself in the ornately framed mirror of the vestibule, admiring the new suit he had purchased in Crescent, a dark silky grey cloth and with it a cobalt blue tie which he knew drew attention to his eyes. He caught sight of Franny in the reflection of the mirror watching him.

'Good evening Franny.' He spun around to greet her.

'Bonsoir monsieur. Patrick. I remember. You are looking very ...' she paused and considered, 'très élégant. Like ...' and there was a twitch of a smile as the steely eyes pierced him, 'Burt Lancaster.'

He didn't quite know why he felt so uneasy with a comparison which he usually found so flattering.

'I should be so lucky.'

69

'Your friend is waiting for you.'

For a flip of the heart he thought she meant Mirrielle.

'He is a very happy man, I think.'

Slocombe, the Chief Engineer, hailed him over to the table with a chorus of cheering jibes at his smart new suit.

Mick proffered a glass of the bubbly and clinked, 'Sláinte! To a thousand smackeroos!'

A girl with dimpled cheeks leant over Mick and pouted.

'You promised you would dance with me.'

'Oh, I'll be jigging soon enough all right!' Mick laughed and pulled the girl in by the waist. 'Paddy have you met Jo Jo, isn't she a corker?'

Patrick nodded as he scanned the room. Where was Mirrielle?

An hour drifted by. Mick slipped away from the dance floor with Jo Jo in tow. Slocombe was asleep. A second hour dragged. Patrick lit one cigarette from the tip of another, his throat already rough and dry. He veered between frustration and anger. He should enquire. Perhaps she was ill. He sat up with a sudden feeling of panic.

A lone saxophone wailed a solemn fanfare. And there she was, Mirrielle. Silver dress shimmering under the dim light. He stood up. Could she see him? He was trapped. Slocombe sprawled on one side. Molyneux with a girl on the other. He raised a hand. But he could not catch Mirrielle's eye. A man moved in front of the table obscuring his view. Mirrielle was no longer in the doorway. He hunted her down with his eyes. She was being led to one of the curtained alcoves by an older man.

As Patrick made his way around the edge of the small dance floor, he felt woozy and light headed.

'You are enjoying yourself, monsieur?'

Franny was in front of him.

'Mirrielle.'

'Ah, this evening she has an engagement.'

The champagne was fizzing and bubbling around his brain.

'Monsieur De La Salle, a film producer; it is wonderful, he thinks Mirrielle could be a Capucine, she will have screen

70

tests; it is her aspiration, to be an actress.'

She clicked her fingers. A blonde girl slid to her side.

'You have met Collette?'

He felt blank, numb.

'She is a very good dancer.'

He shook his head. 'I don't dance'

'I think you will find that with Collette it is not necessary for you to be such a good dancer.'

'Excuse me, Madam.' He was swaying ever so slightly. There was a sudden nausea rising in his throat.

'Perhaps you need some air, monsieur?'

He found that the thick set doorman had a hand on his shoulder and was steadying him.

'You're right, it's a little stuffy in here.' He turned away with as much dignity as he could muster.

In the early hours of the morning he was carried back to the ship dead drunk by a couple of crewmen who found him passed out in a bar on the waterfront. His wallet was empty and he was without the silk tie which had complemented his eyes so well.

Thin sheets of ice appeared on the St. Lawrence overnight. The ship headed for warmer climes as the horn of an ice-breaker echoed across the fog bound waters. Patrick's black mood did not abate even as they dipped down the steamy West Coast of Africa. He was left alone to stew in his melancholy.

The humidity was oppressive. The armpit of Africa they called it. His armpits stank that was for sure, Patrick thought as he rolled dice all night in an Accra nightclub and lost his wages chasing his luck. Emerging into the glaring light of morning a ragged man wearing the ornately embroidered fez of the Muslims held a creature out in front of him.

'Monkey, you like monkey? Good price. I give good price.'

'Here …' Patrick began to unbutton his shirt. 'You want the shirt off my back? It's all I've got. Take it or leave it!'

To his bleary-eyed amazement, the man nodded and

smiled. 'Good shirt. I like.'

It was the eve of St. Jean Baptiste when they returned to Montreal. Patrick wandered the streets, Rue St. Catherine, the Main, the restaurants on the Rue Prince Arthur, Centre-ville, everywhere there were family groups out to enjoy the sunshine and the parades, everywhere the fleur-de-lis were draped from windows and balconies but he was not any part of these celebrations, this was not his city. He had a sharp longing to be sitting on the grass in St. Stephen's Green with Niall slugging back a bottle of Guinness and singing a round of come-all-ye.

His sense of aloneness was compounded when he was forced to donate Peppito to the zoo. The Captain was immovable. Some of the men had birds, and the assistant engineer a lizard, but a little monkey who stole the Captain's pipe and then laughed about it in that chattering way was quite another matter.

For a week Patrick returned every day to make sure that Peppito was being well cared for. By the fourth day the woman at the ticket counter waved him through. He was assured by the keeper that Peppito would be fine, would be able to make new friends, to mate even; it would be a better life, he would be amongst his own kind.

It was heading towards the end of July. Molyneux was engaged to be married to a rather comely looking girl from back home in Pointe-du-Lac. He wanted to celebrate with a stag night.

At dinner that evening the Captain congratulated Molyneux on his good fortune then turned to Patrick. 'And I think Mr Glendon that you also have a cause for celebration.'

He was in the spotlight of a dozen inquiring eyes.

'I see from our records that Mr Glendon will have his twenty first birthday tomorrow.'

There were 'ahs' of comprehension around the table.

After Bar Pigalle it was decided to go on to Franny's Place, 'For old time's sake.' declared Molyneux who was already half cut, 'Because soon I will be an old married man!'

'What difference did that ever make!' Came the riposte and everyone laughed.

Patrick hesitated and said he would return to the ship.

'Oh no you don't lad.' Greene slapped him on the back. 'The night is young and you're a man now.'

Yes, thought Patrick decisively, he was twenty-one, he was a man, time to get over this foolish business of Mirrielle.

Nevertheless, his stomach lurched with tension when they entered. A momentary flicker of recognition from the beefcake doorman, then a nod and down the stairs and the pianist tinkling *If I'm Lucky* ...

The party squeezed into a corner table. It was a busy night and even in the cooler interior of the Club men had loosened their ties and removed their jackets. Jo Jo congratulated Molyneux on his engagement and Patrick on his birthday and called for two bottles of champagne on the house. A pretty girl, Antoinette, with black bouncing curls slid in beside Patrick turning her cupid bow lips into a smile. He excused himself and watched the smile transfer to Molyneux who was already patting the empty space at his side.

Patrick scanned the room. In the dim smoky atmosphere, he could see no sign of Mirrielle; perhaps she was already headed for the silver screen. He felt suddenly that he wanted very much to rub her out, erase her. He regarded himself in the mirror of the bathroom. Was he a man or a mouse? He had been posed the question in the card he had received that morning from Niall. It was meant as a joke of course. A man? Or a mouse? He deliberated. Niall had drawn a little cartoon of Patrick with Micky Mouse ears, so he knew what Niall thought.

What would his father adjudge? There had been a card from his parents and within a letter from his father containing the details of a money transfer and wishing him every success at his coming of age. He was surprised by the amount.

Of course, his father was a man of some considerable

wealth. But nevertheless. There was enough capital to quit seafaring and to set up some small venture if he chose. Not quite enough that it wouldn't be a risk. But that was typical of his father who always made great claims for the benefits of hard work. Patrick wasn't afraid of hard work; he'd always been a hard worker. His mother's cousins on their farm in Mount Mellick could testify to that. But what sort of business? Was it a test of some sort? Or was it his father merely fulfilling his final duty as a parent and washing his hands of him? Either way this could be his big chance to *do* something.

His head was aching with the quandary.

Molyneux came in behind him and headed for the urinal, twisting his head as he unbuttoned his flies. 'There you are Paddy; I was beginning to worry you'd headed off. We've been lining up your birthday present for you.' Molyneux leered and swayed unsteadily.

Patrick frowned, uncomprehending.

'Your fancy girl. Mr Greene says you won't have anyone else.' He shook his head. 'One whore's as good as another to my mind.' A torrent of piss splashed over the white bowl as Molyneux staggered to balance against the wall.

As Patrick slipped into a seat at the table Greene slapped him on the back and grinned. 'Happy Birthday Paddy.'

Mirrielle was slinking over towards them.

'Happy Birthday Patrick.'

She pulled him onto the dance floor. It was that tune again,

If I'm Lucky you will tell me that you care,
that we will never be apart…

They swayed to the music Mirrielle subtly ground her hips into his to the persistent throb of the bass. Patrick could hear Perry Como crooning in his head, smooth as silk. He inhaled her scent and it lent its perfume to the heady atmosphere. He wanted her to throw her arms around his neck, to whisper, *Je t'aime, je t'aime* … she twirled, there was a light air of gaiety about her. He caught her hand and drew her to him.

They were in the same room as before.

'You're looking very beautiful tonight, Mirrielle.'

'Why, thank you monsieur.'

'Do I get a birthday kiss?'

She pecked him on both cheeks in the French way. He pulled her to him and kissed her with all the passionate feeling which was welling up inside. Mirrielle tried to keep her mouth closed, to push him away.

'Non. Non.'

He stopped, confused.

She wagged her finger playfully. 'You know the rules.'

'Sod the rules.' He laughed and tried to kiss her again.

'Let me go. Patrick, let me go.' There was a sharpness in her voice.

They stumbled and half fell onto the bed, he was pinning her down, burying his head in her cleavage, fumbling for the hem of her dress.

'Mirrielle ...' he groaned.

She pounded his shoulders with her fists, 'Tabernac!' She kicked up and pushed him away roughly.

'Mirrielle?'

Her features were tight, 'Don't think because I am in this place that you can do as you like. I could have you thrown out. Even call the police; we have friends there, yes.'

Patrick sat up and ran his fingers through his hair, breathing heavily. 'I'm sorry, please forgive me, I didn't mean to ...'

Mirrielle walked to the window and drew back the curtain to glimpse the dark street outside. She shrugged. 'Oh, you are no better no worse ...   I thought maybe you have some sentiment. That you have respect.'

Patrick crossed the room and reached out to take her arm. She shot a warning glance and he let his hand drop.

'I do respect you Mirrielle. For months all I have thought about is you. That's why I'm acting a little crazy. I love you.' The words tumbling out shocked even himself, he realised that he had never expressed such feelings before.

Mirrielle sneered, 'And what? You are going to whisk me away to your castle, like some Prince Charming? All you have is a berth on a ship; I think it will be very crowded.'

'I have money. We can go away together.'

'Back to Irelande? Introduce me to your parents?' She was prodding him in the chest, upset and angry.

'Come away with me. Come away from here.'

'I don't need to be rescued, Patrick. I do what I want to do.'

Patrick was shaking his head. 'No. You don't want to end up like these other girls, like Franny.'

'What do you know?' There was a fury in her eyes now.

'I'm sorry. I just want …' He realised he didn't quite know what it was that he did want and she could read that uncertainty in his eyes.

'You only want to possess. Well no one possesses me, no one.'

'I want to love you.'

'It's not enough. What else you can give me? Can you give me what I really want?'

He felt a lurch in his stomach. 'De La Salle?'

'Jacques has promised me a part in a new film. Next week I will have the screen tests! Is that what you can give me?'

He sank onto the bed, head bowed, he felt crushed and desolate.

'Patrick, we cannot always have what we want.' She stroked his cheek and sat beside him. 'Let's drink champagne and laugh and forget all this talk.'

He shook his head.

'I think so.' She declared.

Towards the end of October Patrick was back. He had thought that he would find it difficult to see Mirrielle again. But she slipped her arm through his and he felt himself relax.

'I have a present for you.' He whispered and fumbled for the small box in his pocket. It was an emerald set in a gold ring, which he had purchased in British Guiana. As soon as he had seen it, he thought of her cat like grace and her dark eyes. 'I hope it fits.'

'It's perfect!' She kissed his cheek. 'Merci beaucoup!'

She was gay and flirtatious and full of talk. She was to play a hat check girl in a gangster movie. Three lines. *Take your hat sir?* batting her eyelids, *What business is it of yours?!* uttered defiantly to one of the villains who then slapped her face—and then her big screen moment in which she would wear a silk negligée, *I'll wait for you Johnny!* exclaimed with raw emotion.

Filming had been postponed. Jacques was in New York, she said, talking to important people about finance, backers, a distributor, she didn't quite understand how it all worked. Still, she was convinced her career on the screen was about to get underway. To be successful she only needed to meet the right people, to get an agent, to wear the right clothes, it was all very expensive, she complained.

It occurred to Patrick that he could possibly provide finance for the film. The money from his father remained untouched. Each evening as they drank and danced and each night as he spent his lust, delighting in the honey scent of her skin, the idea grew large in his mind. A film producer. Everyone loved films. Everyone loved American films and Canada was a part of North America. In dreary post war rationed Europe, they were crying out for the romance and thrill of American movies. A new decade was about to dawn and he could be a part of a brighter future.

When he spoke his thoughts aloud, he could see the gleam of excitement light up Mirrielle's face. 'Patrick, that's wonderful. A producer. You will make me a star, won't you? We will go to Premieres and walk along the red carpet and sit at a table with—' her eyes shone, 'Clark Gable and … Judy Garland, yes.' She danced around the room trailing and waving a chiffon scarf. Her joy was infectious, childish.

A week later Jacques returned. The two men talked over brandy. It all seemed very simple. Patrick would be credited as one of the Associate Producers, then, when the money for the sales were received, he would have a percentage share of the profits.

'And that's all.'

'What do you mean?'

'Do I do anything? Organise …'

'It's not necessary. We will have a professional crew.'

'But I would like to learn, if there is something I can do.'

'Monsieur Glendon, for this project it is sufficient to be an investor. Perhaps later, monsieur …'

'I see.'

'I must warn you that in this business there is always risk. Who can say with any certainty this film will be successful or this one?' He shrugged in that Gallic way. 'It is always, how do you say, unpredictable.'

'I understand that.'

'And we have no grande actor. Of course, we have some very good talent.' Jacques smiled across the table at Mirrielle who giggled in return. He turned again to Patrick. 'Also, you must not expect to have any return immediatement.'

'I see.' Patrick had imagined that he would be returning to the ship that night to inform the Captain that he was resigning his post. He felt a measure of disappointment as he realised that this would not be sensible. They were due to sail in a week's time before the river became impassable.

'So, Monsieur Glendon, are you interested to be a partner?'

Patrick looked across at Mirrielle's eager face and nodded.

The papers were signed within the week and the investment monies transferred to Le Beau Monde Productions.

He was never to see or hear from Mirrielle again. Nor was Patrick to receive any return on his investment, despite a number of letters to the production company. He was informed, politely, that the film, *Forbidden Assignation*, had after all received only a limited release and failed to go into profit. Eventually his letters were returned, the company had been liquidated. When he did at last have an opportunity to view the film, he could see immediately that it was second rate. Mirrielle was pretty on screen, although her aquiline nose was rather accentuated, but her performance was overblown and unconvincing. He was, however, pleasantly surprised to see that he was on the credits as an Associate Producer, fleeting though the credit was.

Some years later on a weekend trip to Paris with Niall he was dragged into a cinema in Montmartre. Patrick squirmed in his seat when he realised that one of the sirens in the thinly disguised pornography was Mirrielle. He rose from his seat and left with a puzzled Niall in tow.

Unable to give a satisfactory explanation for his abrupt departure, Niall, who was always cruelly perceptive joked. 'Too hot for you in there, Paddy?!'

Patrick woke in the early hours and could not get back to sleep. He was afraid of disturbing Maeve; she would be awake soon enough with the baby. He slipped out of bed and crept to the kitchen for a glass of water. An early morning fog was drifting in from the Pittwater. He shivered inadvertently.

'Da ...' a sleepy voice brought him round.

Nieve was standing in the doorway clutching the old baby blanket which she needed every night as a comforter.

'What are you doing out of bed, Missy?' He asked softly.

Nieve's disheveled face creased as though she was about to start crying.

'Come here macushla, what's the matter.'

She tottered towards him. 'I thought it was the tooth fairy da, but it was a monster and he was going to ... eat me.'

'Come here my big girl.' Patrick picked her up. 'Too much ice cream is what'll be giving you bad dreams.' He grinned.

Nieve frowned. 'No da, not the ice cream.'

'All right, not the ice cream.'

She wiggled one of her teeth.

'Ah, I see. Nearly out.'

'Will the tooth fairy come in the night?'

'Yes. And the tooth fairy is a very nice fairy.'

'And will leave me sixpence?'

'Oh, now I think the going rate is thruppence, isn't it?'

'Carmel Marie got sixpence.'

'Did she now?'

Nieve nodded seriously.

'Well, we'll have to see if these Australian fairies are as well to do as they are in Ireland.'

Nieve threw her arms around his neck. 'I love you da.' She yawned and nestled into his neck.

He held her to him, stroking her back, kissing the top of her mussed-up hair and cooing, 'I love you too darling. It's all right now, no monsters here, everything's all right.'

His daughter, his precious daughter, born out of love. He felt a pang of shame for the lurid fantasies of the night. It struck him—what if a child was to be born of such a conception?

The thought appalled him.

BEN DOWN AND THE WANDJINA

This bird been hanging from gum tree. Not much now. It got no feathers. Red sun coming up but this bird never gonna wake up. Big dead eyes, it skin red, beautiful head feather all gone. I feel sick in stomach and Binni he shaking.

'Is it demons come in the night?'

Shake my head. This Tommy. Young boy in Billangilil, wild one. Auntie Ruby her too tired 'n drunk and bit crazy. Tommy do what he want. We hear dogs bark, camp waking up.

'Can we bury him dad?'

'Sure thing.' I be late for Boss Anderson. But this something important.

I make a place for bark, show Binni how some of our mob do it. Then I lay poor bird on kindling. We walk in circle and put grave sticks around and a few of the feathers we find. I talk to the cockatoo, so he know he can go now, fly away to his father. And the smoke it go up, right the way up into blue sky.

That night Binni he sitting by the fire. He drawing in the dirt. Drawing cockatoo. Binni is upset, he's angry. I don't want him getting in fight with that boy Tommy. Tommy is a bad fella He bigger and he mean. So, I tell Binni about Wandjina.

'Two kids, they been playing with a bird, they think this bird honey-sucker. But they didn't look its eyes. This bird name Tumbi the owl. The boys did bad things, pull out all the feathers from the head and from the tail, blind that bird and throw him into the sky and say 'You fly now!' and that make them laugh.'

'Just like Tommy!' Binni stab the ground.

'But other thing these boys don't know is that Tumbi is son of a Wandjina.'

Binni look up.

'Inanunga the Wandjina sharpen his spears, he angry 'bout what been done. He make lizard from himself, from his, you know, 'tween his legs.'

'From his nob.' Maali laugh. She take yams, wrap in leaves and put them on the fire.

'From out his nob!' Binni laugh too.

'This lizard find the people and it take the Wandjina to the hill above them. Inanunga pull his beard again and again and rain falls, it falls all night, all day, and all the time he pulling his beard.'

Binni jump up and dance around us, his hands pulling at long beard, beard down to the ground. I clap two sticks together. He's good dancer. Maali push the fire around the yams, fire's jumping up like dance now.

'And now everything been flooding and the Wandjina dance on the wet ground and turn it into big swamp.'

Binni jumps and turns in the air and then stamping his feet like in the mud, again and again, I see Binni face in the firelight, angry like Wandjina.

'Then the Wandjina go round and round and push the people into the swamp and they are all drown.'

Binni dance like drowning.

'Everyone drown but not them two boys.'

Binni stop.

'When they seen this terrible rain, they know Wandjina coming, they run away. Then Inanunga he throw lightning out of the sky. Those two boys are really scared you know. The lightening come and they screaming. They see a huge boab tree. This old tree has a big hole. One boy climb in then other boy. It good place to hide.'

Binni and Maali they look at me, waiting. My eyes getting big and I go close up them. 'But these boys don't know, boab tree is Wandjina too! And the big boab tree close itself round them and them two boys crush to death.' My arms are above Maali and Binni, he scream, she laughin'!

Yams smelling good and I go take one from the fire but Maali slap me.

'Wandjina always get them revenge, one way, another way.'

Gun shot somewhere close. It shock us.

Binni look me.

Gun shot again in the night.

'Boss Anderson, he got new fella. He like 'im rifle, Maybe shooting roos. When they finish, I get me one, taste good with these yams.'

We laughing.

But no one from Billangilil be moving round tonight not with these fellas. Maybe shoot us like roo. Happen before you know. Mistake like.

ORANGE DAY

It was only a little white lie. He was thinking of her and the way she would worry over things. He had lost so much on Killpool Hill and then the cost of the move out to Australia. But he'd struck lucky. The chap with the franchise on the North Shore Golden Fleece Service Station, a German called Schmidt, took a liking to him.

Herman was moving across to the south side, his wife preferred it over there, found it more European. Herman needed someone to take over the day to day running of the place. Patrick was impressed; the station had a fresh lick of paint and it was well situated. When Herman asked whether Patrick would be interested in gradually buying out the franchise in installments Patrick grabbed at a chance to have his own business.

Patrick worked like a dog. Business seemed unusually slow at first but he improved the service. He kept the forecourt spick and span. David of Dalkeith, the prize merino whose image was everywhere on the Golden Fleece brand was polished until he gleamed. Patrick always had a smile for the customer. Washed windscreens. Anything. He was full of inventive ideas and advertising strategies for winning the custom. Herman was pleased, the takings were going up.

Patrick on the other hand was only bringing home his wage minus the money Herman kept for the installments. Still and all, Patrick felt the hard work was an investment in his own future, the profits he was making for Herman would one day be his, the sacrifices would be worth it.

He hadn't really meant to tell Maeve that the garage was his. In a manner of speaking it was – or was going to be and owner of the enterprise sounded so much better than simply being the manager on what was after all a rather meagre salary. She looked so pleased too.

All seemed to be going well. The young Norwegian garage assistant, Nils Muldal, agreed a shift pattern which enabled Patrick to extend the opening hours and he hoped to persuade Herman to take on another man part-time. Herman said he'd think about it, he was a cautious man, couldn't see the point of rushing.

Despite these frustrations Patrick enjoyed the work. He could see that, as well as catering to the passing motorist, running a servo put you right at the centre of a community. He felt this was a business that might suit him, it was down to earth and basic, you got your hands dirty, there was nothing pompous or pretentious about running a service station. There was scope for ambition. He might branch out, run a car repair centre, he might even expand to a second-hand car dealership and from there perhaps to a chain. He was running ahead of himself but that was what was so exciting, the possibilities, the potential to grow. His father had been the Great Entrepreneur. Perhaps it was Patrick's destiny to pick up that mantle after all.

The trouble began on the 12th July. A man came into the kiosk without filling up at any of the pumps. That was not unusual, some motorists just stopped off to buy smokes or coolant. He was a big man, his receding grey hair turning white at the temples. The man took his time looking around the kiosk. Picked up a couple of items off the shelves and examined them. A woman came in with her kid, tired and fractious, and paid for her petrol and a lolly to quiet the kid. The grey-haired man waited until they drove away and then he sauntered over to the counter.

'Do you know what day it is today, Paddy?'

Patrick's first thought was to wonder how the man knew his name, but then of course he had heard his accent when talking to the woman customer. His second thought was to place the man's accent. Belfast he would hazard at a guess.

'Thursday, the twelfth of July.'

'That's right.' The man looked triumphal.

'Orange Day.' Patrick muttered under his breath.

'Orange Day. And you know something Paddy? This is the beginning of your Battle of the Boyne. And do you want to know something else? You're on the losing side. So, you can pack your bags and get your Fenian arse out of here.'

'I haven't come all the way to Australia to fight old battles.'

The grey-haired man laughed, a deep rumbling belly laugh. 'That's just what that German shite said! I told that Jerry bastard I'd be licking Hitler's dead backside myself before he'd be welcome around here. That's this lily-livered government for you, letting in all the refos, commies and Fenians.' The last said with particular distaste. 'Not one of yous would put your hand up and take the oath of allegiance to Her Majesty without being lying turds.'

'We're all Australians now.' Patrick protested.

'And I suppose you have a tribe of bare arsed kids as well?'

Patrick wanted to punch the fellow right in the middle of his smug, leering face but he knew if he did that the battle really would be lost. The fellow was trying to provoke him. He must hold on to his temper and let the old bigot wear himself out mouthing his filth. He wondered at the fact you could travel all the way to the other side of the world and still find yourself caught up in old hostilities. That people like this old codger carried their hatreds with them.

'Don't think we don't know what yous are up to?' The man was thrusting a finger in his face now.

'And what are we up to?' Patrick responded, trying to keep his tone light.

'A bloody Papist plot, is what. The Loyal Orange Lodge Institution they've got your number. Oh yes, we know the catholic politicians in this State are bringing in all these papist refugees breeding like rabbits and all these children to your orphanages. Thick as thieves they are with your Christian Brothers and your Sisters of Mercy! Yous are trying to invade Australia, that's what yous are up to!'

Patrick wondered what he could do to get rid of the man.

'It's no surprise to me yous are in bed with that Nazi Schmidt; wasn't De Valera in cahoots with Fritz all through the war. Fenian traitors the lot of yous, while we were getting bombed in the shipyards and our sons were giving up their lives for their country and the Good Lord!'

An old Ford car pulled in at one of the pumps. An elderly woman, tooted her horn for service.

'If you'll excuse me, sir.' Patrick addressed the man pointedly. 'Unless there was something you wished to purchase?' He edged from behind the counter.

The man moved to the door wagging a finger, 'I'm an Orange Man, yous are not welcome here, remember that.'

He was gone and Patrick heaved a deep sigh before going out to help the old lady fill her tank and to clean her windscreen.

The man's name was Frank Hamilton. Herman admitted there had been a little trouble with him in the past.

'Everywhere one meets these sort of people, with their prejudice. I thought that you being an Irishman he would leave the station alone now.'

'There's Irish and there's Irish.' Patrick informed Schmidt.

'So ein Pech.' Herman sighed. 'Ah well, what can we do Patrick? We must hope they grow tired of their little games.'

'They?'

'He has a nephew.' Herman grimaced and shook his head.

'Did you ever call the police out?'

'What can they do? By the time they arrive, these men are gone. And you have no witness or proof, what can they do?'

Patrick left the encounter with a sinking heart.

Early the next morning his heart sank even further. On the freshly painted walls of the kiosk were daubed the words 'Fenian Scum'.

One of the regular truckers jerked his thumb, 'Stone the crows, I reckon you'll be touching up that wall again, eh mate? Somebody have it in for ya?'

Nils arrived for the busy hours of the morning. When he saw the graffiti, he looked glum.

'Kept painting Swastikas before. Want me to go get the tin

87

from round the back? I think there's just enough paint left.'

Before lunch Patrick sent Nils out to buy more, he reckoned they might be needing it.

'Sure you'll be okay Mr Glendon?'

'Yeah sure.'

'Only ...' Nils hesitated. 'That was a reason the station wasn't open such long hours before. After the trouble, Mr Schmidt didn't like to be on his own here. We always worked together.'

'I'll be all right.'

Nils was about to go out the door.

'What do you know about the nephew?' Patrick quizzed.

'Carson?' Nils screwed up his face. 'He's a bad lot. I was at the same school. You didn't mess with him. He's a Bodgie, has this Push, call themselves *The Apprentices*.'

'Very apt.' Patrick snorted. But he didn't like the sound of it at all.

There was no trouble over the next couple of weeks. Patrick could see that Nils was worried so he agreed that he could go back to the old work pattern and he was always there when Nils was so that the lad was never alone. But Patrick continued on by himself into the couple of late evenings which he had set up. A number of regulars had commented on the convenience and he didn't want to mess them around unless he had to. He was beginning to hope that the incident with Hamilton and the graffiti had been a one off.

It was a miserable rainy kind of day and the overcast grey skies gave way to the dank darkness of a winter evening. There weren't many people out and about. Patrick had been doing the books and was about to close up. A car screeched onto the forecourt and braked to a halt right outside the door, the headlights on full beam almost blinding. Patrick was startled and by the time it occurred to him to lock the door and put up the closed sign the first of what he would have called *teddy boys* piled through the entrance. They were in the full gear of their tribe, long drapes, bootlace ties, and beetle-crushers. Hair slicked up in a ducktail.

'G'day mate.' Said the one with pitch black hair. His mouth twitched up into a smile but his eyes were a cold blue and hard. How's business?'

'All right. Can I help you with anything?'

'Just looking.' Piped up a pimply lad and sniggered.

'I'll be closing soon.' Patrick tried to sound businesslike.

'That you will, mate.' The black-haired boy leaned forward with both hands on the counter and stared at Patrick.

Patrick felt the lad was trying to stare him out. 'You wouldn't happen to be Carson McGinnis, would you?'

'My fame precedes me ...' Carson straightened up and adjusted his tie. 'Paddy.' He added with a glint in his eye.

The smallest of the group picked out a coke from the cooler and threw it high up in the air. 'Fancy one of these anyone?'

It was caught by the sniggerer in a flying leap. He threw it back. 'Not really mate.'

The small lad made to catch the returning bottle but let it fall to the floor, where it smashed, coke fizzing and spuming from the debris. 'Aw, look at this mess!'

Carson presented an apologetic face. 'You'll have to forgive Bill, he's a clumsy bastard, aren't you Bill?'

A big fellow who had been standing at Carson's shoulder casually took out a flick knife and flicked it open.

Patrick flinched.

The big fellow began to clean his nails with the tip of the blade. Behind him Bill squealed. 'Oh no!' A bottle toppled off the shelf adding to the pool of dark liquid and broken glass. 'Would you believe it; I've gone and done it again.'

Carson, shook his head extravagantly and tutted. 'Mr Glendon here is going to start thinking we've come to wreck his shop boys if we go on like this.'

'Like I said, I'm closing up.' Patrick's fists clenched below the counter.

'Oh well, we wouldn't want to keep you from your lovely wife. You do have a wife I suppose?'

Patrick kept his eyes firmly on Carson.

'Of course you do. So, I reckon we'll just have to come

back another time.' Carson nodded slowly. 'Okay boys. Rattle your dags.'

They headed for the exit and in their jostle of knocking against each other they flipped maps and cans to the floor with profuse apologies. The pimpled boy began to whistle *The Londonderry Air* as they careened out the door.

Their whoops and laughter echoed around the deserted forecourt as they roared off in the car.

Patrick surveyed the wreckage and called the police. They arrived half an hour later. A constable took notes but after a minute or two, he shook his head. 'Look mate could you say that any of it was deliberate? Did they threaten you?'

'Not in so many words.' Patrick admitted.

The pot-bellied constable closed his notebook. 'They're a bunch of larrikins, Mr Glendon. Don't think we don't know them mate; that Carson is a real troublemaker. I'll pass the word along for the night patrol to keep an eye on the place, they might catch them at the graffiti. My advice would be not to be on by yourself if you can help it. Carson's got a vicious reputation. Would have got him years back for a razor attack; a young fella, sliced his arms, Carson said he'd get his face next time. Boy told us who'd done it but said he'd never testify; can't say I blame him, good-looking fella.' The constable turned to go. 'Sorry mate.'

By the time Patrick cleared up it was after midnight when he rolled into his own driveway.

As he edged between the sheets Maeve turned in to him and slipped an arm around his chest, her head nudging his shoulder. 'Darling, you're working far too hard.'

'It was just tonight, I needed to get the books finished.'

'I thought the advantage of being your own boss was that we might see more of you, not less.'

'I'll try and get home a bit earlier tomorrow.'

'I'm worried that you'll make yourself ill.'

He kissed her and tried to comfort her anxiety as much to quiet his own concerns as hers.

August was quiet. Patrolmen dropped in occasionally to check on him but there was nothing untoward to report. He cut back the opening hours.

At the beginning of September, the station was robbed at knifepoint. A desperado. Patrick hadn't tried to resist or do anything 'clever'. The description fitted an itinerant character not long out of prison. There didn't appear to be any connection to either Hamilton or McGinnis.

Three days later Patrick found that two of the tyres on his mini were slashed. Something which could have been done very swiftly by an innocent enough looking passerby. A week on and *King Billy Rules* was scrawled on the wall of the kiosk.

Patrick didn't tell Herman about these incidents. He worried that Herman would renege on the deal and wish to replace him as manager. He needed time to think, to work out what his options might be. It galled him that all his hard work could be undone by a few outdated taunts daubed on a wall and the threatening overtures of a young ruffian who should have been banged up years before. He wondered if there was some way that he could catch him out.

It was while his thoughts were running along these lines driving home that Patrick found the car behind coming up on his bumper. He pulled over with the intention of letting the impatient driver pass. But the car pulled in with him. In his rear-view mirror, he could now clearly see that it was Carson with his big thug of a mate.

They waited. After ten minutes Patrick could feel the sweat prickling the back of his neck. This was ridiculous. He slammed into gear and shot out onto the road. Up ahead a motorbike pulled out and began to hog the middle of the lane slowing him down. There was Carson again, on his tail. The bike was slowing down even more. Carson was edging up. Patrick looked ahead, the oncoming lane was clear, he'd overtake the bike. He pulled out. As he did so the bike began to increase in speed, just keeping a nose ahead. Patrick squeezed on the accelerator; he was pushing well over the speed limit now.

Coming towards them over the next gentle rise a lorry came into view. Patrick could feel every muscle tensing in his body. He needed to swing back in but either he went full throttle and tried to cut in front of the motorbike or he braked heavily and pulled back in behind Carson. The lorry was blasting its horn, its lights ablaze.

Patrick braked to the floor, grabbed the handbrake and almost immediately began to pull over to the left, his car screeching and burning rubber. He figured that if he was going to endanger anyone else it would be Carson.

The lorry flashed passed, horn still blaring.

Patrick missed Carson's rear by a whisker, continued to brake and to pull in to the kerb. Up ahead, the two boys were waving to him as they carried on their way. Patrick was shaking in every limb; he could still smell the rubber.

The following Saturday, he shut up at midday. He was looking forward to going to the beach with the children. Spring was in the air. It was the bluest of skies. As he passed through the suburbs, he could see that the warmer weather brought everyone out into their gardens.

Drawing up outside their bungalow, he spotted Nieve waving energetically from the tree house next door. His little tomboy. He waved back. John John was running down the drive towards him. He felt his heart loop the loop. This was the new life of his dreams.

A car parked across the road beeped its horn. He turned to see Carson leaning through the driver window. His hand shaped into a cocked gun he took aim, first at Nieve up in the tree and then at John John spilling out onto the pavement. Carson grinned and blew the smoke from the barrel. Patrick clutched his steering wheel white knuckled and realised that his war was lost.

F.J. HOLDEN

The mini car was gone and, in its place, the comely bulk of the F.J. Holden sat in the driveway. John John had liked the mini car, its smallness and its boxy shape, like a big toy. The FJ Holden on the other hand was a real car. He liked the shine of the chrome, the gleam of the hub caps, the horizontal grille, the little chrome fins at the rear and the Holden badge at the front.

'It's a bewdy.' Mr Hal next door nodded, 'Six-cylinder engine.'

Where the mini was cramped the F.J. Holden had plenty of room for them all. He felt a warm glow every time he walked around the new car and thought about the big adventure. An even bigger adventure than coming to Australia on the boat, their da said. That afternoon they were going to buy a caravan. Then they were going to live in it.

They were going to be like pioneers, the da said, and they were going to go out West and they were going to cross the desert and eventually they would reach the other side. On the other side there were beaches and rivers and green forests and it was never cold and this is where they would live.

Mammie said Sydney was beautiful with beaches and forests and the Pittwater, why did they have to leave? Their da said because they would all be happier. Their mammie was quiet then.

John John was glad. Now he was going to live in a caravan. Nieve had always been showing off that she had a gypsy caravan at Killpool Hill. Now he was going to help his da to buy one, not Nieve, because Nieve was at school. Nieve wasn't so glad about the big adventure because she had two new best friends and they were twins and you could not tell them apart unless one wore a pink ribbon and the other wore a yellow ribbon, but then they would swap just to fool you. It was like two for the price of one the da would say when they came around to play.

On the drive to the showroom the da said that when they went on the big adventure, they would see the real Australia. Instead of seeing kangaroos and wallabies and koala bears in the zoo they would see them for real in the wild. John John imagined kangaroos bouncing beside the road as they were driving along with the little Joeys sticking their heads out.

There would be lots of wild creatures and they would have to be very careful. The da bought them a Snake Bite Kit. They had only been allowed to look inside once because it had to be kept hygienic; there was a little knife and something that was called a turnkey. Better not to get bitten at all the da said and they were to tell him immediately if saw any snakes. Their da also bought a slouch hat with a popper on the side, but you could have it not buttoned. It made him look like a cowboy. John John liked to try it on although it was much too big.

The Carapark Hunter was perfect. Outside it was shiny and rounded. Inside was the best, the way you could unfold one thing and have a bed and open another and have a table and cupboard. Mammie said it was tiny and where would they put everything and the da said they had too much stuff anyway but Mr Hal did help him to put the washing machine on the roof rack of the Holden. It wasn't easy to do and there were a couple of teddy boys at the end of the drive who kept laughing.

Mrs Bonnie made a chocolate cake and said she would miss them and they were to keep in touch. And Nieve was a sissy and cried all day and would not come down from Malcolm's tree house until the da said he was going to make her pancakes for supper. John John could not go to sleep with anticipation and when he did eventually fall asleep, he had a little accident and mammie was shaking her head and saying how on earth would she cope if he was going to be having accidents every night in the caravan.

The da said, 'Sure isn't he just overexcited'.

John John couldn't eat his breakfast cereal, it was too early and he didn't feel hungry. Nieve started sniffing and the da said she was to stop that at once and then he said, 'Come here.' And he gave her a big bear hug. John John pushed his bowl away. 'You too.' the da said and John John ran around the table for his bear hug.

Patsy was in the high chair with mush all over her mouth and she was throwing more mess over the side and going 'Am, am, ammmm!' Which meant, 'Look at me!' Mammie came in and groaned, 'Oh Patsy.' And then Patsy bounced up and down in the chair looking at her and said, 'Mama, Mama!'

'Did you hear that?!' The da said.

Patsy grinned. 'Mama, Mama!'

'Who's mummy's girl?' mammie shook her head and wiped all her mouth clean.

John John helped the da to get the suitcases into the boot of the FJ Holden. The mammie came out and said, 'That's everything.'

'We'll be on our way so.' The da shut the boot.

The car drove slowly out of the drive. As they dipped on to the street, they could hear the washing machine rocking up and down on the roof above. The da stopped until it settled.

'Well here we go. Westward Ho!'

The sun was just clearing the dip at the bottom of the street lending a lovely orange glow to the day.

POSTCARDS HOME: THE BLUE MOUNTAINS

Dear Mammie and Daddy

The mountains really are blue—it's the haze from the eucalyptus apparently. Views and spring colours are truly spectacular. The Three Sisters rocks on the front of the card reminded me of you mammie and Aunties Annie and Imelda!

Best wishes
Maeve
xx

MELANESIANS

It was long miles of mallee scrub. After the sight-seeing tour in the Blue Mountains, blooming in the clear air of late spring, with panoramic vistas and pretty little country towns, tea rooms and grand hotels which had all seemed quite European, this was more like the real Australia, Patrick told them.

A land of low scrub. The red earth. The fields of yellow green pasture. Varcoe wind mills revolving gently in the breeze feeding water to the animal troughs. Farmland which survived droughts and the ravages of the rabbit plague. Signs to remind locals of the need for Bush Fire Action Plans. Bare blackened tree trunks and branches like the silhouettes of contorted hand gestures. The thin line of the telephone cable flanking the highway. The huge pipeline carrying precious water; dipping down below ground to allow an entrance to some homestead. Occasional trucks like trains of the road. Towns of wide streets and shop verandahs, red corrugated tin roofs; towns you would drive through in a couple of minutes. Yes, this was more like the real Australia.

Then the Holden broke down and they were stranded by the side of the road with the bonnet open. Patrick thought it might be the Alternator. No one stopped to help. Patrick wondered if this was the real Australia too. Maeve made a picnic of it, set up the little fold up table, it was nearly lunch time anyway. John John kept asking 'Where are the kangaroos?'

Eventually Patrick decided to walk to the next place about three miles up the road. It was a long hot trek in the midday sun. He found a repair garage but the mechanic couldn't come out until after seven, he did however have an Alternator, if that was the problem. Patrick set off back.

The caravan sites were very good, they both agreed. Maeve relieved to find that the facilities, the showers, washrooms and laundries, were universally extensive and well kept. So many people seemed to lead a nomadic life. Wool shearers, fencers and fruit pickers. Whole families living permanently in caravan parks. Some were roughnecks. But most seemed decent enough people, families of eastern Europeans, a few poms, the itinerant Australians.

After an initial reserve you would uncover a certain camaraderie of the road and be invited to join a group or family at their fire for a stubby of beer.

Patrick spent an enjoyable evening with a philosophical Frenchman, Antoine, who ate only fruit and nuts, claiming this was the healthiest and most natural diet for humans. Antoine had traveled widely in the Pacific and lived for many years amongst remote Melanesians. The peoples there had the most exquisite experience of life, Antoine said, because they lived so entirely for the moment and were happy in it. The absence of history and memory amongst them meant that on his return after a year away he had been greeted as a total stranger.

At first, Antoine had been disconcerted to find himself so thoroughly forgotten despite the length of his previous sojourn but he was accepted amongst the islanders with the same warmth and affection as before. He came to admire this freedom from the constraining hand of history. Patrick felt a sudden yearning to wipe clean his own memory and to lose all sense of his past.

POSTCARDS HOME: BATLOW

Dear Mammie and Daddy

Crossing over The Snowy Mountains, JJ disappointed no snow this time of year. Near collision with a herd of wild horses stampeding across road – known as Brumbies. Children very thrilled, P. had to brake so hard thought we'd lose washing machine!

Maeve
xx

POSTCARDS HOME: GLENROWAN

Dear Mammie and Daddy

P. insisted on detour to the last stand of a 'true Irish rebel'—
nothing much to see and from the picture on the front with
the bucket helmet and the iron vest wasn't N. Kelly more an
eejit than a hero—they only had to shoot him in the legs!

Hugs from us all,
Maeve
x

TIGER MOTH

John John was furious. Nieve was sucking a lemon sherbet right in front of him and the day before it had been a three colour ice lolly in the shape of a rocket. She and her new friend Lottie, who had blonde hair in pigtails, collected empty bottles from the men in the caravans and then took the empties to the shop and got money for them. He said he'd tell the mammie.

Nieve jeered, 'Tell-tale tattler, buy a penny rattler!'

Their da said they needed a holiday and they were staying put for a whole week. The caravan site was in a nature reserve. Janine, the lady who ran the place invited them to come and see the baby wallabies. They were living in the pouch of a clothes peg bag. There were wallabies and possums, a lopsided pelican, an old donkey and a spiny ant eater called an echidna. Janine said people brought all sorts of injured animals for her to look after until hopefully they could be returned to the wild. She preferred it if they could go back to the wild, that's where they belonged.

There was a lake of flamingoes and there were other big birds called brolgas, which Patsy called 'bwollies' and they all laughed. There was also a part of the lake where you could paddle and swim and it was sandy like a beach. You could sit on the grass and have picnics or barbecues. Their Mammie liked spending all day on the beach with Patsy, sunbathing and reading. There was a playground with swings and a seesaw and best of all an old airplane called a Tiger Moth, a real one, which you could climb into and sit in what was called the cockpit and pretend that you were flying high up into the sky. Only it was difficult to get a turn because of all the older boys. John John would perch on a swing and watch them clambouring over the wings and the one in the cockpit pretending he was in the war and had a machine gun 'RATT-A-TTAT-TAT!!

John John was bored. The da was giving the F J Holden *the once over* because they would be setting off again the next day, mammie was at the beach, Nieve was stuffing herself with lemon sherbet and the airplane was full. John John went back to the caravan.

His da said, 'Pass me up that rag, there's a good lad.'

John John stood by the car watching his da cleaning the spark plugs, his fingers black with oil. He was wearing a vest and you could see his hair, damp with sweat, curling up to his throat.

'Have you nothing to do?' His father asked. 'Go and fly that plane why don't you?'

He shrugged, 'I'm going to go and get the comic.'

His da winked at him, 'Desperate Dan—always my favourite.'

John John climbed into the caravan. His mammie liked everything to be spick and span but in the caravan that was nigh on impossible. The table and benches were folded into place but he couldn't find the comic. At the other end was where his parents slept. There were clothes stacked up on the bed which had been brought in from the washing line. Perhaps the comic was underneath. The clothes spilled over. Or maybe under the pillow. He picked it up. There was mammie's purse. The soft brown leather one with the patterns pressed in to it which granny had made when she was a little girl.

John John paused. An idea came to him. A terrible idea. It made his heart thump and filled his whole chest. He opened the poppers of the purse. In one section there were notes and in the other section there were coins. Through the open window, he heard his da whistling outside. There were pennies and shillings and two sixpence pieces. His da was starting the engine now, turning it over. He did not think his mammie would miss one of the sixpence pieces. It wasn't fair that Nieve had so many lollies and he had none.

DUBLIN IN THE GREEN

They were following the Yellow Brick Road off to see the wizard, the wonderful wizard of Oz and they were going Along the Road to Gundagai. There were lots of other songs that her da liked to sing; about The Rising. Such as,

We're all off to Dublin in the Green, in the Green
Where the helmets glisten in the sun ...

Which was quite jolly and they all sang along in the back of the car,

In the Green, in the Green!

But another one he sang was very sad, about a young boy that died called Kevin Barry and once Nieve saw real tears in her father's eyes.

Now they really were going to Dublin. Even her mammie was excited. Though she said she was sure to be homesick. This Dublin was in South Australia on National Highway Number One. When her da saw it on the map he said that's where they would stop for a late lunch. Nieve wondered what it would be like? Would there be lots of Irish people? Would it be green? As she watched the passing countryside all flat and dull for miles and miles, eddies of dust rising and swirling across the parched pastures, she thought how nice it would be if it was green in Dublin.

POSTCARDS HOME: PORT AUGUSTA

Dear Mammie and Daddy,

 Still sweltering – even the water in the estuary is too warm
for swimming.
 Stopped in a place called Dublin – what a disappointment!

Best wishes,
Maeve
Xx

THE STRAIGHT LINE

Her father was going to cross the desert by himself. They were to go on a train. Nieve lay awake listening to her parents' low voices. Her mammie had heard horror stories of people veering off the track and being lost forever. Maybe they shouldn't be going out West but settle on Adelaide or Melbourne. It wasn't as if there was a job lined up in Perth. On and on her mother worried until her da grew angry and said that this was the way it was going to be and that was an end of it.

In the morning she awoke to find her mother packing the bags they would need for the train journey whilst her da fed Patsy. She could feel the weight of their silence in the thick warm air in the gaps between their stilted conversation. Her own stomach was a knot with anxiety, sensing a fury which shocked and frightened her.

As they approached the railway station in Port Augusta, Nieve was overcome by dread. She imagined her father lost in a sea of sand, dunes waving endlessly into the distant horizon like the vast rolling oceans over which they had sailed on the Southern Cross. How would they ever find him again? By the time they arrived on the platform, Nieve's fear was a monstrous lump in her throat.

John John rushed ahead to watch out for the train's approach. Her da went off to purchase the tickets. Passengers were filtering through the entrance tunnel. With much honking and shouting an open backed truck laden with crates of groceries drew up on the platform and forced her mother to move the luggage. A trolley cart was wheeled out by a couple of railway porters. The truck disgorged its load and then backed out with as much noise as its entrance and as many oaths. Another trolley emerged from the station office with mail bags and bundles of newspapers.

When her father returned, weaving his way between the clamorous throng, Nieve let out a piercing wail, 'Don't go da, don't go!' and she threw her arms around his waist and clutched at him as though she could physically restrain him from leaving.

Her parents were startled by the vehemence of her outburst. Patsy let out her own echoing wail. 'Da, da, da!'

'Nieve, Nieve what is it?' Her da stroked her hair back from her face and looked across to her mammie for support but found none. He gently extracted himself from her grip and crouched down to face her. 'Nieve, don't be crying, there's a good girl. I'll see you all soon. Sure, you'll have a great time on the choo choo train.'

Her lips quivered. 'Don't go da—you'll get lost and we'll never find you.'

'Away out of that. I'll not get lost, Nieve.'

'Everyone gets lost in the Nullbor.' She was finding it hard to speak for the sob in her throat.

'People are driving over the Nullarbor every day of the week. And shall I tell you something else?'

'What?'

'I won't be getting lost because I've been a sailor, I can read the stars. It's like having another map.' He brushed a tear from her cheek. 'You remember me showing you the stars? Centaurus and The Southern Cross?'

Nieve nodded between sobs.

'You'll know that I can see The Cross and that way I'll not get lost.'

'Why can't we all go with you then?'

Her da blew out his cheeks, 'Well …'

'Because it'll be cooler on the train.' Her mammie interjected. 'We thought you'd all like the change. Come on and say goodbye to daddy now, the train's here and we have to find our seats.'

Sure enough, the train was rolling into the station and John John running back to them alongside it.

Her da gave Nieve a reassuring squeeze. 'I am counting on

106

you to look after your mother for me, Nieve.' He pulled her up into a bear hug and growled and she growled back in the usual way and he winked and let her down again.

She tried to smile but there wasn't a smile there because she still had the fear clawing at her throat and it wouldn't go away so easily.

The train rattled across endless arid scrubland, hour after hour. They soon became bored looking out of the window. Her mother delved into her bag and brought out *The Dandy*. Immediately there was a squabble. John John complained that Nieve always had everything first because she was the eldest and it wasn't fair. A man across the aisle said Ladies should always come first but Nieve noticed that he was looking at her mother when he said this.

'Nieve's not a lady.' John John declared petulantly and sank back into the seat.

Nieve took the comic with a smirk. John John's tongue darted from between his pursed lips. Their mammie gave him a quick slap on his bare thigh and Nieve could see that he was fuming. All at once she felt her conscience prick. It wasn't fair really and John John was doing nothing but getting himself into trouble. Nieve decided in that moment to be magnanimous.

'I'll read Lord Snooty and then you can read it and then it will be my turn again.'

Her mammie smiled at her. 'That's very kind Nieve. Isn't she very kind, John John?'

John John shuffled in his seat. 'I want to read Desperate Dan first.'

Nieve thought for a moment, Desperate Dan wasn't one of her favourites. 'All right.'

The man leaned over and said to their mammie. 'You have lovely children.'

'Thank you.'

'Your husband meeting you?'

'No, he's following on in the car with the caravan.'

107

'Across the Nullarbor?' The man seemed surprised.

Nieve woke in the middle of the night with a crick in her neck and her throat sore from the fug of cigarette smoke in the carriage. She needed a wee. Her mammie was curled protectively around Patsy on the seat beside her, a pillow wedged into the window frame, her head lolling with the rattling of the train. John John was tucked up around his knees with his thumb in his mouth like the big baby he really was. Nieve squeezed her legs together but she knew it was no good. She would have to go down to the far end and she would have to get across the black rubber bit where the carriages joined and which looked like it might chop your legs off if you slipped. She had no choice, the wee might gush out and wet her pants, her dress, the seat and then the shame. John John sometimes wet the bed at night and had a rubber sheet which he hated and her mammie was always saying she was at her wits end.

The lights were a faint amber glow. Grown-ups loomed large and dark on either side. An old lady was snoring, the man beside her shifted in his seat and his eyes glistened out of the darkness as he watched Nieve pass.

In the toilet she reached into the sink cupping the water coming from the tap and splashed it on her face, she felt hot and sticky and she was thirsty but her mammie said they must not drink from this tap.

When she came out the man with his bright pin eyes was there, smoking a cigarette.

'Long journey isn't it?' He said. 'Where ya going?'

For a moment she couldn't recall the name of the place that was going to be better than Sydney.

'Perth is it?' The old man suggested.

'Yes, Perth.' she smiled.

'I'm from Perth.' The man chucked her under the chin. 'You could come visit. Could have a barbie. You like that?'

She wasn't sure. When her da made a barbie the sausages all burnt black like charcoal, and she didn't like to say but she preferred the way mammie did them in the oven.

'I've got a granddaughter, 'bout your age. In Adelaide. She likes it when I tickle her.' He stubbed his cigarette underfoot. 'You like being tickled?'

'No.' Nieve shook her head vehemently.

'I bet you do ... all little girls like it. Give me your hand.'

Nieve shifted uneasily, she wanted to go back to her seat. To her mammie. But the old man was blocking the way and she could feel the toilet door bumping at her back as the train rattled over the tracks.

'Go on.' The man leaned forward; his lips curled in a smile.

She wanted to pull her hand away but his smile enveloped her and his eyes twinkled brightly. He opened her palm and with a finger traced a circle. 'Round and round the garden looking for a farthing ...'

She knew what came next and flinched.

'One step ...' His index finger stretched up along the length of her arm. 'Two step ...' The long bony finger reached to her armpit. '...and tickle you under the arm!'

'No!' she squealed as his fingers prised and probed into the soft yielding underskin and she was losing her balance and they were tumbling into the small wash room. And still he poked and prodded all the way down to her tummy until she was bending over. 'No!' she squeaked.

'Alora!'

It was a Train Guard with a big black moustache. 'Okay?'

The old man straightened up. 'Course, mate. Why wouldn't it be?'

The Guard raised a bushy eyebrow.

'Little girl likes to be tickled, don't ya?'

Nieve squirmed out from under him. Sweaty and flushed.

'No, I do not.'

The man shook his head and laughed and shut the door of the toilet.

Nieve heard the lock click with relief.

'Bambina, you looka hot.' The Guard said. 'You thirsty, you wanna col' drink?'

Nieve hesitated she was not to take sweets from strange

men, but this was a drink and the Guard in his uniform was not a stranger, not like the old man who she thought now was both strange and a stranger. This Guard had kind eyes.

Nieve nodded.

'Is a good idea.' He indicated for her to follow.

They passed through the dining carriage with the Formica top tables, where a man was smoking and another had his head on the table fast asleep. The Guard took her to the snacks counter and unlocked a little door at the side.

'A coke be okay?'

'Yes, thank you.'

Beads of ice-cold water dribbled down the side. He flipped off the bottle top. 'A glass?'

Nieve shook her head. She glugged the coke and could feel it like an icy river passing down her throat and fizzing all the way to her stomach. How thirsty she was. Gulping for breath when she put the bottle down with a satisfied burp. She put her hand to her lips quickly.

The Train Guard smiled, 'Is good for you, the burp. What is your name?'

'Nieve.'

'Nee—ev. In Italia this is a name Nivea, means snow white.'

Nieve's eyes widened, 'Snow White?' Was that her name and no one had ever even told her?

'I am Fortunato, si, a Lucky Man, but now maybe Sfortunato. I have a little girl, Mirabila, my little wonder but my wife take her back to Abruzzo.' The Guard looked sad

'Why?'

'My wife is a … La Lupa, capiche? A wolf.'

Nieve gulped some more coke, had she heard right?

'You don believe me but is true.' Fortunato bent towards her, confiding. 'Many years ago, a neighbour is hunting in the mountain when he sees the wolves above on a rock, he fires his gun. Then, there is another sound that is fantastico.'

'What?'

'A baby is crying. How can this be possible? He climbs to the rock. And crawling out from the cave there is a bambina.

110

My wife.'

Nieve's eyes widened.

'The hunter, Umberto, brings her home inside his jacket next to his heart and I think she has already stolen this heart. His wife meet him, *Umberto, I see you have not killed even a rabbit, what will we eat?* And Umberto says, *But Assunta look what I have caught instead!* And this child of the wolves, Ida, is a great blessing because she mends the hearts that were broken when their son was killed in the Terrible War.

But, on nights when the wolves howl and the village children are crying with fright, Ida goes to sleep like she is listening to a lullaby. When she is older, Ida is not afraid of the forest. One night, I follow her and she is dancing in the full moon with the wolves who are her sisters and brothers.'

Nieve wondered what it would be like to have a wolf for a brother. Not that she had ever seen a real wolf. Then, she supposed that she should be getting back to their carriage, but they would all be asleep and she longed to hear more about Ida.

Fortunato sighed, 'My family, they say, *Fortunato, you must not marry La Lupa.* But, I love her, what can I do?'

Nieve nodded in sympathy.

'Then, everyone is leaving; *You must come with us* they say, *there is nothing in Abruzzo but to be poor.* I read always about railways and I get an idea to come to Australia because here it is the longest straight railway in the world! No bend, no curve, just straight ahead. Is beautiful no?'

'I didn't know that.'

'But La Lupa … she finds hard to speak inglese and she says, *Fortunato, the people call me 'Eye-dah' not 'Ee-da' how it should be.* Then we have a letter that Assunta is very ill and La Lupa goes home to Abruzzo with Mirabila.'

'Why don't you go back too?'

'I must work. They will not come here again even when the old people die because in Australia there are no wolves. Is very sad for me.' Fortunato took a handkerchief from his pocket and wiped away a tear.

111

'I'm sorry.' Nieve patted his huge hairy hand.

'You have a kind heart Nivea. Now we take you back to la mama. Do you know Italiano?'

Nieve shook her head.

'I teach you to count to ten, si.'

Nieve brightened.

'Uno, due, tre …'

As she drifted into sleep Nieve dreamt she traveled deep into a dark wood. She did not know where she was. Above in the night sky and between the looming trees she could discern clouds scudding across the full face of the moon and then the poking branches were crowding around her whispering something in her ear, 'Uno, due, tre …' She pushed her way through the tangle of wooden arms and she was in a clearing. High on a rock, silhouetted against a clear vibrating moon, the wolves were dancing. La Lupa beckoned to her with bright yellow eyes. The wolves began to howl and there was a flash of light and the stars swirled and formed themselves into a man. For a moment she was frozen. It was the hunter; his name was Centaurus and he turned to look at her and he was smiling and it was her father. She held out a rosy red apple, the white of its one perfect bite gleaming in the moonlight.

A horn sounded, loud and piercing.

'Cook! The next station is Cook!' Another Guard was passing along the carriage, older and with a grumpy face.

The train was approaching a small settlement. The horn blasted out its greeting again. Nieve groped into a sitting position, blinking in the sunlight, eyes heavy with sleep.

'Thirty minutes whilst we take on water. Everybody off. When the horn blows you have five minutes to get back on board and believe me you don't want to be left behind!'

There was no platform. You had to lurch down steep steps and drop to the red earth. It was like opening the door to an oven, the heat made Nieve feel dizzy. The grumpy Guard passed the fold up pram down to her mother.

Coming to meet the passengers were the women of Cook,

112

each held out a tray. Freshly baked Lamingtons. Crocheted doilies, jars of chutney and glasses of homemade lemonade. Then running up the dirt street towards them Nieve could see a group of young children holding out little paper flags and drawings, some in crayon and others with splodges of paint. A girl held out a picture of what might have been a kangaroo or maybe a dog with a big tail.

'S'a roo.' The girl stepped back shyly as though she had crossed too far.

'Harry, take a squizz at this.' A large woman wearing a bright, flowery dress said. 'How much do you want poppet, will thruppence do?'

Nieve looked around. She couldn't see her mother. Where was she? She turned again. Nieve ran towards the front of the train. The big engine was throbbing in its own haze of heat. And then one long straight line of railway track. Alongside, like tireless runners in a relay race, the lifeline of poles and wires connecting to a world that was not disappearing over the horizon, over the edge of the world in a scrub of emptiness and desert.

She ran back weaving through the milling passengers, the laden trays and cries of 'Watch out there!' and the children waving their little flags. 'Mammie!' she shouted, as she was blocked by the boxes of tinned fruit and crates of beer being unloaded from the freight carriage.

'Strewth, what a stinker of a day!' said one of the men.

Then, Fortunato was smiling down at her and her hand slipped into his large hairy paw. He led her behind a water butt, on which someone had written

IF Your'e Crook come to COOK

Towards the shelter of a corrugated verandah.

There was her mother feeding crumbs of cake to Patsy and John John licking at the chocolate around his lips.

'Alora! She is here, Nivea.'

'Nieve!' her mammie exclaimed. 'Where did you get to? Thank you very much Guard. I'm so sorry for the trouble.'

'Prego. Snow White is my friend, si?' He winked at her.

John John stared, 'Snow White?'

Nieve stuck out her tongue.

'Nieve, eat your cake now before it's all melting.'

They were bored and fractious. Hour after hour of the endless salt scrub. Nieve pressed her forehead to the glass, she could feel the regular thrum of the train, monotonous and unchanging like the landscape. Occasionally, there would be a railway siding of pens.

They were for sheep or cattle, said Al, the man across the aisle. It wasn't a desert with big yellow sand dunes, but low scrub and now and then, at places like Cook, a few stunted trees.

Then something was breaking the sameness. A small airplane. It was coming down out of the sky. It was flying so low it looked as though it might smash into the red earth. She pressed her nose to the glass. It was still coming down, heading right for the ground.

Her mammie put a hand to her mouth.

Al exclaimed. 'Strewth! Looks like it's about to crash!'

'Those poor people!' Her mammie gasped.

Nieve craned her neck to follow the flight path.

'D'you think it'll explode?!' John John stood looking over her shoulder. 'BAM! BAM!! BAM!!!'

The plane disappeared below the line of their vision behind some stunted trees. They held their breaths.

There was no explosion.

'No worries!' Al grinned. 'There's a runway strip over there, used for emergency landings and refueling.' He couldn't stop laughing.

Nieve wanted to kick him. She decided she did not much like Australians. She preferred Italians. 'Uno, due, tre, quattro, cinque, sei, sette, otto, nove, dieci!' she practiced in her head.

THE NULLARBOR

The asphalt ended and the surfaced road gave way to dusty earth; a track pitted with ruts and rock-hard waves which jarred through Patrick every time the Holden passed over them and set the washing machine on the roof rack rocking up and down no matter how tightly he secured it. His early optimism that he could complete the journey in a matter of a few hard days driving evaporated. With a growing despair he understood how slowly he would need to drive if he wasn't to put either the car or the caravan at risk of a blow out or worse. When he passed the shell of an abandoned car, he knew how right he had been to insist Maeve and the children take the train. By midday the sun had cracked open the sky. All the windows wound down couldn't stir up enough of a breeze to cool a gnat.

By evening he was sick with heat and exhaustion. His shoulders ached, stiff with the exertions of holding the wheel steady over the corrugated ridges. He ate an unappetising meal of tinned spam and wondered whether he might make better progress in the cool of the night. The last rays of the sun sank behind the far-off horizon. All thoughts of driving were then abandoned. The night sky glittered with stars beyond counting but without a moon the darkness which surrounded him was immense.

He felt that he too might drift through the empty blackness of space like a star in search of its constellation. He spotted Centaurus low in the sky, recalling the way Nieve had clung to him on the platform and felt his guts wrench with the missing pain her image conjured. His children, his precious children, how empty life might be without them, without Maeve, an emptiness as vast and lonely as the Nullarbor.

He flipped open a beer, shivering with the night chill. Sleep was tugging behind his eyes and yet he felt a sudden rush of adrenalin, as though the points of his life were converging. He was here now, in the moment, a man surrounded by sky and earth like the first man, an Adam writing God's story in the dirt and across the heavens. He felt what it must have been to be that first man to walk across this red earth, to stare up at this same canopy of stars. Walking in a Dream. Wasn't that the notion the aboriginals had, something about dreaming.

He drained the bottle and lobbed it into the low saltbush. Then a pang of guilt. What was he doing littering the grandeur of this primeval landscape with such cheap detritus? He'd retrieve it in the morning. The first rays of the desert dawn—that'd be a sight to see. He reached for his smokes. Just one more, then he'd have to ration. He would have stocked up on cigs at the servo if the old man hadn't got on his wick.

'You'll get no water here.' The man had growled in greeting through tight lips, eyes narrow slits in his leathery face.

'Right …' Patrick lowered the hand he had raised in salute and turned away to lay out his jerry cans in readiness. Muttering to himself , 'A man'd be crawling out of the desert and get not a drop from the likes of you.'

It was The Last Servo before god knew where. The petrol gurgled up into the glass globe as it was pumped up from the underground tank. The man thrust the nozzle into the Holden's tank.

'Many passing through?' Patrick enquired, propelled by the need to hear himself speak aloud as much as by curiousity.

The old man grunted. 'One or two.'

There was a sorry looking goat tethered to the stand nearby. For the milk, Patrick supposed. The man's only companion by the looks of it. A miserable life for a miserable old sod.

Patrick blew smoke rings up into the air and wondered if indeed he did have enough water with him.

He slept through the first light of dawn and then was thrown for a moment by the absence of Maeve beside him in the small double bed and the children not clamoring for attention. He felt groggy and his head ached. A quick brew and he'd feel better he assured himself, determined to hit the road before the sun climbed any higher but his limbs dragged behind his resolve.

It was late in the morning, a couple of hours into the drive, when he spied a storm of dust approaching on the horizon. Patrick felt unnerved and then realised that it was a large truck. Perhaps the driver would stop, they could exchange a word or two, complain about the heat, already intolerable and it wasn't yet noon. He pulled over, an invitation for the other fellow to do the same. The thought occurred that the trucker might have some water he could spare – being near the end of his journey across the Nullarbor Plain. There'd be no harm to have an extra drop but he'd warn the driver about the old sod at the servo; that was only fair. Patrick stepped out of the Holden, lit a smoko and waited.

The blast of the horn was almost deafening. He could see the driver now, in a singlet, a Jacky Howe they called it, and a shock of sandy hair. The man seemed to give a quick nod in acknowledgement of his wave but he did not slow down, maneuvering the huge vehicle with ease over the contours of the road he roared passed. Patrick was caught in the swirling tail of a thick red cloud which momentarily blinded him and then the truck was lost in the fug of its own making. He coughed and spat the grit from his mouth. As he ran his fingers through his hair Patrick could feel it standing on end with the dry dust. He took a deep drag of his cigarette and stubbed it underfoot.

'Well fuck you too mate!'

Hours later he could still feel the grit in the creases of his neck and the insides of his ears.

Patrick went to bed early that night, hoping to catch a better start the next day. The red dust had begun to permeate the interior of the caravan and even the sheets had a fine rusty tinge. Ablutions would have to be kept to a minimum as he eked out a little water to rub over his grubby perspiring face. There'd be no more shaving.

Sleep was fitful. Dreams came. There was water everywhere. He was standing up to his waist in the sea, it was at Sand Eel Beach, Patrick recognized the curve and shape of the cove, the steep descent. The waves kept knocking him about, seawater bubbling up his nostrils, white spray riding like horses, the Horses of Mannanan, wild eyed, nostrils flaring. The undertow was pulling at him.

He called out, 'Da, da, I can't swim!' His father was puffing on his pipe. 'By Hook or by Crook.' His father was saying. Patrick was climbing up a cliff, Hook Head. He dare not look down, only up, and up. His father peered over the edge. 'What have you to say for yourself?'

Patrick was perched on a ledge, impossibly narrow.

He opened his eyes with a start; a thin shaft of light was sneaking behind the curtain. A fly buzzed around his head, he brushed it away but it would not be so easily deterred.

Still naked he went outside for a piss. An edge of sun exploded over the horizon. He was dazzled looking at it and had to shield his eyes. His shadow thrown long and dark like some mythical titan born in a burning crucible. He felt an urge to roar into the silence, 'FORGIVE ME!' and again, 'FORGIVE ME!'

God did not answer.

It was difficult to concentrate. Hour after hour of saltbush, bluebush and featureless sky. The unending treadmill waves and rucks of the road. Hour after hour the same shimmering horizon playing tricks with the imagination. At one point he thought he saw a sea of golden wheat and felt a stab of pain. But almost always the haze promised water, just out of reach, a beautiful cool stretch of water and once he thought

118

he fancied a sailing boat, its canvas flapping in the breeze.

His thoughts drifted towards the reunion with Maeve and the children. Perth would be the place for them. The climate was good. People said it was a small friendly city. They'd get a house down by the Swan River or by one of the beaches. That would be nice, to feel the cool air coming in off the Indian Ocean.

From the higher fields of Killpool Hill you could see the sea and catch a whiff of salt with a westerly breeze. All those years at sea, he never tired looking at it. Funny that he'd never learned to swim.

His eyelids drooped then there was the sudden sound of cracking vegetation under the tyres. With a waking jolt he pulled too hard on the steering and swung back onto the track, the caravan crunching and clanking behind, tilting dangerously. The car lurched and shuddered to a halt. Patrick took deep breaths of the hot dry air, trying to steady his nerves; then noted the temperature gauge. 'Christ!' It was rocketing. A thin film of smoke seeped from the front edge of the bonnet. He switched off the engine his lips pressed tight, trying to allay the panic which was rising in his gut.

The bonnet was sizzling in the searing heat; you could fry the proverbial egg on it, no trouble. Too hot to touch. He got a rag and released the catch, as it opened, he leapt back from a spume of scalding steam. Hurriedly he propped the bonnet open and stood back. No point attempting to examine anything right away. He got back into the car, his grip tense on the wheel. He would have to wait until near sundown. He felt weary. No doubt about it the heat could take it out of you.

There was a rap on the car roof.

'Yer right mate?'

Another rap, louder.

Patrick blinked. He must have dozed off. A large man in khaki shirt and shorts was standing at the open window, dipping his weather-beaten face into the car.

'Got a bit of a problem have you, mate?'

How many hours had slipped by? The sun was tipping onto the rim of the western horizon.

'Yes, em .. engine overheating -'

'Name's Doug. Let's have a gander then.' Doug moved to the front of the Holden, scratching the back of his neck under the slouch hat, an old Digger perhaps.

Patrick jumped out of the car. 'Patrick. … it was too hot to … Thanks Doug.'

'Yer a Mick are yer? Least your lot speak the Queen's English.'

Patrick bit his tongue; this didn't seem the right moment to pick a fight with a Good Samaritan.

'Lot of these new fellas, don't even know the lingo, yer wops and yer dagos. I just come from Melbourne, visiting the rellies, place is crawling with 'em. Don't hold with it. Yeah, I know all the arguments, Japs on the doorstep, yellow peril and all; but this is a white man's country, we came here, we made it what it is and then this lot comes along wanting all the hand-outs. Same as the abos. Bludgers the lot of them.'

Patrick nodded along to the diatribe. Never mind he felt like Peter denying Christ; anything so long as the Holden could be got back on track.

Doug took his head out from under the bonnet. 'Yer fan belt's gone – got a spare?'

'Yes, I've got a spare.' Patrick responded; and felt like adding, 'I'm not a complete eejit.'

'That'll sort yer, she'll be right, mate. Good car the F. J., she'll see you through.' Doug scratched the back of his neck again. 'Yer all right for water?'

Patrick hesitated. 'Well …'

'Can't really help you there, reckon I'm just about covered myself.'

'I'll be fine.' Patrick assured.

'Righteo then. Gotta go, mate, I'm flat out like a lizard on a log.'

'Thanks for your help, Doug.'

'No worries. Here, one tip from an old desert rat - yer run outa water yer can always piss in the radiator. Be seeing ya.'

Doug returned to his ute and took off in a stream of dust.

'Et tu Brucie.' Patrick waved.

By the time he had finished replacing the fan belt and filling up the radiator, taking Doug's advice in part, there was little point in driving any further. Tomorrow would be another day.

The sandstorm seemed to come out of nowhere. Hitting Patrick hard from behind. He scrambled to wind up all four windows as the flotsam and jetsam of brush and grit assailed him from every side. The car was rocking and rolling, buffeted by the force of the whirlwind, the washing machine creaking dangerously overhead. He wondered if this was one of the tornados which he'd heard speak of, the *willy willys,* and, if it was, whether it could blow the car or the caravan right off the road and toss them up into the air like Dorothy's house in *The Wizard of Oz.* For an agonising moment it felt like the storm could do just that. He slowed to a halt, clutching tight to the wheel.

As quickly as it had arrived the tornado passed away.

Patrick stepped out of the car and checked around the vehicle and the caravan as best he could, cleaned enough of the windscreen to clear his vision. He dared not waste any water. From what he could see debris was scattered everywhere, with red earth banking up in small drifts. The edges of what passed for a road and the desert scrub were no longer so distinct, not that they'd ever been great. He felt his guts wrench. If he could go back, he would, if he could rewind the clock and make other decisions, he would, but he could not. Maeve and the children were waiting for him, would be there in Kalgoorlie even now he supposed. He wanted to curl up into a small tight ball and let come what may, let this cruel god do his worst. But he could not let them down.

He progressed slowly, ever vigilant. At one point the track

121

seemed to run out but veering a tad to the right he could just make out what must be the throughway. He tried to keep the terrifying thought of another tornado at the outer fringes of his mind. He sang. Snatches of old songs and remembered one day driving up in the Dublin Mountains with Maeve when they were courting, he singing full throated.

If I were a Blackbird I'd whistle and sing
And I'd follow the ship that my true love sails in

She'd broken off the engagement. She wasn't ready for marriage; it was all too sudden. She needed time, she said. What was there to think about? He insisted. There was a couturier in Paris, Madame Clert, her assistant had liked Maeve's latest drawings. Maeve could stay with Jean Marie's mother in the apartment in Rue de Versailles. No, no, no, he said. For a week they did not see each other. He telephoned but she was always out.

And on the top rigging I'd there build my nest ...

So, he turned up at the door and she answered it.
'Come for a drive. Just a drive up the mountains.'
It was a lovely day, soft and hazy. Maeve's mother came in from the garden, secateurs in hand, carrying a bunch of yellow roses, she hovered in the hallway.
'Hello Paddy dear.' she'd said, 'Isn't it a peach of a day?'
'All right,' Maeve agreed. 'A bit of fresh air won't do any harm.'

And I'd bury my head in her lily-white chest

A little further along, Patrick was leaning forward, peering through the windscreen of the Holden, was that a cluster of buildings? He shook his head. It shouldn't be possible? His map was worse than useless, a road map for the whole of Australia, little or nothing marked for whole swathes of territory. There were outposts in the Nullarbor, he knew that much. The train would be stopping at Cook. He should really have sought out a proper ordnance survey map, but such thoughts had not occurred to him back in Sydney. It all looked so simple then, a straight line on a page.

The buildings didn't disappear. He was drawing closer. Some outpost after all. The relief was overwhelming. Yes, he could see rippled iron roofing and a Varco mill and fencing to either side of the track.

It was a one-horse town but unbelievably there was a Hotel; called The Shamrock of all things. He grinned like a Cheshire Cat.

'G'day.' He greeted the two men sitting at the bar.

'How are y' Paddy? Isn't it a grand day, right enough?'

Patrick was flummoxed for a moment; the man had a Dublin accent.

'I'm well.' He tendered. 'And y'rself?'

'Couldn't be better, isn't that right Parker?' The Dubliner quizzed the man to his left.

Parker was slumped on his bar stool, his stockman's hat drawn so low over his brow that his features were scarcely discernable. He grunted.

Patrick puzzled, there was nevertheless something familiar about Parker. Had he met him before? He'd hazard that he was in his late forties. Maybe fifteen years older than himself. An associate of his brother John? Or even his father? He pulled out his wallet. 'What'll y'all have to drink?'

'Put that away.' The Dubliner said, 'Tis Parker's shout.'

'Thanks, that's very kind.'

Patrick glanced about him; the Hotel was as basic as most of these places usually were. A couple of rough wooden tables. A darts-board. What looked like an old spittoon. He smiled to see the plaster leprechaun behind the bar and the mock signpost saying, 'It's A Long LONG Way to Tipperary'. Nothing could be more true, and yet he felt at home.

A drink was placed in front of him, blacker than the night

with a thick creamy head. As he licked his lips, he realised just how dry and cracked they were.

He raised the glass. 'Sláinte.' With reverence he took a sip. God, it was good. 'God, that's good!' He declared.

The red-haired barman grinned and turned back to his crossword puzzle.

'Where are ye headed?' The Dubliner asked.

'Kalgoorlie.'

'After a bit of gold at the end of the rainbow are ye?'

Patrick grinned. 'In a manner of speaking; I'm picking up my wife.'

'Oh, a man who loves his wife, isn't that grand, Parker?'

Parker grunted.

'New bride ran off to get family supporter.' The barman muttered loudly. 'Eleven letters. The fifth letter is a 'd'.' He shook his head.

Patrick took a long draught of the black stuff. He felt all the cares of the day dropping away.

'Well there's a pass.' The Dubliner intoned. 'Michael's from Macroom.' He explained, indicating the barman.

'Breadwinner.' The answer shot out of Patrick's mouth.

A moment passed.

'By golly you're right.' Congratulated Michael of Macroom. 'It's an anagram.'

'Will you have another?' The Dubliner turned to Patrick.

Patrick shook his head. 'I should be getting on my way. There's a good few hours driving left in the day. But let me get you fellas a drink.'

'Ah, g'way outa that. Tis Parker's shout.'

Michael, poured a glass.

'Thanks again.' Patrick nodded.

The barman placed the drink in front of him, 'One for the road.'

'And which road will you be taking?' The Dubliner enquired.

'I thought there was only one?'

'He thought there was only one! There's a road in and there's a road out. There's a right road and there's a wrong

124

road.'

'There's a track winding back ...' Sang Michael.

'Well, which way should I go?' Patrick asked all confused.

'Not the road you arrived by.'

'To an old-fashioned shack ...' Sang the barman.

'But not straight ahead either.'

'Not straight ahead?'

'That's the road will lead you nowhere.'

'Along the road to Gundagai.' Sang Michael of Macroom.

'What other road is there?'

'The fork to the left.'

'Then no more will I roam ...'

'Where is it?'

'Right across the street? Did you not see it when you drove in?'

'I must have missed it.'

'Easily done.' The Dubliner acknowledged.

Parker grunted.

'When I'm heading straight for home ...' Sang the barman.

'Will take you straight to the main road and then you'll turn right. Can't miss it.'

'This isn't the main Nullarbor Road then?'

'What would have given you that impression?'

'Christ, I'm lucky I found you fellows, I could have been lost out here in the middle of nowhere.'

'Good and proper.'

The thought filled Patrick with horror.

'Along the road to Gundagai!' Bellowed Michael, his arms extended as though he were the great Irish tenor Joseph Locke.

Patrick drained his glass. 'Thanks a million. For everything.'

'Fare thee well and fare thee well and fare thee well again sir.' The Dubliner hailed.

Patrick waited for a moment by the door to see if Parker would raise his head and he might see the man's face. But he just grunted beneath his hat.

125

Patrick watched the dawn rise orange and golden through the little curtains of the caravan. He'd finished off the emergency bottle of brandy in the night and now he was feeling the dull throb in his head.

Circling high in the sky he could see one of the famous wedge-tailed eagles of Western Australia. Was that a sign that he was nearing the end of the crossing? The eagle dived, swooped and then rose up again a snake dangling from its powerful talons.

Patrick heaved himself from the bed and thought that he should get a couple of hours driving in before the sun began to fry what little was left of his brain. He felt befuddled. As he had lain awake in the small hours of the night, he'd recalled that there was a man called Parker who worked for his father, driving one of the Abbey Mount delivery trucks. And his cousin Joan had been married to a man from Macroom, he couldn't be certain but he'd a feeling his name was Michael.

Patrick sat at the wheel with his head in his hands. Apparently, there were nigh on one hundred hotels in Kalgoorlie. He could believe it. And from what he'd seen so far there wasn't a one of them he would want his wife and children to be staying in. A couple of the landlords said that yes, they could remember a woman and her kids were looking for a room a while back. No one knew where they were. He should go to the police or the Post Office. She might have left a message.

The crossing had left him feeling jaded. Back in Sydney it had all looked so simple. A caravanning holiday across country. A little adventure on the yellow brick road. The children convinced that there really was a Wizard of Oz and that they were off to see him. If he was honest the trip had put them all through the wringer. Maeve had once or twice become weepy in the night and he worried she was heading for the same attack of nerves which assailed her at Killpool Hill. She must trust him. It would all come good. He needed

126

her to believe in him. That was what a wife should do.

First, he needed to find her. She'd be going out of her mind. How many days had it taken him to drive across? There seemed to be one day he couldn't account for. He turned on the engine and shifted the Holden into gear. The Post Office first and then the police station. He was about to pull out when there was a hand on his shoulder through the car window.

'Da! Da! Da!'

It was Nieve, her eyes wild. John John racing in behind her. 'I saw you first Daddy!'

Patrick wanted to cry.

'I've been swimming da!'

'And me.' Added John John, though everyone knew he couldn't swim yet but just splashed in the shallow end.

Maeve, pushing the fold up pram, caught up with them. 'Patrick! I've been out of my mind!'

He was out of the car clasping her in his arms.

'And I can go under the water.' Nieve was tugging at his trousers. 'You should see me.'

Maeve laughed and explained, 'They've an Olympic size swimming pool here would you believe it, and a paddling pool.' The words were tumbling out, her voice high and breathless. 'There's nothing else to do in this god-awful place. At least we keep cool, the heat has us nearly killed.' She grabbed his hand like she would never let it go. He felt the tension in her and then a spring, uncoiling. There was everything in her eyes, blame, anger, fear, relief and love. Yes, love, he could see that, love. Here, in the furthest place from everything they knew, that was all they had to cling to.

'My god Patrick, the car! And the caravan!'

She was taking in the thick red dust that covered virtually every inch of the two vehicles.

'Wait 'til you see inside.'

He opened the door.

She went from drawer to drawer, cupboard to cupboard. There wasn't a space within that the dust had not infiltrated, no surface not permeated.

127

'Come on, you'd have to laugh.'
'Or you'd cry!'

That night as they lay side by side in the hotel room, whispering so that they'd not wake the children, Maeve released all the pent-up fears and dread. It had been awful arriving at Kalgoorlie and trailing from one dire hotel to another, the children exhausted, everyone looking at them. All men, a town full of men. Silent and staring. She had never felt so frightened.

'Finally, this place I had to swear that we'd come in round the back and the children were never to be seen. It's not exactly The Ritz I know,' she said, looking around the grim little room that hadn't seen a lick of paint or fresh wallpaper since the beginning of the century, 'But I can tell you I was thankful for any bed that night!'

Patrick held her tight. He decided then and there that he would only add to her worries to tell her about the breakdown and the sandstorm and the day he seemed to have lost. Or, Parker and the barman from Macroom in The Shamrock Hotel.

THE LIGHTS OF THE CITY

'You look like Billy Bunter.' She sniggered.

Their da snapped at Nieve to shut up.

John John would have laughed if he hadn't been feeling so sick. If anyone should prick him, he would explode, burst like a balloon and lots of yellow stuff would come splattering out and hit Nieve in her smug gob. Except that she was sitting up in the front like Lady Muck and it was his mammie who was sitting beside him with a damp cloth pressed to his brow. The window was full down because he was so hot, burning up, hotter than any of them and they were all moaning with the heat.

His mammie kept asking him all sorts of questions.

'Did anything bite you John John?'

'No mammie.'

'Are you sure? I won't be angry if you've been somewhere you shouldn't.'

He had been somewhere he shouldn't. He had taken the money out of his mammie's purse and bought the pink and white marshmallows in the caravan park shop and hidden behind the wash house to eat them all in one go until the soft mushy powdery sweetness of them made him feel sick. He had thought that no one would ever know but now God was going to punish him because God does know, because he sees everything.

'I don't know mammie … I can't remember. Will we be there soon?' he whined.

They were driving all day, jiggling about in the car and now it was dark and the black night seemed endless. Then all at once there were flashing lights and a siren sounding.

WHA! WHA! WHA!

John John tried to lift himself up to look out of the window but had to flop back. His da slowed to a halt, banging on the steering wheel like he was mad with it.

A policeman appeared at the side of the car.

'Evening officer.'

'You any idea what speed you were doing, mate?'

'Officer—'

'With that carapark on the back? They can jack-knife on yer—and there's a speed limit in these parts!'

'Sorry officer.'

'See your license.'

The da fumbled around looking for it. John John could see the buckle on the policeman's belt and his big hands resting on the sill of the window. He wondered if he could ask to see the gun in his holster.

'This isn't an Australian License.'

'It's an Irish one. I'll be getting the Australian as soon as we're settled in Perth.'

'No point asking you for an address either, I suppose.'

The da shook his head.

'It's a serious offence.'

'Look, officer—' his mammie was leaning forward.

'Officer could I just have a word.' His da cut in.

'I'm listening mate.'

'Outside the car.'

The policeman deliberated. 'All rightie. No funny business.'

Moments later another policeman stuck his head in the window and looked straight at him.

'Kid does look kind of crook, Keith.' He yelled back to the first policeman.

'We need to see a doctor!' His mammie was sounding desperate.

Then the policemen were giving them directions and his father was getting back into the Holden.

'Go easy on the down-hill, mate. Don't want any accidents now do we?'

Around the next bend they crested the Darling Range and stretched out before them lay the twinkling lights of the city.

'Look look, we're here, we're here!' Nieve was jumping up on the front seat. 'It's the wonderful city of Oz!'

The doctor poked and prodded, knocked his knees and got him to stick out his tongue.

'It's mumps, Mr Glendon. Like as not your other kids'll go down with it in a day or two. Keep them indoors, lots of liquids, I'll write out a prescription. A good dose of the Fremantle Doctor will do them all a world of good.'

John John squirmed at the thought of seeing another doctor.

Dr Andrewartha chucked him under the chin, 'That's what we call the breeze that comes in off the Indian Ocean and very welcome it is too. Pity it's late this year—what with the Commonwealth Games.' He turned to the da. 'Opening Ceremony, hottest November day for forty-nine years! I should know, I was doing a stint as a medical. Strewth. Plenty of water, young man.' He nodded at John John, 'Dehydration it's a killer, people don't realise. Do funny things to you.'

The da nodded his agreement.

Even though it was the middle of the night, the da bought him an ice lolly on the way back to the caravan park, with the injunction not to be telling his sister. But when he got back all John John had to do was to flash his yellow tongue for her to know.

POSTE RESTANTE

Patrick made his way up the steps into the Main Post Office. The row with Maeve was still ringing in his ears.

'We've come all this way for what? It doesn't look much different to Sydney only smaller and a million miles from the nearest other city—in the world! Patrick, we're never in one place for more than two minutes. It's hardly worth putting Nieve into the school before the summer holidays because I don't know where we'll be come February! And John John, is due to start. We need to be settled Patrick. I can't take much more of this. We need a home, not a tin can on wheels.'

There was a long queue. People were sending off their Christmas packages and it was only into the first week of December. When he finally reached a counter, he asked for the Poste Restante. A surprisingly large bundle was handed over to him. He saw at once that there was a telegram. It was addressed to Maeve. Telegrams half way across the world were never going to be good news. From the number of letters with a black rim round the edges he had a fairly good idea what had occurred.

Shaking, Maeve placed the telegram on the table for him to read.

22nd November 1962

SORRY. SAD NEWS. FATHER DIED THIS MORNING. PEACEFULLY. FUNERAL TUESDAY. WILL WRITE. KEVIN

Her hand was over her mouth choking back the sobs which were already spilling over. She was trying hard not to break down completely in front of the children.

Nieve was sitting at the fold down table, her face alert and curious. 'Is there a letter from granny?'

The caravan felt impossibly small and crowded. Patrick could see that Maeve scarcely knew where to put herself. Outside, the sun was brilliant in a blue sky. Being the start of the weekend the caravanners were all outdoors. Men were getting loud with beer and Patrick could smell the barbecues on the go. He put a hand on her shoulder and tried to draw her close but she shrugged it off. She wanted to be left alone with the telegram and the letters.

He said, 'The kids are over the worst—why don't I take them for a drive along the coast? They're going stir crazy in here. I'll bring a tin of baby food for Patsy and buy chips and burgers at the City Beach. They can stay in the car, in case of the infection, but at least they'll be out of here. And out of your hair.' He added.

Maeve nodded, her eyes a film of tears.

THE CHILDREN OF LIR

When Nieve saw the black swans, she was reminded at once of The Children of Lir; the children of an Irish king who had been turned into white swans by their wicked stepmother, singing sad songs for a thousand years. Could any of these swans be little black children under the spell of an evil witch? She didn't know and wished that she did. She would like to meet a real aboriginal person so that she could ask but the only ones you ever saw were sweeping floors or looked dirty and scary.

Nieve watched one of the ferries go by and waved to the people on board. They waved back. After all the weeks on the dry dusty road she loved being by the water again, the big fat Swan River. There was water everywhere. Everyone in Perth had a boat. The caravan park was in a place called Como, named after a lake in Italy her da said. Maybe Perth would be like Italy; 'Uno, due, tre …'

Even her mother seemed a little happier as the days passed. Seanathair had gone up to heaven and they wouldn't be seeing him anymore and mammie was very sad but they would all say prayers for his soul.

Her da went to mass with them, which he didn't usually do. It was in Latin but there was a bit in English where the priest talked about the gospel and at the end he asked them to remember in their prayers the dear departed souls of Maureen Kelly of South Terrace and, 'John McMahon of Dublin, father of one of our parishioners'.

Mammie looked surprised and then reached across to the da, she squeezed his arm and whispered, 'Thank you Patrick.'

Afterwards everyone was standing around chatting in the normal way and the priest came over and held her mammie's hand. He was very sorry about her loss and it must be hard to be away from loved ones at such a time and she must come and see him whenever she liked. And her mammie was very grateful.

Then he turned to Nieve, 'And we'll be seeing you soon for your First Holy Communion classes, isn't that right young lady?'

Her First Holy Communion! Nieve looked at her mother who nodded, 'Your uncle Kevin is sending over the dress that your cousin Orla had.'

'And you'll be making your First Confession, where all your sins will be forgiven. But a good little girl like you would have hardly any I'm sure.' He smiled kindly and was gone.

Sins? Did she have any sins? How many? Nieve felt suddenly panicky. Sometimes her mammie slapped her on the back of the legs with the hairbrush for being naughty. Was it a sin when the man tickled her in the toilet on the train? She'd never told her mammie. Would she remember all the sins in time for the First Confession and if she didn't, did that mean that they would never be forgiven?

Now, every night she lay awake, reckoning up her sins. The classes with Fr Clancy were confusing, there seemed to be so many different kinds, mortal sins and venial ones for starters. She was learning the Ten Commandments and there were sins which were easy to understand like not to steal or to murder but there were others that were not at all simple. Then there were ones like the sin of pride or being greedy or thinking ill of others. And then there was the Original Sin which Christ died for but which everyone still seemed to have and never to be able to get rid of even though it was Adam and Eve's fault. Eve's fault really because she was the one had been tempted by the serpent in the Garden of Eden, who was the devil in disguise. Nieve had a vague memory of a dream, a rosy red apple with a bite taken out of it.

As she looked at the black swans drifting by on the

sparkling river, Nieve reflected that her soul must be nearly as black as their feathers. So far, she had counted up a list of nearly twenty sins that she could remember. There were a few she wasn't certain about and she had never told her mammie about the night on the train because something about that felt like a bad thing. But better to be safe than sorry when she made her First Confession; Nieve wanted more than anything else to be in a State of Grace.

LETTERS HOME: PERTH

Dear Kevin,

So good to speak to you! Thank you for taking the Reverse Charges. I'll call as arranged when Mammie is staying with you. A very sad Christmas for all of us without daddy, it has hardly sunk in yet. Mammie sounds as though she is bearing up well. I had a lovely condolence card from my friend Eithne and a mass card from Mary Rose. I feel so far from everything and all so strange.

Thank you for the money order for John John's birthday, I bought him a toy airplane, his latest passion, he is growing so fast and doesn't like to be cuddled anymore, a real little boy! And thank you for Orla's Communion dress, it needs very little adjustment, just a tuck at the waist, (which can be reversed for your Emer if need be) and Nieve looks very pretty in it. The ceremony will be in the middle of January. Fr Clancy is a great comforter. It seems he's a cousin of your friend Brian Clancy the pediatrician.

I have so very much to thank you for Kevin. But Patrick has landed on his feet at last at a large Estate & Lettings Agency and seems to be enjoying the work which takes him out and about all over the city. Perth will suit us very well and now that Patrick is 'in the business' he is hoping to find a bungalow near to the river.

Much love to Sinead and the children.

Your grateful sister,

Maeve

THE SHILLING TOOTH

It was a small dark room at the back of the bungalow which jutted out beside the verandah. She bagged it as soon as they flew through the doors. Her mammie hesitated for a moment, and her da asked wouldn't she rather be in with Patsy and John John. No, she would not! Her mammie smiled and said after all it was a good idea now that Nieve was a little older. The new sewing machine could go in a corner of the living room instead.

So, Nieve had a bedroom of her own whilst John John and Patsy were installed together. Patsy in the cot with mesh all over it to keep out the flies, which Nieve thought made her look like a monkey in a cage at the zoo. Her da told them that he had once had a little monkey for which he swapped a white shirt in Africa. She and John John wanted to know all about Peppito and the funny stories like when he had stolen the ship captain's hat.

Nieve was lying in the narrow bed thinking about pets. At Killpool Hill there had been cats but the cats weren't friendly and a little terrier dog called Flan, but he belonged to Joe, the man who worked on the farm. So none of them had been especially hers. She would like a pet. Her eyelids drooped.

It was very hot in the stuffy little room even with the window open. Her sleep was fitful, half in and half out of dozing. She kicked off the sheet and tossed about. She wiggled her loose tooth absent mindedly, it had been loose for days, and then it came away. She nearly lost it fumbling in the dark but a sharp prick located where it had rolled beneath her arm. She placed it carefully under her pillow. The Tooth Fairy would come in the night and that would be another sixpence for the piggy bank.

Nieve was wondering how much it would cost to buy a pet. *I should have asked Santa for a puppy,* she thought. Instead of which she received the picture book which you painted very carefully with just water and all the colours came out like magic—but a puppy would have been better.

She turned over on to her back. There was enough of a moon to throw a little light through the gap in the thin curtains. The light picked out the cracks in the ceiling and tears in the wallpaper. If she squeezed her eyes Nieve could see different shapes; one bit could look like a squirrel with a big fluffy tail but if you looked another way then there was an ugly hairy monster with one eye. Nieve was a little afraid of the one-eyed monster and the way he seemed to stare at her, it gave her the heebie jeebies. She tried to swivel him into the squirrel but he lurched back.

It was while she was trying to do this that a shadow moved. Her breath stopped. Nieve kept very still. It seemed a long time but then the shadow moved again and she could see that it was a small dark man. He was picking up things on top of her chest of drawers. She could hear the soft jingle of the few coins inside her piggy bank as he shook it ever so slightly. Carefully he turned it upside down so that the pig's legs were sticking up in the air. She wondered who he was. Then a sudden exciting thought came to her.

'Have you come for my tooth?' she whispered.

The little man froze and slowly turned his head to look at her with dark glinting eyes. He looked more like a goblin than a fairy and bigger than she had imagined. But then she had never met a Tooth Fairy so she didn't know what they looked like, perhaps they were more like goblins and gnomes after all.

'Have you come for my tooth?' She asked again.

The man stared at her and nodded slowly.

Her eyes grew large. 'It's under my pillow.' She raised herself on her elbows. Her heart was beating very fast. 'I can't see your wings.'

'We don't have any.' The Fairy was stepping forwards.

She frowned. 'I thought all fairies—'

139

'Shhh.' The Fairy put a finger to his curling lip.

Nieve put her hand over her mouth. 'Sorry.' She mumbled.

'Wouldn't want to wake anyone else, would we?' The Fairy continued in his strange soft lispy voice.

She shook her head.

'We're not meant to be seen, see.'

The Fairy hovered over her with his dark glittering eyes. Nieve thought he looked like the Rumpelstiltskin in her book of stories.

'You've lost a tooth, have you?'

Nieve opened her mouth and showed him the gaping hole. Gently he moved her chin so that he could see the gap by the moonlight. She noticed then that he was wearing gloves. That was something else to remember. She imagined John John's surprise when she told him; *And did you know that Tooth Fairies wear gloves?* She supposed that fairies were strange and funny and sometimes in the stories she read they did strange and even wicked things.

'Did it hurt?'

'A lickle.' She replied with her mouth still gaping.

'Were you brave?' The Fairy asked.

She nodded.

He squeezed her chin.

'Was it you who came when we lived in Sydney?'

He shook his head. 'Must have been one of my mates.'

'Are there lots of you?'

He seemed to be thinking for a moment. 'Yeah, there are.' He squeezed her cheeks. 'You can't tell anyone you've seen me.' He squeezed a little harder.

She nodded, but he seemed to catch the hesitation.

'No one.' He was hissing now. 'Because if you do tell, we dig a hole...'

She nodded, reiterating her understanding.

'... And we put you in it.'

'I won't tell anyone. Pwomise.' She swallowed hard.

He gave her one last squeeze and released her. 'How much you usually get?'

'Sixpence.'

The Fairy frowned. He took a purse out of his back pocket and rifled through a few coins.

'Only got a shilling.'

Nieve bit her lip, she could still taste blood in her mouth.

'Look, I tell you what.' The Fairy whispered in his funny lisping way, 'Have the shilling, but don't tell nobody. See, I could get into trouble. You understand? I'm already in the doodah 'cause you've seen me. You understand?'

Nieve nodded vehemently.

'Good girl.' The Fairy Man placed the shilling beside her pillow. 'Back to sleep.'

A light switched on in the hallway, a thin sliver of the light edging around the door. The Fairy tensed. Nieve watched with horror as from his belt he drew a long dagger.

They heard the bathroom door creak open and shut closed.

The Fairy began to inch back towards the open window with his soft tread.

Nieve sat up. 'You forgot the tooth!'

He glowered at her with his beady eyes.

She hurriedly extracted it from beneath the pillow.

The Fairy took a step forward to take it. 'Remember the hole.' He said and then slipped out over the window sill.

The next morning when Nieve woke she felt groggy. She could remember smatterings of strange dreams, Peppito, the one-eyed hairy monster and a Tooth Fairy who wore gloves. Then she realised that she really had lost a tooth. She wiggled her tongue into the fresh gap and felt the soft little hole. She threw her pillow aside. There, underneath, was a shiny shilling coin. Nieve picked it up and slipped out onto the bare floor, she stuck her head out through the open window.

A few feet away, below her, there was a freshly dug hole in the flower bed which she could see was just big enough for her to fit.

ON THE LOOSE

The police returned to the house in the evening.

'Your husband in? Home from his 'work' yet?' One of them snapped and before Maeve could reply the other spoke.

'Where was he on Saturday night?'

'At home.'

'You sure about that? Not giving us the bum steer?'

Patrick rushed out from the kitchen and his heart sank at sight of the two officers.

Maeve looked confused, 'Is this for the fingerprinting?'

They were fingerprinting everyone in Dalkeith. It was unprecedented.

'We'd like you to come down the station, Mr Glendon.'

Maeve grabbed hold of his arm. 'Patrick what's going on?!'

Patrick took her hand. 'There's some mistake.'

'Oh, I'd say there's been a mistake all right.' The officer jutted his chin. 'Forgot to tell the missus you lost that job at Lysander's, did you?'

'Patrick?!'

He heard the rising panic in Maeve's voice.

Patsy waddled out from the living room carrying a toy airplane. 'Da, da, whoo!' John John running after her, 'Patsy, give me my plane! Patsy!' He wrestled the toy from her chubby grip.

Patsy howled.

John John stared open mouthed at the policemen in the doorway.

Patrick picked up the toddler. 'Ssh, there's a good girl.'

'Come on Mr Glendon, let's not waste any more time, hand the baby over.'

Patrick hugged Patsy before handing her to Maeve, her wailing increased.

142

'Patrick—' Maeve's eyes were large with anxiety.

'Don't worry macushla, everything'll be all right.'

'I'd lock your doors Mrs Glendon, there's a maniac on the loose; but maybe you know that already.' The sergeant sneered.

There's a maniac on the loose.

Ever since Australia Day. You heard it everywhere, *There's a maniac on the loose*. In the back office at Lysander Estate Agents they had all crowded around the wireless for the news broadcasts, even Mr Watkins. A shocking holiday weekend. The police were baffled. There appeared to be no connection between the victims; who ranged from a young student sleeping on a verandah to a retired grocer shot point blank on his own doorstep. Then a couple sitting in a car near the Ocean Beach Hotel had been fired on and were trying to help police with a description of their attacker.

'He's got to be some kind of loony.' Stanford sniffed.

'Monster.' Silvia the secretary was agog at the horror of it all.

Mr Watkins shook his head, 'I'm just hoping it doesn't affect property prices.'

Patrick had an appointment to show a place around the corner from where the student had been shot; he hoped he wouldn't be delayed by police cordons or morbid sightseers. Five weeks into the job and he hadn't quite managed to hit the average weekly sales figures. Mr Watkins conceded it was a slow time of the year.

Everyone was in a flap. He must remind Maeve about keeping the doors locked and perhaps they shouldn't have the windows open at night. But in this heat, they would all swelter in the stuffy bungalow. Still, he reasoned, they would surely catch the man before the end of the week. The police would be going all out and with four separate shootings there must be all sorts of evidence lying around. There would be people who had seen something or who knew who the chap was.

143

'My daughter Lucy reckons she met the life-saver at a beach party.' Mr Watkins contributed. 'Nice chap apparently.'

'There's a maniac on the loose if you ask me.' Stanford sniffed again.

Silvia shivered.

Three weeks later a woman was strangled in her home, raped and dumped naked in a neighboring garden.

'Two maniacs on the loose!' Stanford exclaimed.

'What's Perth coming to?' Silvia wailed. 'You're not safe in your own bed!'

Mr Watkins called Patrick into his office.

A Mr Tweedale had withdrawn his interest in a Subiaco property after Patrick pointed out the recurring infestation problem in the rafters. They'd been trying to shift the house for months. Mr Watkins sighed, 'Look Paddy, in this business sometimes 'less is more'. Do you get my drift?'

'He would have found out at some point, Mr Watkins.'

'Yeah, well you didn't need to hand him the information on a plate. Look, we need a fast turnover. I can't have agents wasting their time showing the same property again and again, you need to clinch the deals quick as you can and move on to the next place, that way I make some money and you make some money. You need to sharpen up your act. You're a nice man, Patrick.' Mr Watkins shook his head. 'Maybe too nice for this business. It's like your heart is not in it. You need to be like a hunter, the buyer is your prey and you gotta nail 'em before they get away, develop a killer instinct.'

'Mr Watkins, I'm sure I can do it.'

There was an uneasy pause.

'I'll get the hang of it.' Patrick was trying to keep the desperation out of his voice.

'I must be going soft—sales, that's what we need Paddy, sales.' Mr Watkins waved his hand. Now get out of here before I change my mind.'

The end came at the beginning of August. Watkins let him go. Two weeks before Maeve's birthday; Patrick couldn't bear to break the news beforehand. He continued to set out for work and came home with tales of the office, Silvia's latest peccadillo and all manner of quirky clients. Maeve was thrilled he was doing so well. He had to swallow hard and spent his days scouring the Employment Agencies.

Maeve had befriended a young mother on the next street, she recommended her babysitter—Mrs Dowd also suggested a good seafood restaurant. They could go out and enjoy a meal on Maeve's birthday, just the two of them.

On 10th August the babysitter was shot between the eyes by a .22 rifle and was found by the Dowds when they returned home. The student's pen was still in her hand and a notebook on her lap.

The press was enraged. What were the authorities going to do about this Monster?!

There was one unaccounted fingerprint in the Dowd house. The police were going to fingerprint every single resident in Dalkeith. Every man in Perth if necessary. That's what they were going to do.

Patrick sat in the interview room. He'd smoked all his cigarettes and was gasping for another. The bastards could see it. Over and over they kept asking the same questions, made the same sly insinuations.

'Strange isn't it how these killings only started after you arrived in Perth, Mr Glendon?'

'They're nothing to do with me I keep telling you.' Patrick drummed his fingers on the table.

'And we're to believe that? You lied to your wife.'

'Or, was she just trying to cover up for you?' The sergeant jabbed.

'Leave my wife out of this.'

'You come clean—we can.'

'You met Shirley McLeod before?'

145

'Before when?'

They waited.

'No. I never met her.'

'But Shirley McLeod was going to babysit for you.'

'My wife never mentioned any names.'

'You don't care who looks after your children?'

'My wife is perfectly capable—' He pushed his chair back; he could feel himself becoming more and more agitated. He just wanted to be out of there. And all the time clanging through his mind, *What'll Maeve be thinking?* And he'd feel sick. 'Have you matched the prints yet?'

'Even if the print isn't yours it wouldn't mean you weren't still a suspect. Killer could have worn gloves.'

'Then it isn't mine?' he asked hopefully.

They didn't respond.

'February the 16th, can you remember what you were doing?'

'That's six months ago how can I possibly remember?'

'Try.'

'What day of the week was it?'

'Saturday.'

'I'd have been at home.'

'You sure about that?'

'I like being with my family.'

'And I suppose you can't recall what you were doing on Australia Day either?'

'Being a Mick, Australia Day wouldn't mean much to you, would it, Paddy?' snapped the sergeant.

'We went to the beach at Cottesloe—home at tea time. My wife likes to have the youngest in bed by seven.'

'So, you're familiar with the Cottesloe area?' The sergeant probed.

'In fact, you know Perth quite well for a comparative newcomer, don't you Mr Glendon? Given your employment at Lysander's.'

'And you didn't work regular hours, did you?'

'Your wife wouldn't know where you were half the time.'

Patrick wanted to wipe the sly grin off the face of the

146

sergeant. His mouth was dry and sour. He could do with a drink. Two hours since the last cup of tea. It was gone midnight. Maeve would be sick with worry. And her birthday now.

'Amn't I supposed to have a lawyer?'

'You feel you need a lawyer?'

'Why would that be?' The sergeant jutted his chin.

'You should be out there catching the maniac that's on the loose. Not harassing innocent men. That's why!' Patrick could feel his cheeks flaring.

'Have you ever used a rifle?'

'I had a farm. Of course I've used a rifle!'

'When—'

'Are you going to arrest me or are you going to let me go?'

'That depends.'

'On what?'

They were silent.

And so it went on. All through the night.

Mid-morning Patrick was finally presented with a lawyer.

Half an hour later he was released but told that he must surrender his passport. On no account was he to leave Perth. He was to be available for questioning again.

When Patrick walked out of the police station red-eyed he was blinded by the sunlight and everything appeared shattered and broken to him.

BEN DOWN AND THE PRIZE FIGHTER

They got a big fair round here. Maali don't want to go; if she don't want do something can't change her. Binni look at me but she's gotta be boss. I go with Mack in his old jalopy and a couple of other fellas. Don't want to go with Roy, Ruby and that mob, you just know they be fighting all night.

At Darinup Fair, farmers come show their sheep and bullocky and the wives make cake.

You can throw hoop over plastic duck—but that gwangy. Those hoops too small for duck, press them down both hands! There's flea circus, but I had enough of them fleas.

No, we fellas go for Prizefighting.

Pete he from place name Malta, He's big fella, got muscles same like rocks. He got job with them fencing mob. He go for prize.

When we get to Darinup they all talking 'bout wadjela Eric Cooke his name. Catch him for lot of murders in Perth.

'Cookie Monster—bad man. Going to hang 'im.'

'Nedlands Monster, Stan, they call him, 'One whitefullah sleeping outside and one answer the door, this Monster don't even know these fullahs.'

'Why the fullah do it?'

'Got funny lip.'

'Uncle Bert he got that hare lip same—he don't go round shooting nobody.' Mack look at us.

'He cut up some girl too and another—' Stan make like strangle. 'That one he rooted after she dead.' Stan shake his head. 'They gonna hang 'im sure.'

Dick say, 'Yeh, crazy like gum tree full of galahs.'

There's noise up in the sky. Small Cesna plane flying around town with big sign in wind say Anderson Crop Dusting. The boss that all he think 'bout, business.

Lot of people coming into the field. Dick say he hungry. We buy hot dog. Hot dog smelling good. All them onion and Tommy Kay make 'em taste good.

Mack go to beer tent, easy for him, he can pass for wadjela. His name McIlvenny but call 'im Mack. He Irish bushranger family, but not like that Kelly mob with iron suit, just thieves 'n cattle duffers.

We looking round fair. Young Jimmy Anderson racin' round track in his go-kart with wadjela kids. He comin' last. We laugh cos winner is girl! All dem boys shame heh!

We come up to big billboard, kangaroo with boxing gloves. Fella in white shirt and bow tie outside big calico shouting 'Who will take on Kangaroo Bob? Come and try your luck. Big prizes for any man can take down Kangaroo Bob!' He point to the Billboard. 'Only five rounds.' He hold up five fingers. 'Five three-minute rounds.' He shout to some young fellas. 'You feeling lucky boys?'

Young ones pushing and laughing. Then Maltese Pete come up, 'I'll take him on.'

Tent is full everyone trying to get a look. We at the back standing. I see Boss and his brother sitting up front. It loud— all the fellas talking and shouting.

The bow tie fella come into the ring. 'Ladies and Gentlemen!' Can't see no ladies 'ere! 'Welcome to the main attraction! Please put your hands together for that most pugnacious of pugilists, the Sultan of the upper cut, wizard of the left hook, Kan-ga-roo Bob!'

Lot of shoutin' and whistling. Towel men come pushing and then man with boxing gloves. He got shiny blue robe with boxing kangaroo on back. All quiet for second—this man is nyungar! One way to make money in wadjela world.

Kangaroo Bob he look real mean, all scarred, but he not young fella now. People throwing money around, betting. Kangaroo Bob come in ring and throw his arms up like he already won the fight.

'Ladies and Gentlemen make way please for the first challenger, Owen Jones!'

All clapping and shouting hurt my ears.

149

'Young Owen works out on his father's two thousand acres. Mighty fit looking twenty-two—in the red corner, the challenger whose family hails from The Valleys, Owen Jones!'

Owen coming in, gloves on and shiny red robe on his shoulders. They all patting him on the back.

'Now let's see what that blackie can do.' Some wadjela say to his mate.

Bell ring. Owen come out, looking mean, gloves up, good boxer-like, he think he gonna win this one.

Kangaroo Bob jumping about the ring, just like roo. Owen don't know where Bob's gonna jump next, he trying hit 'im but he hittin nothin. Now Kangaroo Bob gone punch 'im jaw real hard like. Owen he shock. Kangaroo Bob he go round and round 'im and keep hit them little punches. That young fella all dizzy now. He lucky bell ring.

They all talkin now; this blackfella, not too big but he can move quick like. He can hit 'im hard too.

Fight start again; I'm looking but I'm not ere. Going back. I'm little fella, maybe seven year old. Early morning, orange sun. My murran been teaching me make kulata to catch fish; show me how to fit spear tip with gum from spinifex. He telling me story.

'One time Rainbow down by water pool. Maandi come to take big root of water lilies. She very beautiful—'

'Like ngangk?'

'Yeh, like ngangk.'

I smile his yamble. Don't know any maandi beautiful like my mother.

'Rainbow go in water and change into fish with many colours.'

My murran give me white bit of kangaroo leg, It like stringy. Tell me put in teeth make it soft.

'Rainbow fish swim between her legs and he in love. She see love in his eyes.'

'She fall in love with Rainbow fish, murran?'

'She in love to *eat* that fish for supper!'

My murran funny fella!

150

'Her white teeth smiling.' Murran smile his teeth, front ones knocked out long time. 'Heart of Rainbow fish is going—' My murran hit his chest hard again and again.

I laughing, but string in my mouth.

'She hit her digging stick down like a kulata! But Rainbow fish he too fast. All she do is splash water make hundred little rainbows.'

My murran nod, I give im white stringy bit. He put it round and round tip and shaft, put gum in too. Then he nod, I do same like 'im. Put string round but gum sticking my fingers. Make big mess!

'Then what happen murran?' I ask because I know it is not the end of the story.

'Rainbow fish is angry, *This maandi does not know me!*' he say.

We put earth to cover the sticky string.

'He get bigger and bigger. Maandi not smiling now. Rainbow growing long like crocodile.'

We go walking up the hill. My murran look my kulata. It lookin good and he happy. I waiting 'im finish story. But I am happy too. Murran spear many fish. Take me long time to catch one little fish on my kulata.

Now we walking home. Want show ngangk my little fish.

Murran got long legs, I running 'n my legs tired. He say, 'Rainbow fish come under the maandi she lying on his back now high up like mountain ...'

My murran at top of the hill now. See our camp. I wave to ngangk. She don't see me, too far. See Auntie, she visitin' with cousin-brother, Billy. They gone live mission way. Auntie say, *The Lord Jesus' gonna save us.* Billy, he go school, he help Reverend, 'n play cricket. Murran say he live old tribal way but my mother that her own business. I don't want no school, sit in room, learn wadjela read 'n write, that no good. What 'bout tucker? My murran teach me hunt, how to get water and look sacred place. I do not want to leave our country for wear shorts and dis fella Jesus

Murran stop. He been listening. Mob o' cockatoos fly out bush far away. We hear 'em calling. Murran bend down,

151

touch ground. He feeling it like heartbeat. 'Horses coming.' he say. 'Trouble.'

We hide in big rocks.

Murran call out loud like bird. Ngangk look up but too late—three gunji come from bush.

Auntie go to talk boss gunji.

Murran look me, we come down rock, quiet-like. Near camp, we hide behind bush. We hear talkin'.

'It not right!' Auntie say. 'Reverend he tell you. We live on Mission.'

'You're coming with us crazy woman, like it or not.' one gunjible say.

'Not go.' It my mother. I see her, she pick up burdan.'

'Put that weapon down!' Gunji shout.

'We not go.' Mother say again.

We hear gunshot. My heart stop; want to run, fast, stop bullyman. But murran grab me, put his hand over my mouth. He look sky to say gunji 'im shot in sky. My mother, she not 'fraid.

Bullyman get off horse and call Billy. 'Boy, you come here boy.'

Billy go to 'im 'What do you want. sir?' He polite.

'This what I want.' He put his gun to Billy's head and look my mother.

My mother stick burdan in ground, These bad men.

'Right, so now you behave, hey?' Say boss gunji.

Bullyman put chain around Billy neck. My cousin-brother shaking and crying.

Auntie crying too, 'That my son, he go school. Reverend be very angry.'

You can tell your Reverend to go take a flying leap. We are doing our job and you come with us.'

'We done nothing wrong! Jesus our Lord!' She put hands together and go down on knees.

'Get up. Nobody is saying you done anything wrong—just shut up and come along.'

Then they put chain around her neck too.

My mother run.

Coming near us now. My heart beat fast.

Gun shoot and dust fly at her feet. She move and gunji fire again. My heart jumpin'. Gunji shoot and now he hit her shoulder. Ngangk running but she blood everywhere 'n she fall.

Want scream but nothing come out my mouth. Murran tell me soft-like in my ear, 'Arcoona illa winjawtana.' *There nothing we can do.*

Bullyman fix my mother shoulder. Put her on horse. Boss gunji angry. He shouting *Jesus* and *Christ* but not like Auntie.

They gone, I go to camp and pull spear out from ground. Tip is good, sharp. I want throw it in heart dat gunji boss! I hurting bad. My murran pick up stone and he sit down. He crying loud and he hitting his head. Blood coming down mix 'em tears falling on red dirt.

Kangaroo Bob boxin' next fella, he takin' it easy. But this fella hit old scar up from Bob's left eye, can see it open again. Big punch final round and young fella throw in towel.

Bell ring for break. Got some music blarin'. Fellas shoutin', lotta betting. They see Kangaroo Bob box clever with big fellas. But he done eight rounds

'Kangaroo Bob must be tired.' Fellas say and putting money 'round.

Then next fight is big one we waiting for. Maltese Pete and Kangaroo Bob. Everyone same waitin' for big fight.

Pete look good, 'im fresh. Clever fella too. Round One he goin' slow keep round side. Kangaroo can't jump 'round 'im. Pete keep them gloves up and black fella can't get 'im. Pete hit the scar and it bleeding again. Lot of men shouting now. Round Two Kangaroo Bob he careful now. He want Pete come to him. Not much fightin'.

Wadjela shouting.

'Come and get it ya black bastard!'

'Sock it to him, Pete!'

Money flyin' round, all put money for Pete win. Gone

crazy.

Round Three Pete look mean. He punch him big one in jaw. Kangaroo Bob fall down hard. Ref counting, 'One … two … three …

'Come on nyungarr!' Dick is shouting.

'… five … six …'

Kangaroo Bob shaking his head.

'… eight …'

Get up on 'is feet, grab on rope. Ref hold Pete back.

Big noise in calico—take roof off!

Maltese Pete chasing him round ropes. Bob trying hit him but he missing. Ref push Pete back for hitting low, Pete come again. He smack black fella on the ear like hammer 'n Bob down on mat again.

Ref counting out but bell rings. Wadjela all shoutin and angry. They want blood this blackfella.

It busy in Blue Corner. Kangaroo wiping off blood. Some boss fella is talking his ear. He not happy.

Don't want to stay, but hard to get out now Round Four. Bob cut near eye has lotta blood. Hard for 'im to see. Bob try get away. But Pete come after him. Most time like boxers huggin' and Ref pull them off.

Round finish. All them wadjela dancin, jumpin, They know Pete gonna win. In corner Kangaroo Bob bloody head falling one side then other side. Don't want 'im fight no more. He gotta stop. Give Pete the Prize Money. Boss fellas got plenty money now. Mean bastards.

'Pete's got him now!' Red face wadjela say. Same wadjela I hear callin' Pete a *greasy wop* last week in store.

Bell ring. Last time. Kangaroo Bob getting up slow-like. Ref say, 'Come on get up!'

Pete ready, hit 'im on side quick. Kangaroo Bob fall back to rope. Pete come again but Bob move to side. Pete miss and black fella punch him good on left eye. Kangaroo Bob move away. Pete turn round. Kangaroo he waiting for 'im. He jumpin and 'is long arm punch Pete bang on nose.

Blood running out Pete nose. Pete go for Kangaroo but black fella too quick. Bob punch him again and again. One

154

big one under the jaw. Lift that fella up off his feet. Pete fall down hard. Ref count him out. Wadjela mob angry. Plenty money been lost. All wages gone up in smoke.

Man calling, 'It's a Knockout Ladies 'n Gentleman! In the Final Round! The Winner is—'

Kangaroo Bob arm lifted high, but his face in his chest. He don't look no one. They push him out quick behind tent.

Fellas going back—but I got business. They gamin', say I got woman business. Dick pull 'em away; he want more hot dog.

Look around tent I find caravans. Walk into one.

'Hello Billy.'

He look me like he don't know what happenin'. He punch drunk.

I tell 'im my language name. 'Fellas call me Ben now.'

He nod.

Towel man come in caravan. He hold out bottle o' Bundy to my cousin-brother. I grab the grog 'fore Billy get it.

This man look me strange like.

'Want me to throw him out, Bob?'

Billy shake his head, slow like.

I sit down.

'Long time Billy.'

He say nothin'.

'We been looking for you. Kimberley, Pilbara, allabouts. Went to that Mission place at Kunmunyah. Talk to Reverend Love.'

Billy put out his hand for the bottle.

I take off top but holding it.

'He say you good with cricket bat.'

Billy shuffles in his chair.

'*Billy stand firm at silly mid-off!* Reverend say—don't know what he's talkin' about!'

'Long time ago.' Billy speak soft.

'Where they take you, the gunji?'

'Long way. One place, then another place.'

'But where?'

He look me like I stupid bugger. 'Hospital.' His hand go for bottle again.

I get up look the sink for glass. Give him drink small one and one me.

Billy take some Bundy. Relax. 'Them gunji on Disease Patrol.' He drink again. Shake his head, 'Got money for bringin in black fellas from outback.'

'What disease? My mother not sick.'

'Leprosy.'

I'm shock.

Billy nod slow, 'That's a word still make nyungaa shit.' He finish his rum. 'Whitefullas pissing his pants. Scared as hell.' Billy hold out his glass.

I thinkin', 'Long time back fellas talk 'bout *Leper Line.*'

Billy nod, 'Want to keep black fellas north that line. Some whitefullas get it too, you know. Say it's epidemic. First, whitefulla come with all his disease for our mob, then the chinks bring this leprosy, but it blackfullas get it.'

I give him more Bundy and myself, 'Ngangk?'

'Doctor say she lucky bullet went right through but that arm never same. No good for throwing spear.' He smile, 'She brave woman. She save me.'

I look at 'im. Waited long time to hear this story—but I know it gonna be sad.

'Not enough beds inside hospital. Beds for whitefullas. One doctor. Blackfullas kept in the yard.' He shake his head, 'Old blackfulla come in one day. His face not a face no more. Skin gone here, there. Just bone, jaw 'n teeth.' Billy hug his grog. 'My mother down on her knees praying to Lord Jesus every minute, every day. We moved in a bullock cart, five of us to Wyndham. No better there. Take tests and we wait.'

I don't breathe.

'My mother, she got the leprosy. We know what gonna happen. Lugger boat come, she go to Darwin 'n they take her to an Island like all the blackfullas and forget about her.'

Billy got tears now.

'Sorry 'bout that Billy.'

156

'My mother she says, *The Lord's will be done.* She say she got a mission to be with this mob. Make her feel better. She say, *Go back to Reverend Love, he take care of you*—Auntie 'n me, we can go, see. But I don't believe that Jesus no more. I thinkin' to go Kimberley, find my father.' Billy look me, 'It was bad time, I been 'fraid, Ben. Whitefullas angry we in their town. They hate us. Inside hospital we safe. But we stay there we get sick 'n die.' He shake his head and reach for bottle. 'That last time I saw my mother.'

Outside caravan, it gettin' dark, look like rain, 'What happen?'

'Nearly out that town, it night, keepin' off road; cut across yard 'n dogs come after. Auntie pull me 'n climb on shed. I real scared. Auntie talk them dogs, soft-like and they been quiet but two whitefullas come out, old fella shoutin' come down off his roof. Other fella say, she a leper, he gonna get gunji. Can't see me. Auntie tell 'em hospital let her go. *You're on my property,* old man say, *thieving abo!* He point his rifle.

She look 'em hard 'n slide down off that roof. Walk right up 'n say, *I take nothing.* Then Auntie lift up that hospital dress for them fellas see she hiding nothing; One dog come, lick her foot. She walk right past that old fella 'n them dogs follow her.'

We sit long time, dark now. Better that way.

'Stay on roof all night. Sun come up; I make big jump over fence. Don't want dogs catch me. Hurt ankle but I got away. Wait two days for Auntie, she not coming. I hear trains goin' by, cattle, freight, you know. I saw one blackfulla jump on train. Next train I run 'n get on. Billy look me sad. 'That's all.'

We quiet-like.

I drunk too much grog, try stand up. 'You find your father?'

Billy nod, 'Musterin' cattle. He love bein' cowboy. Got flash shirt 'n ten-gallon hat. What he gonna do with a son?'

Bottle empty now.

'Yeah, what he want with a son? He send me government

place but I runaway. Go here, there.' Billy wave bottle. 'Odd job … stealin' … jail, fightin'— that's road I take.'

'Maybe stop fighting now?'

Billy shake 'is head, 'No, I like it when I get to hit some whitefulla.'

Got lift to Anderson Road. Rain fallin'. Thinkin' 'bout my murran. He don't want live in wadjela country. But he putting on wadjela clothes. We going one Mission, next Mission 'n plenty camps. Long time walkabout looking for ngangk.

In wadjela country everything different, can't hunt, got to eat mission rations, work on farms. I learn fast wadjela way. Five years we lookin', can't find ngangk. Murran getting old.

One day I say, 'Murran, let's go fishing. I see rainbow, maybe can find that waterhole.'

He nod, 'Meenya Janga bomungur.' *Smell of the white man kill us*; he right, you know. We turn 'n go home to born country.

GOING HOME

'Perhaps we should think about going home.'

She meant Ireland of course. The words burned in Patrick's ears. The very thought of return in their present state of hopeless destitution set his teeth on edge.

'Kevin would lend us the money for the fare.'

And take pleasure in it too, Patrick felt sure. No. He would do whatever it would take, he would sell his soul if he had to but he would not go back. He would find a way; he would find something.

He went to the Botanical Gardens to try and clear his head and then sat by the war memorial looking down over the Swan River. The traffic on the Narrows Bridge. The ferries plying back and forth, to the south shore, to Freo.

People going places.

The man at the Employment Office leaned back in his chair as he adjusted his spectacles and looked up at Patrick. 'I don't suppose you've any experience of farming, mate?'

Patrick's face broke into a smile.

This was the lucky country after all.

PART TWO

Inverness

OLD JACK

His father, Old Jack, had arrived in the shire of Darinup in 1901 with a band of other Scotsmen. They drew from a deck of cards for the choice of the half dozen available blocks. When he picked a deuce, Old Jack had to settle for the toughest land. Inverness he called his 240-acres. A last link with the homeland left behind.

He built a humpy with superphosphate bags, opened out and sewn together, stretched over a bush timber structure and cement washed. Roofed it with flattened kerosene tins, below which was a ceiling of hessian for insulation. Basic but comfortable enough with the addition of a cast iron camp oven for heat and cooking.

There wasn't much around Darinup back then. A few scattered farmers. A couple of old timers still working a gold mine, although the mine hadn't given up more than a mean subsistence for years. There was a hardware store, a grocery that doubled as a post office, The Swan Hotel, and a chapel. There was also a fringe camp of aboriginals who could seldom be induced to work.

Without a railway siding within fifteen miles, The Agricultural Bank wouldn't give a full loan to new farmers, it was always going to be a rough trot. But old Jack Anderson had what the others didn't, an iron will. First one and then another of his original companions gave up the struggle against the endless graft, the flyblown heat, the dust and the squalor. The Plague Locust prompted the last of his compatriots to abandon their holding, selling it on to Jack for a nominal amount. No point throwing good money after bad they all reasoned. But in 1907 the railway finally arrived and Old Jack had drawn the Ace card after all with over a thousand acres to his name.

The following year he built a large house of rammed and blocked earth with jarrah framed windows and doors and with a wide shady verandah. Then journeyed to Perth, the small sleepy capital of Western Australia, and found a wife. Jenny Naismith was a plain woman of thirty, originally from Arbroath, she was grown tired of being a teacher at a private girl's school and when her brother, a grain merchant, introduced her to John Finlay Anderson and he proposed marriage the very same day she surprised everyone by accepting. She liked Jack's show of decisiveness. Liked that he was a man of few words. Liked the muscular physique flexing beneath his uncomfortable starched collar.

Jenny took to the pioneering life, could put her shoulder to the wheel with the best of them and dig up a whole field of mallee roots on her own. A spade was a spade and you knew where you were with her. She never complained about the vicissitudes but insisted on a lace tablecloth on Sundays, a highly polished jarrah floor in the living room and no working boots beyond the kitchen. Together the Andersons battled droughts and the unexpected floods of 1917 and Jenny bore three sons, John, Finlay and ten years later, Alex.

Jack heard the story many times how Old Jack delivered him—the nearest doctor being many miles away in the town of Bodenham. Then, taken him outside, the umbilical cord still dangling from his belly, to be held up and told that one day, as far as the eye could see, it would all be Jack's.

Finlay and Alex both had a stake. His brother Alex worked the section of blocks to the south they called Arbroath and lived in a house built over there. As for Finlay, it pained Jack to recall how his mother's heart broke when her favourite son disappeared at age fifteen. Old Jack always certain he would walk through the door one day, the returning prodigal. But Finlay never did return; Alex, only five years old at the time, scarcely recalled the mischievous freckle-faced youth.

The terms of Old Jack's will meant that Alex and the lost Finlay might have income but never own their portion. The land passed lock, stock and barrel to Jack. He had inherited it all, and with it the same determination to succeed, to

164

dominate this country, to make it his own. He'd heard ...
call his father *cunning as a wagon load of monkeys*. Itinerant
shearers said he had extended his borders with the raddle;
that lump of red chalk used to mark the sheep which were
badly shorn and for which the shearer did not therefore get
paid. True or not, the depression in the early thirties saw the
steady accumulation of property. Old Jack made loans to
struggling farmers refused by the banks. Then foreclosed
when they couldn't make the repayments. Gradually
absorbing other local farms until he was the largest
landowner in the shire, the largest landowner in any of the
surrounding shires. Jack liked to think of his father as the
typical *canny Scot*, tough but fair.

Jack continued to add to Inverness and doubled the number
of share farmers on the outer reaches. Indeed, he felt himself
even more enterprising than his father with the
transformation of one poor stretch of land into an airstrip and
his new sideline in crop dusting with the young Dutch pilot
mechanic he had hired. His property was like a patchwork
quilt with only the odd gap here and there.

His latest acquisition was Ken Duguid's block, over
towards the salt lakes. One of those blocks given out to
Diggers after the War. Jack had taken on the drunken fool as
part of the sales deal but once Ken's brat of a girl was
grown, he could give him the heave ho without too much
fuss. Next, Jack had half an eye on the adjoining Stiller
place. Al Stiller's only child, a daughter, had run off to
Melbourne with a geologist, it was only a matter of time.

He was doing it for young Jimmy, of course. Jimmy, for
whom he had waited fifteen long years into his marriage, his
son, his pride, who would one day inherit it all, land as far as
the eye could see in any direction and then the same again
and again. Twenty-five thousand acres.

Sam Kirkwall sittin' at my fire, stabbin' stick in ash, 'I'm a citizen of the world.' he say, 'That's what I am. A citizen of the world, Ben!'

Sam old friend, work together up Pilbara. He been passing through look for work but not much luck. Hair like bushpig's backside—put people off. But he's good worker, you know.

Sam talking 'bout them Big Wigs down in Perth, 'bout the voting. Like, we black fellas can vote in State Elections, even Federal, we been enrolled.

'They're saying I can vote now, just like the wudgebulla – but vote for what?'

'Yeah, what black fella vote for?' I say.

'Big bloody deal—what they want? Like we all gonna bust a gut vote for their lousy ratbag politicians?'

'Like back that time after Big War.'

'Too right!'

Sam got bottle of Bundy. Maali don't like the grog, but she say nothin', stay in humpy. Sam's my friend, visiting at my fire.

'Too right!' he say. 'Buggers give with one hand, take with the other. What good it done those fullahs in forty-four went up for the certificate? Tell me that, Ben.'

'Didn't do no good, Sam.'

'Civilized life!' Waving the bottle 'bout. 'You think these wudgebulla got civilized life?' Shake his head. 'Ben, I like that Mozart fullah well as any man, 'specially that Clarinet Concerto one them mission sisters like to play on the wind-up, *Listen to this children ...*' he sings high voice, '*... the most beautiful music in the world.* But where's your beautiful music and civilization when those Germans killing half of Europe mate! That's what I wanna know!'

166

Sam slap me on shoulder. 'I seen pictures, old photos, black fullahs in top hats, women done up in big dress and bonnet. What good top hat and big dress out here mate?'

I see Maali, corner of my eye. She's squat outside humpy now 'n she been listening every word Sam say. Nod her head. Tomorrow she be on at me again 'bout leaving Boss Anderson.

'Come in from Bush, they say, give up Tribal Law, they say, wear wudgebulla clothes they say, you can be Australian too. These people take our country and then they say we don't belong, our kids don't belong us, not citizens. I'm a citizen of the world that's what I am and this here …' Sam stagger up on his feet and arms wide open wide. 'This my country.'

Over in Billangilil one them dogs set off barkin' and another.

'Can make a black fullah angry Ben.'

'Yeah, I know Sam, only thing—anger eat you up.'

'They had no guns we would have beat those wudgebulla, they'd been all gone now.'

'Here now, too many.'

'Yeah, they're here.' Sam look sad. 'They weren't here I wouldn't be born! My grandfather come from that Scotland place, where they wear them skirts.'

'Yeah?'

'Kilts—that's it. Surveyor he was. Surveyed my grandmother and liked what he saw.' Sam laugh, he gettin' drunk. 'She say he's not bad man. Stayed long time out our way. Four kids they had.' Sam look me. 'Know Ben, not many you full bloods left.'

'Yeah, gotta go up Territory.'

'Sometimes don't know what I am. You think if I go to Scotland and say, *'G'day, I'm your cuz Sam.'* They gonna say, *come sit at our fire, have a glass of whisky, cuz!.* Nah, I'm too mixed up, muda muda, don't belong nowhere—not even an Australian!

Sam lie back on ground. Rum all gone. 'Citizen of the world, that's what I am.'

167

'Im snorin' now.
Get blanket. Night gettin' cold.
I look at stars, big world, you know.

LETTERS HOME: DARINUP

12th October 1963

Dear mammie,

I was so glad to hear that your stay in Skibereen was blest with an Indian Summer and you had the trip to Garnish Island. I always remember the gardens as one of the highlights of my honeymoon. I'm sure auntie Imelda was great company for you, she's always so jolly.

We now have our first experience of the country life in Australia. The farm is called *Inverness* and from that you will gather that the family originally hailed from Scotland, but are long settled here. Jack Anderson is a rather gruff character with a face you could chart a map of the world on and tight lipped; I find it difficult to understand what he is saying sometimes—but apparently that is the way they all speak, so as not to let the flies in!

Patrick talks of nothing but wheat and sheep and what might be done out here once he has a grasp of the Australian way of farming. The station (as they are called) is so vast it makes Killpool Hill seem like a cottage garden in comparison!

The station is at full stretch with the sheep shearing—quite a sight to see, the shearers are so fast and skilled. Spring comes suddenly, we had a couple of days of rain and the wildflowers burst into bloom overnight. Sunsets are very spectacular with the huge vistas, so I have taken quite a few photographs—I enclose a couple.

I haven't met Mrs Anderson yet, her daughter in Sydney has just given birth to the first grandchild. There is a son, Jimmy, two years older than Nieve, and he has called round to play marbles, which seems to be the latest cra

THE INK RUNS OUT

Maeve shook the pen and then scratched at the paper but the ink had run out. The kerosene lamp flickered. Was that about to run out too? Everything was running out and then there would be only darkness. She felt unable to move. She felt that she too had run out. Mr Anderson turned the generator off promptly at nine o'clock each evening. Then sure enough the kerosene lamp sucked in its last breath and died.

It was the kind of darkness you might rightly call pitch black. There was no moon and on such a night out here in this wilderness the darkness was pure and infinite, unpolluted by light.

TOM POM

There was a scent about Mrs Glendon that Tom liked from the first time he met her; she reminded him of his mam. Something sweet but not too sweet, not like the cheap perfume the local girls wore on a Saturday night for the Drive-In. Tom hadn't thought of his mother in a long time, not in a remembering kind of way. She was tall his mam with startling green eyes, fair and willowy; as a youngster he was always hoping that he would grow up to be tall one day even though, right from the start, everyone remarked on how small he was, like his father. Small, dark and handsome was two out of three, his mam used to say about his father, which wasn't bad going for a girl from Rochdale.

Corporal Massimo Martinelli, 'Marty', was a G.I. from Chicago. But before he was a yank, he came from Italy, Corinaldo, which was a castle on a hill. This is what his mam told him because Tom never met his father. The letters just didn't come after a while and that's when his mam knew Marty was dead, like so many others, and he died before they could get married.

This part of the story, Tom didn't know until later when Uncle Ray came to collect him from the house in Manchester and said Tom's name wasn't Tom Martin but Thomas Martin Bradshaw, because his mother wasn't Mrs Martin she was plain Lily Bradshaw and he was her *greasy wop bastard*. Which was the reason the family never came to visit. His mam was in The Hospital and they said that eight-year-old Tom would be better off in The Home.

One rainy day, when he was ten, a tall man with thin greying hair came to see him. The supervisor said it was his grandfather.

'They say thee can go to Australia.' He said with a strong,

thick accent. 'I think that's for t' best.'

Tom didn't know what to say.

'Will mam go too?' He ventured at last.

'Forget about thee mother.' His grandfather fiddled with a pipe. 'Tha'll not be seeing her again. Best make a fresh start lad. Some place where nobody knows thee. Best all round.'

Tom noticed the dank fetid smell of the overcoat carried in with the rain, the smudge of ash on the collar. His grandfather rummaged in an inner pocket and pulled out a worn leather wallet.

'Here take this for t' journey.'

It was a ten-bob note.

'Good luck lad.'

In The Home Tom learnt what a bastard was.

His mam never cared what anyone said, Tom was her little Prince and Marty was a Man of Honour. Tom puzzled over the things his mother used to say and how she'd get angry and *just have a snifter*.

Tom's childhood had been filled with talk of his father. Marty was always telling Lily stories; for example, the one about the Polenta Well.

In the old days the people of Corinaldo were preparing for a celebration and they were going to make a polenta— whatever that was his mam said. Big enough to feed the whole town. The town had an excellent well with water as clear as crystal and all the neighbouring villages were jealous. So, the people of Corinaldo decided to bring all the polenta and the meat and the gravy to the well and they threw it all in and then one man said that he would jump in to make sure that it mixed up well together. The people waited but the man did not reappear and they were getting very hungry, so someone said, *that bastard he is eating it all for himself!* and he jumped in and then another until all the people of the town had jumped into the well. And even today in Corinaldo they will slap you hard if you tell this story.

Tom Bradshaw got taken on at Inverness at fifteen, as soon

as his time was done at The Fairbridge Farm School in Pinjara. It was the usual orphan story, the boys provided labour for the stations, and oftentimes the remote ones where no one else wanted to go. It wasn't such a bad life. He liked the outdoors, and after half a lifetime in dormitories he preferred to keep to his own company; which was just as well because a boy who needed the warmth of society could have died of loneliness out on a spread like Inverness. Young as he was there was no special treatment from Boss Anderson or show of motherly concern from Cissy Anderson who had three of her own and was caught up in the whirlwind of marrying the eldest daughter Jenny to some East Coast toff.

Tom was usually shepherding at the section run by Anderson's brother Alex whose wife had a condition of some sort and had moved to Perth for treatment. Alex complained that the house in Perth cost him an arm and a leg but truth be told he liked the arrangement well enough. Until the Flying Dutchman and his wife arrived the only female presence at Arbroath was an aboriginal cook and domestic, Jari, and Sally Duguid, eleven years old and practically feral the way her drunken father let her run wild.

Tom shared a room off the sheds with another boy, Boswell. A couple of worn blankets over a slim mattress on each iron bedstead, a wooden plank stretched across two kerosene cases for furniture and a tin tub for bathing in. Spartan as this was, they were both used to the rigours of institutional life. Boswell was a scrappy looking lad. He'd drifted about since leaving the catholic Boy's Town; tossed out into the world without even the annual follow up that Tom had from Fairbridge.

Boswell dreamed of making a break for the bright lights of Perth or even out East to Sydney, but it was mostly talk. There was something inert about Boswell, he lacked gumption and could scarcely read or write. Tom wondered what they'd been teaching over at that place in Bindoon because Boswell wasn't entirely stupid, he could see that. Boswell liked company, or rather, he didn't like his own very much. Liked a drink and most of all he liked to gamble, which was unfortunate because he lost more times than he won which meant he was always skint. Tom got used to seeing half his own meagre wages on permanent loan to Boswell and that little disappearing down the Swanee come Saturday nights.

Boswell was also light fingered. Tom had known kids like that. Filching was like a nervous tic, something they did without even thinking about it. Mostly food, like he didn't know where the next meal was coming from. Tom made allowances. Something made him feel sorry for Boswell. At least Tom had a mother. Boswell was left at the gates of a convent in Peckham. Cuthbert Boswell was like something out of Dickens Tom thought, the Artful Dodger transported to Australia, except he wasn't very artful and not much of a dodger either, Tom had seen some of the scars on Boswell's back and buttocks.

The old farm hand, Stubby Croker, taught Tom everything there was to know about sheep, about footrot, the staggers, worms and pink eye, you name it. Alex was ostensibly their boss but it was Stubby knew the Merino.

Stubby was a pom like Tom and Boswell but he'd been on the farm since before the Anderson brothers were even born so no one ever mentioned that fact, at least not in any derogatory way. Besides which, everyone knew that Stubby had killed a man once.

Stubby gave Tom a Kelpie pup, from his own bitch Bisley, and Tom named him Spike. They trained him up to respond to Tom's whistle and hand signals. Spike was a big dog for the breed but quick and intelligent, as adept in the pens as he was out on the open plain. There was nothing Tom loved more than spending days out on the pasture with just Spike and his horse Cobber for company.

Two years in, Tom was moved up to Inverness and his own one room shack out the back of the main sheds. That's when he met The Whipcracker. He had come in as a temporary hand for herding. He could make a whip sing, make it swirl and twirl in the air and snatch a crack a half inch away from your ear. At the annual Fair in Darinup The Whipcracker had given a demonstration in front of an admiring crowd, his whip dancing to the beat of its own music and Tom, admiring from the sidelines.

On the day he was to leave The Whipcracker came to Tom's shack early, he held out a brand-new polished whip, the cow hide leather soft but strong, plaited to a tapering tip. Tom held it, gaged the weight, appreciating the grip, marveling at the workmanship and knowing the man had made it just for him. Tom bit his bottom lip, emotion welling inside. The man cuffed him on the cheek.

'Watcha, mate.' He said as he backed away.

It was a pleasant breezy Sunday morning after rain, Tom's eighteenth birthday, but no one else knew that. He had ridden out by a waterhole to practice, far enough away from the jibes of the other men. That's when he had encountered Jenny Anderson. Only she was Mrs Nancarrow since she'd married a cousin of one of her posh friends. And here she was riding into his arena in slacks and a tight little blouse, blonde as Marilyn with honey gold skin and the sheen of good living and she didn't look anything like an old married woman.

'Impressive.' She eyed him with amusement. 'You got any other tricks?'

Tom whistled Spike back to his side and rolled the whip back up, 'Maybe.'

'Catch this.' She threw something up into the air and with lightening reaction he plucked it from the sky. Her packet of cigarettes.

'Sorry, might have crushed them, miss.'

'Never mind, I enjoyed the show. You wouldn't have any smokes, would you? I'm gasping.'

She could see very well that he did, the packet was poking out of his shirt pocket. He fumbled and drew them out, offering them up to her.

She jumped down from her horse. 'Light one up for me will

you.' Her blue eyes sparkled with mischief. He fiddled with his zippo while she tied up cock-eyed Popcorn alongside Cobber.

'Tom Pom, right?'

'Tom.'

'You've grown, Tom.'

He flinched at that, thinking she was making fun of his height, like the other fellas did, calling him Tom Thumb when they weren't calling him Tom Pom.

'Not up the way but out the way if you know what I mean.' And she smiled winningly to make up for any slight. Adding, 'I don't go much for tall men myself, get a crick in my neck looking up at them all the time.'

He held the burning cigarette out to her.

'And fed up with them looking down on me.' She continued under her breath. She took the cigarette from him and Tom found he had to concentrate hard to control the tremor of nerves which seemed to be taking hold of him.

'No, I'd say you're about right for a girl of my height.' She eyed him provocatively, taking a deep draw on her cigarette. 'You got a girl Tom?'

'No Mrs ...' He fumbled with the strange surname, felt awkward, tongue tied, felt like a great gallumph and part of him wished she'd bugger off and leave him in peace and part of him couldn't take his eyes off her and the way her hips swung when she moved and her breasts strained against the tight little blouse.

'Jenny, call me Jenny for God's sakes.'

He nodded.

'You're not much for conversation, are you?'

'Guess not.'

'I'll bet you're shy, the ones to watch. Toby, my husband, now he's the life and soul of the party. Guess that's why I married him, I wanted to be at the same party, seemed like fun. And it is. One long party after another, one fancy cocktail after another. Only when the lights go out, he's got this tendency to run out of steam. They say the booze can do that to you.' She blew out a long fume of smoke. 'Why did I

176

tell you that? I haven't told anyone that.' Then she paused and caught the quizzical expression on his face and half laughed, 'D'you understand what I'm talking about?'

Tom felt himself blush and hoped his dark complexion disguised the fact. He realised she must be talking about sex and he'd never met a woman who talked about sex. Not a proper decent woman.

'You can keep it under your hat though, can't you? Toby's little shortcomings?'

Tom nodded, 'Sure, no worries Mrs Carrow'

'Jenny. No worries Jenny.'

'No worries Jenny.' And they'd both smiled.

'You should smile more often, suits you.'

He shrugged.

'I guess that old bastard, my dad, doesn't give you much to smile about.'

His looks were about to protest.

'I know he's a bastard.' She stubbed out her cigarette like she was stubbing Jack Anderson underfoot. 'Say 'hi' next time you see me Tom, okay.'

She retrieved her horse and rode off with a back handed wave and he watched her go until she was a whisper through the thin scrub and patchy trees.

Next time he was feeding the horses, pitching fresh sweet-smelling hay from the back of the ute into the North Paddock. She appeared, looking at him from the other side of the open truck door.

'Hi.' He said, digging his pitch fork into another bale.

'Looks good enough for a tumble.' She watched him spear the straw with his quick deft economy of movement. 'Do they give you a smoko around here? I owe you one.' and she dangled a packet in front of him.

'Sure, Mrs—'

'Jenny.'

He stopped, leant on the fork and their eyes locked and he found that he felt remarkably steady.

'Jenny.'

That night when he heard her soft rap on the door, he realised that he was expecting her, listening out for just such a sound. Spike padded to the door and let out a low growl which Tom quickly hushed.

'Don't turn on the light.' She whispered.

But as she stumbled in the dark he reached over and flipped open the zippo and by the light of the thin darting flame they acknowledged each other. She slipped out of her cotton dress and he found his heart pounding as she searched out his face in the flickering light making sure he was watching as she unclipped the hooks of her brassiere and let it slide to the floor. He could feel the heat rising, pumping between his loins as she edged between his rough sheets into the narrow bunk, his back pressed against the wall to allow her room, feeling momentarily embarrassed by the size and urgency of his erection.

She lifted the sheet and smiled to see him, stroking the tip and then suddenly gripping the shaft so firmly he let out a strangled moan and the lighted zippo dropped between them. They flurried to put it out and then giggled like naughty school children in the plunging darkness. He wanted her then, fiercely, and she responded, pulling him to her, helping him yank the panties down below her knees, finding his mouth and pushing her hot sticky tongue in to meet his. His whole bodied tensed and wracked with the desire to pummel into her and when at last she guided him there he gave way to the thundering beat of his lust groaning with a mixture of relief and then despair because he knew at once that it was too soon. He'd heard the men laughing about blokes who *shot their load* and failed to perform for the ladies. His sense of failure was immediate and acute.

The tension gave way to a gulping sob, 'Sorry, sorry ...' and he could feel tears stinging at the back of his eyes.

'Shush, shush ...' she crooned cradling his head into the crook of her neck running her fingers through his thick black hair. 'It's all right ... it'll be all right ...'

And it was. They talked in low murmurs for a while and

178

then she teased him in a playful way for his impetuosity and led him in a slow exploration of her body, her need, and this time he felt the movement of her body, attuned to her rhythm, felt her climax beneath him before he let himself follow.

She was to return to Sydney in six days, the day after Boxing Day, and each night for the remainder of her visit she crept out to the shack. Tom's love making grew more assured and on each successive night Jenny became more demanding. She striped his back with her nails and bit into his flesh as she drove him on and Tom felt himself being sucked inside the ravenous void which she was attempting to fill. In the day he found himself nodding off as he plodded the range on Cobber and once or twice, he caught a suspicious glance from the station manager.

On Christmas Eve she presented him with a small leather box, He opened it to find a set of engraved cufflinks, engraved with the Ace of Spades. He was speechless. The last person to give him a proper Christmas present had been his mother.

'I bought them for dad, but he makes me so mad at the moment, I changed my mind. They're real gold by the way, not plate – in case you'd ever want to sell them, I wouldn't want you to get ripped off.'

'I don't have anything for you.' He stammered.

'That's okay. I know what you can give me.' And she poked him in the ribs and winked and they had to hide under the blanket to smother their laughter.

When at the end of the week he surreptitiously watched her departure amid a flurry of farewells Tom experienced a loneliness never felt before. More than the lovemaking he found he missed the whispers in the night, her stifled laughter, her giddy sense of fun. He realised that she took away with her more knowledge of his past, his dreams for the future, his intimate thoughts than anyone else. For the first time he was aware of a need to share his life.

Over the weeks the empty feeling shifted to a more comfortable place and his days resumed their familiar patterns but he was aware of it nonetheless.

A year later Jenny returned; this time her husband accompanied her. Tom felt the shock of seeing him and realized he had never allowed himself to imagine Toby Nancarrow as a real person. Toby was tall, well over six foot, and blonde like Jenny. Everything about him was sharp, from his sharp suits to his sharp enquiring eyes and his even sharper wit. A person would never feel directly insulted by him but somehow, he could make that person feel small, feel that Toby was in some way laughing at them from his superior position.

He brought with him the smell of old money, the polish of breeding. He made everyone a little uneasy. Mrs Anderson had after all only been a shop girl at Woolworths before her marriage and Jack Anderson, for all his great wealth, hid behind monosyllabic gruffness and the excuse of supervision out on the station to absent himself. But it was the way Jenny herself behaved around Toby that most struck Tom; she was brittle and edgy. And there was something behind her forced gaiety, a fleeting plea in her eyes. He'd seen that look many times before in the orphanage and later at Fairbridge, it was fear.

He tried to keep out of the way but Mr Anderson instructed him to groom and saddle up the horses whenever they were needed. Tom had never been made to feel like a lackey before. A hired hand but not a servant; Toby made him feel like a servant.

'Thank you, Tom.' Jenny smiled without looking at him as she clutched the reins and tried to steady Popcorn. 'Sorry.' She added in a whisper and he knew what for.

'That's okay.' He patted the jittery horse, calming him with soothing sounds.

Tom watched them ride off down the track towards the uncleared bush which skirted the creek.

They returned mid-morning. The sun was already burning a hole in the sky.

Toby heaved down from his sweating horse.

'I need a shower! This godforsaken place, Jen. Damn dust gets everywhere. And the flies! You didn't tell me about the flies!' He swept his Akubra around his face and stomped towards the house.

The next morning Jenny was alone. She rubbed Popcorn's nose and gave him a couple of sugar lumps. 'Good boy, good boy.' The horse nibbled at her ear with a gentle snort.

'Ride out with me Tom.'

'I don't know about that Mrs—'

'Jenny.' She eyed him.

'Jenny.'

'It's Christmas Eve, Tom. You work too hard.'

'Maybe.'

'You still got those cufflinks or did you sell them?'

'You want them back?'

'No, stupid. I'm glad you kept them. How old are you now Tom?'

'Nineteen.'

It had been his birthday the week before, not that the anniversary of his birth had been an occasion for celebration since he was eight years old. On that birthday his mother had taken him to the Belle Vue Speedway track. His mother and two men.

'Tom meet Andy, he's from work, got us the tickets. And this is Larry.' Something in the way she said 'Larry' made him sound special and not just because his skin was the colour of treacle.

They made a fuss of Tom, bought him lemonade and a bag of hot nut brittle. He liked the Speedway with all its noise of roaring bikes and screeching tyres. The air was thick with the fog of their breath because it was a bitterly cold day. But he didn't care and everyone was happy and everyone was shouting on their team.

On the way home they called into a new ice cream parlour and ate sundaes with glacé cherries on top. Then Larry had pulled a small parcel out of his pocket and said, *Happy Birthday, Tom.* Tom had been amazed because he'd never met Larry before and inside was a YoYo and that was even more amazing because that was something he really wanted.

Another special thing about Larry was his voice. Larry worked at a biscuit factory but at night in *shebeens* he played guitar and sang. He would practice in front of Tom and his mother. Big Joe's *I Won't Be In Hard Luck No More* and they'd all sway to the music and Larry would tap his foot to keep the beat. And the one Tom really liked *Wild Cow Blues.*

If you see my wild cow baby tell her hurry home
because I had no milk and butter
since my wild cow been gone.

'Nineteen. Is that all?'

Tom flushed.

'You've already saddled Caesar; he needs a decent ride. Not somebody pulling his mouth every which way.'

Tom hesitated still.

'Do I have to order you?'

Tom shook his head and helped her up into her saddle.

A golden light lay across the land as they rode out, their long shadows following them. A flock of white cockatoos flushed from the trees and spread across the field like a fall of ticker tape to their own screeching accompaniment. Out to the salt lake. A flat sheen of white pink crystals with here and there the tracks of some animal. In the middle of the lake a local wit had placed four half tyres of different sizes to look something like the humps of the Loch Ness monster. Tom and Jenny grinned, everyone always did, no matter how many times they saw the joke. They rode on to Reynolds Lake, it was fed by a spring all year round but despite this it had also turned from fresh water to saline – in summer some of the townsfolk would come out and sail home-made dinghies but there was no one there on that Christmas Eve.

182

'Do you like swimming Tom?'

'Yes, I like swimming.' It had been one of the pleasures at Pinjarra. He remembered the day he had been thrown off the jetty and the blind terror and panic as he had thrashed his limbs trying to keep his head up above the water and somehow managed to doggy paddle until he felt stones beneath his feet. Mr Cole grinning at his shocked expression. But he had lost the fear. From then on, he learnt to float, to crawl, to dive. Deep down beneath the surface, feeling the cool murky silk of the water on his limbs and the sense of freedom it gave him.

'Fancy a dip? Some people reckon it's good for ya, like the Dead Sea.'

'I wouldn't know about that.'

'Or, we could go on to the Darinup Lake.'

'Won't you be expected back soon?'

The sun was above the trees now whiting out the light and draining the colour from even the earth itself.

Jenny shrugged, 'I don't think I'll be missed.' She gave Popcorn a spur and took off. 'Race you.'

Tom smiled, he'd give her a head start, the way Caesar was pulling he was ready to be let loose. They came in neck and neck but only because Jenny decided where the finishing line was, just before he overtook her.

Over on the other side of the lake there was a family fishing and preparing a barbie. Jenny waved. They waved back. 'I think it's the Osbournes.'

Tom was fairly certain that it was. He could just make out a large woman in a floral print dress with a straw hat. The three boys. And her daughter Nancy. Nancy had sidled up beside him at a youth dance a month previous at the Masons Hall, but he was two left feet when it came to dancing. He hadn't counted on her obstinacy and when the last slow dance was announced she grabbed his arm and it would have been churlish to refuse. They shuffled and swayed about like everyone else, her face right into his neck.

'I love the smell of after shave.' She murmured.

Boswell had slapped a dab of Old Spice around his chops

183

before they left. Tom thought he reeked of over ripe fruit.

The lights grew dimmer, she brushed her lips against his and he felt obliged to respond. They were surrounded by couples smooching and snogging. She was slim and pretty although you could tell that one day she would be as big as her mother if she let herself go, which she probably would.

'Maybe we should be heading back.' He suggested.

'No way, I haven't been skinny dipping for years.'

'Skinny dipping?'

She laughed at the look of horror on his face.

'Well I didn't think to bring my bathers.' She was already unbuttoning her blouse and kicking off her boots. 'Last in's a sissy.' She taunted.

'What about …?' Tom nodded in the direction of the Osbournes.

'I am jumping in this water right now. You can turn away if you feel embarrassed.' She wiggled her hips with a grin as she began to slip the tight breeches off her waist.

Tom looked away and out across the rusty red water with its supposed medicinal qualities. How could he resist. Let Nancy think whatever she liked.

Fresh from the lake Jenny wanted to make love under the shade of a River Red. Tom couldn't help feeling uneasy as shouts occasionally drifted across the lake. Tom suspected that Jenny enjoyed the edge of risk, the possibility of being discovered and that worried him. He couldn't get Toby's face from his mind and his smirk when they had been introduced by Mr Anderson.

'Tom Pom? You look more like a dago than an Englishman for my money. Sure one of your ancestors didn't have an encounter with the Spanish Armada?'

Tom wanted to punch him right then and there but somehow Toby managed to just take the edge off the insult.

'I've always thought one of my forebears didn't put up much resistance to the Viking invasion.'

'Don't think about him.'

It was as if she could read his mind.

'You know your trouble? You worry too much and you're too young for that.'

She was right. What did it matter to him? She was the one offering herself up. She slid on top of him, still wet and slippery from the swim and all he knew was that he wanted her badly.

When they returned, Toby spotted them from the verandah and wandered over to the paddock, long glass in hand.

'That was some ride. Had fun darling?'

'Super.'

'Your mother was getting worried.' He raised his glass and eyed her through the clear liquid. 'Time for another pre-prandial, I said. Tom Pom looking after you, is he?'

'He knows how to handle a horse.'

'And the fillies too, I'll bet.'

Tom sensed that he was in the middle of some game that the two of them were playing. No one had bothered to tell him the rules. He couldn't wait to lead the horses away. Tom knew then that, much as he desired Jenny Nancarrow, she was using him and he'd never love her.

SISTER GOBBLESHOE

The cockatoos were screeching high in the tangled trees and ruffling their yellow feathered crowns as the orange pink dawn cut through the gap between the cotton print curtains of the children's bedroom and danced on Nieve's face. On the darker side of the room John John stirred. Nieve rubbed her eyes and turned over, savouring the comfort of her bed. And then she remembered. It was the first day at her new school. Her stomach tightened into a little knot. This would be her sixth school and she was only eight years old.

There had been the school in Wicklow with kind old Sr Eukaria, then Muckross in Dublin, the school in Sydney, two in Perth; and now Jimmy said they would be going on a bus which would take about an hour because of the pick-ups on other stations. Jimmy would be on the bus but they would not be going to the same school. At the last minute her mammie had found that there was a Roman Catholic school after all. Apparently, they were a miracle. The school was run by two nuns and they only had thirteen pupils, aged from five to fifteen. The school was about to be closed down but with the arrival of Nieve and John John they would survive, if Patsy hadn't still been in nappies, they would have taken her too the da said.

Mrs Anderson drove them to the entrance gates of the farm and minutes later a rickety bus pulled in and they jumped aboard. Jimmy immediately went to sit with a friend at the back and ignored them for the rest of the journey. Nieve and John John sat together near the front. John John was clutching her hand and she knew it was because he was nervous too; at the school in Perth he had wet himself on the first day, it had embarrassed her because he was her brother but she knew that the three weeks at the school had been a nightmare for him with the teasing he'd endured. The bus stopped and a group of six children got on. A girl of about ten glared at Nieve.

'That's our seat y'r sitting on ya great galah.'

'Oi leave 'em alone Netta, strewth, it's their first day for cryin' out loud.' The bus driver winked at Nieve as he drew out into the road again.

Netta grumbled under her breath and plonked herself in the seat behind Nieve. She leaned over breathing in her ear. 'Heh, yous Poms?'

Nieve shook her head.

'What then?'

'We're Paddies.' John John offered, bright and friendly.

Netta laughed, 'You'll be thick as two short planks then.'

Someone else on the bus laughed.

John John frowned, not quite sure what was meant but catching the sneer in Netta's words.

The driver slowed down and a boy sitting at his shoulder gave a yelp of excitement.

'Snake! Carpet snake right across the road.'

Children began to crowd up to the front of the bus to get a look-see. Nieve and John John pressed their noses up against the window pane and could just see the slow-moving undulations of what Nieve figured must be an enormous snake, the biggest she had ever seen.

The driver stopped completely, the bus juddering and vibrating as it idled.

'Run him over Ted!' someone shouted.

'Yeah, run him over!' echoed the boy at the driver's shoulder.

'Leave it out why don't ya, guys.' Ted wiped his sun glasses clean as he leant on the wheel.

'Run him over. Run him over!' A chant was underway and growing more furious and persistent.

'All right. All right.' Ted sighed and shifted into gear. The bus lurched forward, the children still screaming him on. 'Bunch of savages!'

There was a whoop all around as the snake disappeared

under the wheels and the children raced to the back of the bus to see the results.

'Bewdy!' Nieve could hear Jimmy exclaim.

'What a rip snorter!' said his friend.

'Oi watch your language back there.' Ted shook his head and glanced into the rear-view mirror.

'Nieve!' John John was tugging at her sleeve to let him out into the aisle so that he could go and see for himself.

Nieve shook her head vehemently. She felt sickened by the image which had formed in her head. A giant snake with two perfect tyre tracks running through its body.

John John shook her arm petulantly, 'Nieve.'

Nieve pursed her lips, 'Mammie wouldn't like it, it's cruel.'

'Rotten spoilsport.' John John moaned as he sank back down into his seat.

The school had two classrooms. Children up to ten years old in one classroom. Older children in the other. There were only two teachers. Two nuns. Nieve and John John were put into different rows. In all there were three rows in the juniors, one for the nine and ten-year olds, one for the seven and eight-year olds and one for the five to six-year olds. In Nieve's 'middle class' there was just one other girl, Maria. Maria had a round face and her long black hair was in plaits. Their teacher was a young nun with freckles and twinkling green eyes. As it was their first day, she had given John John and Nieve tests to assess their ability.

To Nieve she said, 'I can see you're going to be a star pupil at the reading and writing Nieve, but your maths is pretty lousy to be honest.' And she smiled making it seem all right to be lousy.

Nieve thought Sr Gobbleshoe was the nicest teacher she had ever had.

At lunchtime they all collected their lunch boxes and sat at a table in the shade of the verandah. Nieve opened the plastic container feeling a hunger suddenly gnawing at her insides. Her mammie had made their favourite sandwiches, salad cream for Nieve and vegemite for John John.

'Yum!' John John grabbed one and crammed a huge bite into his mouth.

Nieve nudged him. 'John John don't eat so fast!' Which was what her mammie said to him all the time.

Nieve glanced into Maria's lunchbox; as well as sandwiches, she had biscuits and a packet of jelly babies. Her own mammie had packed an apple each along with the orange squash. Nieve felt a twinge of envy but also a sudden flush of shame, what would Maria think of them because they did not have fancy biscuits and sweets?

She had once heard her mother saying to her da before they left Dalkeith, 'We're poorer now than the church mice!'

Nieve looked around the table and saw that other children had biscuits and cakes too, she bit her lip and nudged the lunch box closer in between herself and John John in the hopes that no one would notice the shortfall in theirs. Instinctively she began to eat her second sandwich more slowly to stretch it out. She was still nibbling at the sandwich when most of the children had finished their lunch and hurtled into the yard to play. John John was yanked away by his new friends, Tony and Brian to play Catch; his unfinished apple discarded on the table.

Maria opened up her packet of jelly babies, she regarded Nieve for a moment and then held the sweet packet in front of her. 'Want one?'

Nieve hesitated.

'I don't like the yellow ones.' Maria explained. 'You can have all the yellow ones if you like.'

By the end of the lunch break Maria decided that they were going to be best friends forever. Maria said her father worked at the Rural and Industries Bank in Darinup and her mum was French Lebanese. Nieve didn't know what that was but she might seem stupid if she asked. An older boy with funny metal contraptions on his legs was Maria's brother. Vincent had Polio. Nieve didn't know what this was either.

In the afternoon Sr Gobbleshoe got out her guitar and suggested that the new pupils should be welcomed with a

189

song and what would everyone like to sing.

'*Ging Gang Goolie Watcha!*' the children shouted at the top of their voices.

Nieve listened closely but the words made little sense to her.

> *Oh Hayla! Oh hayla-shayla!*
> *Oh hayla shayla roo.*

She was reminded yet again that people in Australia spoke another language and she felt nervous because it seemed that she would never catch up.

The bus was full for the first part of the journey home. When Nieve and John John and a couple of kids from the catholic school got on the kids from the State School were already on board. Netta had reclaimed her seat and glared at Nieve as she passed by. Nieve looked about for somewhere to sit but there weren't two seats together so she left John John across the aisle from his new friend Tony and she went back up the bus to the only free seat. A much older boy, tall and lean, was resting his head against the window, a faint shadow of dark hair on his upper lip lending him a semblance of adulthood. Nieve hesitated, uncertain whether she would be committing yet another mistake by sitting next to him. The bus lurched from the bus stop, Netta and her friend sitting behind giggled as Nieve staggered and grabbed the seat back. The older boy glanced briefly in her direction and indicated for her to sit down before turning his attention back to the road.

After a while Nieve felt a sharp tug at her hair, she turned around but Netta was innocently leaning over her friend to look out of the window. Puzzled, Nieve settled back, it happened again but harder this time so that Nieve winced, and again Nieve swiveled round to see who the perpetrator was but this time Netta was looking at her friend's comic. As she turned away, they started to snigger. Nieve blushed knowing that their laughter was directed at her. Minutes later her head was yanked right back with the force of the tug.

She turned and mustering her courage addressed Netta, 'Please don't do that.'

Netta looked up at her with surprise, 'Do what?'

A low voice interjected, 'Cut it out Netta.' The boy sitting at the window spoke without turning to look at them. He gave a little impatient strum on the window. Netta stuck her tongue out at the back of his head and folded her arms but sank back into her seat.

When Mrs Anderson finally deposited them outside the shack the two children staggered into the house with their satchels and slumped into the one armchair, practically falling on top of one another. Nieve felt almost too tired to eat supper and too tired to answer her mother's questions about all of the events of the day. Before she could help herself, she found that she was crying and she couldn't stop.

BEN DOWN AND THE BLACKBIRD

Maali got newspaper she pick up 'bout Wiradjuri girl. Father he's a sheep shearer. This girl win at tennis, a kid. All dressed up in them white clothes with all them wadjela girls. Maali read.

> *Aboriginal girl Yvonne Goolagong, one of the State's top junior girl tennis players, is pictured with blah blah at the Mattara Northumberland tennis age championships at District Park yesterday. Yvonne comes from Barellan, near Narrandera, and flew to Newcastle for the championships ...*

I say, 'Show our mob do anything.'

Maali say that girl grow up wadjela same. Say that girl been blackbird like she. Wadjela use her up 'n throw her away—then where that Goolagong girl gonna be? Won't know her own mob, won't belong nowhere. Start drinking grog, lotta kids, end up bad place.

I say, 'Girl do what she want, she big grin.' That girl Goolagong she beat wadjela—then she good fighter.

Binni say, 'What's tennis?'

'You hit a rubber ball over net with string bat.' Maali say.

'Bet I could do that. Then I could be a champion, right dad?'

'You already a champ, Binni.'

And we laugh, Maali same.

COFFEE ROYAL

They were harvesting the wheat, acre after acre. Straight rows, up and down with nothing on the horizon but the line of a fence, the sharp edge of land and sky and only a solitary mulga tree to keep you from losing all sense of scale. After the rolling green hills of County Wicklow, with their patchwork of pasture, hay and barley fields bounded by dense hedgerows full of small birds and burrowing animals and blackberries picked for jam at the end of the summer, these fields were a great emptiness of space.

At first Patrick found it disconcerting, scarcely to be able to see one end of the field from the other, the lack of feature, the apparent absence of wildlife, the monotony of trundling on the same groove for so long. Killpool Hill had always assaulted his senses, the colours muted or vivid, the smell of the earth after rain, from one field a sight of the sea, from another the mountains and in the lower field an ancient stone with faint markings of ogham script, around which farmers had been detouring with their ploughs for hundreds of years.

Here on the edge of barrenness there was nothing but the movement of a cloud and that only if it were not a cloudless sky. Initially Patrick felt unsettled by this blankness, his mind desperately seeking some points of interest and finding none his thoughts then spiraling inwards to the images conjured by memory and reflection. But he dare not let these thoughts wander far unchecked; unless he kept guard over them, they would worm there way back to that summer's day in 1939.

It was a day which had begun as brightly as the first days of a long summer holiday should and you are a week away from your twelfth birthday and your older brother, home on a short visit from the seminary, has promised to take you out

193

to the Charity match at Old Belvedere. Their team had won, he remembered that. The wild cheering of the fans. A walk along the Dodder on the way home with the crickets singing; the running tackles over a tin can.

'Did you see that pass from Clancy? Wasn't it a cracker?!'

Then James tussling him to the ground and into the long grass. The quiet of the big house on their return. Everyone out for the day. Or so James had thought. Then that splintering moment. His father's face in the doorway.

No, Patrick could not allow himself to venture there he could not hear those words, the exchange of glances, the look on his father's face. Most of all the look on his father's face. Patrick could feel his heart thumping, thump, thump, thump. Anything, anything, anything but that.

There was something Maeve had said at breakfast. 'Isn't that a funny thing Patrick?'

'What's a funny thing?' He sipped his tea and turned to face her at the kitchen table.

'Nieve, tell your da what the name of your new teacher is.'

'Sister Gobbleshoe.'

'Sister Gobbleshoe?'

Nieve nodded solemnly.

He'd looked at John John with a quizzical expression.

'Sister Gobbleshoe.' John John repeated emphatically, like his da was slow or something.

He and Maeve looked at each other with the laughter twitching at their lips. 'Well isn't that a funny thing.' He'd said. 'I never knew there was a Saint Gobbleshoe.'

'Perhaps it's an Australian saint's name?' Maeve had suggested mischievously.

Patrick mulled that over, 'You could be right, along with St. Dingbat and St. Widgie and St. Bodgie.'

'St. Bruce and St. Bonser?'

Their faces creased with the laughter bubbling up into their cheeks and he had delighted in the twinkle he'd seen in her eyes, which had been absent for so many weeks.

'What's so funny?' Nieve pouted. 'She's the best teacher, ever.'

194

'Oh, sweetheart we're not laughing at her, it's just—' Maeve floundered, 'Are you sure that is her name?'

Nieve nodded, 'Every morning we have to stand in our line and then she says, *Good morning children,* and we have to say, *Good morning Sister Gobbleshoe,* and then we put up the flag and sing the ant hymn.'

'Good morning Sister …' Patrick repeated slowly, and then grinned widely, 'Go – bles – choo … God Bless You!'

Maeve hugged Nieve and explained what they had misheard. Nieve looked like she might cry.

'I prefer Sister Gobbleshoe.' Patrick declared, 'We'll always call her Sister Gobbleshoe in this household!'

And at last the children laughed too.

He smiled to think of it. 'Good morning Sister Gobbleshoe!' He called out to the acres of rippling wheat and the empty sky, the solitary mulga in the distance his only landmark.

When he came to the fence he stopped, turned the engine of the harvester off and jumped down to stretch his legs and have a swig of his coffee royal, the blend of brandy and black coffee which he had been assured would help to assuage his thirst in the heat. Without the rattle and throb of the engine the stillness was immense. If only his mind could be so still.

He stood for a while, willing it to be so.

BEN DOWN AND YAMA THE STORYTELLER

We sleepy—stomach full. Maali put smoke bush on fire, keep mozzies away. Binni curl up with Maali, head in her lap, she stroking his hair. Remember me long time back, same same with my ngank. Them nights we listen to story. My murran live long time, he tell lotta stories. Murran got stories like women get lily root in dilly-bag. Old murran sit at fire 'n tell story every night.

It been hard day. Crutching sheep. Flies bad, reckon we need be doing sheep every six weeks not be fly blown. I tell Boss he maybe think 'bout mulesin', less work long run.

He look me hard, 'If I want your opinion Ben, I'll ask for it.' Then he spit in dirt 'n walk off.

Old Stubby he say, 'Them Andersons mean as hell.' Laugh 'bout that all day. Old Stubby been working for them buggers long time, fifty years more.

Wadjela, Ken, he got big laugh too—but mean, got bad temper. I call 'im *karrang*. Wadjela think I can't say 'Kenneth', but black fellas look me 'n smile, know what I say.

I gotta work with karrang on the crutchin'. He shakin', been on the grog. All his sheep jumping, scared like, you know. Karrang curse 'n swear like his shears bust. Nothing wrong with them shears. I say I take his place, he have mine. Karrang angry man then! End of day Boss say, 'Why's the job not been finished?'

Karrang look Boss hard, 'You want to look at who you are hiring, mate.' Then 'im look me mean.

Boss nod, but slow like, you know, not look me in eye. 'Ben, you better shape up tomorrow.' He say.

Karrang clever fella like that, you know—he know Boss

not gonna argue, not for black fella. Karrang one them fellas throw you in fire. He no good worker. Why Boss not fire 'im? I don't know.

Binni say, 'Tell us a story, dad. A really mean one, dad.'

''Bout the pelican babies?'

He shake his head.

'One 'bout Wan trick Mullian to step on kangaroo bone spear?'

Binni grin but shake his head.

'One where Wan building humpies?'

Binni got big grin now.

I sit up, laugh—same story I love my murran tell, 'Wan the Crow very lazy fella. But 'im good lookin'—like me.'

Maali laugh.

'Wan a clever fella, could make up stories, make different voice, make women laugh 'n women do anythin' for 'im.'

'Stupid women!' Maali shake her head.

'Wan never go huntin', he make women lazy, listen 'im all day. His mob say he gotta go away. So Wan he go away—but not go far.

'Because that Wan a lazy fella!' Binni grin.

'He make humpy. But Wan getting hungry now. What he gonna eat? He got idea. Make 'nother humpy 'n 'nother. Make two long row humpies. Then make big fire in his camp.

Evening come, Wan's mob been goin' back to their camp, been huntin', stop and see new humpies, *'This 'nother camp, big camp, who this mob? Maybe bad mob, no good!'* They moving on, quick like. Then last hunter comin, he tired, got him big kangaroo on his shoulders. See this camp 'n big fire. Kulamandi think—maybe I give bit roo to this mob 'n we sit at fire.

First humpy he hear baby cry. *Wah! Wah! Wah!* Go in—but there no one there!

The kulamandi hear children playin' and women shoutin' but same, same, he enter humpy and—'

'There's no one there!' Binni grin.

'Last humpy 'im hear a young woman sing, beautiful song,

197

and he already in love.'

Maali grin 'n she look me.

I take deep breath,

Women's hands are deft 'n quick
With fire-stick 'n diggin' stick

Maali and Binni roll 'round on ground, Laughin' 'n holdin'
bellies. I don't look them, carry on with woman's song.

Seekin' yams 'n fruit to eat ...

I make noise to stop 'em laughin'. Binni put hand on his
mouth.

Then Maali look straight face, 'Go on, tell the story.' She
say.

'This hunter, 'im look in humpy, but no young woman in
humpy—only Wan the Crow.

'What you want?' Wan ask.

'I hear girl singing.'

'Can see, no one but me.' Wan say.

'I hear big mob here.'

'Only me.' Wan laugh and come to kulamandi, he got arms
out wide wide.

Kulamandi step back. 'This place no good, bad spirit here.'

Wan jump on 'im. Spin round 'n round and throw that
hunter in the fire. Wan laugh like kookaburra—'

'Cack, cack, cack, cack!' Binni make good kookaburra.

'Wan got plenty roo, now. Cook 'im kangaroo 'n eat 'til
can't eat no more.'

I stir ash in fire.

'One week, two week. That mob thinkin'—what been
happen all the hunters? Then, Mullian the Eagle come back
from walkabout. Mullian tell them he find kulamandi.
Mullian see many tracks go in this new camp but only one
come out. Mullian know them footprints. *Wan the Crow.*

Mullian him clever fella. He hunt wallaby and come to new
camp. First humpy he hear baby cry; *Wah, Wah wah!* He

198

look in humpy.'

'There's no one there!'

Binni turns; it's a voice outside our fire. I look. Little Witiyana 'n Winston Goody sittin' under gum tree. I nod 'n wave them boys come sit at fire. Boys come little bit.

'There no one there.' I say again.

'Next humpy Mullian hear old fellas talkin' up.

Hey you know that big fish I caught when I a kulamandi? Strong one 'im, two day to catch it. One fella say.

Ha, ha, nah! You caught little fish—it pull you in river!

Mullian look in humpy—'

'There's no one there!' The boys say.

I smile. 'There no one there.'

Witiyana come little closer, I see big eyes in fire light.

'Mullian hear kids laughin' and women been calling but he go in humpy and—'

'There was no one there!' Binni shout loud.

'Then, Mullian hear singin', sweet like.'

I look them—all look me. Winston he come close now.

> *Cloud fly past 'n east wind blow*
> *So, the dry time come and go*

My singin' get high high. They all smiling up now, Teeth all white in the night.

> *West wind bring the big big rain*
> *Fill the thirsty earth again ....*

Witiyana laughing up now, he holdin belly and rollin' on ground with Binni.

I stand up for end of story.

'Mullian the Eagle go in that humpy. Only Wan look him, hands on his hips.

'What you want fella?' he say.

'Oh Wan, that no way talk to brother? I hear girl singin'.'

'Hey Ngulyar—you just marry my sister!' What you doin' lookin for young girl?

199

Wan come to Mullian. Mullian step back back in middle of camp.

'Wan, what you angry?. Look 'ere I kill wallaby—we can eat at fire.'

Wan come to push Mullian in fire. But Mullian he clever fella, him move side 'n trip up Wan!'

'On his bum!' Binni laugh.

'Catch his ankle 'n whirl him around and round like bullroarer! Throw that fella Wan in fire. Flame get big and Wan get small small. His ashes dancin' in fire.

I dancin' around our fire 'n Binni with me.

'Them ashes come together, flew up up come out white crow. That how Wan is white crow. But he still lazy and bad. Then he turn black crow but that—'

'—is another story!' Binni clap his hands.

'Not tonight.' Maali say. 'Time for bed.'

SLOUCHED HAT

Tom found himself watching out for her. If he was working around the homestead in the day, he might see her going to the woodpile to collect firewood or to the outside dunny situated discreetly beside it. Or she might be stoking up the fire under the old copper. Or wringing out the endless nappies in the mangle. In the evening he might see her watering her pots of geraniums. There was one occasion when she had been collecting wood from the surrounding bush when he offer his assistance to carry the wood back to the yard. She smiled then and asked his name.

'Would you like a cup of tea, Tom?' she invited.

He could see old Van der Berj with the Flying Dutchman working on the Case tractor which had broken down yet again. He might be able to spare ten minutes before they would notice his absence.

The house was quiet. Tom could see it was well scrubbed. He felt he should take his boots off but removed his hat instead and walked lightly on tip toe.

They sat at the large kitchen table and she offered him dried biscuits with the cup of milky tea. Mrs Glendon had tried to make Irish soda bread the day before, she explained, which she liked to make with sultanas and was lovely with lashings of butter but she still didn't have the hang of the Coolgardie Safe after years of a refrigerator and nothing seemed to keep fresh for long as the days were becoming hotter. She had tried to sour the milk for the bread but in twenty-four hours it had so gone off it was full of maggots. She joked they were living on tinned meat and frankfurters.

Tom listened to her flow of words and liked the soft melodious quality of her accent, so different from the harsh nasal tones of the local women. He thought that he could sit at this table and listen to her and admire her all day. She was the most beautiful woman he had ever met, her nose just a little crooked but in a way which gave her face character and strangely enhanced her features. Her movement was graceful and fluid, almost languid. He was thinking all these thoughts when he realised that she was waiting for an answer.

He flushed.

'Sorry, if I'm being nosy.' She said. 'Only, Betty mentioned that there were two of you on the station that had been sent out to Australia as orphans.'

Tom nodded, and then blurted out, 'My mother went to hospital.'

'I'm sorry.'

'My grandfather thought Australia would be for the best. I don't know what has happened to her, my mother. They didn't say.'

Mrs Glendon frowned, 'But that's … that's terrible.'

Tom gulped the dregs of his tea. It was his pain, why had he told her this? He had only ever told Jenny, in the first days of their relationship, and she had shrugged it off and poked his ribs saying if he hadn't been sent to Fairbridge then he wouldn't be at Inverness and they wouldn't be rooting like rabbits and what a shame that would be and he'd forced a smile in response and put the pain back in the box.

'How old were you?'

'Ten.'

'Can't you … write and find out?'

'Never get any answer.'

He saw his sorrow reflected on her face. Immediately he wanted to cast its shadow aside. 'I like it here though, in Australia. Like the space.'

'There's certainly plenty of that.'

'You can …' How to explain the way he could ride through open bush and sit in wide rimless pastures all day and let his mind wander across some invisible threshold into another world, roaming without impediment. 'You can dream.'

'What do you dream about?' her eyes brightened.

He shuffled the biscuit crumbs on the plate.

'Sorry, I'm being a dreadful nosy parker. Dreams are ...'
She hunted for the right description. 'Like a sacred country.'

He darted a look at her and his heart leapt. He wanted to
tell her not just about having his own spread one day or the
prince in the castello but the way he sometimes composed
poems and had once sent one to a newspaper in Perth under
a pseudonym and Grace Smithers in the post office had
raised her pencil thin eyebrows when he had gone in week
after week asking if there was anything for 'Slouched Hat'
until one day it was there, the letter of acceptance from the
newspaper and a postal order for ten whole shillings.

The baby started calling then, a cranky, 'Mama, maamaa!'

'Oh dear.' She'd said. 'That'll be Patsy finished her nap.'

He nearly knocked the chair over rushing to his feet. 'I'd
better be off anyway. Thanks for the tea.'

'Mammaaa!'

'It was lovely to meet you Tom.'

He was half way out the door. 'And you Mrs Glendon.'

A week later Tom was riding by her yard while she was
putting washing out on the line. She waved and then he'd
seen it, head raised and neck flattened. He gave Cobber a
quick kick and flicked the reins even as he reached for his
whip. She looked startled as he thundered towards her with
the whip circling in an arc above his head and then cracking
down to the ground at her feet. She was white as the sheets
on the line by the time he wheeled around. Then she had
seen it, split in half not a foot from where she was standing,
the distinctive black and yellow stripes of the Tiger Snake,
and she was breathing hard and fast and he thought she
might faint. He jumped from the horse and pulled her away.

'It's okay. It's okay.' Calming her.

Her breathe was turned to gulping sobs and she was
clinging on to him.

'I can't ... can't ...' she'd cried. And then over and over,
'Patrick, Patrick, Patrick.'

UNDER THE BED

The dragon crept out from under the bed and eyed him with evil intent, its eyes slowly blinking. Then it flattened its body, spread out its mane and opened wide its mouth all yellow and pink inside. John John could feel his heart pounding. They were coming out from under the bed. That was where they were every night. Under the bed. The deep forked tongues flicking in and out. Their cold dead eyes waiting. The slimy slithery scales uncoiling and weaving around and about each other until you couldn't count how many there might be. Lizards and goannas. Snakes and dragons. A writhing mass of reptiles.

John John couldn't move. He was trapped. If he put even one toe out of the bed they would lash out with vicious claws and bite him with sharp little teeth and sink their fangs into his flesh and they would poison him. Tiger snakes and copperheads, huge carpet snakes and stumpy bobtails. Racing horse goannas and sand goannas standing high on their back legs. The hissing blue tongued lizard and the bearded dragon. He had hoped that he was safe on top of the bed. The dragon was moving closer. A mulga snake slithered across the foot of his bed.

He was screaming and screaming.

'Shush, shush, darling ...' His mammie was gently stroking his damp forehead.

'Mammie ...' It was Nieve, whining, groggy with sleep.

'Go back to sleep Nieve, there's a good girl.'

The screams which were loud in his head were strangled yelps now.

'It's only a bad dream, John John. Shush, mammie's here.'

His hair was plastered to his scalp.

'You're wringing.' mammie said and pulled the sheet back.

The warm damp wee was spreading under his bottom. 'Oh John John, not again!' His mammie sighed and lifted him out of the bed.

He whimpered, 'It was going to get me, mammie.'

'Come on, let's have you out of these wet jammies.'

His mammie wiped down the rubber sheet, the gloves and a bucket of disinfected water in the corner of the room ready for the purpose and then she changed the bedding. He slipped under the top sheet in his fresh cotton pajamas.

'Mammie, they're under the bed.' He whispered.

She caressed his cheek. 'There's nothing there, John John.' His mammie made a show of looking under the bed with the torch. 'Nothing there.'

His face creased with anxiety, 'Are you sure?'

'I'm sure darling. Now get some sleep.'

He nodded, but he knew he would not sleep again that night until the thin sliver of sunlight reached his corner of the room and promised safety from the darkness of the night and the glittering eyes of the bearded dragon.

They were everywhere, John John came to realise. Under the house, which was built up on short stumps; to keep the house cooler his da said and the metal frill around the stumps was to keep the ants out of the house. But it did not prevent the lizards and the goannas or the snakes from getting in.

One day, shortly after their arrival on the farm, when they returned from shopping in Darinup there had been a monstrously huge goanna on the porch outside the front door. The da shouted at it and waved his hat but it seemed in no hurry to leave. This creature was like some sort of prehistoric monster, its tongue darting in and out, with thick scaly legs ending in enormous talons. His da ran at it, shouting again. Slowly the creature lumbered to the end of the porch and disappeared. John John found that he was clutching his mother's hand and she was squeezing it.

'It's a Perentie, Jimmy told me; they are the biggest ones.' Nieve's eyes were large with wonder.

A month later on the patch of rough ground behind the big machinery shed two of them were fighting. Their long tails lashing back and forth like whips. He watched with awed fascination.

'It's 'cause they're mating.' Tom nodded to him and leant against the fence, his big dog Spike at his heels. 'Showing off to the lady goannas. Sorts out which one is the boss. Mostly show. Lot of animals do that.' Tom smiled and added almost to himself. 'Humans too, I reckon.'

They watched for a while in companionable silence. John John felt safe with Tom. Tom had killed the snake that was going to kill their mammie. He had a whip. It was wound up and hooked on the saddle of his horse.

'I'd keep out of their way, though, they can be nasty buggers.' Tom advised.

Spike edged in between them and allowed himself to be patted by John John. He wished he had a dog. He'd feel safe with a dog like Spike.

It was on the third day at school that Tony and Brian took him to the drainpipe in the lunch hour. Brian had a stick, he said, 'Watch this.' Brian whacked the drain pipe again and again. A small lizard darted from the lip but Tony was ready and waiting. Quick as lightening he grabbed the lizard as it emerged. He whooped, 'Bullseye!' and held the lizard up. Its tail flicking wildly. Tony squeezed hard around the neck and shook his hand. The lizard went limp. Tony and Brian laughed; their eyes bright with delight.

Then Tony threw the lizard at John John, 'Catch!'

John John instinctively ducked out of the way and the dead lizard fell at his feet. He eyed it with horror.

'Chicken! Chicken! Chicken!' Both boys chanted.

Brian rushed forward and picked up the lizard. He waggled it in front of John John's face. John John wanted to run away but he knew the boys would think he was scared. He wanted them to stop but he didn't know how to make them. He didn't want to have to touch the dead scaly creature with its broken neck.

'John John!' It was Nieve, calling for him in her bossy voice. 'John John!' she was insistent.

He was grateful to her for once. He looked at Brian and Tony apologetically, shrugged and ran to her.

It was only to eat his crusts. Mammie had said he was to eat all the crusts. Nieve stood over him to make sure he didn't try to throw any away.

From that day John John dreaded the moment in the lunch hour when one or other of the boys would pick up the whacking stick and head for the drainpipe, he ate more slowly, he began to collect marbles hoping to be allowed to play with older children, he suggested joining in with *Simple Simon Says* even though only the girls played. But he knew it was only a matter of time before he would be forced to touch the lizards, to catch the lizards, to kill the lizards.

BY DE GRIS

Maeve chewed the top of her pen, she had struggled for weeks to finish this letter, adding little bits here and there. The more she wrote the more she could see the gaps between the words, the chasm between the lines. What could she say? Tell her mother what it was really like in this barbaric landscape, this Outback? A wilderness of rough uncivilised people, dust in your hair and the folds of your clothes and flies that would drive you crazy every time you stepped beyond the fly screen. It was known as *the bush salute*, the constant waving them away from your face. Maeve tried to imagine her mother visiting this house which was a rough shack that the pigs wouldn't be kept in back in Ireland, never mind a home to bring up children.

And she was tired. At night one or other of the children would need her in the early hours. She worried about John John, the frequency of his bed wetting and the nightmares. She placed a lamp in the children's bedroom overnight and this seemed to allay some of his night terrors. With the arrival of dawn, just as she might be drifting into sleep, the light didn't steal into the bedroom so much as invade it along with a raucous chorus of cockatoos and galahs.

In the day there was little enough time to get anything done. Everything was an extra effort, to cook the food, to wash the clothes, to trek out on a Saturday to the local town for provisions. It had taken a couple of weeks to clean the house; which had been lived in by a man and his two sons. The father had died, keeled over one Saturday night at The Swan Hotel, glass still clutched in his hand, and the sons had moved on. The filth was unimaginable. It took Maeve days of scrubbing and a bucketful of disinfectant to make it even habitable.

The old Kooka wood stove was an ancient monstrosity ingrained with years of grease and burnt sauces. She asked Betty how on earth she might get it clean. *By De Gris,* was the reply and Maeve had looked for the brand in the store only for it to dawn on her that Betty had meant the cooker could only be cleaned 'by degrees'. It seemed that she was forever misunderstanding people, nodding along in a vacuum of incomprehension.

Slowly but surely the ingrained dirt gave way. But she grappled with the lack of mod cons. It was like living in another century, the Coolgardie Safe and a bath for which you had to heat up water in the copper and then hope the children wouldn't knock the plug out as you tried to scrub them one after the other. Endlessly feeding the fire under the copper, that was her life. No wonder she was so completely exhausted. Betty told her that you got used to the outback, it got easier. She was a scrupulous housekeeper with time to bake cakes and to teach Maeve how to make pavlova with the cream fresh from the cow. But would Maeve ever get used to a life like this? Even by de gris?

Ever since the incident with the snake she sensed that despite her somnambulant state she was waking up. All of it had been in a trance, the long voyage out, the harbour and the bridge, the migration west, the shuffling around the Swan River, and then to this. She looked beyond the rough contours of the house, which no amount of scrubbing could disguise, beyond the fly screen door to a world turning to the colour of rust. She who had been spoilt and petted by four distinguished older brothers. Who had been the belle of the Ball at The Sheridan Hotel. She who had …

Maeve felt a rush of anger. She had meekly followed Patrick like one of those millions of sheep out there on the stubbled pasture. He had brought her to this back of beyond where her slender hands had become red raw, where the sun would ravage her face and dig premature lines down her cheeks, where no one had heard of Proust or sat in the stalls at the opera. Where was he leading them? His share of his father's fortune was gone, the misbegotten venture at

Killpool Hill was gone, the Golden Fleece franchise was gone, the caravan was gone, even the Holden was gone, replaced by an old van forever breaking down. What was left? The few trinkets of jewelry she still had. Were they to go too? Was she to follow him on a road to nowhere? To disaster?

Pride. That was what drove Patrick Glendon. She could see it in his eyes, in the toss of his head. He was too proud to admit defeat, to ask for help, to return home. Ireland. It was like a hungry fire this pride of his, consuming him with one great false hope after another. She had seen that look before, at a casino on the Riviera when summering with her cousin Helen and a couple of Dublin friends. An Englishman, the Honourable somebody or other, won a great deal of chips at roulette and everyone clapped. With a show of flamboyance, he began to place larger amounts on the table, made small gains but steadily lost, chasing his luck across the green baize until with a jut of the chin he placed his last few chips on zero. She had seen the thin smile on the croupier as he span the wheel and closed the betting. The Englishman did not even wait to see the little ball finally settle, bowing to people on either side as he left as though it were a trivial affair. Two days later he had drowned off Antibes, a tragic accident the French police reported.

She would have to think. Start thinking for herself. And this was something new, Maeve realised. She had been called willful and high spirited as a girl but she had never really thought for herself. Her parents and brothers had thought for her; Patrick had thought for her. Now she must start thinking. Thinking for both of them and for the children. But what would she think? She felt utterly hopeless.

Maeve scrunched the letter up and tossed it aside. It was all lies. She must start to speak the truth. At least to herself, slowly but surely, she must learn to open her eyes, to see, to scrub away at the debris of lies and illusions until the way ahead became as clear as the bright-eyed kookaburra which had emerged on the enamel of the Kooka stove after hours and hours of scrubbing by degrees.

210

THE AWA CONSOLE

Jack had come in that evening after a day at the Bulk Bins to find them all crowded in front of the new AWA television console. One hundred and nineteen guineas plus the delivery and the aerial and the installation fee. He blamed Alex. Ever since his brother had purchased his own television set, Cissy had pestered Jack on an almost daily basis. And this was the upshot. Here she was with a sitting room full of women, all glued to the 'goo goo box' as he had come to call it. Joan Smithers, fat Ethel Osborne with her daughter Nancy and if that wasn't enough, she had let in Betty Van der Berj and the Irishman's wife with a toddler on her lap.

The furniture was rearranged. Everything now faced the console, the armchairs, the couch, half the straight back dining room chairs commandeered. Cissy ensconced in prime viewing position in the armchair which used to be his armchair. Where Jack would sit by the fireplace in the winter months and listen to an hour or two of the wireless and browse through one of the agricultural machinery catalogues before lights out at nine o'clock.

They were watching the Funeral. No doubt it would go on all evening, he'd be mithered to keep the generator on. Endless reruns of the cavalcade, the assassination footage. The bloodstained dress. The speculation. The sonorous interviews. Women weeping. The endless questions. Why? Why? It was a terrible thing of course, an assassination. The Irishman had tears in his eyes. Anyone would think Kennedy had been a relation. Maybe he was, come to think of it. But what did it have to do with them? What did it have to do with Australia? Nothing. That was Jack's opinion. The markets might twitch and shudder, but next week it would be business as usual and the new guy Johnson looked steady enough; less flash than Kennedy and maybe that was not a bad thing.

Jack worked hard. He was a hands-on kind of a man like his father. Was it too much to expect to come home to a little attention from your wife and a meal on the table? Cissy hadn't even turned her head when he walked into the room.

'You gotta hand it to her she's really got style.' Fat Ethel was opining, her mouth full of Twisties.

The sideboard was littered with empty tea cups, the debris of sausage rolls and biscuits and cakes. Jack helped himself to the one remaining slice of Betty's chocolate cake, to which he was very partial. He'd often wished Cissy had the same light touch with pastries and sponges.

'Poor little fella, he must be missing his daddy so much.' Janice Smithers was sniffling into a handkerchief her eyes already red and her face blotchy.

The boy was buttoned up in a fancy coat on the steps of some cathedral. The funeral cortege was about to set off to the cemetery. Jack turned away. He'd seen enough.

In the kitchen he found Jimmy sprawled at the table doing a jigsaw with Paddy's girl and the boy with the ridiculous name. They were so intent on the emerging fairground carousel that they didn't even look up from the table.

'Here's one with a horse's nose!' The girl pounced on a loose piece.

'Where's Dinah?' Jack asked, thinking maybe the house girl could at least rustle him up something.

'Aunt's crook over in Wubin.'

'I didn't know she had any relatives.'

'Here, I got the tail!'

Jack grabbed a beer from the Coolgardie and went out onto the verandah for a smoke-oh. All the talk that day had been of the planned construction of a 14,000 tonne horizontal A type wheat storage facility at the Goomalling receival point. He'd talk to the CBH, one day he felt sure he could put Darinup on the map with something similar.

BEN DOWN AND HOW THE GOANNA GOT ITS STRIPES

Binni angry. Someone stole his marbles. He say, he have marbles in humpy in morning. Been looking at new one when wake up. Red 'n green. Turn it round 'n round look at colours. Now he's back from school, marbles gone. Maali makin' damper in mornin'. After that she dig yam 'n get wood for fire. That when marbles stolen. Binni very angry. He got good idea who took 'em.

Tommy not been at school. His tummy sick, he say. Binni won that red and green marble last week. Tommy, he's angry but can't do nothin'—other kids watch that game in the yard and saw Binni won that marble.

I give Binni stick of gum, 'Saturday we go Darinup get new marbles, any colour you want.'

'It's not the same.' Binni say. He say all his marbles special; big blue one that been Danny Yamatji, yella one and green speckle one he buy with bottle money, silver-grey one he been find in street, orange one he win off Winston Goody, big orange one with scratch Sam Kirkwall give 'im and other marbles all got own story. Not the same buy new one, you know.

'Tommy—he be Goanna Dreaming.' I say. 'Goanna his brother.'

'He should be punished for stealing!' Binni shout.

'That how goanna got his stripes.'

'Bugger the goannas!' Binni kick drum of water.

'Binni –!'

'Bugger the goannas!' Binni shouting angry, run off in gums.

Maali look at me from humpy, you know, got her arms cross.

'What I say?'

'He want you to go Auntie Ruby and get marbles back. He wants you punish Tommy.'

'But Auntie Ruby gonna say Tommy don't have Binni marbles.'

'I know that.'

'I say, *Don't mind I look for them-like;* then Auntie Ruby gonna throw bottle at me 'n swear.'

Maali nod.

'All them kids gonna run 'round, laugh, Tommy make big noise. Wake up Uncle Roy.'

'Yeah, and Tommy he real loud.'

'Uncle Roy be madder than a cut snake.'

'Yeah, he be mad.'

'Mean too—itching to fight then.'

'True.'

'Auntie Maggie be up shoutin'. And Albert and Big Joe.'

'And Rooter.'

'They want to see blood spill on ground.'

'Your blood.'

'Yeah.'

She come to me, put her hand on my face, soft-like.

'Best get it over with.' I say and head for the mob at Billangilil.

Next evening, I get back to camp been loadin' at silo all day. Binni don't look happy. Tommy at school and ask Binni to play marble match and Binni say he got no marbles. Tommy singin' then, lookin' mean 'n pointin', *Binni lost his marbles! Binni lost his marbles!*

Binni come and give me hug. Soft-like. I got plenty bruises.

We sittin' at fire. Damper cookin'. Getting dark. Binni been quiet-like.

I hear footsteps and turn look who coming camp. In the gums some boys and girls from Billangilil, with dogs. Kids look me, look Binni, not laughin'.

Witiyana sit near Binni. Put down marble for him.

'This purple one.' Witiyana say. 'Nan Myrtle give me two for present long time ago. Light purple one like the sky after it rain sometime. This one is for you.' He wipe his snotty nose with back of hand. ''Cause you my friend.'

Witiyana get up 'n walk back. He push girl to us.

Her name Sunny, maybe twelve or thirteen. She look at me bit frighten, my eye is half-close. Sunny hold out one hand, then other hand then open. We see marble in each one. 'Don't play no more Binni, you gotta keep these ones, got them up Kimberley.'

Binni took the marbles 'n put them next to purple one. He say, 'Thanks Sunny.'

'One more girl drop speckle marble in Binni's lap. She run away laughin', shy-like. Binni pick up 'n put with marbles. He smiling up, maybe he like this girl.

Winston, same age Binni, come with big grin, 'Remember this one Binni!'

It big white marble with black line.

Binni nod, 'You won it from me a month ago.'

'Walala! It's a bewdy don't ya think?'

Binni nod again, 'My second best.'

Winston put this one with marbles. 'Bet I can win it back again next week!'

'Not on your nelly!' Binni grin.

More kids come with marbles for Binni. All them marbles got a story and they all a gift.

THE RETURN OF THE PERENTIE

Despite the summer heat Nieve had a cold and she was going to stay in bed all day reading her books. John John said he might have a cold too but his mammie would have none of it.

'It's enough to have one chancer in the family.'

'It's because she's got a maths test.' He griped as they lurched down the track in the old van.

Mrs Anderson had taken Jimmy down to Perth to buy his new uniform in readiness for boarding at Christchurch Boys College; the upshot was his mammie had been driving them all week. She still did not have the hang of the gears or the clutch and at the end of the track would make a wide circle to avoid reversing. After the New Year she was going to have to deliver them down to the school bus every day and the da kept saying he'd give her lessons but there never seemed to be enough time. He called her his bunny girl the way she went hopping down the track in the van.

'Bunny mummy!' Patsy exclaimed all excited.

'Funny bunny mummy!' Nieve chanted.

John John could see his mammie did not like that so he poked Nieve and told her to shut up. Mammie said, 'Quiet, the pair of you.' But he had seen her smile.

'And you've Father Sweeney over today for the Holy Communion preparation, so you'll just have to lump it whether you've a cold coming on or not.'

The van gave a strangled moan and ground to a halt within sight of the gates. His mammie banged the steering wheel. 'Lord, I've no time for this!' His mammie cursed the day they'd ever let the Holden go. It was a long walk home with Patsy to find help to fix it with the blistering morning sun rising fast in the sky. 'You'd better trot along to the end, you

216

know the bus won't be kept waiting.'

Sure enough he was a hair's breadth away when the bus drew in. 'Run now.' His mammie shouted.

'I've got a cold too!' John John insisted as he jogged towards the waiting bus. 'Funny bunny mummy!' he called back even though he knew she couldn't hear him above the impatient honking of the horn.

Brian and Tony cornered him in the lunch break on the way back from the dunny.

'Chicken, chicken, chicken.' They hissed.

'Am not.' John John insisted.

'Yella, yella, yella.' They persisted.

'Am not.'

'Show us then.' Tony prodded him.

'He's too scaredy, aren't you, Jo Jo?' Brian shortened his name with mocking emphasis.

'Not got your big sis today, have you?' Tony's eyes bulged up close to John John.

Tony had the whacking stick in his hand. John John snatched it from him and ran around to the side of the building, the other boys hot on his tail. He paused for a moment staring at the drainpipe. Then he began to whack it. His face red with the fury of the action. Whack. Whack. Whack. Part of him wanted there to be nothing lurking inside and another part of him, with nerves on edge, was ready to grab at the scaly creature.

When it emerged, small head darting a quick reconnaissance, John John grabbed out blindly. He could not miss, there would be humiliation in that too. It was the tail he clasped. The lizard swinging and flailing to free itself. The suddenness and the fright of it ricocheted through John John's small body. He swung the creature up and then down on the ground and round against the wall, again and again. His teeth barred, grinding. It had to be dead, it would have to be dead. He must kill it. He wanted to kill it.

Brian whooped; eyes gleaming.

Tony shrieking, high pitched.

John John flung himself around and slapped Tony across the face with the smashed carcass of the lizard.

'John John!' It was Sr Veronica. 'John John!'

The command in her voice stopped John John in his tracks. His chest heaving so rapidly it might burst open. The remnant of the scaly creature dangled in one hand; the whacking stick still clutched in the other.

There was a man with her in a black suit with a white dog collar. The priest. Brian and Tony edged away, trying to distance themselves from the field of carnage but not so far as to miss out on the fate of their classmate.

'He just went a bit loony, Sister.' Brian proffered innocently in his retreat.

'Is it a little Heathen we have here?' Fr Sweeney regarded John John with steely eye. 'What's your name boy?'

John John stared fiercely in return, the blood bubbling in his brain driving all coherent thought out of it.

'You've a devil of a one here, Sister.' The priest's eyes narrowed.

Sr Veronica bent forward, her voice calming, 'Let it go now, will you? Will you do that for me, John John?'

After a moment her words seemed to reach him. John John dropped both stick and creature.

'You know that's a wicked thing you've done?' She was trying to catch his eye. 'Don't you?'

John John quivered; the heat in his head moving in waves down to the tips of his fingers and his toes.

'Answer the Sister young fellow me lad before you feel the back of my hand.' The priest glared.

John John opened his mouth but any decipherable words were choked in his throat.

'This boy needs a good lesson in manners as well as in common decency.' The priest indicated the tattered remains of the lizard with the point of a polished toecap. 'Will you look at this … obscenity. You'll be made an example of—mark my words.' The priest turned to Sr Veronica. 'It might be best for me to take care of it, Sister, you've been distressed enough. I've experience of boys of this mien. He'll learn a lesson all right.'

Sr Veronica shook her head sadly. 'It's not at all like him Father.'

A tear rolled out onto John John's cheek. 'I'm sorry Sister Gobbleshoe ...' He gulped. 'I'm sorry Sister Gobbleshoe.'

Sr Veronica extended a hand to his shoulder. 'God Blesses you too John John and all the poor creatures of this earth.' She sighed, 'How could you have done this—?'

John John brushed the tear from his cheek.

'—to one of his blessed creatures?'

'I don't know Sister.' He was shaking and gulping still.

'Oh, he knows, right enough. Plain devilment. It's the devil that's in him and wants to be thrashed out.' Fr Sweeney's eyes tightened. 'You spare the rod and you spoil the child.'

Sr Veronica flinched. 'Have you ever done this before John John?' She quizzed.

'No, Sister.'

'You're heartily sorry, aren't you John John?'

'Yes, Sister.'

'And you won't do it again?'

John John shook his head. 'I don't want to.'

'Father, I think that on this one occasion if John John prays for forgiveness ...'

The priest stiffened. 'You've provenance here of course Sister Veronica, but I'd watch this young fellow like a hawk, one step out of line.' He bent towards John John towering over him like a black bird of prey. 'Remember young man, God sees all, remember that. And you'll not avoid his judgment!' The priest wheeled away.

Sr Veronica took hold of both his shoulders to make him look her in the eye. 'John John, I want you to pray. That's what we do when we are really sorry. Ask God's forgiveness.'

'What will I pray Sister Gobbleshoe?'

'Well, I think if you kneel and say one *Our Father* out loud before you go to bed tonight then I am sure He'll be very pleased with that.'

'I won't go to hell?' He whispered.

Sr Veronica frowned. 'God wants us to do good, He wants us to come to him in Heaven. If you're a good boy you've no need of such worries.'

That evening when he arrived at the gates of Inverness Tom was waiting for him in his old jalopy. 'Jump aboard mate!'

The van needed a new part apparently. Tom had offered to do the pick-up. He tapped his nose. 'Just don't let the Boss know.'

When they pulled up outside the house, the first thing John John saw was the perentie swaying across their yard. He stared at him in horror, the malevolent eyes, the deeply forked tongue, had the serpent come for him? In retaliation for what he had done?

Tom switched the engine off. 'That old devil back again!' He stepped out of the jalopy and set about running the giant reptile out of the yard.

That night by the light of the kerosene lamp which his mammie kept lit for his sake, John John knelt by his bed and pressed his hands tightly together. *'Our Father Who Art in Heaven ...'*

Nieve stopped her dramatic coughing and stared at him wide eyed with surprise.

ON ANGELS WINGS

When Patrick came in for supper, he heard Nieve's high plaintive voice from the verandah. 'Mammie we need it for tomorrow.' He entered the kitchen to find her on the verge of tears. 'Everyone else will have cotton wool.'

'Whisht, we've run out, all right.'

Maeve was feeding Patsy. Mash splattered all over the high chair as Patsy tried to grab the spoon. Patrick could see from Maeve's unkempt hair that it was an *end of the tether* day. Her period had started in the night, a week late and a cause for relief but her periods knocked her sideways, particularly with the heat of an Outback summer getting into gear.

'We could go and ask Betty?' Patrick ventured.

Nieve's eyes lit up. 'Auntie Betty will have cotton wool.'

Maeve sighed. 'We're forever asking for this or that.'

'It's only a bit of cotton wool.'

Nieve was already heading for the door.

Maeve looked at Patrick. He knew the look.

'We'll be out of the woods soon, I promise. I'd better catch up with Nieve, thank Betty myself.'

Sure enough, their Dutch neighbour had cotton wool to spare and they returned with a slab of chocolate cake to boot.

A couple of days later he arrived home to find Nieve and John John helping Maeve to string up a line of cut out angels, their wings stippled with wisps of cotton wool; and there were other decorations made of silver gum nuts and red ribbon draped around the pictures on the wall. Nieve was grinning from ear to ear. Patrick saw the gleam in her eyes and knew there was something else.

'Tell your daddy the news.' Mammie prompted.

221

'Guess what da?' She spluttered.

'You've come top in the maths?'

'No da!'

'You've a new dress?'

'No da!'

He held out his arms and she rushed into them.

'Will I tell you da?'

'I'm dying of the suspense.' He squeezed her tight.

'Sister Gobbleshoe,' who they had all learnt was really Sr Veronica, 'says I'm to be in the Nativity Play—and I'm to be Mary Mother of Baby Jesus!'

'And I'm a shepherd!' John John piped in, not to be forgotten.

Patrick held her close, arms wrapped around his neck. 'Mary, sure, isn't that grand?' He tried to swallow the cold metal taste in his mouth. It was sticking in his gaw and he could feel the nausea rising to meet it.

'It was between me and Maria but she is going to be the Innkeeper because she is good at pulling funny faces and making people laugh and Sister Gobbleshoe said I was good at learning lines and I have lovely kind eyes for Our Lady.'

'Great news altogether and John John a shepherd.'

John John sidled towards him.

'But listen, if you're all in the Nativity Play who will be watching?'

'You will da!' They chimed one on top of the other.

'Is that right?' He tickled their ribs. 'Is that right?'

'Will the boss let you off?' Maeve interjected.

'He will and that's a fact.' Patrick promised.

He tossed in the bed that night. *It's an honour, Patrick.* Br Anthony had said, *To play the part of Our Holy Mother.*

In a school of boys to be the one dressed up in the blonde wig, the blue dress and with the smudge of lipstick. Quinn had called him a soft girl for running off home; is that what they all thought, that he was a soft girl?

Holy Mary, Mother of God.

BOMBS AWAY

Maeve was deliberating between spam or frankfurters, neither did she relish but without a refrigerator they could seldom eat fresh meat. She replaced the spam on the shelf. For days she had felt troubled.

They had all been invited to spend Sinterklaas with Betty and Bram. Their daughter Saskia had arrived up from Perth with Dirk and their three young children. After an initial shyness her three were soon racing around the yard, over excited, full of cake and lemonade and awaiting the arrival of Dirk as Santa and young Paul Vermeer from the Davidson place, who was to play a character called Zwart Piet.

Maeve sat next to Mieke, the wife of Pieter, The Flying Dutchman. Maeve admired the fabric of Mieke's frock, the vibrant colour and her simple line. Mieke flushed and owned to making her own clothes. Maeve could see she had an eye for quality. They moaned about the limitations of shopping, even in Bodenham, with little beyond endless floral prints.

Maeve began to wish that they could live on the same station; that would have been something welcome, she realised, the opportunity to have a friend nearer her own age.

'I thought about training to be a designer.' Maeve confided. 'But I was terrible for parties in those days and then before I could say Jack Robinson I was married with children and feeding chickens on our farm at Killpool.'

'You had a farm?'

'Patrick – I wish he'd told me before we got wed that he'd always wanted to be a farmer!'

'But then why—?'

'We lost it, over-extended.' Maeve interjected.

'And now you are here.'

'Yes, now we are here.'

223

John John came crashing into her then. 'Mammie, mammie he's coming! Santa's coming!'

Dirk rode up on a piebald horse in the red robes of Saint Nicholas followed on the ground by Paul, blacked up and looking like a scarecrow.

'Why is there a gollywog?' Nieve asked, puzzled.

Mieke explained that Zwart Piet was black with soot from climbing up and down chimneys for Saint Nicholas.

Presents were distributed with much joking as a list of the children's misdemeanors was read aloud and promises were extracted to be good in future.

Bram stood and addressed the youngsters. 'And now that you have all promised to be so well behaved and deserving of your gifts from Sinterklaas I think that it is time for bed!'

Amidst much protestation Saskia ferried her children away.

Patrick, offered to take their brood, insisting Maeve stay a little longer, she did not often have the chance of company.

The sun was dipping over the rim of the horizon. The adults settled on the verandah and enjoyed the breeze which ruffled through the lemon trees in Betty's small orchard.

Dirk shuffled out of the heavy costume jacket, removed the white flowing beard and mitred hat and wiped the sweat from his brow. Bram was already pouring a large glass of beer for him now that he was out of saintly character.

'To Sinterklaas.'

A clink of glasses echoed around the verandah.

'To good friends.' Bram enjoined, his face glowing as much from the many glasses of *bowl* as from the heat.

The murmur of chatter started up again.

'I'm learning to drive, properly, after Christmas.' Maeve said. 'Perhaps you might like to come over for lunch one day, Mieke? I could collect you.'

'That would be very nice but you must not go to any trouble and Pieter could bring me.'

Mieke glanced over at her husband. He was politely listening to Mr Vermeer prattling on about the best way to make Gouda.

'They come all the way to Australia these people and all

they ever talk about is tulips and cheese.' Mieke whispered with a smile to Maeve.

'The Irish are the same, only its potatoes and stout.'

'So, Mieke, where are you from?' Dirk cut in.

'From the Arbroath block, it's about five mi—'

'No, I mean in the old country.'

'From Amsterdam.'

'You are not from near Gouda, like Pieter?'

Mieke shook her head averting her eyes, 'Amsterdam.' she averred.

'But that is not where you were born, is it?'

Mieke blinked. 'No, but—'

'Not where you spent the years of the occupation.'

Maeve felt a ripple of tension on the verandah. The murmur of voices began to subside.

'I know who you are.' Dirk's eyes glittered.

'Dirk?' Betty frowned. 'What is this?'

'This is Sinterklaasvond. We must all be held to account.' His features hardened, 'Isn't that right, Mieke De Wolf?'

Mieke flinched. Across the verandah Pieter jerked to his feet knocking his chair over.

'But what is another lie—'

'No!' Pieter was pushing towards them.

'—to a Nazi collaborator!' Dirk denounced triumphantly.

All colour drained from Mieke's features.

'You are the daughter of Jacob De Wolf?' It was Bram, and the question escaped as a whisper. 'Is it true?'

'How does it feel to betray your own people?' Dirk prodded.

Pieter was standing between them now, his fists clenched.

'Dirk, enough! These are our guests.' Betty implored.

'It's a vicious lie.' It was Pieter. 'Jacob is not a Nazi.'

'But a Wrong Dutch? A collaborator?'

'Dirk.' Betty silenced him. 'It's enough.'

Bram's face crumpled in on itself. 'It must not be forgotten.' There was a plea in his voice.

'He's right mama.' Saskia insisted. 'Great uncle Simon, cousin Lena, they all died in the camps. Papa only just

225

escaped to England, even a half Jew would have been sent to those death camps.' With anger welling Saskia was confronting her mother. 'They could even have taken me mama—and Lisbeth too.'

'No, we are Reform Church, nobody knew Bram's mother was a Jew.' Betty shook her head as if to shake off all this unpleasantness. 'When did you know this about Mieke? You have planned to do this? Here, like this, at our party?'

Saskia glared at Mieke, 'You should know who you sit down to eat bread with mama!'

A tear trickled over Mieke's eyelid.

Pieter placed a hand on her shoulder. 'Come Mieke, we must be leaving, it is late.' He helped her to her feet, bid goodnight to the assembled party, and guided her down the verandah steps.

Maeve found herself mulling over the years of the War. She had been fourteen when the peace finally came. In neutral Ireland all the horrors of war had seemed beyond the boundaries of her world of school and piano lessons. On occasional evenings her parents had listened to the wireless, the latest news or Lord Haw Haw; but Maeve found it all very boring and preferred to engross herself in her book of scraps.

When Eleanor Solomon and her family arrived as neighbours she thought little beyond the prospect of a new friend. Then Kevin told her how they came to be there. The Germans had conducted a bombing mission over Liverpool and on their return journey had swung past Dublin and emptied their bombs. A warning, Kevin suggested. A house in Rathdown Park had taken a direct hit. One of the bedrooms crashing right through to the floor below but miraculously the Solomons had survived. Now they were renting whilst their house was rebuilt. It was the drama of the survival which made her regard Eleanor with a kind of awe.

Eleanor was someone with whom Maeve could discuss

Hollywood stars and go to the flicks. Their trips became regular and they afterwards sucked lemonade through straws at Hennessy's tea rooms with Eleanor's friends. The youngsters would sometimes venture talk of relatives in Europe and rumours about work camps.

'But we are safe here in Ireland, aren't we?' Eleanor exclaimed,

A boy called Sammy glared at the table, 'We will always be treated like dogs until we have our own country.'

They had all been silent as though a great truth were pressing down on their young shoulders.

That evening Maeve was helping her mother, shelling fresh green peas, every so often popping one into her mouth, when her father and Sean Og, entered through the back door into the adjoining vestibule. Maeve overheard them talking business and her father complaining, 'That Jew boy Stein is driving a dreadful hard bargain.'

That night she lay in bed and wondered how it might be to be a Jew and to never feel safe even in your own home. A passing moment, Maeve now reflected as she decided finally on the spam over the frankfurters, when the ugliness of the war had intruded into the even temper of her days.

Patsy hurtled through the fly screen and clasped her around the legs. 'What is it darling?'

'Jo Jo hit me!'

'Have you been naughty again?'

Patsy stared up with eyes large and innocent and shook her head, the pinch of her lip the only give away.

Maeve smiled ruefully as she grappled with the tin opener. For Patsy this Australia would be home; Ireland not even a memory. She would be an Aussie through and through.

Maeve paused and considered that this barren country would never be home to her and she would always be made to feel like *The Wandering Jew*.

GOLD RUSH

Stubby Croker dreamed of gold, cascades of gold. He was knee deep in it. He dreamed of his brother Hayden. The gold rippled through Hayden's hands like water, gleaming and sparkling in the way of fool's gold. Hayden was laughing, his golden curls bouncing around the dazzle of his smile. He was calling. What was he saying?. Laughing out loud. *Look to here, Ash!* The gold streaming through his hands.

Stubby stirred from his slumber. A dawn light was shivering through the cracks in the weatherboard. It took him a while to get his bearings, muggy in the stifling heat, feel the dull ache in his back and the effort of sitting up. He looked around his decaying shack, the cluttered shelves, the cobweb corners, all the detritus of fifty years. Ashes to ashes, dust to dust. The familiar bunk, the tattered curtain but with the same old question never answered, *Where am I?*

No better off than his father had been after his mother's death that was for sure. When the labouring on farms in the Slad Valley slid down the length of a bottle of cider. Along with the tithe cottage. Bart Croker forced into the workhouse in Gloucester and made to work like a drudge on the docks. A man from the parish council arranged that the eldest boys, Hayden and Ashton, get a passage to Australia on some assistance scheme for rural workers.

It felt like an adventure to the two boys, that their lives were all before them and they were going to the land of opportunity, far away from the scrimping poverty of the five valleys. Worth the cramped berth in the dank fug of steerage and the stomach-churning seas of the Roaring Forties, they assured each other.

What a lark it had seemed.

The reality was bondage on an outback farm felling trees

228

and clearing land. Broken backs in the killer heat. The flies and the mozzies sucking the life blood from them. They ran away from a farmer too rough and ready with his fists. Broken their bond to the Assistance Scheme; felt like criminals. Laughed about it. It was the Wild West. Two boys on the run, working as casual hands for a square meal and a bunk until word of the Gold Rush to Kalgoorlie enticed them to try their luck at prospecting their own few square yards.

They joked that when they struck it lucky, Hay would make hay on Hay Street with all those good time girls. There were endless days of filling your lungs with dust and grit, and shanty town squalor and the girls on Hay Street were mostly sad and frightened creatures as much in bondage as they themselves had been. They built a rough shack with Hessian walls stiffened with paper in imitation of their neighbour—and only just saved it when it caught fire. The surface gold strikes were tailing off but there was plenty of disease. The outbreak of plague scared the wits out of them.

Hay was drinking by then, developed his father's taste for golden ale, cheaper than water in Kalgoorlie and that's a fact. It was water that was like gold, Ash thought when the thirst was on him. He was for leaving, getting a job on the railroads, something like that, but Hay said their luck would change; he could feel it in his bones. And then Len Goodji, came in from the bush with a surface nugget hidden deep in his pocket. Got to talking with the boys. Aboriginals were not allowed to keep their finds of gold. They did a deal, a fifty-fifty split.

Hay was on the ensuing bender when they staggered into Donovan's billiard hall.

Hay dead at twenty in a drunken brawl. An argument over a game. The big Norwegian was looking for a lump of trouble from the outset.

Ash just seventeen and on his own in a vast friendless continent. Lost without Hay and his golden smile. A drifter, he drifted. Worked as a Broomie then ended up on The Rabbit Proof Fence Number 2, busy staking its way like some Chinese Wall along the edge of the wheat land, keeping the invaders out. Then he wasn't Ash anymore; that lost too. He was Stubby, his growth stunted like his heart.

Old Jack, saw him on the section of Rabbit Proof straddling the east of Arbroath. Stayed because where else was there to go? Without Hay? Hay was the one with the dreams, the golden boy with dreams of gold. He was just little Ash, always in the wake following on. Where could he go with no Hay to follow? Home to the Slad Valley? What home? His father dead he was sure. There would be his sisters, Lucy and Agnes, married no doubt; that or domestics. And sickly Keynes, would he still be alive? In some Barnardo's home? No point thinking about any of it. The way your life could slide away from you until it didn't feel like your own life at all but a covering that you'd slipped into to pass the time.

He'd died too that night in Kalgoorlie in 1898. The knife in his brother's chest, cornflower blue eyes rimming red. That was the last Ash could recall, the look of bewilderment in his brother's eyes. Later in the courthouse he heard how he had taken up the billiard cue and like a creature possessed gone after the big Norwegian, who'd been wrong footed by the frenzy, caught his head when he fell. But Ash couldn't remember any of it, only those cornflower blue eyes and his brother's look of surprise, the way your luck could change. Two dead in one night. Calls for law and order and a seventeen-year old boy standing before a judge. A glassy eyed boy beyond caring about life or death.

What did Stubby Croker have to show for any of it?

The carpet snake coiled in the rafters, lifted his head and tasted the air with his flickering tongue. Other roustabouts didn't understand how Stubby could live with such a tenant, but he found the large snake companionable enough now that his bitch Bisley was passed away.

'Happy Christmas.' Stubby saluted the giant reptile and the snake flicked his tongue in reply.

BUSH TUCKER

It was the last field. At the outer reaches of the Anderson empire. In a halo of dust and chaff the giant harvester trundled down towards the red ridged road at one end, the one they called The Thirty-Six Gate and up towards the border with the bushland natural flora and fauna reserve at the other; under the shadow in the distance of Mount Stuart. Even further afield into the ranges there were supposed to be ancient rock formations.

Patrick had heard talk there were plans to turn the bushland into a proper Park, with designated nature walks and a purpose-built scenic picnic and barbecue area by the creek, an information kiosk even. It was a place where travelling gold miners had habitually camped on their way out to the Yilgarn goldfields. That practically made for an historic monument in these parts and the rusty old tin cans the gold diggers had left in their wake were like archaeological treasure. He could picture the ostentatious display case, *baked bean container circa 1892,* and chuckled.

He imagined walking under the shade of the gum trees, pointing out one plant and another, different acacias and wattles, naming this bird and that lizard, passing on knowledge of the land to his children, just as he might have done back in Wicklow on a mellow summer's evening. Only there he would know the names, would recognise hawthorn, ragwort, know a raven from a blackbird and a crow. But here? Would he ever have the gist of this strange land with its primeval plants and creatures?

On the far side of the field he could just make out the second harvester. An aboriginal chap, Ben. Black as the ace of spades. No front teeth. But Ben knew his way around a harvester that was for sure, and a good worker, Patrick could

231

see that in the grudging respect which Anderson gave him above all the other blacks.

Ben Down. Was someone *taking the Micky*. Van der Berj said many of the aboriginals were named by the missionaries, florid, biblical or fanciful names, Samson and Delilah, Pontius and Pilate. It was hard not to think there was a joke or two intended amongst them. He could hardly ask; bring Ben's attention to it. He shuddered. Ben Down. No that was not a thought to conjure with.

They spoke little, locked in their own small cabins atop the harvesters, only meeting for the midday halt. At least out here, skirting the bushland reserve, there was some shade to be had from the killer heat of the noon day sun. Under the speckled shelter of a wandoo, Patrick tucked into the sandwiches which started to curl at the edges the moment he took them from their waxy wrapper. Thick white slabs of bread you could taste the preservatives. None of Maeve's home-made soda bread out here. He smiled remembering the early days of their marriage, watching her hands covered in flour talking aloud her mother's recipe for the first time.

'What does she mean by a smidgeon of this and a smatter of that?' Her brows creased in an exasperated frown. 'And what would you reckon a knob is?'

He had been unable to suppress a guffaw.

'What? Are you laughing at me, Patrick Glendon?' Kneading the thick dough.

He'd wrapped his arms around her from behind. 'No, never you macushla, never you.'

She tried to smack him away with a floury hand as he pressed himself against her, finally getting the joke, but he saw the twitch of a grin at the corners of her mouth too.

It was a sad burnt thing which came out of the oven.

'It's supposed to rise, at least a little.' Her face deflated.

He took a slice of the dense brown loaf with a spread of butter. Her eyes on him. But the butter couldn't disguise the concrete dryness. 'Mmmm.' He assured trying hard to swallow and lathered some more butter on the remainder.

'Is that a slice of bread you're having with your butter?'

232

'Nooo, only a knob.'

And they'd laughed and laughed and taken the bread down to the park and tossed chunks to the ducks.

'They'll be constipated for weeks.' Maeve observed.

Ben was holding something out to him.

'You wanna try, Paddy?'

In his hand Ben held out a shiny red fruit, redder than any Patrick had ever seen before. He marveled how Ben brought no lunch box with him. Every day he seemed to find sources of water and sustenance in the midday halt, roots and grubs, all manner of strange fruit most of which didn't look edible at all.

'What is it?'

'Quandong. Taste good.'

And it was too. A little acidic but pleasant nevertheless. He must remember this one. Quandong. Show it to Nieve.

'Can make medicine. With roots and leaves too'

'Jaze Ben, how do you find it all?'

'Bush tucker. My murran show me.'

'Your father?'

'Grandfather.'

It was pitch dark when they finished the field but there was little point leaving half a day's work. Anderson came by and said as much.

Patrick felt every bone in his body aching by the time he got back to the compound but there was still his cow to be milked, it was not something he could ever ask Maeve to do. As he headed towards the milking sheds his path was blocked by Ken Duguid pissing up against the wall. He had a bottle of Bundy in one hand and his cock in the other.

'Paddy is it?' Ken swung the bottle in greeting, staggering back slightly. 'The new blue-eyed wonder is it? They say you're smart. Anderson, he thinks you're smart. Smarter than old Ken, that right?' Duguid swiveled to face him, the last dribbles of the pissing torrent spraying Patrick's boots.

Patrick backed off with a look of disgust.

'Whadda … you fucking Irish …!'

Patrick held his tongue. He seldom encountered Ken Duguid but he knew of his belligerent reputation. Knew too that he had fought in Malaysia and been a POW. Then he had been granted a block of land as part of the Soldiers Settlement scheme and married a waiting sweetheart. But she'd died in a car crash and he'd gone to pot and hit the bottle. It hadn't been long before he was absorbed by Anderson and now worked as a general roustabout.

The man was obviously stocious.

'Ken, I just need to get to the cows.'

'Ken is it? I'll 'Ken' you boy. Ken you this, you Paddy nonce.' He fumbled angrily with his zipper. 'That what you are? They say you had your own farm. Lost it. Not so smart then after all. You and me both there, mate!' A last glug of the Bundy. 'Think you know a thing or two? Don't know bugger all!' Finger jabbing towards Patrick. 'Bog ignorant Paddy.' Duguid chuckled over this witticism. 'Bog Man.'

Patrick stood, undecided. Should he back away? Give it ten minutes and return? The weariness felt like lead in his limbs. From inside the sheds he could hear the cow lowing; the cow Nieve called Minnie the Minx, but he had to remember to call her Dolly when speaking with Anderson.

Then Ken had him by the scruff. His mean, tight lipped face pressing closer to Patrick. 'Listen to me, Bog Man—'

'I am not after any trouble, all right.'

'Listen good. Bog Man ...' The empty bottle smashed against the side of the wall, whether by accident or design. 'I fought in a War.'

'I know you did.'

'Three years in a Jap camp. Know what that means, do you? Do you?! What did you do? What did you Irish do? Hide out in that shitty bog of yours, Bog Man?'

From the corner of an eye Patrick could see the jagged neck of the bottle still clutched in Duguid's fist. If it came for him, he would strike, he was ready.

'Mr Duguid … Mr Duguid …'

It was the young lad, Tom.

'I sorted the bedding out for you.' Tom came up beside him, 'We got an early start on the silos tomorrow.'

Ken grunted, his eyelids beginning to droop at the mention of bed, but his grip tightened on Patrick momentarily. 'Back to your bog, Bog Man!' Then he released him with a flourish and lurched away, waving the broken end of the bottle.

'Thanks Tom.' Patrick took a deep breath.

'No worries. Ken gets like that, like that with everyone.'

'Thanks all the same.'

They felt the first spots of rain. There was thunder in the air and the static of lightening. The wheat had been harvested just in time.

BEN DOWN AND THE INITIATION

I keep down-wind. Bubai don't smell me. Sun settin' pink sky. Binni got his wurlie, not bad little humpy, you know. Roo eatin' grass, maybe fence broke someplace.

Binni makin' fire. He been rubbin' fire stick like I show him. Usin' dry animal shit.   I smile—see little smoke. Binni blowing 'n blowin', catch them spark, put on grass and gum sticks. Talkin' to fire, callin' up fire, soft like. Smoke comin'. Gotta work hard make good fire.

Dog barkin' 'n want to play-like. Binni shake his head.

This dog make me laugh. Bubai a little dog. Pup from Billangilil. Last for milk, live on scraps. Binni find 'im one day when he walk to get mission bus and Binni give him little food. Next day same—keep something for little dog and dog wag his tail and follow to our camp. Binni run him away—Maali don't want a dog. She thinkin' we leave this place.

Young dog sit under gum tree, pink tongue hangin' out 'n bright eyes look in camp.

'You not feeding that mongrel, are you? Got fleas.' Maali shout me. She want Binni to hear.

I shake my head. 'That dog one of Billangilil mob.'

'Then what it doing at our camp?'

'Smell your cookin', I reckon.'

'He hungry.' Binni say.

'Can stay hungry.' Maali say.

We sit quiet, eat tucker.

Next day little dog same place. Maali throw stone, to scare dog. Binni tell me, I workin' at railway in Darinup loading grain.

Dry wind come that night—sometimes make fellas crazy. Rooter been gambling, won little, got a stash 'n drinking.

Rooter got an eye for women; how he come by his name. And he gets in his crazy head Maali feelin' lonely. He pick up bottle and go for visit.

Maali and Binni sleepin'. That don't stop Rooter. Maali look like a Krubi he know. Krubi a name for one woman in his mob, most beautiful. Rooter he lie down with Maali, he singing, call her his Krubi 'n touchin' her. Maali wake up and she on her feet shouting at him, but he drunk—only hear sweet words. He been pullin' at Maali, she kickin' him. Binni wake and see Rooter smilin' but him hitting Maali, say keep quiet. Binni 'fraid; Rooter a big fella.

Then little dog come running barkin' and teeth bare and he biting Rooter on leg. Rooter been kicking that little dog. Dog's hurting but he come back 'n bite Rooter ankle.

Maali got a knife now. She stab at Rooter, tell him get out. He swear 'n pick up Bundy and leave our camp. Little dog barkin' at him. Rooter cryin' now for Krubi, his old love.

Next day, Binni helpin' Maali, poundin' yam; he know Maali been hit, hurtin' bad. Maali cookin' on fire. She take food and say give it little dog. Binni look her, he shock. 'Don't mean he belong here.' Maali say.

Every day, little dog get close to our fire and he get food. Binni not 'fraid 'n play wit him. Sometime he mischief but Maali look 'im angry like. He stop, look with 'im big soft eyes. He don't have name; but Maali call him Bubai—*little one*. Little dog but got big heart.

Binni got fire going good 'n Bubai sitting with him. Young wadjela ride up on his horse, got kelpie dog runnin' next him. Binni wave 'n Tom come close. Bubai barkin' and run to kelpie, he want to play. Binni got big grin, he happy, you know, been walkabout. They talk 'n Tom give 'im stick of gum. Then Tom give salute and ride away. He pass me; he see I been lookin' at Binni, first walkabout, you know. Tom smile 'n whistle his kelpie.

Binni got dilly-bag for tucker. Damper, quandong, desert raisin—good for one day. After, he have to hunt 'n look for

237

tucker. He got lot to learn.

Think 'bout first time my murran take me hunting. After he got wallaby, he stick knife in his arm, blood fall on the ground. Murran say gotta pay-like for taking from land. It's old way.

Miss that old fella. End of life, he near blind, he know not long 'fore he go with spirits; talk 'bout his Right Death. Long time among wadjela we been looking for my mother. Now time to be with his mob 'n he want me initiated with that mob. They happy we come. My murran say it time for me to be a man. Take long time get ready. Murran tell me stories 'bout warrior fella, Mamru.

Initiation, can't talk about, that big secret. It hard.

I look Binni cookin' his tucker, first walkabout, been doing good. He not my mob, you know, not our Dreaming, but I can teach him be a good fella.

THE SILVER STAR

Nieve's Silver Star six shooter nestled securely in the holster which was strapped tightly in place over her shorts; she patted it to make sure. The cowgirl set was the best present ever.

Her da grinned from ear to ear watching her tear through the wrapping paper of the big box. 'Looks like Santa got it right this year, heh Nieve?'

The Annie Oakley Cowgirl set. A black cowboy hat with white fringe. A red cord waistcoat and skirt, though if truth be told she wasn't too bothered about the skirt, and best of all, the gleaming Silver Star six shooter with revolving barrel, belt and holster.

Nieve drew the gun and practiced twirling it around on her finger. Popping it back in the holster and then drawing it again as fast as she could. Pow! Pow! She took aim at a red-tailed black perched on the roof of an abandoned truck and fired. The cockatoo screeched and flew off into the clear blue sky. The hammer clicked and clicked. Time to reload. Nieve dug into her pocket for the roll of caps.

Freshly loaded Nieve pointed the Silver Star at an ugly goanna which was stretched lazily over a rock. She squeezed the trigger slowly. Crack! 'Got yer!' She breathed in the whiff of sulpherous gunpowder.

The goanna looked back at her with disdain and blinked slowly. Nieve stuck her tongue out at him and kicked the door of the old truck, which was sometimes used for play, she or Jimmy sitting behind the wheel pretending to drive even though it didn't have any wheels. The floor had completely rotted away under the pedals. There was no passenger seat and the driver's was slashed with the back broken.   In the compartment under the dashboard Nieve noticed a Red Back, she stiffened, and pictured the poison extraction kit in the kitchen with its sharpened steel knife. She shuddered and fired at the Red Back.

Pow!

This was dangerous country, just like The Wild West, and here she really could be a cowboy. Only Aussies had different names, stockman or ringer or jackaroo and jillaroo. Which sounded like they should be carrying buckets of water up and down a hill.

Thinking of danger, her mind ran to the quagmires. The day before Tom the Pom had said, 'Be careful now and don't go anywhere near those quagmires, lost a sheep last week.' Maybe the sheep was still there with just his woolly ears sticking out.

The first time Jimmy had taken Nieve she was petrified by the strangeness. He swooped around her, took hold of her hand and dragged her right up to the edge of the quagmire then made a pretense of pushing her. She screamed with sheer terror. Jimmy whooped, confident in his greater strength that she would not attempt the same trick on him.

But together with the fear Nieve also experienced a tingling excitement. A strange temptation to feel the warm oozing slime sucking her in. She and Jimmy would crouch on their haunches and stare at the expanse of mud, covered with flies and struggling primitive vegetation. Parts of the surface were hardened and cracked. They would break up the surface with their sticks and prod and dig into the glaucous gluey mass. Throw stones or old beer cans and watch them being slowly sucked under; they never ceased to be fascinated by these experiments. Somethings might remain on the surface for days so that they would have to beat them in.

Nieve broke off a small dead branch, it snapped sharply, brittle and dry in the hot season. The branch dragged along the ground leaving a trail of raised red dust. When she reached the quagmire, she squatted at the edge and tried to break the surface crust with the poking stick. She wondered if it would be possible to walk across when the top was drought hard like this. She dug the stick in until her hand was completely covered. The mud felt warm, she wriggled her hand about, the mud made a sort of popping, glucking sound. She felt a heaviness drawing her in and pulled her arm up abruptly in alarm, this time a louder noise.

Nieve stood up, a little shaken, she'd have to scrape off the mud with something before going home for lunch – it was her gun hand too. She would have to find a patch of yellow grass or a bit of rag.

She searched about, shading her eyes in the glare. Her gaze snagged on a figure crouched behind an outcrop of bushes. Nieve squinted to make out a pair of khaki shorts, a lime green T shirt and bright eyes.

'G'day' she called.

There was no reply

Nieve noticed that although the crouching figure had blonde hair, he was honey skinned with the flattened features of the aboriginals.

'Scuse I, you from Billangilil?'

The boy poked his head above the bush and nodded and shrugged so it wasn't clear to Nieve if he was saying yes or no. He pointed at her arm and grinned.

Nieve blushed, feeling a bit of an idiot because he must have seen everything. 'Yeh, I was just messing. My mum'll have a fit.'

A young dog padded out from behind the bush, tail wagging furiously, barked and came to sniff at her hand. The boy broke off some gum leaves and brought them to her.

'Thanks' She pawed at the fast caking mud.

The boy gave a hand, he was quick and careful. 'Yer alrighty now?' he said with satisfaction.

'Yeh' Nieve paused and stared at him, never actually having spoken with an aboriginal before, Dinah who worked at the Anderson house didn't really count; she had laughed when Nieve asked about boomerangs and digeridoos; said she preferred Elvis Presley.

'My name is Nieve.'

'Niv.' the boy repeated, 'I'm Binni Jumurrula.'

'That's a funny name.'

241

'So's yours.'

She could see that Binni was eyeing her gun from the corner of his eye. Nieve slipped it from the holster.

'She's a real beaut.' The boy whistled.

Nieve fired off six caps in a row. A Rosella flew up into the air in a flutter of colour. The dog barked and scampered around them. The satisfying commotion made her feel generous.

'Here you have a go.' she pushed the gun into Binni's hand.

Binni looked at her in amazement. He handled the gun gently and with great care. He took aim, squinting his eye down the barrel as he fired.

'Walala!'

Binni made to give Nieve the gun back but she shook her head.

'Have another go. You can twirl the revolver.'

Binnie span the revolver section and then had a try at spinning the gun on his finger, the gun dropped to the red dust.

'Crikey, sorry mate!'

For a moment Nieve didn't know what to say. Then, 'It's okay I was always dropping it at first.'

Binni picked up the gun and blew the dust off and using the hem of his T shirt vigorously polished the weapon until it gleamed and handed it back. 'Thanks.'

They sauntered towards the mire. Nieve picked up her mud baked stick and tapped the crust.

'What y'er doing round here?'

'Walkabout.'

'Walkabout?' She and Jimmy watched *Whiplash* on the new telly; about an American cowboy with a whip just like Tom and he was in Australia and there were sometimes aboriginals in the stories and they did Walkabout.

'What d'you have to do? Just – walk about?' Nieve snickered at her own wit.

Binni prickled. 'Make a journey, hunt your own grub, make fire and shelter.'

'Can girls do Walkabout?' Nieve enquired, her curiosity

roused.

Binni shook his head. 'Girls help with cooking.'

'That doesn't sound fair.'

Binni shrugged. 'You have any brothers and sisters?'

'John John and Patsy but she's only little.'

'A yudu.'

'Yudu.' Nieve repeated carefully.

Binnie hesitated, 'Only been gone one day. Got a wurlie over there.' He pointed to some distant trees. 'You can visit tomorrow 'fore I go.'

'How far you going.'

'Over Mount Stuart, then another place my dad showed me ... I can't tell you, it's secret.' He added.

'Secret?'

'Sacred.'

'Like a church?'

Binni grinned. 'Yeah, it's a big cave, lotta pictures.' He rushed on then. 'My dad he's always going Walkabout. He can tell lotta stories about the old times. Wi'tig the python. Wan the Crow. I can tell you some if you like. The ones that aren't secret.'

The boy told her the story of the Rainbow Snake and Nieve found it hard to pull herself away but she was late for lunch and her mother would be starting to worry.

She skipped and jumped her way back towards the compound feeling the thrill of having met a real aboriginal.

Auntie Betty called out to her as she was passing, 'Niv! Niv! I have some herbs for your mother, will you take them home with you?'

Nieve nodded and ran over to old house.

'You look thirsty – I just made some lemonade, want some?

The drink was cool and refreshing. Nieve swung gently back and forth on the double swing which hung in the verandah as Auntie Betty sorted the herbs, put elastic bands round the different types to separate them and then placed them in a brown paper bag.

'You had a good holiday, Niv?'

'All right.'

'No one to play with?'

'John John just spoils everything and Patsy's too young.'

Auntie Betty nodded, 'And Jimmy's got his sister Susan home from Perth. It can be a lonely life out here on a farm.'

'Auntie Betty do you know any proper aboriginals?'

'No, not really. You see them about the station, of course. Once a long time back, Bram took me out to Billangilil. They don't care much for hygiene is what I saw. An old woman gave me some potion for rubbing on mosquito bites.' Auntie Betty gave a little laugh, 'Smelled something rotten but it did the trick.'

'Do they have houses?'

'Well, just a shanty sort of place. They got a water tap. And children everywhere and dogs. I don't know if they go to school – I guess nowadays they must have some kind of schooling. What are you so interested in the abos for?'

'Oh nothing.'

As she approached her own house Nieve could see her mammie taking down the washing, flipping the sheets over trying not to stir up any dust as she went along. Patsy was running across the yard pulling a little wooden truck, yelling 'Brrmm, brmm.' The truck would fall on its side each time it was yanked over a bump but Patty did not bother to set it right and continued to pull it along until it was bumped back on its wheels.

Nieve snuck up behind and grabbed her up into her arms. Patsy screamed and kicked. Nieve dropped her hurriedly. 'Ugh, you nasty little girl.'

'Nieve! Where have you been!' Her mammie shouted from the washing line, 'And look at you, you're filthy! I don't know how you manage to get so covered in dirt.'

Nieve offered the brown paper bag, 'Aunty Betty said to give you this mammie.'

Her mammie nodded curtly. 'That's kind. Bring Patsy in will you and wash her hands and face—as well as your

244

own.'

Patsy did not want to go in and started to cry.

'Oh, come on, don't be such a baby. Nieve dragged the red-faced toddler up the steps.

'Hey what's all this!'

Nieve looked up to see her da. Patsy stopped crying almost immediately.

Her da patted the toddler on her head. 'No more of your squealing little pup.' They entered the dark shade of the house.

'Nieve would you like to go to Bodenham tomorrow? And you too little monster, heh?'

Nieve brightened, Bodenham was a long trip and a real treat, looking in all the shops and having lunch in the hamburger restaurant. Then there was the park with its slides and swings and seesaw.

'Well would you like that? We'll all go, heh?'

Her mammie came in with the laden basket.

'Maeve, Anderson wants me to pick up some new fertilizer sample in Bodenham. Thought we'd have a day out.'

'I don't know, there's a lot to do.' Mammie replied testily.

'Oh, come on, take a day off and we'll go to the Drive-In on the way back?'

'Yeah!' shouted John John his mouth full of peanut butter sandwich.

Her mammie smiled 'Really? We can do that?'

'Good-O.' her da beamed at them all.

Nieve danced around with Patsy, all thoughts of trekking out to visit Binni at his camp lost in the excited prospect of a trip to the Drive-In movies.

BEN DOWN AND THE TRIBAL LAW

Last days of my murran, sad time. He gone with spirits. After that sad time I find first love.

There a maandi I like. It time for me to have wife. She kin I can have for wife. Heart dancin' every time I look her. I see she look me too. Gwangy smile when we think no one look.

Then one day uncle come to me 'n say, 'That girl been promise to Juberji.'

Big shock. 'Juberji an old fella, he got a wife.' I say.

'This one not for you, find other one.'

My heart break, like, you know.

One day I been cuttin' kali from mulga this maandi come to me quiet like. She scared mob see us. She ask me run away. She don't want Juberji. Maandi eyes big, like pool 'n I want to dive in.

It hard for me, big pain in my heart, 'I cannot.' I say. 'It the Law.'

I angry with maandi.

Look her feel hurt. She with Juberji. Now I must go from my country.

FIRE

I

There had been no breeze for days. The house never seemed to cool down but stored up heat like the old range oven. Nieve kicked the sheet from her, sticky with sweat. She could hear the nasal twang of John John's heavy slumber. The soft open-mouthed rhythm of Patsy's breathing. A bird call in the night, a mopoke maybe?

She couldn't settle and she was thinking about Netta. How Netta ambushed her when the two schools had been joined for a nature walk over at the Darinup Lake. There was a talk from a local expert on flora and fauna and then the children had been given a worksheet and had to identify the plants on it and tick them off and on one page they had to do a drawing of their own choice. It was her fault that she dawdled, fascinated by the Christmas Bush with its profusion of orange yellow flowers, a gaudy seasonal display that seemed to light up the bushland just like a Christmas tree, and she had learnt from the expert that it wasn't a tree at all but a parasite living off the roots of other trees around it, sucking away all their moisture and nutrients. She was thinking how she must remember all this to tell her da.

Netta and her cronies surrounded her before she realised what was happening. The other girls made a screen so the grown-ups could not see the way Netta prodded her, goaded her to fight and when she wouldn't, called her chicken, knocked off her sun hat and tripped her down to the dusty ground. Her knee scraped and the new pale brown gingham frock became stained and grubby as the girls kicked the sandy dust into her face. They knew she wouldn't squeal on them; she would have to blame some unseen tree stump that had sent her sprawling into the dirt.

Her mammie's groans were ringing in her ear, 'Could you

247

not have kept the dress clean at least until the weekend!'

She knew her mother hated washing in this weather. Having to stoke up the fire under the old copper, the sweat dripping down her nose. The endless stirring of nappies and sheets. Her mammie was desperate to have Patsy toilet trained, for John John to stop wetting the bed in the night and here was Nieve adding to the load. She wanted to tell her mammie about Netta, about the jibes on the bus now that she was without the protection of the older boy who had left school. She wanted to tell her mammie about the time Netta flicked chewing gum in her hair and Maria had to get it out with a pair of craft scissors and she hoped her mother wouldn't notice the little clump missing from her hair.

She needn't have worried; her mother didn't seem to notice anything these days. Her mammie was always saying things like, 'don't you think I've enough on my plate', or 'I'm at the end of my tether', or, 'that's the last straw'. When they had first arrived in the Outback their mammie used to hop around the kitchen with them singing along with the radio, *Tie me kangaroo down Sport, tie me kangaroo down!* Now, she would sit at the table with a pained expression staring at the dirty supper dishes and ask them to keep the noise down; Patsy, over excited, waving her podgy arms, bouncing and yelling, 'Roo down! Roo down!'

No, Nieve would not tell her mammie about Netta, or her da for that matter, her da who was forever out working on the farm. She would have to deal with Netta herself.

When the Southerly came and gusted through the open window Nieve felt its soothing breathe on her brow. Her eyes began to droop at last. The kero lamp guttered on top of the chest of drawers as the Southerly gulped and sucked through the gap of the open window, rattling the fly screen. Through a blur of encroaching sleep Nieve caught the way the curtain sailed up and flapped around the lamp, heard a tinny sound and then the fluttering and the way the orange blue flame leapt suddenly and licked along the hem of the curtain.

II

John John snuffled awake; the acrid smell of smoke tickling his nostrils. Then his eyes flew open, startled by the blazing strip of curtain gusting into the room, skittering down and settling onto the rag rug beside his bed. A sheet of flames caressed the dry tinderbox walls.

'Mammie. Mammie!' A low guttural cry escaped his sleep-strangled throat.

Then he saw Nieve, the look of mesmerised horror on her face as she crouched, pressed hard against the bed head.

'Nieve! Nieve!' He shouted, angry and scared; why wasn't she moving? Why wasn't she getting help? It was as if the flickering flames held her in some spell. The room glowing with a witch's fury.

Patsy awoke, crying and pulling herself up the side of the fly-screened cot which was like a cage.

Nieve looked at him, her eyes suddenly alert with panic and fear. 'Go. Go.' she said.

The rag rug was smouldering between them, a curl of smoke rising up to meet the swirl of smoke billowing back in. He was nearest to the door and before he could even think about dragons he was out of the bed and yanked it open.

'Mammie! Mammie!' he yelled, over and over.

A kero lamp in the kitchen cast a dim glimmer of light across the table, doing little to lift the deep shadows in the corners of the room. But he did not need its light to know she was not there. Was she asleep?

He ran to the door of the main bedroom, banging as he went through. The room was curtained and dark but by faint moonlight he could see that the big bed was empty. His mind raced with confusion. Where was she? Where was his da? The door to the bathroom was ajar, the old clawfoot tub a gleam in the pitch.

John John pushed through the creaking fly screen door. 'Da! Da!' He yelled into the emptiness of the night.

Then it wasn't empty. Then he was swept up off the verandah and strong arms held him tight.

'Da!' He screamed and could feel tears pricking at his eyes.

'Where's your sisters? Where's your sisters, mate?' Tom was shaking him, urgent.

John John pointed back into the house, blubbering incoherently.

III

Patrick skidded into the yard jumping from his van before the engine cut. There were men rigging up a hose. Others with buckets of water or any other container they could find. The Southerly had dropped and a thick pall of smoke draped over the house.

'The children!' Patrick shouted.

The lad Tom jerked his head to the dunny and the huddle of small figures crouched outside. Patsy cradled in Nieve's arms wailed a plaintive, 'Daddy!' as she recognised him.

Patrick looked about frantically confused, 'And my wife?'

Tom shook his head, the bucket slopped over, full and heavy.

Patrick's breath caught short, a look of horror spreading wide his eyes.

Tom at once realised the misunderstanding. 'No, she isn't here mate, she isn't here.'

For a moment Patrick looked bewildered. Then he began to move towards the verandah with urgency. 'She must be.'

Tom caught his arm. 'No mate. I've checked mate, honest. It's too dangerous in there.'

Patrick was shaking him off but then suddenly there she was racing towards them, Bram Van der Berj close on her heels and Patrick was gulping down the sobs which were threatening to break like tidal waves through the fissure of his mouth.

REPAYMENT

Maeve felt there wasn't any price she could pay that would be too high. She had left her children unguarded. Abandoned them because Slim Dusty was singing that godforsaken *The Pub With No Beer* on the radio for the umpteenth time. Abandoned them because she was being driven mad with loneliness.

Most evenings Patrick would wolf down his supper whilst he chatted and joked with the children and then he'd be off out again to milk the cow. Then there were the nights when he would be late altogether or have to stay over on some other block. And they were both so dog tired they scarcely spoke to each other, even in the whispered intimacy of the bedroom. She had reached that last straw. It was nearly a week since she'd had a decent adult conversation. Maeve didn't quite know what possessed her but she passed out of the fly screen door, stood a moment on the verandah observing the rising moon so full and luminous you'd feel you could reach out and touch it and then she set out to visit Betty Van der Berj.

When Patrick told her that Mr Anderson wanted compensation in full for the damage to the decrepit shack that was their home and when, white faced, he told her the estimate for the repairs she absorbed the body blow and all that it implied without demur.

Thank the Lord the young lad Tom had been so near to hand, was her only thought. Taking a stroll with his dog, catching some night air and the Southerly breeze. She envisaged him now as a kind of Guardian Angel watching over them all, watching over her.

THE HEART OF THE CABBAGE

Soft words, that's what he would have, soft words to all.

All the time that he had stood before Jack Anderson, as a dawn light began to sear the night sky and the boss had brazenly insisted Patrick pay the full whack to restore the clapped-out ramshackle wreck of a house which had scarcely been fit for human habitation; Patrick bit his tongue and made with the soft words.

He could hear his cousins in Mountmellick with their store of sayings ringing in his ears, 'Soft words don't butter no parsnips,' Donal would say, 'but they won't harden the heart of the cabbage either!' Liam would finish like a double act.

Even as Patrick saw the little savings they had disappear in the last wisps of smoke from the fire, even as he saw himself indentured to Anderson for god knew how long, he spoke in soft words to the heart of the cabbage. It was a kind of penance he realised, and he would give it all up for her, because he had witnessed the look on Maeve's face in the moment that she had seen their children wide eyed and shivering despite the heat of the night.

BEN DOWN AND THE EMU DREAMING

Been real hot—country drying up. Fellas talking 'bout drought. No water 'n emus movin' west. No water same long time go, emu come this way. Boss Stiller field no good now, emu run all over. All 'long Rabbit Proof the emu broke wire. Boss Alex 'n Karrang 'n other wadjela every day been shootin' emu.

They been laying poison wheat but now they shootin' 'em. Roy, Doubleday 'n Rooter loadin' emu in ute. Most they burn but mob here in Billangilil eatin' emu steaks 'n thinkin' it Christmas. I say Maali she grab some free tucker, cook em up for her 'n Binni. She say no.

Emu my totem, like Brother, initiated man don't eat his Brother.

COCK-EYED BOB

Jack sat on the verandah rocker enjoying a cool beer. Rocking steadily back and forth he was mulling over the Presidency of the local branch of the Merino Breeders Association. Jack wasn't one for the limelight, he'd been happy to stand in the shadows behind Bill Davidson for years but Davidson had let it be known that he was going to retire, doctor's orders. Jack deliberated over the vacuum which would be left. He reckoned Ron Hammond would be jostling for the position, a voice for the smaller farmers and he might have a chance of support. Unless Jack put himself forward. Then Hammond's following would fall away.

Or Alex. He could get Alex to stand. Now there was an idea that might work. The notion grew on him rapidly. It would kill a whole flock of birds with one stone. Stop his younger brother griping the way he always did; make Alex feel like he was a somebody. That had always been half the problem with Alex, being forced to play second fiddle. And boy, could he be sour about it. There were times when Jack wished his father had split the place, left Arbroath to Alex and had done with it. Alex was as much a millstone round Jack's neck as the reverse might hold true. Then there was the business with this Duguid girl. He'd heard snatches of ribaldry amongst the roustabouts, didn't seem to have traveled much further yet, but it would.

Jack had seen Sally grow from a precocious and insolent eleven-year old into an even more precocious gum chewing fifteen. That bugger Duguid's relationship with the bottle had deepened over the years to the extent that Jack wondered why he kept the bastard on – it was for the girl of course. He should have brought her to the attention of the Welfare people a long time back. Now, Sally had left school and aside from keeping house for her father, her sole interest in life seemed to be going over to watch the telly with Alex of an evening. Was it any wonder there was speculation? A forty-two-year-old married man and a sassy teenager. Jack shook his head. God give him strength.

The Breeders Association would be something to shift Alex focus and there'd be a brotherly word about image and public standing. President of the local branch of the Merino Breeders Association might just do the trick. Alex could lord it over all at the next Ram Sales in the Spring, strut about the exhibits at the Perth Royal Show. Jack smiled to think of his younger brother puffing himself up like some bigwig fool.

All of this Jack was thinking just as a squall in the North Paddock caught his peripheral vision. Not just a squall, a real dust devil, gathering intensity and heading straight for the house. He saw that Cissy had noticed it too for she was scurrying down the side steps towards the rotary line.

'Cissy!' he called her back.

She waved a hand irritably to quiet his admonishment.

Jack could see the vortex swirling up off the paddock. So what if the line of bloomers, panty hose and whatever else out there had to be washed all over again – Maggie and Jari would be up in a couple of days and he'd see if they could do a little more about the house until he got a replacement for Dinah. The damn girl had got herself hitched with some cousin over in Wubin; all those times to her crook auntie, Jack's arse! He noted with relief that the Willy Willy was veering sideways, it would likely miss the house itself.

Instead the force of the small tornado hit the chicken sheds full on.

THE GIRL WITH GREEN EYES

Tom was standing in the patchy shade of a sugar gum.

'Looks like Bob finally got his revenge.' A portly woman declared.

'Bob?' the other puzzled.

'Cock-eyed Bob.' The first woman tried to keep a straight face, tickled by her own wit. 'You remember Bob Strick, Under Manager at Woolies, he and Cissy were sort of unofficially engaged. Then Jack Anderson comes sniffing up her skirts, because I suppose Cissy was a bit of a looker back then and with Jack's dad rich as he was, Bob is history! Poor Bob, he was cock-eyed and all; never did get over it, went under a bus a month later and that's not easy in Bodenham, not back in those days when there can't have been one bus a month!'

People were spilling out of the Church in their different shades of black, fanning themselves with the Order of Service. It was mid-February but felt as hot as any day they'd had in a long dry summer.

Tom had witnessed the *Cock-eyed Bob*, seen its destructive path across the parched North Paddock. He'd been pitching hay, it whirled up and blew around him like straw ticker-tape. He tried to calm the horses, and saw the tornado leap and bounce, twist and dive and then hurtle towards the Anderson house veering at the last across the back yard. Tom had a gut sense of disaster, he ran hell for leather across the paddock, eyes squinting shut as grit and dust rose up in his face. He clamboured through the jagged broken remains of the wooden post fence and then seen the devastation all right.

She was splayed in the dirt. Jack Anderson standing over her. He had placed an undergarment, a slip of some kind,

256

over what would have been her face if she still had a head. Already the blood splatter was drying in the hot dusty wreckage of the feather strewn yard and Tom could see a little way off a section of the rippled iron roof of the chicken shed, upended against a lemon tree in the small orchard. All Tom could think was that he was glad young Jimmy had started at his boarding school; this was not something any child should see.

They were all here now. Jenny, ashen, propped up by Toby and clutching her baby, the two younger ones, Susan and Jimmy, looking bewildered and uncertain in their smart funereal rigs.

The church was packed to the rafters, everyone from Inverness, every farmer and his wife from miles around the shire and then this coterie of women; former shop girls from Woolworths who had worked alongside their girlhood chum Cecilia Evans. Amongst the swish of fans and mewling cry of the baby there had been the occasional sniffle and even a stifled sob from Mrs Osborne when they stood for the hymn *Abide With Me.* The congregation sang full throated. Each no doubt imagining that no one could know the minute or the hour when death would come, such a random misfortune could be anyone's lot, the mighty and the good included.

Jenny was passing close by the sugar gum, her baby in her arms. In amongst the condolences Mrs Van der Berj was cooing and fussy over the infant.

'Such beautiful eyes she has.'

The baby squirmed and stretched out her chubby little arms.

'She wants me.' Toby said proprietarily and Jenny gave her up without qualm. 'Come on poppet, who is daddy's girl?' The softness in his voice surprised Tom.

Tom's eyes met Jenny, she raised a brow and then seemed to dismiss him.

'A sort of green, aren't they? Quite distinctive.' Mrs Van der Berj continued.

257

Toby laughed. 'Yes princess, we're talking about you!'

The baby gurgled happily.

Toby grinned enjoying the attention his little daughter was commanding. He held the baby up showing her off to the gaggle of women who were honing in on the group and in that moment, Tom saw the green eyes for himself and was startled to recognise them immediately. The green of the eyes, the shape of the head. A flash of memory. His mother bending over him, eyes twinkling.

'Tom.' Alex Anderson was at his shoulder.

'Yes sir?'

'Better start getting cars organised to ferry this lot to the cemetery.'

EVERYTHING IS GREEN

The rain came in the night through thundering skies. Sheets of it.

John John came running into the Van der Berj kitchen the next morning. 'It's green.' He shouted. 'Everything is green!'

And it was true.

Overnight the red straw coloured landscape had turned green and the long hot summer was finally over. The repairs were nearly complete and they would be moving out of the Van der Berj house and back into the old home, only it would have been made new and fresh and his mother would be happy again.

SANDGROPERS

Patrick was ploughing up the Silver Vale Block at the far north eastern end of the Anderson spread; it was all to be left fallow over the autumn. The soil was sandier up at this end of the Shire and an infestation of sandgropers had taken hold, shredding the roots and turning the young wheat yellow until it wilted and died leaving bare thin patches of crop. Fallowing for several weeks would help to reduce the numbers of these underground tunnelers; but to ensure less damage to the next crop they were going to plant oats instead of wheat.

He examined the strange little insects who spent nearly all their life underground, marveled at the short strong almost flat legs to the side of the head designed for burrowing, marveled at the amount of damage which they could do. At every turn Patrick was learning something new; the problems of soil, pests and drought all so different to the conditions back in Ireland. He was a keen student and Anderson had been more forthcoming than usual, the death of his wife seemed to have knocked the gruff edge off him.

Patrick remembered the summers in Mountmellick with Liam and Donal where the learning had been like a game with his mother's cousins always joking. On his first visit in the August of 1939, the summer he was twelve years old, Liam said, 'Will you give me a hand there feeding the pigs Paddy?' And he carried one of the buckets of peelings and swill and gawked at the size of the sow with her small pinpricks of eyes which seemed to look quite through him.

'You've not had a good year of it I gather?' Liam probed.

Patrick froze then. Did Liam know what had happened? Did they all know? Were they watching him to see what other guises the devil might assume?

260

'Ye ran away from the Brothers?'

Patrick's heart was pounding.

'Before Christmas I hear tell you jumped over the wall and skidaddled all the way home to Dublin?'

Patrick nodded slowly, 'Yes, Mr Fogarty.'

'Jaze will ye less of the Misters round here, call me Liam will ye.'

Liam was older than his own father, all his five sons were grown, it seemed unthinkable for a twelve-year old boy to be so familiar. But Liam and Donal were always full of surprises. On Sunday he discovered they never went to mass.

'We favour our mother.' Donal explained. 'A Quaker, one of the original families that founded the town – but a shortage of men had her marry Daniel Fogarty – and maybe it was a bit of love too since they eloped and she still in her school uniform!'

They would all come home at lunchtime to great steaming plates of champ, potatoes mashed with chopped scallions and lathered in butter, and there'd be hunks of boiled bacon and the green leaves of cabbages cut fresh from the garden. Liam's wife Denise seemed always to be in the kitchen at the stove or hoisting the washing on the overhanging rails near the range and there was always laughter and a pot of tea on the go and the smell of warm soda bread and if it wasn't the tidiest house, it was far too busy and easy going for that, it was the warmest and safest place that Patrick ever knew.

All through The Emergency of the war years he spent his summers there and it suited everyone. It was there he learnt his love of the land, the sweet loamy smell of the earth. It was there he felt a joy in the hard work, using his hands, no time to dwell or think.

Anderson swung by in his ute, pleased to see the speed of progress. 'Come by the house when you've finished Paddy, tell me what you think about this new fertilizer we're trying out. Have a beer.'

Patrick knew that the older man was finding it difficult to

cope, though he would never admit it. His daughter Jenny stayed on for a while to help sort through her mother's things and Patrick had seen her a number of times when she was out riding looking red eyed and wan. The middle girl, Susan, had gone back to her boarding school within the week but young Jimmy moped and claimed illness. Nieve went up to the big house one day to play cards and keep him company and Jimmy had started to cry, then begged her not to tell; he said that he didn't want to go back to school because he was afraid of what the other boys might say if he was to weep there.

Patrick could understand those fears, the long nights he had tried to stifle his own tears. Soft eejit, Nancy Boy and the rest; nicknames could be cruel, he knew that well enough from his own schooldays.

Sandgropers was the nickname for Western Australians. Having seen the insects and the way they lived underground Patrick couldn't quite see the connection with the tough outdoor people of the State.

GIANT OF THE BUSH

Nieve finished reading her birthday book, *Giant of the Bush*. It was about a boy and his horse and his adventures. When she closed the last page, she knew what she wanted more than anything else in the world. She wanted to learn to ride. Why had she never thought of it before? To be a cowgirl she would need to be able to ride a horse.

After a month in mourning Jimmy had gone back to his boarding school and would not return until the Easter break. She could not ask him to teach her or to let her ride Gulliver. Could she ask Mr Anderson? He always looked so stern, that she was afraid to go anywhere near him. She thought about Mrs Anderson for a moment with morbid fascination. Maria said that Mrs Anderson had her head chopped off, the sort of thing that usually only happened to kings and queens. Nieve regarded Jimmy with a kind of awe after she learnt this snippet of information.

After supper Nieve took to running over to the North Paddock where she would find Tom the Pom pitching hay to the horses or rubbing them down. Once he had just returned on Cobber with Spike at his heels and she observed carefully whilst he unsaddled the big horse.

On the next visit she ventured to ask him what all the parts of the saddle were, the girth and the stirrups, watched him remove the bit from Cobber's slobbering mouth. Tom explained that the saddle they used was called an Australian stock saddle with a good deep seat to make it more secure and the pads at the knees were called Poleys and it was designed for long days on the range. The blanket underneath the saddle he called a numnah.

'Numnah', she rolled the word around her tongue as she fed the big horse a carrot and Tom brushed the sweat from his rusty red coat.

'Gonna be a jilleroo then, are you Niv?'

'I'm going to be a cowgirl.'

'Not much call for that round here – it's all sheep, you'd have to go up to the Kimberley for the cattle.'

Nieve frowned and adjusted her Annie Oakley hat, would sheep count the same she wondered.

'Tell you what, you come along first thing Saturday morning, we'll put you on Gulliver and trot you round on a lead. He's getting fat since Jimmy took up with his go-kart and now gone back to Perth, old bugger needs more exercise. Truth is, Jimmy's grown out of him; boss'll be looking to sell, could do with getting him fit for the yards.'

Nieve nearly fell off the fence with the rush of joy.

Saturday saw her shoveling her breakfast cereal into her mouth in double quick time. John John was glowering at her over the rim of his bowl. When she insisted that he could not come to the paddock he said she would fall off the pony and land on her big fat bottom, ha ha ha. Her da made him apologise for being mean. This was Nieve's riding lesson and John John would no doubt get his turn one day.

'It's very kind of young Tom, isn't it?' Her mammie said. 'Remember you're to thank him properly.'

Her mammie cleaned the Annie Oakley fringed waistcoat especially for the occasion. Then they deliberated over the most suitable footwear and decided the leather buckled sandals might afford the best grip in the stirrup.

'Maybe, if you get on alright with the riding, we could get you a proper pair of riding boots.'

Nieve felt absolutely certain that she would get on alright with the riding.

Nieve had always thought that Gulliver was small, and compared to the other ponies and horses he was, but when you were sitting up in the saddle and bouncing up and down,

264

your legs splayed around his fat girth, he didn't feel small at all. And the ground seemed quite a long way to fall. She was glad of the riding helmet, its covering bleached to an indeterminate colour. Tom had ferreted it out for her and she reluctantly relinquished her black cowgirl hat. He insisted and she was glad of it now.

She clutched the reins and the pommel too. Tom said it was okay to hold on to this when you were first learning if it made you feel safer, even hang on to the mane.

'Only saddle we got for Gulliver's this English one; Jimmy was keen on show jumping for a while but you know what he's like, never sticks at anything long. You sit tight in the saddle you'll be alright.'

Nieve wanted to believe him. Gulliver snorted and jerked and flicked his head. Flicked his tail. His nostrils flared and Nieve caught a wild stare in his eyes.

'You need to feel the rhythm of his movement Niv.'

It all sounded so simple but the reality seemed far from simple as the pony twitched and jerked under her. As he seemed to dance to the right and pull on the lead rope her left foot slipped out of the stirrup and she was lopsidedly thrown to one side of the saddle, she could feel herself keeling over and grabbed around the pony's neck.

'Whoa!' Tom reined in the pony and walked her to a stop.

'You alrightie?' He asked, helping her foot back into the stirrup.

Nieve nodded despite the wobbly feeling in her legs.

'Had enough?'

Nieve hesitated, she didn't want him to think her afraid.

'One last walk around and that'll be enough for today I reckon.' Tom assured.

She allowed herself to relax a little as she swayed back and forth in time with the steady stride.

'You done well for your first time, Niv; hasn't she Gulliver, old boy?' He patted and calmed the pony and then gently eased Nieve to the ground.

'Thanks Tom.'

'You give me a hand rubbing him down and he'll get used

265

to you. Won't be so flighty next time.'

There very nearly wasn't a next time. When she arrived at the paddock the following Saturday there was no sign of Tom. Susan Anderson was saddling up another of the ponies, Popcorn. Nieve was puzzled to see her, it was another two weeks before the Easter break, what was Susan doing home at Inverness? Nieve shuffled by the fence uncertain whether or not to stay and wait for Tom.

Susan finished saddling her pony, patting his flank. Then she put her thumb and forefinger in her mouth and gave two loud sharp whistles. She glanced over her shoulder to Nieve, 'Tom can't make it, gone with dad, buying a ram.'

Nieve couldn't disguise her disappointment.

'Said I'd take you out with me on a lead.'

Moments later Gulliver trotted up from the far end of the paddock in response to the call.

'You get the bit in, alrightie? I'll saddle him up. Not got any boots? Bound to be an old pair of mine up at the house, maybe a bit big but nicely worn in. We'll pick 'em up when we get back for next time.'

Nieve nodded her thanks. And felt a kind of relief too. She had heard her mammie worrying about the cost of the shopping again.

Gulliver snorted and his lips curled back over his disturbingly large yellow teeth. She hesitated with the bit, afraid he would bite.

Susan gave him a sharp rap. 'Grrr, Gulliver!' She tightened the girth. 'Just shove it in, he's all bark and no bite!'

Nieve wasn't so sure but she couldn't look a sissy, not with Susan. She pursed her lips tight and somehow managed to catch the metal bar into Gulliver's jerking mouth.

Susan picked up the rest of the reins. 'You'll learn.'

Nieve nodded her determination.

'Here, Tom said you'd need this too.' Susan proffered the riding helmet, her tone implying that this was for babies. 'Better put it on.'

Once they were up on the saddle, Susan led Gulliver through the gate on the safety lead and latched it after them. 'Gulliver's getting fat, lucky you got long legs for your age, what are you? Ten?'

'Nine.'

'Righto. Thought we could go down to the waterhole.'

This seemed a long way off to Nieve but perhaps not so far on a pony.

They sauntered through the compound at a leisurely walking pace. Susan sitting back languidly in her saddle one arm loose at her side dangling the lead. Uncle Bram saluted as they passed. Nieve spotted her mammie stoking the fire for the copper and wished that she would look up. She did and waved across the yard, a big smile creasing her face. Nieve bit her lip, clutched the reins awkwardly into one hand and dared to raise the other and return the salute, beaming with pride.

It was surprising how quickly they left the farm buildings behind as Susan increased the walking pace on the dusty track. A few fluffy clouds rolled overhead and there was a pleasant breeze ruffling the wisps of hair which escaped the helmet. Nieve allowed herself to look from side to side. The red rust soil turned over and ploughed into furrows on her right and pasture to her left, a Varcoe watermill feeding the trough for the cows, she spotted their own cow Minnie and was tempted to try another wave but this seemed foolish.

'Ready for a trot?'

Nieve swallowed hard and nodded, surreptitiously clutching at the pommel.

'Hup.' Popcorn rose into a gentle trot and Gulliver pulled before shuffling and jerking into the rhythm; Nieve bouncing unevenly on top.

'Lean into it!' Susan ordered sharply. 'And stand up in your stirrups. That's it, now 'up', 'down', 'up' ... feel the horse.'

With grave concentration Nieve found the rhythm of movement, up and down, up and down, unfamiliar muscles straining to hold her position on the pony's back and not to hurtle to one side.

'Good, a little faster now, up-down, up-down!'

Nieve gulped, her hands clammy with sweat, helmet slipping forward.

'Grip tight with your knees.'

Easier said than done.

'Alrightie?'

Nieve gave a whimper in reply, all her energies focused on clutching onto Gulliver.

'Now stay up into the canter.'

'Canter?' Before Nieve had time to consider what this might entail Susan gave a little kick to Popcorn and an urging sound to Gulliver and the ponies seemed to lift from the ground and the posts of the fencing on the pasture side of the track began to rattle passed her vision. Her heart was racing uncontrollably, breath heaving in her chest, but it was like flying, flying like the wind!

She caught sight of Susan grinning at her. She wanted to smile back, let her know how amazing it felt but scary too and everything was clutched into the urgency of clinging on as the ground sped out from under her.

'Whush, whush ...' Susan drew the ponies back into a trot.

Nieve slammed back onto the saddle.

'Whush, whush ...' slowing to a walk.

Nieve could feel herself shaking and shivering, her bottom throbbing with the force of her landing, and a sense of relief too, she had felt her sandals begin to slip in the stirrups.

'Have you out on the range in no time, Niv.'

They walked the ponies in companionable silence until the waterhole came into view, glistening amongst the salmon gum.

The ponies were tied up in the shade. Susan opened a saddle bag and brought out a packet of biscuits and a flask of orange squash.

'Put it in the water for a bit, cool down.' She kicked off her boots. 'That's where I'm headed too, coming?'

Nieve was standing on the edge of the small wooden jetty jutting out into the waterhole, sure she had caught the flash of a fish in the still dark waters. Before she knew it, Susan was rushing past without any clothes on and yelling a high-pitched yodel as she bombed into the water. Nieve flinched to dodge the spray.

Susan emerged shaking the water from her dirty blonde hair. 'Bonsa!' Then she began to flick water up at the jetty. 'Come on slow coach!'

Nieve smiled uncertainly and wished that she had togs with her. The water, although murky, looked tempting and cool. Susan struck out for the other side and Nieve took the opportunity to divest herself of her clothes, hesitating only at her knickers and then whipping them off to jump in, holding tight her nose. The cold shock brought her gasping to the surface. 'It's freezing!'

'Don't be a sook!' Susan shouted from the far bank and began to return with a quick fluid crawl.

Nieve paddled furiously to warm her limbs until she floated into a smooth breast stroke and felt the soft brown silkiness of the water enclose her.

Susan was up on the jetty and positioning herself for a dive. Nieve couldn't help noticing the soft bulging pads of her burgeoning breasts and pert nipples and was reminded again that one day her body would change in this way.

Crouching low and taking a deep breath Susan sprang upwards and sailed out over the water to pierce the surface with the sharpness of a blade. Moments passed, Nieve turned her head about this way and that. Where was Susan? Had she become caught on something in the depths? Perhaps hit her head on something and was even now drowning beneath her. Nieve thrashed about, uncertain which way to turn. She'd never been very good at swimming underwater but she'd have to try. Puffing her cheeks up with air she stuck her head underneath and peered below, wide eyed, but all she could see in the gloom was the blur of drifting plant life. She surfaced, hoping desperately that Susan would be there, yelling to her from the other side. But she wasn't.

'Susan. Susan?' Panic escalated within her, catching at her breath, 'Susan.' she wailed. Something had hold of her ankle, she was being catapulted up out of the water. Whush!

She had just enough time to speculate whether crocodiles or other monsters might lurk in the depths of the waterhole when a great roar assailed her ears and she crashed back into the water.

'How long was I under?' Susan panted to regain her breath. 'I think that was a record.'

Nieve had swallowed a lungful of water and was lashing out for the bank, coughing and spluttering, relieved and annoyed all at once.

They were sitting on the edge of the jetty sharing the biscuits and orange squash. Nieve had decided to forgive Susan for giving her the fright of her life but wary now in case the older girl would think it funny to push her off the jetty, especially now she had her vest and knickers back on.

Susan was telling her about the school in Peppermint Grove, the silly uniform and the snobby girls. Even her cousins had become stuck up, she said. Susan would much rather be back at home at the school in Darinup.

'I've been suspended.' Susan grinned and it was clear that this punishment didn't bother her at all. 'Caught me having a smoke-oh round the back of the gym building.'

'Oh. What did your da say?' Nieve was shocked.

'Reckon he's too busy to notice.'

Susan shuffled over to the saddle bag and delved into the bottom to pull out a packet of ciggies. She lit one up.

'Want one?'

Nieve shook her head vehemently, trying at the same time not to look scandalised. 'How d'you get 'em?'

'Boyfriend. Well, I let him think he's my boyfriend 'cause he sneaks me what I want over the fence. Bruce's fifteen. Got caught speaking to him once, got a lump of trouble.' Susan took a deep drag and then began to blow out smoke rings.

Nieve's eyes widened. She wished that Susan did go to the school in Darinup and then Netta would never dare to pull her hair again.

'Time to pack up little squirt.'

270

They were back in the saddle and ambling through the gums, the midday sun high and hot overhead. Susan was telling her about Bruce and how he was going to join his dad out on the boats fishing for prawns.

They were caught by surprise when the snake hissed up in front of them disturbed by the fall of Popcorn's hoof. The pony reared back awkwardly and Susan, without her boots in the stirrups, jerked off his back and crashed to the ground, the lead rope slipping from her grasp. Gulliver pranced to one side as Popcorn bolted clear. Nieve was clutching to the mane as she desperately urged Gulliver to calm. With a toss of his head Gulliver settled.

The snake slithered back into the brush and disappeared.

Susan wasn't moving. And she wasn't making any sound either, just lying in a funny position on the ground. What should Nieve do? Go and get help? First, she needed to know if Susan was still breathing, she looked very still. A word flashed into Nieve's mind, this felt 'omm-inn-ooous'.

Nieve slipped out of the saddle and dropped to the ground. Keeping hold of Gulliver's reins, she looped them around a sapling gum.

There was still no movement from Susan. Nieve crouched and gently lifted the hair from Susan's face. She could see that there was a cut on her forehead, a small seep of blood.

'Susan?'

There was no response. Nieve put her hand in front of Susan's mouth. She thought she could feel her soft breath but wasn't sure. If you had a mirror you could tell. Then she remembered that doctors and nurses looked for a pulse; how often had she done that with Carmel Marie in the old gypsy caravan, but that was just a game. Nieve took Susan's wrist between her fingers. with a rising panic. Was it her own heart beat she could feel? It seemed to be thumping and racing so loudly she felt like telling her heart to shut up.

Tears were pricking at her lashes. If Susan was dead would it be her fault? Everyone was dying. Mrs Anderson and now

Susan. Nieve tried to concentrate on the wrist. Why was it so hard! She moved her thumb around and pressed a little harder. There? Was that a beat? Yes? Maybe? The tears began to spill over her cheeks.

'Susan ...' It was no use. She was no use. She would have to get help, that was the only thing to do.

Nieve un-looped the reins. Gulliver eyed her implacably as she tried to throw them back over his head.

'Shush, okay boy, okay Gulliver.'

Nieve had seen Tom and Susan just swing up into the saddle in one motion but she had always been helped. You put one foot in the stirrup and then swung. She held the saddle with one hand and tried to lift her foot to the height of the stirrup. Gulliver stirred restlessly. She was hopping on tip toe and straining every fibre. At last her foot caught into the metal frame of the stirrup but she was still hopping madly on the other foot. Teeth gritted she pushed off the ground and clutched both hands to the edges of the saddle, clawing and grappling her way over until she was looking at the ground on the other side of Gulliver's girth. Carefully she swiveled about and slid her loose leg over the rear. She was up! She felt about with her right foot for the other stirrup, at the same time realising that the left one was twisted. It would have to do.

Nieve clutched the reins tight. At least Gulliver was facing in the right direction. 'Giddyup Gulliver.' The pony pawed the ground and remained stationary. Nieve flapped the reins. 'G'wan!' She shouted to no avail.

She tried to kick. Gulliver was so fat it felt like kicking the air. Gulliver lowered his head pulling her forward with him until she felt like she might slide down over his head.

'Gulliver!' Nieve yanked the reins as hard as she could. Tears and snot were streaming down her face. 'Gulliver, please, please, we have to get help. We have to save Susan.'

As if this was all that he had been waiting for Gulliver moved forward.

They found Popcorn at the edge of the trees. He nudged up alongside them.

Nieve urged Gulliver to move faster. 'Hup, hup!' she enjoined. Popcorn began to quicken and in response Gulliver at last began to lift his legs.

'Up, down, up down.' Nieve felt for the rhythm and then suddenly the two ponies were lifting off the ground into a canter and she nearly slipped back but jerked herself forward in time and was gripping the mane, her right foot slipping in the stirrup. Faster they went, her foot finally sliding out of the stirrup grip Nieve flung herself forward and thrust her arms about Gulliver's neck, no longer able to see where they were headed. The dust swept up into her eyes from the galloping hooves until all she could do was close them tight shut and pray. 'Please, please, please ...'

They stampeded into the compound and it was the Dutch pilot who caught hold of Gulliver and brought him to a stop as they circled the yard. She was slipping over the side of the saddle, her left foot still twisted in the stirrup and he was catching her and she was shouting, 'Susan! Susan!'

The Dutch pilot flew Susan down to Bodenham, an ambulance was waiting. She was going to be all right, a few bruised muscles, concussion and a broken collar bone. Mr Anderson was going to drive down to the hospital and before that he wanted to thank Nieve for getting help as quick as she did.

'Hear you came galloping into the yard, only your second time out. Reckon we've the makings of a Jilleroo, heh.' And he chucked her under the chin in his awkward way.

'Well, aren't you the little hero!' her da grinned.

Susan came home a couple of days later with her neck in a brace. It would be awhile before she would be back in the saddle and in a way Nieve was glad about that.

A TIPPERARY TAN

It was Anzac Day. Begrudgingly Mr Anderson gave all the old diggers the day off. They were undermanned as a consequence. And so, it was only Patrick who could be spared to take the ute into Darinup and load up the barley and wheat seed waiting for collection at the railway station. By himself it took all morning hoisting the heavy bags onto his back and flipping them onto the tail of the ute, every three or four bags he'd clambour up, drag them to the front and lay them out neatly one on top of the other. He'd been glad of the chill westerly which was blowing as he worked up a sweat but his back was killing him. Every so often he'd get a painful surge down his lower spine and into his legs. When last Maeve had dragged him along to the doctor, the man had warned he might develop sciatica. But what could he do? The job had to be done.

By two he was finished. Across the tracks he could see The Swan Hotel. He would drop in for a pot of beer and there might be a pie to be had. The thought of a long cool drink brought the moisture back into his dry, parched throat and he licked his lips.

They were all in there. All the diggers in their slouched hats and medals pinned to the old khaki. The old battlers, was that what they were called? Or maybe it was the pioneers he was thinking of, there was a name for everyone out here. There'd been a bit of a march in the morning, Patrick gathered as he moved through the swell of bodies, a few words spoken, wreaths laid and flags raised with a band from the local secondary school. All the formalities wrapped up the diggers then repaired to The Swan Hotel.

The usual taciturn silence of the bar was replaced with raucous laughter and in one corner a couple of old mates were singing the chorus of some lewd wartime ballad. Patrick signalled to the landlord who was taking his time and not to be rushed even by the prospect of all this custom.

'Bloody poms!!'

'Yeah, always giving us the shit jobs!'

'Remember Gallipoli!' one old timer was wagging his finger.

'What about Malaysia?'

'You want to have been in Burma mate!'

'Bloody Japs!'

'Shoulda nuked the lot of 'em.'

Patrick signalled again to the landlord who seemed to have chosen to ignore him.

'Yeah, Bloody Poms, left us to rot in those stinking camps.'

'Listen mate it's taken me twenty years to get this paunch back!'

'Starved we were. Walking bloody skin and bone, fellas dropping like flies and worse, I could tell ya.'

'Yeah, Ken mate, bloody awful. Come on, let's raise another glass for all the old diggers!' The man lurched up against Patrick and elbowed onto the counter. 'Here Stan, set 'em up again.'

Stan lumbered over. 'How many's that Fred?'

''Scuse me sir.' Patrick jerked his chin towards the landlord, 'Any chance of some service here?'

'You want me to stop serving these old soldiers, mate?' The barman eyed him and the question hung in the air.

'I'm just saying ... I've been here awhile.'

A hand grabbed his shoulder. 'Is that Paddy?' Ken Duguid, his face as florid as any *Tipperary tan* Patrick had ever seen, swung into him. 'If it isn't little Lord Haw Haw himself!'

'You been in the wars then mate!' Alex Anderson chortled when he caught sight of the livid colouring around Patrick's eye.

Alex certainly hadn't, Patrick thought bitterly. From what he'd heard old Jack Anderson had bought his youngest out of that war. Alex Anderson had been *essential* for work on the land alongside his older brother.

'Didn't venture into The Swan on Anzac Day did ya, mate?' Alex continued grinning. 'No one warn you? Those old diggers are only looking for a blue on Anzac Day, they'd fight their own grandmothers with a keg of Tooheys in them given half a chance—and I'm tellin' ya round here it's the grannies would come out on top mate!'

'Yes, well, some wars are never over, are they?' Patrick hoisted the sack of seed onto his back and headed for the barn and he thought about Ken Duguid and the years the man had spent in a Japanese POW camp and reckoned that was war enough to last a lifetime.

THE WILD WEST

There was a rodeo visiting the neighbouring shire. Tom had read in the advertisement that along with the bucking broncos, the lasso displays and so on, that The Whipcracker would be giving an exhibition and Tom was determined to go and see him. He had made a promise to take Boswell along with him. Half way there Tom was beginning to wish he hadn't. Boswell was rattling on like a two-bob watch. All he could talk about was how young Sally Duguid had got herself up the duff.

'What a bloody shower, eh!' Boswell exclaimed with leery eyed relish.

Tom slowed down behind a petrol tanker.

'You shoulda seen old Ken! Mad as a cut snake! Mad as an effing rattle snake! If Sally hadn't half bled to death in that hospital in Bodenham, he'd have bloody killed her hisself!' Bert Boswell slapped his thigh with the delight this notion obviously brought. 'Expecting twins! Imagine that! Bloody twins!' Bert shook his head at the wonder of it. 'One was a gonner but they reckon they've saved the other little tike.'

Tom edged out to see if he could pass the tanker.

'Much thanks she'll be giving them doctors and nurses for that!'

All Tom could see was a road works team up ahead, he dropped back in, sniffed the giddying smell of tar in the air. They came to a halt. The engine of the old jalopy cut out; it had been doing that lately. Tom thought he might ask Pieter to take a look at it next time he was over in Inverness.

'She's in a shit load of trouble mate.' Boswell shifted a booted foot up against the dashboard. 'Police turned up and all asking questions. She's not sixteen 'til next week for one. Then Doctor reckoned it's a botched abortion see. Sally's

277

swearing blind it's just a miscarriage. But no one's buying that. Police want to know who dun it. Put the squeeze on the Dutch woman. She was with Sally down in Bodenham when it happened. Supposed to be on a shopping trip—we all know what they were shopping for.' Boswell smirked. 'I'll bet she was really wetting herself, that stuck up old crow when Sgt. Brooks comes knocking at her door.'

Tom frowned, 'Mrs De Vries? She'd never be involved in anything like abortion.'

'You wanna bet? Twenty says you're wrong.'

'Not with you Boswell.' Tom conceded.

'At one point, I thought old Ken was coming for me. Wednesday avo just brought Sally back from the hospital, he hit the bottle straight off and by the time I've come in from the paddocks the old bastard's hammered. Comes over to the bunk house, starts kicking and bashing down the door, ranting and raving and calling me out for a stoush. I keep telling him. *Ken, you've got the wrong bloke! It's not my head you want to be breaking mate!*'

The road was up. They bumped down onto the rough red dirt and immediately the dust raked up by the tanker in front was misting the windscreen. They rolled up their windows. They'd be lucky to get to the rodeo by midday.

'Won't tell him, you see. Sally, won't tell him who the bloke is who knocked her up.' Boswell regarded Tom slyly. 'Reckon we might all take a guess at that, eh Pom?'

'You might.'

'Oh, I know all right. Too right, I know mate.'

They bumped back up onto the sealed road crawling behind the tanker on the incline.

'He'll deny it. All the way down the line. No bloke's going to admit to knocking up a fifteen-year old. And Sally's not stupid.'

'Got herself pregnant.'

'We can all make mistakes.'

'Yeah, we can all do that.'

'She's a goer that Sally.'

'I thought you liked her?'

278

Boswell shifted awkwardly in his seat. 'I reckon she's an all right Sheila.'

Tom always figured Boswell had an eye for young Sally, there was a rough untamed attractiveness to her.

'Boswell admitted, 'She needs a shoulder to cry on I reckon a bloke can give a hand, mate.'

Tom smiled, Sally had never given Bert Boswell passing consideration, now he just might have a chance to be her knight in shining armour.

An hour later they were pulling in under a headlining banner.

AUSTRALIA'S VERY OWN WILD WEST SHOW!

A BIT OF THE BLACK

In August, six months after Cissy's funeral, Jack returned to Inverness from a winter break with the new Mrs Anderson in tow. They had married without anyone knowing anything about it, in a Registry Office in Perth. After which they had taken a short honeymoon down the coast in Mandurah. Jack said they were both too old for any kind of fuss, besides which it wasn't the first time around for either of them.

The children took it in different ways. Jenny was refusing to speak to her father, and didn't want to meet her new stepmother, she warned Jack that he might never see his granddaughter Emma Cecilia ever again. Jack assured Maddy that Jenny would come around eventually, she was never going to accept any attempt to replace her mother easily. Susan on the other hand was blithe; reckoned her dad wouldn't be putting up with Maggie's cooking for much longer anyway. Jimmy said nothing.

The citizens of Darinup were intrigued to find that Jack and Maddy had met at the funeral. Maddy Prior nee Blomard had been one of the former shop girls from Woolworths. Shortly after her arrival at Inverness Maddy Anderson, as she now was, had been browsing the limited stock at Jessups Groceries when she overheard two locals.

'Woolworths, that's right.'

'No. What does he think—you can just pick them off the shelves, Pick and Mix?!'

The other woman tittered, 'Oh well, I've had the blonde hair and ruddy face I think I'll try the brunette with the tan next!'

Jack laughed along with Maddy when she relayed the joke and mimicked the look of horror on the women's faces when she stepped into the aisle and the women realised their faux pas.

It amused Jack, the extent to which his remarriage assumed a scandalous air amongst the good women of the shire. He was not so amused however when he overheard Ron Hammond muttering in a huddle of small farmers after the quarterly meeting of The Merino Breeders Association.

'I hear she's tarred with *a bit of the black*, imagine Jack Anderson marrying an abo!'

Jack faltered at the threshold to the bar. Osborne coming along behind him slapped his shoulder. 'Buy you a drink Jack?'

'My shout Phil.' Jack stepped through into the throng of sheep farmers and raised his voice. 'In fact, drinks are on me fellas.' He stared steely eyed at Hammond. 'I'd like you all to join me in a toast to our new President of the local branch.' He nodded towards his brother, already ensconced at the bar. 'My brother, Alex Anderson.'

'I'll second that!' Somebody shouted enthusiastically and was joined by a round of cheering.

Hammond pursed his lips sourly.

For days Jack couldn't get the phrase *a bit of the black* out of his mind. An ancestor of hers was French, the surname originally De Blomard, Maddy'd boasted. Was there any more to the olive skin, the full lips and the dark eyes than that? Hammond was just spreading malicious rumours, sour grapes because he'd lost out on the local Presidency of the MBA. Still, it rankled with Jack and he wished it didn't. Made him think about things to which he hadn't ever given much thought. What if she did have a bit of the black? What if her great great grandmother had been the native girl of some whaler or convict under license? Maddy's father had moved down from Broome where the family were in the pearling business, plenty of abos up there, plenty of all sorts up in Broome.

He'd recently heard of a girl from the missions, girl who was practically white, being married off to a station owner's son on a remote cattle station up north. Rules stopping whites and abos getting married were bound to get a bit fudged now and then when the blood line got diluted. Where did the line get drawn? That was the muddle. He'd often thought that the co-habitation laws should have been done away with years ago, when he'd bothered to think about it at all.

Jack was sitting alongside Maddy on the verandah enjoying a sundowner, a chill in the air but a golden light and the fresh scent of spring on the breeze. Peaceful. The kind of evening when you could feel it was good to be alive. He glanced across, could he see the abo in her? She was a handsome woman and no mistake. Passionate too. He'd imagined that he'd said goodbye to all that a long time back. He and Cissy had slipped into a regular drill and even that less frequently once Jimmy was born. Job done. No more need for the procreative act her expression seemed to say. But Maddy liked sex, initiated it. The pleasure she gave him took his breath away. Sex never had been to do with children for Maddy. She told Jack straight away. No children. At forty-five it wasn't beyond the bounds of possibility, but she was clear on that point; it had been the one agreement in her rocky first marriage as well.

If there were aborigine in the ancestry would it change how he felt about her? It mattered to some people; Jack knew that. His father would have had something to say. All those bastions of the White Australia Policy. Well, that was in shreds. Australia learnt a big lesson during the War. She stood alone. And that lingering fear of how close they had come to a full-on invasion put the wind up all the Anglo-Saxon, Scots-Irish Big Wigs in the Federal Government, if they were going to defend a country the size of Australia, they needed a population to do it. All very well taking in every orphaned bastard from London to Glasgow, the Tom Bradshaws and Bert Boswells, any fool could see that wasn't going to be enough, not even your Ten Pound Poms were going to make the difference. For better or worse Australia needed to open its doors, Italians, Greeks, Maltese, stretching ever wider, the olive-skinned Mediterranean extending to the Lebanese, the Turks and on it went, he'd seen a turbaned Sikh walking down the street last time he was in Perth.

They were a mongrel country. Nothing would stop the interbreeding. Maybe they were the better for it. Didn't he see it on the farm? Your thoroughbred was the one always notching up the vet's bills. Australia was a tough land; *a bit of the black* might not be a bad thing. It was a country that needed tough men and women; it was a country that needed mongrels. When he looked across at Maddy and caught her warm brown eyes smiling back at him, none of it seemed to matter.

'There's a light supper whenever you're ready Jack. Thought we could take an early night.' She added with sleepy-eyed suggestion.

Hammond could go to hell with his insinuations. He, Jack Anderson, was the leading farmer of this shire and they would all show his wife respect or pay for it. Still, if he was honest, if he was really honest, he was thankful that there were no such doubts about young Jimmy's racial heritage.

It had been a long day herding sheep from one block to another. The sun already set by the time he was back in the yard and rubbing Cobber down.

'Tom.' It was Boss Anderson.

'Evening Boss.'

'Any problems.' The Boss patted Spike on the head.

Tom shrugged. 'A ewe looking a bit lame, just a shard in her hoof, nothing serious.'

'Good. Those bloody fencers have the Dingo netting up along the Eastern border?'

'All done boss. Done a good job too.'

'Bloke telephoned. From Fairbridge. On his rounds. Reckons it'll be your last. Better stay around the homestead tomorrow. Plenty of work cleaning out the sheds.'

'Righto.'

'How long you been here now, son?'

'Five years Mr Anderson.'

The Boss nodded. 'Five years, you done good. Good with the horses, good with sheep.'

'Learnt a lot from Stubby.'

'Anyway, I'll be telling this Fairbridge bloke I've no complaints.' The Boss scratched his head under his hat.

'Thanks, Mr Anderson.'

'Fact is there's a future here for you, Tom. Good hand like you could be a station manager one day.'

Tom paused, the brush resting on Cobber's flank. 'Thanks, Mr Anderson.'

The Boss nodded and walked away across the yard. Tom watched him go. Cobber stamped and nudged him. 'Whoah boy.' He resumed the rub down.

Tom chewed over Boss Anderson's parting remarks.

Increasingly he'd been feeling restless. Maybe it was Mrs Glendon who had him on edge. Knowing she wasn't the type of woman who would be staying long at a place like Inverness. Wondering how he could ever get to know a woman like that. Or maybe it was seeing the baby. The sight of the child with his own mother's eyes had eaten into him. He was a father. That was something you couldn't get your head around overnight. That and knowing she'd never be allowed to know he was her father. Emma Cecilia. It had a nice ring to it. He hoped she'd have a good life. All that money. Didn't always bring happiness of course, but she'd have choices, that was something.

He'd be twenty-one in December. Some accounted that the point you became a man. Time to start thinking about where he was headed. Fairbridge had organised the job for him at Inverness and the years had gone by not giving much thought to anything beyond each day's work. Was this what he wanted? Years as a jackaroo and then maybe one day promoted to station manager to Mr Anderson, or more likely, young Jimmy. Was this the sum of his ambitions?

'I remember you now, Haig Seven.' Mr Cardwell from Fairbridge met with Tom outside the main house, they were walking down the drive towards the yard.

'Yes sir, Haig Seven.'

At Fairbridge Farm School they'd all had a number; a Cottage that they belonged to and a number. Tom had been in Haig Cottage and he was boy number seven. Not all the teachers and Cottage Mothers called their charges by cottage and number but some, like Cardwell, did.

'Standing on your own two feet now heh?'

'I reckon, sir.'

'Mr Anderson seems pleased with you. Credit to your old alma mater.'

'Sir.'

'Haig ...' Mr Cardwell nodded, 'Kitchener Cottage they've always been the sporty ones. And we've a boy in Rhodes shaping up as a sprinter.'

'Mr Cardwell, I wondered if there was any news come from England, about my mother? I wrote a while back to Pinjarra.'

Mr Cardwell stopped. 'You have a mother?'

'Yes sir. I've tried writing … I just wondered if Fairbridge might have any information? Could help me find out?'

Mr Cardwell shook his head. 'If you've heard nothing back then your best bet is to put the past behind you. That's my advice. You're an adult, near enough, and Fairbridge has given you a good start in life. You're one of the lucky ones, I hope you appreciate that.'

One of the lucky ones.

He remembered the terror and confusion of his first days at Pinjarra. How remote it seemed from the rest of the world. How far from the familiar red bricks and smog of Manchester. The way they took your shoes from you. The cuts and jabs his tender feet had endured until they hardened up. The ice-cold shower in all weathers. The endless scrubbing and chores. The sounds of strange new creatures in the lonely hours of the night.

He was young, he had adjusted. There was an outdoor life, he welcomed that. There were small kindnesses. A Cottage Mother who shared her hearth if not her affection with the boys in her care.

One of the lucky ones.

MY FAIR LADY

All the talk was of the Fair. Betty invited Maeve and the new Mrs Anderson over for coffee and chocolate cake. Whilst the women sat on the sofa sipping the hot sweet coffee Patsy was amusing herself with her two battered dolls. Daisy the Rag Doll and the other, known as 'Baby'. Maeve would overhear Patsy's high-pitched little voice engaging in bizarre three-way conversations as the dolls were dressed and undressed, scolded or praised, had tea or went to the shops or any other kind of outing the two-year old might devise. Maeve gave thanks that her youngest was so easily amused and wasn't the tear-away toddlers that the older children had been.

The Field Day was the social highlight of the year, everyone dressed to the nines. Ladies were expected to wear hats and gloves and it was the hats which were the real centerpiece of any outfit. Maeve thought of her dove grey velvet French hat and coat packed away in her trunk which she had not yet had an opportunity to wear in the whole of her time in Australia, perhaps she might consider it now.

She remembered buying the outfit in Brown Thomas whilst staying in Dublin for a week with her parents. Patrick driving up for the weekend to join them, edgy at leaving the farm for the first time in Joe's care. But he clapped his hands and declared that they were off to the races the following day, just the two of them.

She smiled ruefully to remember her excitement at the opportunity to try out the new outfit and the image she had of herself poised on the grandstand in the members' enclosure, binoculars in hand.

As she emerged down the stairs to join him the next morning Patrick greeted her with a huge grin. 'Aren't you the picture!'

'Like Jackie Kennedy.' her mother smiled.

The papers were full of photographs of the Kennedy's campaigning for the Presidency. The whole of Ireland was agog at the notion of a Catholic President and a son of Erin to boot. Kennedy had almost attained sainthood and his wife, the lady Madonna of both fashion and motherhood. Maeve pinked at the welcome comparison.

It was a bright day with a little nip in the air that lent it freshness. They drove north out of the city and the further they progressed the more confused Maeve became.

'Which race track are we heading for?'

Patrick tapped his nose. ''Tis the most spectacular course in the whole of the country.'

By the time they reached Julianstown she was wondering if they were on the way to the North itself, but here they turned off. Then, as if from nowhere it seemed, they were snarled in traffic and horse boxes and crawled to the outskirts of a small coastal town where people were being directed into a makeshift car park. Patrick turned in with them.

'Welcome to the Laytown Races.' a man held out a ticket for the parking. 'Isn't it a grand day for it?'

Patrick grinned. 'Time enough to check out the contenders and have a little flutter wouldn't you say?'

They joined the throng of excited country people milling through the town. Heads turned as they made their way down the thoroughfare. A wolf whistle even. The local girls giving her the critical once over. Maeve snatched at Patrick's arm, anxious not to be separated in the jostling mayhem.

'God but you're looking gorgeous!' He exclaimed.

A view of the sea opened out before them, the tide swept out beyond the long wide strand which stretched all the way up to Bettystown and beyond. She could see the little flags and the fencing posts which had been set in to the damp sand, which, Patrick informed her, could only be outlined on the day and took a practiced and experienced eye.

As they drew into the main centre of activity they were confronted with all the hurly burly and hullabaloo of a typical race meeting and then something extra. The bookies with their long jackets and trilbys wedged firmly on their heads, surrounded by ruddy cheeked Meath farmers counting out wads of filthy money. Children tugging at their father's sleeve begging for him to buy a bottle of red lemonade and a packet of Taytos and to have a go on the hoops at the bit of fairground. The strident hurdy gurdy music. Ice cream vendors, candy floss and the smell of fat greasy chips wafting on the breeze and mingling with the salt tang of the sea. A cacophony of laughter, from shrill to full throated. Stewards with bands on their sleeves, steering the crowd.

Maeve took it all in, flinching at the rough and ready gathering. She felt the high heels of her stilettos puncturing the sand and had to hold Patrick all the tighter.

'You never know who might be here, there was The Aga Khan himself one time.'

'Here, on the strand?'

'Above. That's where all the nobs are, in the field above drinking champagne.'

As Maeve cast her gaze upward, she could see what must be the members enclosure, a splash of colour in a hat or two and even a top hat. So, what were they doing down here on the beach with the hoi polloi?

'But sure, who'd want to be up there and out of it all.' Patrick was smiling from ear to ear. 'We'll have a bite and put a few bets on and go on over to those dunes and have the best view of all for the main event.'

She felt like spitting nails. Why couldn't he be like all the other men she'd ever known? Why must he always be surprising her? Catching her off guard and out of step.

'Now, the thing with the two mile on sand is making a good start, the horse that gets out in front is the one most likely. A sprint start and stamina. No fancy tricks.' He explained as they lurched through the loose sand up the slope.

She had to take off her shoes and carry her French fashioned grey velvet hat after a gust off the sea nearly took it away and her hair felt limp and dishevelled in the salty air. They passed not one but two canoodling couples in the dips and hollows before Patrick found a satisfactory perch. He took off his jacket and laid it on the sand with a flourish. 'Your majesty.'

Maeve sighed at what felt like the final nail in the coffin of her hopes for the day. Well, what was done was done, she thought as she lowered herself on to the jacket.

Patrick was pointing out the field heading to the line-up. He produced a hip flask for the 'nip in the air'.

'There'll be horses preparing for Galway, so a good field but the tip I've had from Niall is a dead cert over the two miles, *Nancy's Boy,* the one in the grey and pink. I'd good odds as well. See now, they race down to Bettystown and do a great sweeping U turn and back to the finish here at Laytown.'

And so on and so on, passing her the binoculars as he discussed each horse and rider; with the seagulls screeching overhead and diving down on to the beach to tussle over abandoned chip wrappers.

Even from the distance they were at you could feel the tension in the atmosphere as taut as the dense knot of people squirming to position themselves along the fence. Then there was a crack and a roar and they were off. And *Nancy's Boy* was in the first six and Patrick was up on his feet. And she felt the keenness of his excitement.

'How much did you put on Patrick?'

She could tell by the press of his lips that he'd rather she hadn't asked that question and her heart sank. Their first year on the farm had been costly. The old farmhouse was run down, draughty and damp and would take years to repair and restore to its former Georgian glory but when they had realised the extent of the leaks in the first heavy downpour there had been no option but to fork out for roof repairs. Then most of the machinery was old and had to be replaced, like the gleaming new tractor which had arrived that summer.

She felt sick in the pit of her stomach. 'How much?'

'Alright, a ton.'

'Each way?'

290

'To win.' He raised the binoculars to his eyes and strained to pick out the grey and pink as the strung-out field approached the sweeping turn nearly a mile down the strand.

She got to her feet and squeezed his arm. 'Come on Nancy's Boy!' she shouted into the breeze that was gusting onshore and carrying away her hopes and dreams.

She felt the gladness in him.

'They're coming around now ... he's neck and neck at third ... it's very tight at the front ... jeez will he find the space ...'

'Go on Nancy's Boy!'

'He's pulling wide.' Patrick shook his head.

She could see the white-knuckle grip on the binoculars.

She yelled the horse's name again and again, her throat straining and hoarse, she dare not even look at the beach, it was to heaven she was shouting, willing an act of divine intervention. 'Nancy's Boy!'

'God, but he's overtaking on the outside! He's behind the leader! Will you look at him go! Keep your head down Boy, watch out on your shoulder ...   G'wan! G'wan! G'wan!!' Patrick was pumping the air with his fist. 'That's it! That's it! You're ahead!! Hold on!!! Yeeeeh!!!!!'

He threw the binoculars aside and pulled her into his arms and they were swaying and tumbling down onto the sand, laughing, his face alive with triumph.

'We've won. We've won macushla. Eight to one!'

'My coat is ruined.' She smiled through her tears.

'Sure, can't I buy you a hundred new coats.'

Then they'd kissed and cuddled until the sun began to dip behind them and it was time to hit the road. And on the drive home he shared his plans. Face aglow with the possibilities. The new harvester he could put the deposit on, his plan to move lock, stock and barrel into wheat, the fortune that could be made if they invested in a modern, well run farm. He could take on more men. The two of them could put their feet up and live off the fat of the land.

'... I will show you, if you like.' Maeve was brought back to the present chatter, 'I bought the hat when I was down in Perth with Saskia, you know they are expecting another one

Maeve, four children, it's like the Irish!' And unable to conceal her excitement Betty went off to get her new outfit for their perusal.

It was the first opportunity for Maeve and the new Mrs Anderson to observe each other.

'If you don't mind me saying, Mrs Glendon—'

'Maeve, please.'

'Maeve. I would not have you down as the Outback type.'

'No. I wouldn't either.'

'I see. So, you'll be moving on soon, I guess.'

'We won't be going anywhere for a while.'

'Your husband likes it then? Men – always get their way!'

'There was a fire at our house, it was my fault. We still owe Mr Anderson a good deal for the repairs.'

The new Mrs Anderson raised her eyebrows. 'I see.' She regarded Maeve thoughtfully and Maeve willed herself to hold her gaze. 'Perhaps I could have a word with Jack, it seems a little unfair—'

'No.' Maeve cut in abruptly. 'I'd rather that you didn't.' Her tone softened, 'Thank you for the kind thought but we'll find a way to pay the debt.'

'Of course.' The new Mrs Anderson shrugged. 'I try and keep out of Jack's business. Hard enough being a stepmother. I worry about Jimmy. You can see the kid really needs someone to talk to but I've hardly had two words out of him.'

'Harder for boys I think.'

'I suppose so.'

Betty reappeared wearing a wide brimmed hat with floral trim and holding up a sunflower yellow print frock with a matching short jacket.

'What do you think girls?'

On the other hand, Maeve, thought, this might not be the occasion for the simple sophisticated lines of the dove grey velvet French coat and hat. She sighed as she saw the opportunities to find the right occasion recede into the distant ether.

SWEET CHARIOT

John John saw something glittering in the dust. A coin. He stooped to retrieve it. In the same moment another hand swooped down and snatched it from the ground.

'Find a penny pick it up, all the day you'll have good luck.' Nieve held the shiny new penny out in front of her triumphantly. The young Queen's profile catching the light.

John John felt a hot stab of fury at the injustice of it.

'Give that penny to a friend and your luck will never end!' She was offering the penny to him with a beaming smile on her face.

John John hesitated, was there some trick in it? Tentatively he reached out and accepted the coin.

'Am I not your best friend!' The da exclaimed with mock affront. Why aren't you giving me the luck?'

Nieve laughed and leant into the da, 'Daa! It's me who gets the luck for giving it away. John John just gets the penny!'

John John had been done out of the luck but still he was the one with an extra penny to spend at the Fair. A penny to add to the shilling their da had already given them.

As they moved through the crowds streaming into the center of the grounds John John's eyes darted from one possible attraction to another. To one side there were the pens of livestock and a ring where they were being paraded before judges. There were tents of produce, huge vegetables in competition and jams and honeys and cakes, displays of plants and floral arrangements. Charity tombola stands. An arena that had been set up for the events, the go-kart racing, which Jimmy had come home to enter, the exhibition of whipcracking from Tom, the sheep dog trial and on and on. His mammie was reading from the programme and hanging on to Patsy's reins with the other hand. At the far end of the field there was an exhibition of old agricultural machinery and John John could see that Brian was amongst the boys clambouring onto one of the old tractors.

On the other side there was the Fair. Stalls with hoops, rifle ranges and coconut shies. Hot dogs and candy floss. Tea and cakes. Lamingtons. Tents with different shows, mirrors, a boxing ring and on one he could make out the word 'circus' in the sign. That made his heart quicken. John John was nearly eight years old but he had never been to a circus. All he knew of them was from story books. The Ringmaster, the clowns, the trapeze artists and the high wire, the elephants and the lions.

'Da, da.' He exclaimed with excitement. 'Can we go to the circus?'

'Of course.' His da looked about and frowned. 'But I don't see any big top around here.'

'Over there da, over there.' John John was pulling on his da's shirt sleeve and pointing to the sign.

The sign was rounding into full view.

'The Flea Circus you mean?'

John John's face fell. A flea circus. Was that it? A circus of fleas? He suddenly felt a fool. Of course, the small grubby tent wasn't big enough for elephants and lions, for trapezes and acrobats. It was only big enough for fleas. How could he have ever imagined that it was a proper circus.

'Ugh! I'm not going in there, daddy.' Nieve was being snooty, she always said 'daddy' when she was being snooty.

'I'm afraid I won't be risking it either.' His mammie looked horrified.

Patsy was straining at her lead. 'Circus. Circus ma ma.'

'Why don't we go on over and see the flower show? Won't that be pretty? Nicer than a bunch of old fleas!' His mammie looked at the da. 'Yourself and John John go to the circus we'll meet you for tea and cakes in an hour.'

'You and me for the fleas!' His da said and jumped about pretending to scratch himself only making John John feel even more of an idiot.

They could still hear Patsy shrieking in protest as they

queued up for the tickets from the large woman at the entrance. A sign beside her warned, POSITIVELY NO DOGS WILL BE ADMITTED TO THE SHOW

They were the last to squeeze through for the 10.30 performance. An audience of twenty. At a tinny fanfare they were all ushered in. It was pitch black except for a small spotlight on a sawdust ring. The circus was on a stand at about the height of his father's waist and perfect for a boy of John John's stature. There were no seats. The small audience crowded around in a semi-circle, children in front of adults, a curtain at the back of the ring. John John was mesmerized at once. It was a circus in perfect miniature already laid out with trapeze and tightrope and hoops.

As the music came to a crescendo the curtain was pulled back and a wizened man sporting a top hat and red waistcoat appeared under his own spotlight.

'Ladies and gentlemen, boys and girls welcome! Welcome to the Greatest Little Show on Earth! The most Flea-mazing, the most Flea-tastic, the most Flea-mendous circus in the world! '

The tinny circus music struck up again.

'You will be dazzled by the Flee-atellis and their daring high-flying display on the trapeze! You will be awe struck by the colossal feats of strength of the Great Fleemo! You will wonder at the acrobatic dexterity of the Fleekovich Family! You will laugh at the antics of Fleabo the Clown! And you will thrill to the chariot race finale, a race to rival Ben Hur!!'

A couple of older boys began to snigger. John John wished that they would shut up. More than anything now he wanted to be amazed, he wanted them to be amazed.

The Ringmaster, who was wearing a short-sleeved shirt, held the bare forearm of his left arm out under the spotlight. 'But first let me introduce you to our star performers!'

The circle of audience were suddenly still as they took in the scene and then craned forward to get a better look. A colony of well-fed fleas appeared to be living on the man's flea-bitten arm.

John John could see that the boy beside him was goggle eyed. 'Are those things real!' He exclaimed.

'Every last one of them named and known to me personally.'

Some members of the audience took a step back as though to distance themselves from the colony.

The Ringmaster grinned. 'And if you're thinking they might desert me in favour of taking up residence with you, you've no worries, believe me. These fleas feed exclusively on my blood, as I am demonstrating to you now and you can see with your own eyes; blood which I keep well-nourished with a protein, iron rich diet. These are the best fed fleas in the whole of Australia, if not the world!'

He nodded at one of the lads. 'So, no worries mate, you can stop your scratching unless you've brought your own brigade in with you!'

This was greeted with a round of laughter.

'Allrightie everyone – let the circus begin!'

An hour later over coconut lamingtons and lemonade John John still held the image of the tiny little racing chariots, each one pulled by a single flea, lapping the sawdust ring and heard again the shouts of exultation of himself and his da when the green chariot which they were supporting had crossed the winner's line.

Nieve refused to sit near him, making a big fuss about catching fleas and she was gloating over her win of a set of Spillikins on the Children's Tombola. 'See, I've got the luck already!'

John John held his tongue and smiled his secret, Nieve might win all the prizes she liked that day but she had not seen the Greatest Little Show on Earth.

BEN DOWN AND KANGAROO BOB

Same man, same white shirt n' bow tie, outside calico, shouting, 'Try your luck. Five rounds with Kangaroo Bob. Win lotta money'. Plenty fellas in line to look them boxers beat up. Not me this time, got Binni.

Binni got pink candy. He tryin' get his tongue 'round candy floss. Big, sticky, pink sugar smile. Binni big eyes look everywhere. All that gwangy hoopla. We been looking sheep shearing competition 'n Binni shock how quick these fellas. Shearers comin' down this country. It spring n' soon they at Boss Anderson and we driving sheep in to sheds. Lotta noise, all them shearin' machine goin', sheep crying out', fellas cussin n' swearin'.

Binni pull my arm, point at game to win coconut. He reckon he can win one them coconut. Reckon he can—got good aim. I say, first got business, got a relly to visit. Want to get Billy to give up the fightin', come with us, look out for him. Maali gonna have a blue, but he my brother.
 At the caravan got *Kangaroo Bob* painted on it. Towel fella's there, seen 'im last time. He look me suspicious like, you know.

'What you want fella? Nuthin' back here mate.'

'Lookin' for Billy.'

'Ain't no Billy, mate.'

'Kangaroo Bob.'

'What business you got?'

'He my cousin-brother.'

'Come back after.'

Shake my head. 'Got to see 'im now. Ten minutes, boss.'

Towel man come close. 'We don't want our boy upset now. Not before a show.'

'Just ten minutes, boss.'

Fella look Binni with big candy floss smile.

'Ten minutes.' He tap on the door. 'Bob! Got some your mob 'ere.'

We hear noise inside. Towel fella tap again. 'Couple of minutes. Got to get your gloves on mate.'

Door open and bad smell—like old sock 'n smokes 'n other bad stuff. Young blackfella look out.

'Lookin' for Bob.' I say.

'Whaddya want?'

'Say g'day.'

'Who this fella, Ed?' The kulamandi ask towel man.

'Said he was your brother.'

This new Kangaroo Bob. Ask 'im. 'Where blackfella was 'ere last year?'

'Dunno mate.'

I look to towel man, 'Know the one, mate? 'Im move on?'

He say to Kangaroo Bob. 'Go take a piss Bob, I'll be in in a sec for the gloves.'

Kulamandi shut door.

Towel man he walk away, nod for me to come.

'Look mate, thing is ...' he speak low, 'We didn't know his mob, he never talk about his family. So, don't go blowing off.'

'What you say?'

'Your brother ... after we left here, next place we went, he was having a bad run ... end of the show I knew somethin' was up. Starts fitting, here in the caravan. I ses, we need a doctor ... but already too late. Doc ses it was brain haemorrhage. Nothing to be done.'

Billy dead. Hit me like below the belt.

'We buried him decent, mate.' Towel fella look me. 'The boss won't want no trouble.' He nod at Binni. 'And you're not after none I can see that. So, why don't I have a bit of a word, yeah? He'd have been owed something that Bob; not much after all the funeral expenses, but ...'

Shake my head. Look at Binni, we walk away.

Binni quiet-like. He know somethin' bad happen.

298

'What's a haemorrhage, dad?'
'Like someone switch light off.'
'Oh.'
'Come on Binni, Bet I could get one them coconut too.'
He give me big, pink smile.
In the end we got us three.

THE QUAGMIRE

Sheets of water were pouring over the edge of the verandah. A constant drilling of raindrops on the corrugated roof. The school bus had been canceled because of flooding on the Anderson Stiller Road. John John sat at the kitchen table most of that day playing Ludo with Nieve, who always won, and they ended up having a big fight when Nieve said he was cheating and he said it was just a joke.

All through the next day he copied out pictures of dinosaurs from his book in the Wonders of the Natural World series and stared glumly out of the fly screen door. Nieve tried to make treacle toffee from a recipe in her girl's comic and ruined one of the mammie's pans. Even Patsy, with her sweet tooth, spat it out on the floor. Finally, on the Saturday morning they woke up to a barrage of sunlight breaking through the curtains.

The road was still flooded so they wouldn't be able to risk going into Darinup in the old van. Nieve was up at the Big House with her new best friend Susan, who had been expelled for getting in a fight with another girl. The evening before, his da said they would go fishing, just the two of them, and they might catch supper. But then Uncle Bram turned up at the door and said there was a problem with a fallen tree that was blocking a track and he needed the da in the tractor.

John John wandered down the rutted path on his own. He wondered if they had fish in Australia like the Salmon of Knowledge and then he would get all the brains and be famous like Finn McCool and that would show Nieve. That morning, before he was called away, his da had ferreted out some line and tied a weight to it and found a hook, which wasn't a proper fish hook but which he had sharpened a bit

300

and said might do with the right bait and if they flicked the fish out of the water quick enough. They were to find the makings of a rod along the way. And it was for this that John John had his eyes peeled.

He found one stick which was a bit thick but would do as a snake stick to tap along the ground and let the King Browns and Taipans know to keep out of his way. Before he knew it, the hunt took him down onto the track that led to the quagmires. He stopped to think. They were forbidden. But Nieve had been there, he was sure, he'd seen the smart alecky smirk on her face. Tom had said one of the flock had strayed and was sucked in. John John worked that image over and over in his mind, the sucking of it, until the quagmire had become a great blobby alien monster from outer space ready to suck in any passing life form, suck, suck, like when you were trying to suck up the last bit of lemonade or milkshake through a straw with mammie complaining about the rude noise.

He'd just have a peek, sneak up so as not to be spotted, just see if the sheep's head or feet which might still be sticking up out of the Quagmire's mouth. He imagined the lonesome 'baaa ... baaa' of the sheep and was listening out for it as he drew nearer.

THE LOST BOY

They were rounding up the early lambs that would be going to the sale yards when he spotted the broken section of fencing. Roos again, Stubby reckoned. Alex was talking about getting electric fencing but Jack wasn't convinced it would be worth the outlay. There'd always be lost sheep one way or another, you factored it in. No point splashing out for the heck of it. Count the pennies and the pounds would look after themselves, Old Jack used to say. Mean old bugger he'd been, Stubby grinned at the recollection, but fair in his way. John Jack was like his father that was for sure, mean bugger. Fair, now maybe that was another matter. The ground was still soft after the rain and it was easy enough to follow the tracks of a ewe and her lamb, he'd give it ten minutes and then he'd get back to the round up.

Count the pennies and the pounds would look after themselves; that was something his mother would say. Where would Stubby be now if there had been buckets of pennies? If their mother hadn't passed on with the tuberculosis when he was scarcely ten? Would he still be in the Slad Valley? A little stone cottage tucked cosily into the hillside? His own small business? Dry stone walling; he'd been good at helping with that. Along with his brother Haydon perhaps? He laughed aloud. No, Hay would never be still, he'd have roamed the length and breadth of the five valleys at the very least. Perhaps, Stubby mused, he'd have married. Violet Coldrick, she'd have been the one that he wanted. Had children of his own. There was a thought.

Closest Stubby had come to children was the Anderson boys, John Jack and Finlay, hardly a year between them. He could see them now roaring and yelling round the yard, him chasing them with the sloughed skin of some snake.

302

Laughing. Sweeping a pitch, setting up stumps, trying to teach them how to play cricket, John Jack powerful on the bat, Finlay the joker, trying to disguise the ball, he'd get the edge, eventually he'd get the edge. Stubby had been like a big brother, fooled around, never been an 'uncle', always a playmate. And Mrs Anderson standing on the verandah calling them in for supper. He remembered the pride in her two boys always shining in her eyes even when she was stern, which she could be. Sundays, Stubby would be invited in to the big kitchen; clean shirt, boots polished. Finlay making funny faces at him across the table trying to make him snigger into his gravy.

Finlay, he hadn't thought of Finlay for how long? The lost boy. Lost boys, lost sheep. Factored in. No, that wasn't right. The loss absorbed but never accepted. He recalled with a pang the sad tilt around Mrs Anderson's eyes, the empty place at the table, never set but always there would be 'one for the pot', a portion for Finlay, just in case of a knock at the door, the cheeky grin on a freckled face, the lost boy returned.

Once or twice, Stubby almost said, 'He'll never be found Mrs Anderson, he's dead Mrs Anderson, dead, dead like Hay, not coming back, no prodigal son.' But he didn't because he was the one who had said to John Jack, 'You can trust me!' Shaken John Jack until he could see the comprehension in the boy's eyes, 'You can trust me!' Not two boys lost but one, only one. That was something.

He had made the right decision; it was the only decision.

The ewe was gutted, soft underbelly ripped open and ragged. The eyes gaping holes, pecked out. The lamb was nowhere to be seen. A dingo perhaps or a feral dog, there were a few that had been spotted in the shire.

THE GOOD SHEPHERD

John John hadn't imagined it after all. The bleating was a little lamb. He could just see its woolly head as he passed through the trees and came out by the quagmire. It was truly a strange, queer place, with a steaming mist lifting off the glaucous surface after all the rain and the pong in the air was thick with flies. You could imagine it the lair of any kind of beast. It made the hairs stand. His ears were tingling too with the sharp, piercing 'baa baaa...' John John edged into the clearing and each step brought him closer to the suck suck suck. The little lamb saw him and flailed his one hoof still above the yellow brown sludge, splashing the thin film of rainwater, straining his neck, eyes bulging. Baa ... baaa ...

John John knew he must turn around at once before the monster reached out its tentacles and drew him in to the same horrible fate.

Baa ... baaa!

John John caught his breath; the little lamb was pushing urgently towards him. It wasn't so very far out. It had simply slipped down the edge; he could see that now. If the little woolly creature could just get a grip on something.

'Come on little lamb!' he shouted. 'You can do it!' He banged the snake stick on the ground. 'You can do it! Come on Silly Billy! Silly Billy!'

Baa ... baaa! The little lamb fell back, exhausted.

John John took a step back. 'Your fault, it's your fault!'

Baa ... baa ...

'Billy, billy, billy!' John John inched forward. The glucky pond shimmered in the light breaking through. A large black bird wheeled down to the other side of the mire and, with its beak tilted, strutted impatiently along the far edge.

John John swatted at the flies around his head. 'Go away!

304

Go away!' He wanted to cry he was so angry. The little lamb was going to die and it wasn't his fault. He would try once, that was all, and then that would be enough.

He dropped down to his knees; the fear gulped back in his throat. He held the snake stick out in front of him; if he crawled very carefully forward then he would not slip and fall in, not like the silly billy lamb.

FOR THE LOVE OF MAISIE

Jack was the first to see old Stubby emerging through a break in the fence, he was carrying a slime-encrusted lamb, whispering soft words to it. Jack nudged Caesar towards them. The pungent smell of rot and decay was wafting towards him. Stubborn old goat. That was Stubby. Never liked to lose any of his flock. They'd finished loading up the truck already. He could see Ken over by the gate having a smoke-oh. This one would have to be cleaned up and go in the next transit.

'The ewe's a gonner.' Stubby called over. 'But this little fella's had a lucky escape.'

'Good man.'

'Not me, Master.'

Jack wished the old codger would leave out the 'Master', they weren't in his damn Cotswolds now, tugging forelocks to the Lord of the Manor. Why couldn't Stubby simply call him 'Boss' like all the other men.

'Not me.' Stubby stroked the woolly head.

Baaa ... baaa

What was the old man saying? Jack was sure there was a touch of the crazies about him these days.

Stubby jerked his head backwards, his mare was ambling along the bush track behind him and sitting astride the saddle was a young boy. The boy smiled uncertainly, a gap tooth smile. The dirty smudge of a freckled nose. That reddish tint to the hair sticking on end with the mud caked through it. This boy was how old? Seven? Eight? He was not fifteen. Not fifteen. Jack did not believe in ghosts. When they tried to creep into his nights, he faced them down and beat them away.

The boy was swatting at the flies swarming in his wake.

Little devil. Lord of the Flies. His mother had a way of Bible talking. All the demons of hell, the curse of Eve and the mark of Cain.

Jack gripped the reins tight. *It was an accident.* How many times had he wanted to tell his mother that as she moped over the stove with her, 'One for the Pot.'? *We were only fighting in the way that boys do, ma. Finlay always joking. A small matter to laugh when it is not at your own expense. He could never keep his blasted mouth shut.* Jack could feel his gall rising. *It was an accident!* he wanted to shout.

'Bit of an accident.' Stubby jerked his head again. 'But he'd not let go of this little fella. Had to tug the both of them out.'

'What were you doing there boy?' Jack glared.

The boy's smile dropped like a lead weight and he flinched.

'Haven't you been told it's forbidden?!'

'Heard the lamb, that's all, Master John, heard the crying.'

As if on cue the orphaned lamb let out a plaintive bleat.

After Finlay and the quagmire, that's when it had started, the 'Master' business. 'You can trust me, Master John. You can trust me!'

'Please don't tell mammie.' The boy was whimpering now.

What will I tell ma? Young Jack had sobbed.

And Stubby stared at him a long time. Had he seen that push? It was meant only to teach Finlay a lesson, to take the goading smirk from his face. Make him eat his taunting words. *Maisie Davidson ses you kiss like a bush pig's arse!*

It was a day much like today, a day after heavy rain and Finlay stumbled awkwardly through the sludge onto his back, arms flailing and then twisted into the shock of the soft oozing mire, a look of sudden horror on his face. Jack had done what he could. He had done what he could. He had broken off a branch, his face puce with the effort and urgency. He had stretched out from the edge and Finlay grasped the other end; he could see the look of relief on his face even now. Then, the tugging against the sludge, yanking and pulling with the desperation of a drowning man, the look of pure panic and disbelief.

'We won't tell your ma.' Stubby patted the mare. 'Will we

Master John?'

The Glendon boy looked anxious.

Jack grunted. 'Just this time, you mark?'

Could he have saved him? No. NO. He himself was slipping over the edge there had been no choice but to let go.

The boy nodded and chanced a tentative grin.

Even now on the rare occasions these days when Jack would see an old Reo truck he wanted to believe, like everyone else, the story which Stubby had told. Of seeing Finlay walking out on to the main Tin Creek Road, thumb outstretched, and getting picked up by a stranger in a Reo. Someone passing through.

EARACHE

John John was up all night, crying with the pain in his ear. They tried everything. An adult dose of aspirin, warm oil in his ear and cotton wool. Nothing seemed to alleviate the agony.

'We've to get him to a doctor.' Maeve pleaded by the first light of dawn.

The doctor's surgery in Darinup was a weekly affair and wouldn't be due for another three days. They looked at each other in desperation.

'That means Bodenham.'

The impossibility hurtled through Patrick's mind. The old van had broken down yet again and was awaiting a replacement clutch but for the moment it might as well be a useless piece of junk. The Van der Berjs were visiting their other daughter in Geraldton. Maddy Anderson was also away, on a shopping trip to Perth.

'You'll have to ask Mr Anderson to take us, or at least borrow his truck.' Maeve voiced the remaining options.

Patrick nodded in agreement and wondered why he didn't feel any confidence.

'Look Paddy I don't have time right now for some day trip to Bodenham because your kid's got a bit of an earache. I'm the one getting earache right now!'

'He's in agony Mr Anderson.'

'There's just too much bloody work to be done before the shearing. We're short as it is with Bram off dipping his toes in the Indian Ocean until the end of the week. Tom and Boswell are over on the Stiller Block and I need you at the pens.' he jabbed with his finger to emphasise the word 'you'.

Patrick felt a heaviness in his chest. He wanted to punch Jack Anderson right then and there, tell him to stuff his bloody job where the sun don't shine but there was all the money he still owed for the fire damage. What could he do?

Anderson had already turned away.

'I can go Boss.'

It was Ben Down.

Jack wheeled about and glared at the black man.

'Doubleday got old jalopy that go all right. Work Sunday 'stead Boss.' Ben was staring Jack Anderson straight in the eye and there was something in his stance which would not be denied.

Patrick could see the tight lip of Jack Anderson flickering with fury.

'If you can let Ben go, I'll work Sunday too, Mr Anderson. No pay.' Patrick interjected his eyes darting anxiously between the two men.

'Get out of here before I change my mind, Ben.' Jack turned and strode away. 'You Paddy, come with me.'

Patrick gestured his thanks to Ben. His gratitude immeasurable.

Ben grinned his wide toothless grin. 'No worries mate.'

THE BLACKFELLA

They had not known what to think when the black man came to the door. His hat clutched in his rough calloused hands.

'Take Missus to Hospital.' He simply said.

He was the blackest man John John had ever seen. Even blacker than the magician and not that glossy black of the African which shone straight back at you but a dense black which drew you in towards the deep-set eyes.

Nieve was dropped at the top of the track to wait for the school bus and even through the distraction of the excruciating pain John John felt in his ear, a pain the like of which he had never experienced before, he could see the green eye of envy in her parting glance.

This was the closest he had been to one of the aboriginals on the farm. He was sitting right beside him because his mammie was at the passenger window of the ute with Patsy on her lap. Nieve had whispered one night that she had met a real aboriginal boy who was on a Walkabout and he had told her the story of the Rainbow Snake.

Tell me then. John John demanded but Nieve rather pompously said that she couldn't because it was a secret. John John did not believe her. Nieve was always making things up. Like when he lost his front tooth, she said that Australian Tooth Fairies did not have wings and wore gloves and looked more like goblins than fairies. He tried to stay awake in the night to see if she was telling the truth but drifted into a strange dream where he was flying over seas and green fields and high mountains, someone was holding his hand but he could not see his face. In the morning the sixpence was there under his pillow and he knew he would have to wait until the next tooth fell out to catch the Tooth

Fairy.

Ben did not have his two front teeth and John John wondered if sometimes they didn't grow back.

It was a long way to Bodenham in the rattling old truck which crunched through the gears. At first, they drove without speaking, just the sounds of John John whimpering as he leant against his mammie and occasionally Patsy strained to look out of the window. 'Roo roo— Looka roo Joh Joh!' she insisted, but it was only the misshapen stump of a burnt tree.

Then his mammie said, 'Do you have a family Ben?'

'Yes Missus.'

He had a son called Benny and Benny was very good at school but the mission people were closing down.

'That's a pity.' His mammie said.

They were silent again.

Then John John had an idea. 'Do you know the story about The Rainbow Snake?'

Ben grinned his wide toothless grin. 'Know lotta stories.'

'Do you know one about a magician?'

Ben nodded and told them a story about a magician who turned his two brothers into swans and forgot to turn them back again and how those swans ended up with black feathers instead of white ones.

'I know a story too.' John John offered.

'Like to hear that story.' Ben said. 'My murran knew story for every day of year.'

'This one could be the October the twenty third story.' John John suggested helpfully, as that was the date it was. This one is about birds as well.'

Ben looked pleased. 'Emu—he my brother.'

John John wasn't sure he had heard Ben properly; he was sometimes a little difficult to understand because of the missing teeth and his accent. He didn't want to sound silly asking, 'Did you say you have a brother who is an emu?' Perhaps his brother had been put under a spell like the swans.

'Storwee, storwee!' Patsy chanted.

'Once upon a time.' John John began. 'A long time ago in Ireland all the birds got together to decide which one was going to be the King. There was sparrows and Robin Redbreast and—'

'Cockatoos?'

'No.' John John shook his head.

'Emus?'

'No.' John John looked at Ben like he was crazy.

'Galahs?'

'No.' John John broke into a smile.

'Eagles?'

'Oh yes, eagles!' John John sat up. 'This is a story about an eagle!'

'That right?'

'The eagle is the biggest bird and he says the only way to find out who is the King is to have a contest. The other birds thought this was a good idea. The swallow said it should be the bird that could fly the furthest. No, said the eagle, that contest would take too long and who would be the judge? It should be the bird that could fly highest and then everyone could see. The birds twittered, they all knew that the eagle could fly higher than any of them. *Well?* Said the eagle, looking fierce. *Don't you think that is the best idea?* The other birds had to say it was.

A sunny day came when there wasn't a cloud in the sky and all the birds rose up in the air; like a big giant cloud. Higher and higher they all went.'

'Hiyer! Hiyer!' Patsy echoed waving her arms above her head.

'One by one the birds got tired until the only bird that was left in the sky was the eagle. The eagle thought, I will fly right to the top of the sky I will touch it with the tip of my wing and then they will all see who is the King of the Birds!

So, the eagle kept going up and up and the other birds all looked amazed.' John John's eyes widened. 'They all shouted, *The eagle is our King!* Eagle was very happy because he had no strength left and his wings were slowing almost to a stop and the sky had no end. Then from under his

313

wing flew a wren—that's the tiniest bird in the whole of Ireland.' John John explained.

Ben nodded, 'Lirra lirra, same like, little bird.'

'Lirra lirra.' John John repeated. He would remember that. That would be something else to tell Miss Know-it-all.

'So, this wren, like a lirra lirra, it had been hiding under the eagle's wing all the time and now it flew up above him and the eagle was livid, really livid, but he was too tired to follow. And all the other birds were shouting because they could see that the little wren was dancing and singing at the very top of the sky.

Look! The sparrow said, *It's the Wren that's the King of all the Birds, because he is the cleverest!* And that is the story of how the littlest bird in Ireland became a King!' John John declared with a big wide smile, because he had almost forgotten his earache.

Ben chuckled. 'That a good story. I tell that story to Binni. Eagle will be name Mullian and it been Wan the Crow hidin'. Jump out 'n win contest. That sort of trick Wan like!' Ben laughed again.

Then they were at the Hospital in Bodenham and the journey hadn't seemed so long after all and already John John was looking forward to the stories Ben would tell them on the way home and Nieve would be livid, and *livid* was his new favourite word.

314

THE STOLEN ONE

The van had been fixed up at last and Maeve was determined that the first thing she was going to do was to show her gratitude to Ben. She wondered about writing a card of thanks in the interim but Patrick wasn't sure Ben could read, it might be awkward if this was the case. After much deliberation Maeve decided on a cake. She had perfected Betty's chocolate cake recipe but of course that would not do, it wouldn't last the trip to Billangilil without melting all over the plate. For she was determined to visit Billangilil and introduce herself to Ben's wife.

More than a year at Inverness and she had never visited the aboriginal fringe camp. Why would she, she supposed? She had scarcely spoken two words to an aboriginal before the dash to the hospital with Ben. If she was honest, she was afraid. They seemed so different, so *other* and they were spoken of with such contempt and distrust. And then of course there was her stupor. The way your mind became addled by the constant struggle against heat and flies, the grind of daily domestic tasks just to survive in the face of this penny-pinching poverty.

How her life had turned itself about. From the spoilt young girl in Dublin, beloved of parents and brothers alike, with little thought beyond her own fancies and pleasures and certainly little thought of others. How easy her life had been then and how hard it was now. There was an expression in Ireland, The Hard Life, the sort of life you associated with the Gaelic speaking indigents of the west coast, people so poor they lived on seaweed. Well, these aboriginals were the self-same dwellers on the fringe of the civilized world. What she had learnt, she felt, was that the line between her former life and this one was so thin as to be invisible and at any moment you could cross over and find yourself on the wrong side of it, side by side with the aboriginals of County Clare or Western Australia. Here it was of no consequence that she was the daughter of the late John McMahon or that one of her brothers was a leading heart surgeon and another had his own company, she was as nothing here. And the only thing that mattered, she divined, was kindness.

She had spent the most of her life being thoughtless and careless of other people. She determined to be a better person, to be kind and caring. If there would be one thing that would come out of all this hardship, that would make the Odyssey worth the suffering, it would be to truly *be*. To see the world around her for the way it really was. To judge others neither by the money in their pocket nor the colour of their skin. To have … what was the word she was struggling for? Compassion. That was it; that was the crux.

She would write to her brother Kevin, she would tell him the truth of their condition, she would hold nothing back and she would not be ashamed of it any more. This life had given her something more precious than gold, than fame or position, it had brought her to wisdom. All these grand thoughts swirled about through Maeve's mind as she beat the eggs for the lemon drizzle cake.

The cake was warm in its tin when she dropped Patsy off with Betty. Betty was full of talk of a nice little bungalow for sale near Greys Beach, not far from their daughter Trudi—just what they were wanting when Bram retired and Betty confided that she was trying to persuade him they could afford to do it now. She tapped her nose. 'I think I've succeeded, but keep it under your hat.' Then she looked squarely at Maeve. 'You're really going over to Billangilil?'

Maeve nodded. 'It's the least I can do.'

'Wouldn't you wait for Patrick to go with you?—Or, he could take the cake.'

Maeve explained the difficulties and pressures of time and children; this way she would be back before the school bus.

'Well, you be careful. And hold on to your bag, that mob'd have the tyres off the van quick as a flash.'

316

Maeve couldn't deny that she felt a nervous flutter as she turned off the Anderson-Stiller Road and over the grilles heading down the track to the enclave which served as an aboriginal workers camp for the area. A wild pack of barking dogs raced up to greet her as she pulled into the rubbish strewn compound of dismal looking corrugated iron huts interspersed with the occasional lean-to. Maeve clutched the steering wheel and wondered if she should just turn around. There was no way she could step out of the van with these rabid dogs at her heels.

A man lolling under the shade of one of the flimsy structures yelled and a couple of the dogs loped away but the rest persisted, one young dog jumping up and scraping at the van door. The man did not move. The camp seemed otherwise deserted and then Maeve noticed a huddle of women sitting in a circle under a shady gum, she waved to them and called, 'Hello.'

They ignored her or chose not to hear.

Maeve was beginning to feel ridiculous. All her good intentions fast ebbing away. No wonder people said these people were lazy and ignorant and did nothing to help themselves, she could see this now for herself.

'Yous from the Welfare?'

It was an elderly woman, who had come up on the passenger side. 'Yous from the Welfare?' The woman repeated with a note of hostility.

'No, no.' Maeve reassured; whatever *The Welfare* was. 'I'm looking for Mrs Down?'

The old woman appeared blankly uncomprehending.

'Ben's wife? Do you know where I can find her? I have a gift for her.'

'Auntie Maali?'

Maeve felt hopeless.

'Not here, missus.'

'Oh.' Maeve sighed, exhausted with disappointment.

The old woman pointed into the bush. 'Got them own camp

317

that mob.'

A small boy with a shock of dark curly hair and bright eyes appeared beside the woman.

'You lookin' for Binni's mum?'

'Benny, yes Benny.' Maeve agreed eagerly.

'I can show you. Got to walk.' The boy paused then. 'Not from the Welfare, are you?'

'No.' Maeve smiled. 'I have a cake.'

'A cake?' The boy's eyes lit up.

Maeve opened the van door with the cake tin clasped to her chest.

The boy shouted and waved at the dogs to keep back.

'What kinda cake?'

'Lemon drizzle.'

'Walala!' He grinned a toothless grin.

Maeve followed close on the boy along a track through the bush. The boy said his name was Witty Anna and the babble of his chatter distracted Maeve from the dry crackling sounds of the bush, the whoop whoop of birds overhead and her fear of snakes.

A small, terrier sprang towards them baring his teeth with a low fierce growl.

'Bubai!' A young woman was calling the dog back, he gave a last dart forward with a yap of triumph and then turned back wagging his tail in a friendly way and immediately returned to the shelter which Maeve could now see in the clearing ahead.

At first glance this camp seemed even more primitive than the previous, there was no corrugated iron roofing only simple structures of branches and bark. But on second looking Maeve could see that it was swept clear around the fire pit and all was kept very tidy and orderly.

A young woman stood by the main shelter, eying Maeve with undisguised hostility. Despite her brown skin tone what struck Maeve immediately was the European cast of her features. The woman folded her arms across her bosom and continued to stare.

'Mrs Down?' Maeve ventured.

Still there was no response. Maeve was reminded of the sort of dumb insolence of which one of her classmates was habitually accused by Sr Perpetua; a bad end had been forecast and indeed the girl disappeared over to England as soon as she was of an age to leave home.

Maeve held out the round tin. 'It's only a small thank you. For Ben's kindness.'

'It's cake!' Witty Anna leapt forward. 'Lemon-drizz cake!'

Obligingly, Maeve opened the lid to display the contents. The warm smell wafting in to the clearing.

'Walala!'

As if from nowhere another young boy appeared.

'Binni!' The woman shouted in alarm, but he was already half way across the yard his nose rushing ahead to greet the sweet, sharp smell of the lemon.

'For us missus?'

Maeve beamed as much from relief at the break in tension as at the sight of the wide gleeful smile of the boy with his honey skin and blonde curls. Was this Benny? Maeve mused. Could he really be the son of the black man?

'Benny?'

The boy nodded furiously and ogled the cake. 'Look mum, for us!'

Maeve handed the tin to the grinning boy.

'Thanks missus. You Niv's mum?'

'Yes, yes that's right.'

'Niv is my frind.'

Maeve nodded slowly understanding that this must be the boy who Nieve claimed to have met on his Walkabout. She felt a prang of conscience for having doubted the story.

'Well.' said Maeve. 'Many thanks again to Ben. My son has made a great recovery. And do please keep the tin.'

Maeve took a step back, ready to leave, although the return she suspected would lack an escort as she noted the smaller boy, Witty Anna, hovering hopefully at Benny's shoulder.

'You want to sit? Have a drink.' A frown still lingered on the woman's face but her eyes had softened.

A woven mat was produced and Maeve watched fascinated

319

as Binni, face concentrated, lit a fire using what they called a *fire stick*. Maali, as the woman introduced herself, showed Maeve around their small camp and answered Maeve's queries with a shyness lurking behind the apparent bravado. Maeve genuinely marveled over the patterned weave of the dilly bags.

As they sipped the strange but refreshing tisane and the children eagerly licked the lemony crumbs from their lips, Maeve felt emboldened to more personal enquiry. From which she learnt that Maali and Ben had come down from the north. When she asked about other family there had been a silence. Then, haltingly Maali explained that as a small child she had been taken from her mother and brought to a Mission Settlement. They rubbed soap in her mouth to force her to speak English. At fifteen she was sent to work on a remote cattle station in the Pilbarra.

'Treat us like slave, like they own us.'

The look of anger which flashed across Maali's face made Maeve feel ashamed. Ashamed for all the sins these white people had visited on Maali. A memory came to her, a conversation in Sydney. With Bonnie? She couldn't remember, but whoever it was had explained that the aborigine were dealt with by the Department of Flora and Fauna. The woman made a joke about native wildlife. To her shame, Maeve remembered that she viewed the information as little more than a peculiarity of their new country.

'You must come to visit.' Maeve blurted. 'For dinner.'

Maali's face creased up then and she laughed, her whole body shaking with mirth. And the children, although clearly not certain as to the joke caught the laughter like a contagion and were soon rolling about the ground exciting the tan terrier who rose from his slumber and yapped in and out of their heels.

Nonplussed for a moment at this response to her invitation Maeve felt the infectious laughter tickle at the corners of her mouth, then bubble up in her throat until it heaved between her lips and came spilling through her nostrils. Round and round the laughter seemed to go, with a catch of the eye and a slap on the thigh to keep it spinning like the plates in a circus ring. Maeve's eyes watered as the laughter exploded through her like an uncorked well of feelings unexpressed.

She only half noticed the dog stand stock still, ears pricked, then dash off up the track

The laughter was gulped down in fits and starts by the time Maeve heard the fierce yapping of the dog they called Bubby and then a harrowing squeal.

Binni was up like a rocket. 'Bubai!'

'Binni!' His mother was calling him back, a wave of panic crashing through her voice.

It was too late.

As the boy stooped to pick up the limping, whimpering dog which returned into the clearing he was gripped by the scruff of his T shirt by a large white man in uniform.

'Hang on to him Len!'

'Alright Sarge.' The young constable called back up the path and grabbed the squirming boy around the chest, pinning his arms and lifting him off the ground.

Sgt. Brooke rolled into the clearing mopping his brow. 'Annie Murphy. I got an order to take this boy down to Mogumber.'

Maali was already on her feet, launching herself at the big young constable, a heart-rending scream strangled in her throat.

'Mum, mum!' Binni kicked.

Maeve caught the look of terror in little Witty Anna's eyes as he upped and bolted for the trees. She felt herself in some kind of nightmare as she turned in time to see the constable swat Maali away with a vicious elbow full to the face which knocked her to the ground.

'Look, let's have no trouble Annie, no point with the argy bargy.' Wearily Sgt. Brooke waved a piece of paper. 'It's for the boy's own good.' He nodded towards the struggling child, 'Boy like him don't want to grow up with a loada good for nothing blackfellas.'

Maali was clawing at the constable's legs, a stream of barely decipherable oaths gushing from her lips. Len tried to shake her off, kicking out with his boots.

Maeve found her feet at last. 'Sgt. Brooke!'

'Come on Len, we haven't got all day.'

Len caught Maali under the chin with the full force of his boot and staggered back still clutching the wriggling, crying boy.

'Sgt. Brooke!'

The Sergeant glanced round as though taking in Maeve's presence for the first time. 'You from Welfare?'

'Sergeant, this can't be right. You can't just take the boy away from his mother like this.'

'Orders is orders.' The Sergeant shrugged, shifting the belt around his portly frame.

'But there must be some mistake, this boy is well cared for, he has a good mother and I know his father—'

'Not from these parts, are you Mrs?'

'No, but—'

'I'd advise you stay out of things you don't understand then.'

'I understand enough to know that this is an assault on human decency!'

Binni yelped as Len grappled him tighter and headed towards his sergeant.

Maeve stepped out into his path. 'Can't you see you're hurting him!'

Len halted, momentarily, caught in the flashlight of Maeve's piercing blue eyes.

'Let him go, you're hurting him!' she accused again, scarcely resisting the urge in herself to lunge out at this great hulking brute with his strained and bulging muscles.

Perhaps it was the prospect of another Fury launching herself at him that occasioned Len's grip to falter, loosening a fraction. Enough for Binni to seize the opportunity to wriggle free. As his feet touched the ground, he flew across the clearing.

'Mum, mum – run!' He shouted. But Maali was out cold on the hard earth.

Len was momentarily stunned.

'For crissakes Len – go on and catch the little blighter!'

Len lumbered after the disappearing boy.

Maeve found that she was trembling through her whole body whether from anger or shock she did not know.

Then Sgt. Brooke was pressing his florid face up to hers, his piggy eyes narrow and hard. 'You are under arrest right here and now Mrs Whoever-the-hell-you-are for obstructing an officer of the law in the performance of his duty!'

THE OPEN INVITATION

Patrick was still in shock. He had arrived back at the compound to find a distraught Betty running out onto her verandah and waving them down. Leaning in at the passenger window she explained that there had been a call from Mrs Anderson telling her the Irish woman had been taken into custody. Betty was looking after the children.

'Maeve, arrested!'

'Shush, keep your voice down, I don't want to alarm the children. I've told them their mother had to go into Darinup. They are curious beyond belief, of course.'

'Thanks Betty. I'd better get going – do you know why? Did they say why!?'

Betty shook her head. 'No. But your van is still over at Billangilil.'

'Billangilil!?'

Bram shifted into gear. 'Come, I will take you.'

And now here they were drawing up outside the police station. Patrick leapt out with the ute still in motion.

Sgt. Brooke himself was at the desk.

'Ah Paddy, been expecting you.'

'My wife?'

'Your wife is a proper little tiger, mate. Been shouting the odds all avo. Threatening to call up Ambassadors and God knows what. You want to keep her on a tighter leash mate.' The big man snorted. 'Kept us all entertained, mind you. Makes a change, a fine Sheila like her in the can.'

'You have her locked up! Will someone tell me what the blazes is going on?'

Sgt. Brooke puffed himself up to his full height.

324

'Obstruction. Possible Accessory—'

'What are you talking about?'

'We have the orders right here.' He tapped the desk. 'Half-caste kid over at Billangilil, Protector of Aborigines wants him in. You need to talk to your wife about the way things are done around here.'

Patrick took a breath to curb his anger, 'I will.' he assured, desperate to see Maeve.

'Well then ...' The Sgt. hitched his belt. 'You're lucky I haven't had time to write out an arrest sheet. Let's leave it at a warning this time.' He wagged his finger. 'A very strong warning mate – and you can tell your wife, there's an open invitation for her here.' He jerked his thumb behind him. 'If she so much as—' He left the words unspoken. 'Got it?'

'Yes Sergeant, thanks Sergeant. I'll tell her.'

'Len!' The big man yelled back into the hinter regions of the station. 'You can let the Queen of Sheba out now!'

'I want to go home Patrick.' Maeve declared as they emerged into the twilight, brushing back a tear she had been so obviously straining to keep at bay.

'That's where I'm taking you right now, macushla.'

'No. I don't mean here. I mean our real home. Ireland. I hate this country, Patrick, I hate its mean hard people that can do that to a child.'

He sighed, 'Now Maeve ...'

'I mean it, Patrick.' The tears were brimming now.

He tried to put his arm around her but she pushed him away.

'We'll be out of this fix before you know it and then—'

'Then what?' she sniffed, trying to force the tears back.

'I'll make it up to you, I promise you, for all this hard times. Our luck will change.'

'It isn't the hard times Patrick, its ...' her voice trailed off hopelessly. Then she turned to him stopping him in his tracks. 'Kindness. The world needs more kindness in it. That's what's important.' The plea in her eyes cut him to the quick.

He resolved that he would try and spend more time with Maeve and the children. He was working all the hours that God sent to try and dig them out of the debt but he could see now it was at the expense of the love and affection which Maeve craved. He had neglected her. Taken her for granted. And this was the upshot.

He would take the weekend off. They'd all go on a picnic, the one he had been promising for so long in the nature reserve.

BEN DOWN AND THE FOOTSTEPS OF THE ANCESTORS

Me and Doubleday get back to camp. I see Irish fella's van, that funny. Why he comin' Billangilil? Roy step in front of car—Doubleday got to brake hard. He been on the grog.

'Come take them gunji.' he shout.

Ruby she come over, say I got to get to Maali quick.

I run. Something happen bad. I know. Bubai don't come to meet me.

There is a fire. Smell medicine 'n Auntie Maggie stirring pot. In the humpy I see old woman she bending over Maali, Auntie Ivy singing old song. My heart beating hard, something bad happen.

Maali is beat up. Face all swollen 'n cut. One eye closed. She confuse but she see me. She try sit up.

'Binni? Gunji get Binni?!' Maali ask.

I look at Aunties. Where Binni?!

Old woman shake her head, 'Gunji don't get Binni. That boy run fast. Sergeant Brooke 'im mad like cut snake!'

Auntie Maggie laugh. ''Is face red like bush pig bum!'

Binni gone. Think fast fast. I nod to Maali, 'I know where Binni gone. Good place. Binni be safe.' I take her hand. 'You gotta rest up.'

'No.' Maali try sit up again, try to speak, 'We go. We gotta leave this bad place.'

'Two, three days I be back, then—'

'Now.' Maali say.

I shake head, she look beat up, hurtin' bad. Maybe can't stand, can't walk. Maali look me.

'Maali ...'

Auntie Ivy nod, 'Gunji come back. Make big trouble.'

Maali spit blood. 'She's right, Ben.'

I nod, 'We go.' Even if I gotta carry her.

Maali sound in bad pain.

'Lie still.' I say.

Old woman keep Maali down.

'Gotta clear camp.'

Maali laugh, 'No need do that!'

'Told Boss Anderson I clean up when we leave.'

'Don't need do nothing for that waipela.'

'Make promise.'

She doesn't speak. Bad pain. Auntie Maggie bring medicine.

I look at camp. Been big trouble. All kicked about. Bowl and biscuit tin and cake. Not much to take, maybe one bag. I tell Aunties take the rest.

'What we gonna tell Boss Anderson?'

'Tell 'im we gone Walkabout.'

'Got wages end of week.'

'Tell 'im to give Doubleday.'

Auntie Maggie laugh. I laugh same. Them wages stay right in Boss Anderson pocket.

Noise close by. I see Bubai lyin' in grass. Little dog beat up real bad. Stroke him, feel his broken body, big eyes look me, say he done all he can. Anger hot in me but I say soft soft like in his ear. 'Bubai ... Bubai ...' I know what I gotta do. Hold him close—make end quick-like.

Getting' dark we leave that camp. Maali won't wait. We walk long way on road to Thirty-Six Gate, then there is bush.

Maali cursing wadjela, she say we find Binni, keep moving, up country. I know her. Muda muda woman, belong no place. Annie Murphy her name. Mission send her to cattle station. She runaway. Found her mother on the grog. No help with child she carryin'. She want this baby dead but he born anyway. Binni—he take her heart even he look like his father; wadjela come up took her in chicken house and leave 'er cryin' in dirt.

Maali don't want nothing to do with wadjela no more. You

328

know, wadjela done bad things our mob. One time I see skull in truck, on dashboard. Wadjela laugh say, *That your brother mate!*

Sun come up, I say we gotta stop, rest up. Maali in lotta pain. Stop, have some tucker. First chance I got to think—thinkin' Binni gone to caves, sacred place I been show him. But what if he gone back to Anderson land, him 'fraid? Maybe back at Billangilil? He seen our camp gone. Aunties don't know where we go. One bad fella Roy wantin' get reward give Binni to the gunji.

Worry now. When Maali safe, get back double-quick. I got Binni's marbles; leave message, make picture with marbles Wan the Crow. Big rock next to cave. Binni name it *Crow Rock*. Look like Wan sitting up gum with beak tucked in and one eye look at us—we tasty nuf to eat!

Thinkin' 'bout Binni, that time, make me smile. We put sticks in hair 'n laugh, say Wan think we echidna now, all sharp-like, no good for tucker! Binni be at the caves; feel it like song singing in my bones.

We rest up 'til avo. Maali little better but she been hurt bad. Bone maybe broke in 'er face. One side her body she got lotta bruises. She lean on me for walkin'.

This bush got plenty good tucker. Old times good country for our mob, Wadjela take all the good country. Now all wheat 'n sheep.

We walking near creek. Can see wooden table under river gum. Got barbie, it still smokin'. Swings for kid. Good place for swimmin'.

There one family in the water. It's the Irish fella. His boy Joh Joh got bit bark like canoe. It going down creek. He shout, 'Look mammie!'

She smilin'.

Irish fella got little one 'n dipping in and out water like sheep. She happy shoutin' too.

One more girl. Binni see this girl on walkabout. She got long stick stabbin' in water—she not gonna catch them fish that way!

We stay close to trees, they don't see us. Then I stop.

Quiet-like I put five quandong on table. Irish fella know it gift.

Night we rest again. Put medicine on Maali. She sleep. I hold her, sing soft-like. Thinkin' first time I see her; young maandi then. Walking on dirt road. Little fella on her back. I had old car, been workin' the Kimberleys. Left my mob long time back. I stop car to look this maandi. She walk right pass. I shout, 'You want lift?'

She shake her head, don't look me. I drive but that old car playin' up, I cursin' 'n bang steering wheel. She come up again. She take little look, I see she got smile, like I silly fella. Little one he pointin' at me. I grinnin' funny, make 'im laugh.

'Where ya goin'?' she ask.

'Nowhere quick-like. Where you goin'?'

'Some place got no waipela.'

I nod. 'Nowhere you get quick.'

'You real black fella?'

I nod.

'Initiated?'

I nod again.

'Should be with your mob.'

'Trouble with woman.' I say.

She don't like that, shut her mouth tight.

'This way good campin' 'bout mile up. I make good camp.'

She don't look me. Keep walkin'.

'Got plenty tucker too.'

Old car start again, drive to camp place. Car hot. Wait for cool down then I open bonnet. Clean up old fire and rubbish from last mob. When mandi come I got fire 'n makin' fresh wurlie.

She feeding her baby. She look me, 'You show me how to make?'

I grin. 'Make one just for you.'

She look me—not sure.

'And little fella.' I say.

'Binni.'

'Binni? Binni a good name.'

Maali she learnin' fast, hungry for old ways. Then the dry come. I say we got to go back wadjela country. Maali not happy. Got no choice, you know.

I look. Maali awake, she hurtin'. She want go my born country and never come back; she worry wadjela take Binni away—same like she took from her mother.

Sun high now and I see Crow Rock. My heart beatin'. Is Binni here? Him safe? I know Maali 'fraid, she not good, need plenty rest. I call out like kookaburra. Listen. Insects buzzin' loud. Call again, like crazy kookaburra. Listen. Then thump, thump, animal running. Strange black animal got spikes come runnin' from bush.

'Dad! Dad!'

This wild animal jump in my arms. I hold him 'n look. Binni got black charcoal on his skin, in his yella hair, even 'im shorts and he got sticks in his hair. Sticks make me grin.

His eyes big, he happy and 'fraid both. 'Won't want me now, will they dad? Now, I look like black fella, won't see me, will they?'

I grin, 'You are black fella Binni, 'n now look handsome fella—like me!'

Then he see Maali, her face beaten up, and she bendin'.

'Mum!'

She shake head. Open arms wide wide.

Binni run to her. She hold him. They cryin', big tears.

This place sacred. Back in old time ancestors come here. They paint stories in this cave. Ancestors, they part of this country, part of this rock. Kangaroos, birds, lizards, some half-fella, half-bird. Hands painted too. All over, feel them pushin' in the rock. I put my hand on the ancestor hand and he talk to me.

331

Next day I show Binni; put charcoal in mouth and blow black-like—round fingers 'n hands. Three hands. We leave our story here with the ancestors.

ON PARADE

Nieve had been entered into the junior long jump and the high jump, due to her long legs rather than any proven ability. Indeed, she had never even attempted a proper high jump with a frame and a bar. John John was in the Boys Relay team along with Tony and Brian. The inter-schools' games were to be held at the brand-new stadium in Bodenham. A school bus would take all seventeen of them and Sr Gobbleshoe and Sr Joseph their headmistress. Even Vincent, Maria's brother who had polio, was entered into the shot put for which he had been practicing assiduously. A pennant had been made with the name of the school and one of the older boys, Philip, would be carrying it at the head of their small group in the parade.

For weeks they marched up and down the school yard. Sr Gobbleshoe kept time and Sr Joseph admonished them to keep their chins up and to lift their feet – with the exception of Vincent who would bring up the rear. They marched in pairs, Nieve with Maria of course. No one expected them to win anything, not up against all the bigger schools with their gyms and sports facilities but they were exhorted to carry forth the honour of the school. Nieve was more excited than she could have imagined. She had never attended anywhere long enough to feel that she belonged. Mammie bought new white gym shoes, which, with her brown gingham frock freshly pressed, was to be the uniform for the day and she would wear it with pride.

Her mammie traveled down to Bodenham with Maria's parents; Nieve only wished her da had been able to come along too so that he could see them marching around the track of the stadium.

The schools were all being lined up behind the grandstand in readiness for the opening parade. A woman with a clipboard was trying to organise the order in which they would enter whilst overexcited youngsters were still milling into their squads. St. Pius RC, was to come directly behind the school in Darinup.

'Oww!' Nieve felt a sharp twinge in her left arm followed by a thump.

'A pinch and a punch for the first of the month!' Netta accompanied her assault with a smirk.

Nieve cradled her aching arm and winced at the pain.

'And a slap and a kick for being so quick!'

They were all taken aback by the suddenness and vehemence of Maria's retaliation. None more so than Maria herself.

Who knew how Netta might have reacted if the officious woman with the clipboard had not noted the different uniforms, 'Come on girls you should be with your own school by now!'

'I'll get yous later ...' Netta hissed.

A fanfare belted out across the PA system. Then, an announcement officially opening the games followed by a loud and strident marching tune vibrating through the speakers. Up ahead the first of the schools set off and were announced to tumultuous applause.

Nieve's breath quickened as Philip hoisted the pennant above his head and began to shout the time, 'And one and two and march two three four, hup two three four!'

They were moving as one, heads held high and proud just as Sr Joseph had taught them. Through the tunnel into the stadium and the cloudless sky overhead. Nieve was sure that she could hear her mother calling her name in amongst the cheers and whistles and clapping. She had played Mary Mother of Baby Jesus in the nativity play but it did not compare to the hundreds of eyes that were trained on her now, she felt herself flush, if only the da could see her too.

'Hup two three ...' beside her, Maria kept the rhythm

through gritted teeth as she raised her knees with military precision.

A light breeze came up behind them and ruffled Nieve's hair across her eyes. She should have clipped it back as her mammie had wanted but she hated the tight tug of the hairgrips and the way they accentuated her widow's peak. Suddenly her left knee was not coming up, she was lurching forward, flailing to retrieve her balance and heard the gasp from Maria. As Nieve tried to keep her head up she had time to see that the shoe laces of her left gym shoe had come loose.

'Two, three ...'

She was against the beat. The left going up when it should have been the right. And then another stumble and Tony was kneeing the back of her legs and she heard the curse under his breath. And worse, laughter and a catcall from the stands.

'Three, four ...' Maria louder beside her. 'Left, right!'

A cheer and a whistle accompanied the ripple of laughter spreading along the North Stand in their wake. Nieve wanted to melt into the track with the shame. Rising and falling on her tips hoping not to trap the loose shoe lace. Lip nearly bitten off with the effort to concentrate all her body on keeping in time with the rank and file. And then at last the tunnel came into sight again and the snake of marching schools was swallowed up into its dark anonymity with a final blast of triumphal music.

Sr Joseph simply glowered, which was almost worse than a reproach. But Philip stuck his pointy nose in her face, 'Are you the big baby who can't tie her shoelaces?!'

The PA crackled into life again and the Announcer was declaring calling for the first athletes.

Sr Gobbleshoe took her shoulder. 'Let's try a double knot.'

John John and the other boys came last in the first heats of the Boys Relay. The Games were nearing their end and St. Pius had won nothing, their best result had been Vincent's fourth in the Senior Shot Put; 'Almost a medal!' Sr

Gobbleshoe beamed.

Netta gained a Bronze in the Girls Long Jump, sneering at Nieve's efforts and guffawing every time she fell backwards onto her bottom.

Now it was the Junior Girls High Jump and Nieve was St. Pius last contender in the Games. They all gathered to watch. She surprised herself in the early round. The girl ahead of her leapt up to the bar like a hurdler, one leg extending over and dragging the other behind. The better ones threw themselves a little to the side. Her heart was beating a tattoo as she made her own run up with scarcely a notion which leg would give lift off, wondering if it would hurt when she hit the bar and then to her amazement she found her body twisting backwards over the bar her legs kicking up behind her and she flopped with a thump onto her bottom on the pile of mats. Netta shrieked with laughter but as Nieve looked up to her amazement she saw that the bar was still in place.

'Whatever way was that?' Maria gawped at Nieve when she came back to the line-up.

'A bottom flop!' came John John's response.

Nieve flushed and grinned to herself.

Netta poked her in the ribs. 'Little miss RC, let's see you land on your RC good and proper next time!'

They raised the bar. Would it work again? It did. Her face thrusting skyward, sailing through blue, applause ringing loud about her ears. It was the greatest moment of her life.

With bursting pride Nieve strode up to receive the silver medal behind the lanky girl from Bodenham and, on her tail to collect the Bronze, Netta's whispered taunts and jibes were ignored.

THE RADDLE

It was the final day. All day he had been channeling the sheep from the pens towards the shearers. The pressure was on. The shearers would be loading into their vans and jalopies and on to the next shire tomorrow. Patrick looked over the pens and wondered would they get through them all but the shearers seemed to have shifted up a gear with the lure of the cash in hand at the end of the day. Patrick marveled at their speed and dexterity. He could see Boss Anderson watched them with a beady eye. They joked, even to his face, about how legendary Old Jack Anderson had been with the raddle.

'Strewth, I hear tell the bugger near enough built this station with that bit of red chalk!'

'Meaner than a Dutch Uncle!' an old timer added.

They were all seasoned professionals and when one sorry sheep did receive the raddle, they guffawed with the hilarity of it, until the Boss, rattled, went off and left Alex in charge.

Patrick observed it all from the corner of his eye. He liked the easy way these men had. They were beholding to no one. They had a demand for their skill and the freedom of the road. He envied them. If he were a younger man. He had chosen the sea to do his roaming but not been his own master.

Then he saw Nieve and John John watching enthralled from behind a fence where Tom was helping to stack the wool for baling. What was the freedom of the road compared to their love? They saw him and jumped up and down waving frantically, their faces bright with excitement. He flushed. He wanted more than anything that they should be proud of him. It had been there for the taking, Killpool Hill, his heart sank at the memory. So close he had come to the fulfillment

337

of all his dreams. What pride was in that wheat and how bitter was the fall. Now, here he was, the heat of an outback summer already a promise in the air, a paid labourer. A debt still to be paid and a wage that barely kept them all alive. He could feel his bile rising, what more did God want of him? Was the luck never to be his?

He was teamed with Ken. Patrick could smell the whisky on his breath from the little nips took all day and the effects were showing, he was slowing down, stumbling over the sheep. Patrick was fed up trying to cover for him with Alex breathing down their necks. Everyone wanted the job finished. He had scarcely taken ten minutes over his sandwiches at lunch, whilst Ken disappeared for half an hour. And now Ken had disappeared again for 'a slash'. Alex was fuming. Some of the shearers complained they weren't getting the sheep fast enough, the language they used was choice. Alex moved one of the aboriginals, Doubleday, alongside him. A taciturn man, he didn't speak much but could handle sheep. Alex was swearing how he'd shove Ken's 'smoke-oh's' up his arse. Ken never did show again. Dead drunk somewhere, Patrick reckoned.

The sun was past setting by the time the last run of sheep was sheared and he was dog tired. As he queued up to collect his monthly pay packet alongside the shearers who were stuffing fresh rolls of banknotes into their pants a chap called Doug slapped him on the back. 'Good-oh Paddy, you done a grand job. Fancy a beer, mate? Reckon I could down a couple of kegs!'

The smell of the lamb stew being cooked up in the cook house by Maggie and Jari wafted over to them. He'd told Maeve he would be late, that a cold supper would do. Now the prospect of hot stew, a cool beer and the company of these good-natured rowdies grabbed him by the throat. How often did he have the opportunity of an evening amongst men and their talk?

The stew revived him. Not a patch on the succulence of the

Irish Stew which Maeve could conjure up even out here in the Outback. Too much gristle and salt in Jari's pot, still he put his plate out for seconds like all the rest and the thin light beer the Aussies favoured took the edge off his worries. Patrick leaned back, stretching his stiff joints. The talk was all of 'that bastard Cooke'. The Nedlands Monster; for whose killings Patrick had briefly, but devastatingly, been suspect. Would Eric Cooke finally face the hangman's drop or would some other Appeal, some new *death bed confession* serve to extend his stretch?

'He's a cunning little shite.' said one.

Another shook his head. There'll be a mob will lynch him they don't do it quick – and I'll be first in the queue!'

'Mad bugger. Can't figure why he'd do it all.'

'Said he wanted to hurt people.'

There was a silence for a moment.

'His wife says she knew nothing about it ... '

'He'll drop for sure. Monster like that.'

Patrick could feel the tight ring of anger around the table. He hadn't thought too much about Eric Cooke lately, not since the days after they captured him. The relief he'd felt that the coppers were finally off his own back. The press were full of the lurid details, the confessions, the queer pugnacious little man glaring off the covers of the newspapers. What shocked Patrick, almost more than anything else, was that Cooke had seven children, a family man, how did you square that with the murdering maniac?

He remembered with a shiver the morning Nieve leaned over his shoulder to peer at the crooked face, 'That's the Tooth Fairy.' and then put her hand to her mouth and whispered, 'I wasn't to tell.'

'Tell what?'

She shook her head, alarm in her eyes.

With coaxing he drew out the story of the shilling tooth. It made his blood run to ice but he did not let her see this.

'Your da will keep you safe.' He'd said. 'Your da will always be here to protect you.' Hugging her in close.

Good job of that he had made. Only the other day she

339

returned from the Schools Games her dress ripped, tear stained and her arms covered in shocking bruises.

Maeve stopped his questions and put all three to bed in a strange silence, even the normally ebullient John John.

Then Maeve sat with him at the kitchen table and turned her hands one inside the other. 'Sr Joseph is threatening to expel Nieve.'

He leapt from his chair.

'Sit down, Patrick.'

He put his hands on the table leaning over to her. 'What happened?'

'There was a fight with a girl from Darinup. Just after the closing ceremony. Sr Joseph said Nieve was like a mad thing, she had the girl strangled by the throat and was squeezing the life out of her. The girl was kicking and punching to be let loose but Nieve wouldn't let go. It was only Sr Veronica got them apart in the end. The officials were called by the girl's family. There was even a policeman.'

Patrick had been unable to digest it all.

'That was when I got there, all set to congratulate Nieve on her big prize!' Maeve shook her head, there were tears pricking at her eyes he could see. For a moment she couldn't speak. He reached over to hold her hand. 'If you'd seen the state she was in. White and trembling head to foot. And that big lump of a girl screaming that Nieve had tried to kill her.'

Maeve sniffed back the welling tide. 'Her friend Maria said it was this Netta started it, there was no one denied that.'

'That's alright so.' He heaved with relief.

'No, Patrick. It wasn't just some playground scuffle. Don't you see, Nieve nearly killed that girl, it was like a madness in her, nothing would make her let go – you've seen the bruises for yourself!'

'Macushla ...'

'This other family weren't going to let up. Sr Joseph was very shaken with it all. She said Nieve would be punished. And then Netta's mother said Nieve was a loony and she should see a doctor.' Maeve swallowed hard. 'She's not said

340

a word since, Patrick. What are we to do?'

'Nieve, does not need any quack. The girl attacked her, a bigger girl you said. Nieve was protecting herself; alright in the heat of it she didn't know to let go, she's a child!'

And so it had gone on, urgent whispers across the table until he soothed her nerves whilst inside, he boiled and fumed.

'.. the Game.'

Patrick emerged from his reverie to see Bert leaning over him with a gleam in his eye. 'Game?'

'A couple of these cobbers asked if we'd like to stay for the Game.'

Patrick was none the wiser and looked it.

'Poker.'

'No. I'd best get home.'

'They'll be long in their beds.'

Poker. Patrick hadn't played Poker since the long nights on the ship coming up from Buenos Aires. With Mick. He shook his head and laughed. 'I've only ever played with matchsticks. I don't have the dosh.'

'We're not playing for Sheep Stations.' Bert laughed. Then seeing that Patrick did not comprehend the phrase, Bert explained as though to a child. 'There'll be a limit on the stake. Only a bit of fun mate.'

Patrick hesitated. A couple of hands, just for the craic, what could be the harm in that and when had he last allowed himself to enjoy the company of men.

BEN DOWN AND THE BORN COUNTRY

Maali want to move on. Afraid of gunji. Like it better when she angry. Tell her Sgt. Brooke he not find us. Gunji don't track up in hills.'

'He lazy bugger. ' I say.

Want Maali rest up. She look brave but I seen 'er movin' 'bout hard.

Binni like to live in cave, like time we together. I been hunting 'stead of dipping sheep. It all big adventure to Binni. But night he cry in sleep, wake up all sweat. I know he 'fraid wadjela come steal him.

Been working hard for Boss Anderson—but not thinkin about Binni. Wadjela can take him—anytime. No good. Break our heart and we all crying, crying. Binni he clever fella but Moore River teach 'im wadjela way, They think he only half man.

Maali say we go my born country where wadjela not look. .

'We go there.' she whisper in night. 'Go to your born country.'

I nod. Make her happy.

THE DEADMAN'S HAND

A halo of smoke hung over the poker table. There'd been a couple of tables at the start of the evening but now there was only one. Just as he'd been about to withdraw, Patrick had hit a lucky streak which started with a flush. He played it coolly, no sudden big raise, just let the pot build steadily. He felt bad when he saw Bert hazard the last of his month's wages, Patrick could tell by the twitch in the lad's left eye that the game was become too rich for him and from the way he kept sneaking a look at his cards anyone could see he was thinking to bluff in a last desperate attempt to claw back some winnings. Alex Anderson wasn't doing much better but there was a deeper hole in his pocket.

With each round Patrick vowed it would be his last, quit whilst he was ahead. He could hear Maeve whispering in his ear, *come away*, and himself responding, *one more round macushla and I can have us out of here*. It was well after midnight and he was still in the game. Next to him Doug slammed his cards down after a string of rags, groaning that Lady Luck was a floozy. Another shearer simply keeled over dead drunk.

Somewhere outside a man was strumming an old bushman's tune on a guitar and Patrick could hear Stubby singing along, his voice cracked but surprisingly sweet.

Patrick had two Aces in his hand and the Queen of Hearts. The dealer was looking to him for a decision. Would he buy three or two? Poker was not a game for sentiment, Mick taught him that. An older shearer, Digger, had his narrow eyes on him, could smell the hesitation he was sure.

'Two.' He would keep his Queen of Hearts.

He waited until the other three picked up, looking for any glimmer of a sign. The Digger might fancy his chances. The groan was already in Alex face. Woods, the dealer was harder to read. Patrick edged up the corners of his cards. Two eights. Aces and Eights, the Deadman's Hand. He could feel the beads of sweat gathering on his brow under the heat of the spirit lamp suspended above the table.

Patrick fought the impulse to throw in his hand, perhaps it was the lateness of the hour, the rush towards one last fling, the way the Queen of Hearts looked at him, he went in strong. There was a flicker of uncertainty on the Digger's brow and then he raised.   So, it went around and around, an end of the evening recklessness setting in until Alex threw his cards down.

'I'm out boys' Alex leant back in his chair and fiddled in his top pocket for his zippo.

The dealer, Woods, hesitated imperceptibly and then followed suit.

Patrick raised.

The Digger splashed the pot with his remaining stack, to shaking heads all round and claimed a raise.

It was his for the taking. Patrick had only to see and raise again. It had been agreed. No I.O.U.s. Hope was dancing a merry jig as he laid his last stake.

The Digger glared at him across the table.

'You've wiped us all out then Paddy!' Alex blew rings of smoke above their heads.

'Fair play.' Doug added, from his position as an onlooker.

'Not so fast.' Digger was chewing his lip.

'Digger?'

'Woody'll vouch for it. The deeds, I have them in my kit.'

'Mate ...' there was a plaintive plea in the dealer's voice.

'Deeds to what?' Patrick ventured.

'Two hundred and forty acres.' The leather faced man tapped his cards. 'That's what I'll pay to see your hand Paddy.'

A silence of expectation hung over the table and those shearers still awake caught a whiff.

'Up to you Paddy.' Woods shrugged.

'Forget it, Glendon.' Alex stubbed out his cigarette. 'It'll be some fly blown piece of crap doled out by the government in the Back of Bourke, not worth the ink on the paper!'

Patrick calculated, never taking his eyes from Digger. Aces and eights. Would Mick have taken such a risk? Digger needs only three twos to beat it and maybe that's exactly what he has. There were enough notes stacked up at Patrick's side now to pay off Boss Anderson and to see himself and Maeve out of there. He could give Perth another shot. There was no need to accept this stake. Alex would back him up. But the money and a farm. His own farm again. When might that chance come around again?

'Well Paddy?'

He nodded, 'Alright.' And laid his cards face up on the table.

'You bastard!'

A shot whistled past his ear.

Alex was knocked backwards out of his chair.

'You bloody perving bastard!' Ken Duguid reeled in the doorway of the shed, his face puce with rage. 'I'll blast your effing balls off for you, mate!'

Ken staggered forward and the shearers, seeing the dangerous gleam in his eyes and an argument not with one of their own, parted like a red sea. Ken raised a boot to kick the table out of his line of fire. A shot misfired off into the corrugated iron roof overhead.

Alex whimpered on the ground clutching his shoulder, which was seeping blood, his eyes rolling back with the shock.

Patrick stumbled out of the way like the rest but as Ken swung around and tried to regain his balance Patrick knew he must sprint forward and wrestle the rifle from him before he could reload it. Someone will help surely.

Ken was surprisingly quick. The butt caught Patrick squarely in the side of the head and sent him sprawling to the floorboards, the sudden pain rattling through his brain. His eyes squeezed shut.

'You and all Bog-man!' Ken steadied himself, 'Anymore heroes?' he challenged the congregation as he deftly reloaded the rifle. 'No?' The rifle snapped back. Ken stepped forward sneering down at Alex who was curled up into a tight foetal ball of fear.

'That's right you little snake, you bloody squirm.' Ken took aim. 'You think you own us? That it? Take my girl just as you like? Well you're the one that's going to bloody pay!'

A shot reverberated through the swimming darkness as Patrick swooned into unconsciousness.

JACK IN THE BOX

He had lost one brother, was he about to lose another? With a gruff nod of gratitude, he took over from the shearer and shoved the rag hard against the bullet's entry hole to stem the gush of blood. Thoughts were rushing helter-skelter. All his life his father had towered over them. A long bony reach extending far beyond the grave. It was time to step out of the tyranny of his shadow. This was his land now to do with as he would. Old Jack had bound them all together with his obsession to keep the land intact; but there would be lawyers to pick that apart. Finlay would be declared dead. Then he would build a memorial of some kind and bury the ghost. Beside his mother's last resting place. The idea soothed him. After all the years of resentment he could face it head on, his mother loved Finlay above all. Finlay, not steady and capable like John, not bonny looking like Alex, but with the way to make even their stern father smile.

A smile twitched at the corner of his own lips. *A bush pig's arse ...,* even as Finlay had made the jibe Jack had known it was a cod, Maisie Davidson would never have been so crude. Finlay, Finlay ...

Alex groaned, his eyelids fluttering.

Then he would find a way to release Alex. Alex would own Arbroath outright, be his own boss or Jack would give him the going market valuation. Alex could do what he liked, join his wife and daughters in Perth—whatever he damn well pleased. And then perhaps, there might be a day when they could face each other as brothers, as equals.

'The doc's just pulling in.' It was Bram.

He would be alright. Alex would be alright. Stupid horny bastard that he was for raising the skirts of that brat Sally Duguid. Jack groaned, that would be the next mess to be

347

sorted. She'd given birth to a bastard boy. It was seeing her in the agony of labour that set Ken off on this rampage.

Sgt. Brooke was standing over Ken's body. Someone, the Irishman maybe, for he seemed to be one of the few sober men in the place, had thrown a sheet over it. The barracks were crowded with shearers but most were flat out snoring on their bunks, the drama of the hour had palled.

'Self-defense, clear and simple. Duguid was half-cut as usual, went berserk and this sorry bloody outcome. What else could Stubby do?'

Jack tugged at his earlobe. Did the man want a pat on the back for this piece of deduction?

'Coroner will want to take a look, what with Ken being shot in the back. Got a van coming to take the body down to Bodenham.'

Jack nodded. 'Whatever I can do ...'

'Got Stubby out in the cop car. Have to bring Alex in for questioning too, Jack – when he's patched up proper, of course. But it's clear as mud, far as I can see.'

Jack baulked at the familiarity; the way Brooke made it sound like he was doing Jack a favour. He'd always loathed the man.

The Doc pushed his way through and Jack released his brother. He would be alright. That was the important thing.

'Len's made a start collecting statements. No need for you to hang around Jack, seeing as you weren't here.'

Jack gave a curt nod. He suddenly wanted to be out of the fug of smoke and the smell of unwashed men. Outside he could see that the skies were bunched and clouding over. Promising a good rain.

The Irishman stubbed a cigarette underfoot, 'Mr Anderson sir. I'm sorry for your trouble.'

'A bloody shower alright. Hear you tried to step in? Got yourself a shiner. I'm grateful for that, Paddy.'

The Irishman shifted uneasily. 'There's another matter ...'

'And what's that?'

'I have the money I owe you. And a month's notice.'

Jack sized the man up and down. Taking stock. He was a

decent bloke no doubt about it, his sort of bloke.

'And what if I was to tell you that Bram's leaving soon – got himself some retirement bungalow up in Geraldton. What if I was to say, you can make a go of it here, move into his old house, my right-hand man, Paddy?'

'I'd say that was a good offer ...'

Jack held out his hand ready to shake on it.

'But I'll have to decline, Mr Anderson.'

Was the man a fool? Station Manager on the biggest spread in the Shire. Jack pursed his lips. The Irishman was playing a close game, had already heard that Bram was leaving. He even wondered if the claim to have the remainder of the debt was a clever bluff. He allowed himself a smile. What of it. The House always won, wasn't that what they said. 'You'd start on Bram's wages if that's what you're after.'

'No, it's not that Mr Anderson. Thanks for the kind offer but I'm striking out with my own place.'

The Irishman turned about and walked away.

Kind! Jack felt like spitting nails. First the abo gone bloody walkabout, then Bram about to up sticks, that drongo Duguid getting himself killed, Alex and now Paddy all leaving him in the lurch with the wool bailing, the dipping and then the harvesting and the fencing along the Creek Road. Was this the thanks he got. Bastards the lot of them. The first spots of rain pattered at his feet.

'Tom ...' The boy was coming out from the kitchen.

'Boss.'

'Made your statement?'

Tom nodded.

The boy wasn't much for talking that was for sure. So be it.

'Better turn in then, we'll need an early start. And Tom ...' The boy turned back. 'You done a good job this season. I'll see you right.'

'Thanks Boss.'

He'd give the young Pom a rise, Jack decided there and then. Loyalty should be rewarded. Loyalty, that's what counted in the end.

PART THREE

The Back of Bourke

THIS RED HOT SAND

Ninety degrees is nothing you know
A hundred degrees everyone knows
A hundred and fifteen, a record please
A hundred and twenty, complaints are quite free
A hundred and thirty, the fools will exclaim,
A hundred and forty, no one's to blame,
A hundred and fifty, that's mine, I claim.

You exalt this place, who've never been here,
And do extol from an office chair
That, 'There's no place like it (this side of hell)
Why not send the migrants there.'
While you, your dirty filth and smoke,
Your corruption and your joke
Will sit, and sneer, and finally choke.

Do not excuse nature's spree,
These are the facts, don't hide them please,
The horrid dryness is there to see.
Of endless bush, bush and dire salt bush,
Of ants and ants and flies and flies.
This red hot sand, you dare not trod,
Is life, is real, is mine you see.

It's all I have, and mangy sheep,
Enough I have and just my keep.
But look, the difference you see,
I enjoy it and here am free.
The hot wind, amid swirling dust and sticky sweat,
Believe you me, is quite a treat,
There's something here a man can't cheat.

By Slouched Hat

THE END OF THE RAINBOW

Stubby Croker got back to his old shack after the short sojourn in Sgt. Brooke's lock up to find a note on his bunk. In an awkward hand it read simply,

I Owe U the Tin mony
Bert Boswell

The Tin was still under the bed where it had always been kept but sure enough it was empty of his life savings, all those pennies which had turned into pounds.

Stubby looked up at the carpet snake. 'Much use you were.'

The next day word was flying around the station how Sally Duguid and Bert Boswell had done a runner and Sally left the baby with the Dutch couple. The pilot was saying he was the father and he was ashamed for what he had done having taken too much drink and not being in his right mind; but his good wife was sticking by him and they were going to keep his son because it was the right thing to do.

Everyone agreed you couldn't find a more decent bloke than Pieter De Vries and his wife seemed so happy with the baby, it would be a crying shame to take the little chap from them. The general feeling was that it would be an easy matter to sort out the paper work. They'd wink and under their breath say what a close shave that had been for Alex Anderson!

Most figured the young lovers had gone to Perth, lured by the bright lights of the city, and wondered how they'd make out without a brass sou to rub between them.

Stubby knew better and he would shake his head and chuckle every so often. 'Over the rainbow, that's where they's gone.'

Jack grumbled about the old man getting crazier by the day.

One morning Stubby's back was so bad he couldn't lift himself up off the bed. Doc said he needed rest and plenty of it. Jack griped but Alex pointed out that Stubby had never taken a day off work in all his years. He got Jari to see to all the old man's needs.

Alex found that he took a strange comfort in sitting with Stubby some evenings. He fixed up an old lounger on Stubby's porch and the two of them would contemplate the stars in companionable silence with a beer. Or Stubby would listen whilst Alex puzzled over why Jack had suddenly decided to cede him the Arbroath station. The big decision now was whether he should stay or take the price Jack was offering.

Mostly, Stubby liked to be left on his own. His waking hours were filled with dreamings and imaginings. He dreamed of little white bungalows with green lawns and picket fences. He dreamed of a smart car and an open road. He dreamed of cruise ships and far-away places. Airplanes and bright lights and swanky hotels. He dreamed of all the things that could be done with a lifetime's savings. And he imagined young Sally and Boswell enjoying all the fruits of his labour and he grinned and whooped with the pleasure of his imaginings.

THE BACK OF BOURKE

Life were but a little thing worth the gambling. Where had he heard that? Patrick couldn't remember. It felt to him that his very brains were fried in this searing heat, baked within the oven of his skull. Worth the gamble. He looked around the homestead from a high spot on the low range of hills bordering his property. From this vantage you could see a large part of its acreage. To one side lay a low rise and a line of gums below alongside a spindly creek. And then pasture-land and scrub abutting the rock-strewn hills. He had few neighbours, a man called Hobbs to one end and to the north another abandoned property. A scattering of watermills, a ribbon of cockatoo fences hardly worth the name, a lopsided weather-beaten shack with a roof of rusting corrugated iron strips. The interior home and shelter to any number of native inhabitants who Patrick thought wryly had more claim to it than he did.

He was glad to have settled Maeve and the children down in Perth. A small bungalow in Subiaco on a short six-month lease, the rent more than reasonable. Mr Watkins at Lysander Estate and Lettings Agency said that Patrick was doing him a favour; the new owner wasn't ready to move in yet and as he reminded Patrick these short rentals were more trouble than they were worth. That gave him a six month start.

He had come on ahead to get the lay of the land. Passed through a dusty one street town twenty miles back and then bucked over the grille and left the screeching gate open behind and he had the measure of it. It was the Back of Bourke all right, no doubt about it. The question was could he make something of it?

THE REPRIEVE

It was a relief to be back in a city that was comfortingly familiar. The Gardens. The Swan River. The beach at Cottesloe. Although Subiaco was yet another new suburb, another rented house to scrub and clean, new school, new neighbours. She despaired for the children, the constant shifting could not be good for their education never mind the evident distress Nieve was experiencing at having left behind friends in Darinup and her beloved Sister Gobbleshoe.

And herself? Maeve felt how alone she was. No family or old friends close to hand. Little time or chance to develop anything more than superficial new connections. Patrick was her be all and end all. But where was he? Always either going on ahead or consumed by work, the garage, the lettings agency, Inverness and now what? She scarcely dared think about what lay ahead. Maeve loved him and when she was in his arms there was no doubting it, but she felt less and less sure that she knew him.

She needed to be strong for the children but Maeve felt herself nearing collapse every time she considered the new venture. In daylight hours she would keep herself busy and distracted but alone at night those fears would steal up on her until she trembled in every sinew.

The future had been theirs to determine. Or, so she thought fleetingly on the night when Patrick finally returned from the end of shearing.

She had found herself tossing in and out of fitful dreaming. Sounds, a sharp crack, faint but distinct. Then a car roaring over the rough road with its headlights sweeping through the thin curtains woke her. Anxiety overwhelmed her. Where was Patrick? It was gone midnight. She went to sit on the verandah. Dim lights through the gums came from the direction of the shearing sheds. She twitched with indecision as she tightened the thin wrap over her nightgown; she longed to know that Patrick was all right but there would be all those men and he would think her foolish. Clouds were massing overhead. A few fat globs of rain splattered on the steps up to the verandah.

A figure approached out of the darkness.

'Patrick?'

'Mrs Glendon.'

It was Tom and she was running down to meet him. 'Is everything all right!'

He doffed his hat. 'There's been a fight, an accident—'

'Patrick?!'

'Mr Glendon is fine, will be fine.'

'What do you mean?'

That was when she learned of the confrontation between Ken Duguid and Alex Anderson, that Patrick had bravely tried to intervene but been knocked out, that shots were fired, that Ken was dead.

There was a thunderous rumble from the distant hills. The heavens opened overhead and rain came down in sheets drenching the thin fabric of her nightwear. But she did not care, her eyes frantically hunting out the darkness and then she caught sight of him running towards her.

'Macushla!' He swept her up into his arms.

She was horrified at the sight of the lurid gash at his temple, the dark swelling bruises.

'Patrick, what's—'

'Never mind that scratch!' He was laughing and kissing her and holding her so tight she felt her bones might crack. 'We're rich Macushla—we're rich!'

Her mind flailed about for sense. There had been a fight, a man dead; Patrick himself could have been killed and yet here he was dancing them through the yard, cock a hoop.

The night had been a roller coaster of emotion. Joy and relief that they would be able to pay off the debt to Anderson and leave with money in their pockets. Fury and recriminations that he had risked so much in a game.

'Sure, I knew the luck was with me and wasn't I right?'

She could not help but be caught up in his giddy triumph.

He stopped mid-twirl. 'You're soaked through! Let's get out of this. And celebrate!'

Maeve changed into a dry nightgown and joined Patrick at the kitchen table where he was pouring a generous shot of whiskey for both of them.

'Sláinte.' He raised his glass and they clinked.

She choked as the fiery liquor rolled through her body. Patrick bristled energy even as he sat and she knew there'd be little sleep. Her mind too was fizzing with possibilities. What would they do? Dare she imagine there was enough to take them back to Ireland?

Maeve's mind raced to images of her mother, a visit to Daddy's grave as soon as they returned; images of Dublin, walking down Grafton Street, coffee in Bewleys, St. Stephen's Green, trips to Dalkey, on and on the images streamed. On a tide of optimism, she broached the possibility.

'Patrick, do you think maybe now we can go home, back to Ireland, now that we're rich?'

'Macushla, but isn't that the beauty of it! I've been saving the best for last.' From his jacket pocket Patrick pulled out a piece of paper. 'Signed, dated and witnessed.' He pushed it across the table with a triumphant gleam in his eye.

Maeve frowned. 'What's this? Some sort of I.O.U.?'

'More than that, it's the instructions to the solicitor to make the Deeds over to me!'

'Deeds?'

'Our land. Ours outright.'

Her head felt suddenly woozy with the whiskey.

'Up beyond Mount Magnet the fellow said. Still in W.A.' Patrick added by way of reassurance.

'And will we be able to sell it? Is that the riches?'

Patrick shook his head indulgently. 'Don't you see, darling? It's not just a house, it's a farm. No more working for the other fellow, this will be our own spread. Everything I could have wanted. Can you believe the luck of it!'

What could she say? Patrick was brimming over with his good fortune. It was infectious, his joy. You could be carried away with it. But someone had to talk sense.

'Patrick, you haven't even seen the place.' She knew there was a whine in her voice and wished there wasn't, wished she sounded sensible and strong.

'Mammie, I had bad dream, mammie ...'

It was Patsy entering the kitchen, hair disheveled, rubbing her eyes.

At once Patrick bounded from his seat and gathered her into his arms. 'My little Princess. No more bad dreams for you—aren't you going to be the princess now!'

Patrick worked out his notice at Inverness, with Anderson grumbling the whole time about the way he was being left in the lurch by all and sundry. Truly she wasn't sorry to see the back of the place and his mean hard ways. She tried one more time to dissuade Patrick from the venture but he was sweet reason itself.

'I'll give it six months, Maeve. You're to stay in Perth, I have it all arranged with Mr Watkins, he was always a decent bloke. And we'll have Killpool Vale fit for a queen by the time you come up.'

'It sounds very far out Pat. Couldn't you sell? And at least have the pick of somewhere closer to Perth.'

'Look, we've the bird in the hand that's worth two in the bush; in six months I'll have fixed the place up so we can make a real go of it. Or sell. What have we got to lose?'

She had no retort. What could she say? This isn't what I want. What did she want, other than to go home? It was Patrick who had a clear sight of the road ahead. And it was for her to stick by him, to support, to encourage. And yet. And yet her stomach heaved every time she thought of it.

BURIED TREASURE

Nieve tried so hard not to cry. But the tears would not be kept back. The whole of that first day at the new school Nieve cried, great rackety sobs. Miss Dale did not know what to do with her. The proficiency tests were abandoned. Nieve moved to the B Class where Mr Chidgey shushed the murmurings of her curious classmates and sat her at the top of the class beside his desk.

That evening her mother hugged her close. 'My poor, poor darling.' she said over and over. 'It isn't fair on you.'

John John rolled his eyes. 'Big Baby!' he mouthed.

The next day a girl called Collette offered to be her friend. Nieve shook her head. 'I don't want any friends. We'll be leaving soon.' She explained.

There was a school library. She spent her time reading. *The Famous Five*. Mr Chidgey found her there in the lunch hour. 'You should be in the A Class, Nieve.' he said.

She looked up at him dismayed, and shook her head.

Then he reached onto the shelves and pulled out a book. 'Try this.' he proffered. 'Stick with it.'

She had. And once she had grappled with the odd language and the slow build to adventure on the Island, the shifts and turns about of fortune gripped her so tightly that she had to secrete a torch into the bedroom and read under the sheets hoping not to wake Patsy in the room they shared.

All day on the beach at the weekend, even when Patsy hit her with the spade demanding help with the sandcastles and John John wanted to dig home to Ireland, Nieve read and eked out the last pages of Long John Silver's scheming and Jim Hawkins' fate.

A HANDFUL OF DUST

That afternoon they finished jacking up the east side of the house where it had begun to list. One of the supporting posts needed to be replaced urgently. They worked well together, Tom realised. The Irishman was an easy-going boss. He'd make decisions, know what he wanted but then again take the time to listen if you had another opinion on the matter. Mostly they worked side by side in a companionable silence. In the evenings they might discuss the work to be done the following day, the weather, or now and then a political aside as Patrick tuned in the wireless. They wondered aloud if Menzies would ever give up his stranglehold on the government.

'Tomorrow we'll make a start on the supports.' the Irishman said.

Tom liked that Patrick was a man of few words and didn't pry into another man's life. Back on the Anderson place the view he first formed was coloured by his feelings for Mrs Glendon. It made him fume with anger that Glendon had ever brought her to such a place, a lady like her; subjected her to the unforgiving heat of the summer months, the flies and the indignities of that crude shack which she struggled so hard to make a home with her unrelenting toil. Tom raged within. Let it all pour onto the pages of his exercise book, page after page. His poems of the Outback. About the dried-up billabongs and peeling bark. Splinter-eyed prospectors scratching their pans. Leather-faced women stoking the copper. Thin lipped diggers saluting flies. The red red sand.

After the fire which had swept through their home, he had seen the exhaustion in Mrs Glendon; the lines of care etching deeper into the grooves around her eyes. Above all, witnessed her hopeless despair. He wanted with all his groaning heart to rescue her, to lift the heavy burden from her hands made cruelly rough and red with labour and to … to what? What could he offer? Scarce more than a boy. With not much more than a saddlebag of possessions to his name. Nothing. Less than nothing. He pondered this as he beat together the ingredients for the steamed date pudding he was making for supper, *plonk* they used to call it back at Fairbridge. What had he been able to offer? His care, that was all. To watch over her and to keep her from harms way. His withering despise of the Irishman fostered and nourished.

When news of Patrick Glendon's great success at the poker table spread like wildfire about the station Tom felt a hard lump form in his throat. He could scarcely swallow. The Irishman was paying off all his debts. Had told Boss Anderson to stuff his job where the sun don't shine, they said. The man wasn't a loser but a winner after all.

All at once it seemed to Tom that everyone was going or gone; Ken Duguid was dead, Stubby in jail, Mr Van der Berj would soon be following his wife to the seaside bungalow in Geraldton, Alex Anderson was recuperating with his wife and family in Perth, Bert and Sally were who only knew where, and the Irish family preparing for pastures new. But he, Tom Bradshaw, Tom the Pom, was left behind. With Boss Anderson madder than a cut snake.

It was a few days after that eventful night, Tom was helping Mr Van der Berj drive some of the sheep back up to the sixty-five block when Bram laughed out loud. 'That Irishman!' He spluttered.

Tom whistled to Spike to keep a sharp eye on the ragged edge of the flock then kicked Cobber a little closer to catch what it was that amused the station manager so much.

'He's not the full shilling!'

Tom made a sound to encourage explanation.

'Plans to farm that digger's block.' Bram snorted. 'Actually means to give it a go. He hasn't a Buckleys!'

Tom frowned, 'Where is it, this block?'

'Some godforsaken outpost, north east of Mount Magnet.'

363

'You tell him?'

'That Irishman's not for listening. All he can think is, he's got his own bit of red dirt now.' Bram heaved in his saddle, 'I told him, *Paddy, you take my advice, sell up, get a few bob if you can and you'll be quids in.* But no, reckons he knows all he needs to know about the sheep and the wheat.'

Tom spent the rest of the drive stewing over the Irishman's folly. A boy at Fairbridge, Doug? No, Denny. Had been sent out to an old digger's block on the edge of nowhere and at the first annual visit the man from Fairbridge brought Denny back and all their eyes popped out of their heads. He was skin and bone, his hands calloused and raw, the spark beaten out of him. When he was fed and recovered Denny regaled them with the horrors of the far outback, the backbreaking labour in searing heat, the plague of locusts that near destroyed the crops, but above all the mind crushing loneliness of it all.

Was this the sort of place the Irishman would take Maeve and the children to? The lump that was lodging in Tom's throat swelled. The Irishman must be made to see the madness of his dreams. They could return to Perth. The man was a hard worker, Tom had seen for himself that he was no shirker, there would be some other opportunity now that he had money.

His opportunity came at the weekend. He went to make his deposit as usual at the Post Office when he saw that the Irishman was three ahead in the queue. At the counter Grace Smithers flattered with a smile.

'Hear you got lucky Mr Glendon?'

He nodded. 'This is to go registered post to the solicitor in Meekatharra.'

'Yeah, hear your bit of property is out some. Planning a sale, are you?'

'How much will that be?'

'We'll all miss your lovely wife and the little ones. Strewth, I'd be thinking of leaving myself with these shootings and the like! What is Darinup coming to these days—making the front page of the Bodenham Herald! Hear your wife had a bit of trouble with Sergeant Brooke as well—'

'Thank you, Miss Smithers, that'll be all.' The Irishman rapped on the counter and Tom could almost imagine the scowl he fixed on Gracie to silence her.

As the Irishman hastened from the Post Office Tom fell into step beside him, 'Mr Glendon ...'

The Irishman stopped abruptly and Tom caught the tail end of his ferocious glare.

'Yes, what is it?'

Tom gathered his resolve, 'Is it true you're going to—'

'What?'

'Going to farm that block?'

'It's nobody's damn business if I'm taking a trip to the moon!'

'Only ...'

The Irishman shook his head and turned away.

'Only you might need a hand.'

It seemed the only way. There on the pavement, outside Jessups, the old men squinting up at them from their bench and swatting at flies, he threw in his lot with Patrick Glendon. He would hand in his notice to Boss Anderson. He would leave Inverness. He would swim on the surging tide of fate knowing not where it would take him. But he would watch over Maeve.

He planned to dissuade the Irishman from the enterprise altogether. His heart almost rejoiced at the sight of the broken shack you could scarce call a house, had skipped a beat alongside the twisted fences and tumbledown paddocks. The lack of water was a serious setback, with the dams near dried out and overgrown. To make something of this? With only 240 acres of poor grazing and dashed prospects for farming wheat? Surely the man would see the impossibility of it. Tom thought it a matter of days before the Irishman would admit defeat. He had not counted on the steely purpose of the man.

'Six months, we'll give it six months.' Patrick declared and

Tom could see no point of protestations.

They bent their backs to it. He helped the Irishman choose two strong horses along with the dairy cow at the nearest auction. They rode the perimeter surveying the most urgent works. Tom shot a feral goat, skinned and butchered the meat. They dined for days on goat curry and stews. Tom kept his eye out for the goats; you could make a bob or two selling them on.

Long days were spent digging posts into the hard earth. Fencing and repairing the stretches which were still serviceable with taut lengths of wire. Their neighbour Hobbs drew up alongside and observed them with a cynical eye.

Two days later, as the sun was dipping in a blue gum haze, Hobbs drove up to the lopsided house past the new sign on the gate which renamed the property Killpool Vale.

The Irishman placed the glasses on the table whilst Tom fetched the bottle of whiskey.

'Your good health.' The Irishman saluted Hobbs.

Hobbs knocked his tipple back and nodded his appreciation of the malt. 'And yours.' He smacked his lips. 'You'll be needing it.' He was one of those weathered Aussies that looked a good ten years older than he probably was.

The Irishman winked at Tom and responded. 'You needn't worry on that account.'

Hobbs scratched his stubble. 'Cattle or sheep?'

'I see you've cattle.' The Irishman rejoindered.

'I've more land.'

The Irishman poured a second shot.

'Relative, are you?' Hobbs probed. 'Of Quinlan?'

The Irishman shook his head.

'Never thought the stubborn old bastard would sell. I made him a fair offer.' Hobbs continued.

'Is that so?'

'I could save you a broken back with the same.'

There was a silence then for a moment. The two men eyed each other across the table. Tom looked on and tried to keep his own desperate hope at bay.

'I'll take my chances.' The Irishman downed his whiskey.

'I can wait.' Hobbs offered. 'But the price will drop.'

Three days before Christmas Tom drove Mr Glendon on the long road down to Meekatharra to catch the train to Perth for the festive season. On the return they would attend the New Year ram sales. The Irishman apologised for leaving Tom on his own over Christmas but Tom assured him that he would be happy enough in the company of Spike and the horses. Furthermore, he intended to tackle the repair of the mechanism of the Southern Cross watermill in the home pasture. The structure had toppled over in a past storm and Tom was determined to get the rusty old contraption going again. The bearing would need to be rebuilt and he'd use a grub screw to hold it.

The first morning, Tom stood on the verandah yawning and stretching in the glowing dawn light, it was his twenty-first birthday. He was truly on his own, he realised, for the first time in his entire life. The thought exhilarated him. He allowed his imagination to roam over the land spread out before him under clear skies and claim it for himself. In the free rolling days which followed, he began to appreciate the allure the farm might have for a man. He intuited that he and Patrick might not be so different; that in many ways they might be cut from a similar cloth.

On the twenty eighth he drove into the one-horse town to fetch supplies and to deposit the wage which the Irishman had left. At the post office counter, he was surprised to find an envelope waiting. Puzzled, he opened it. Within was a Christmas card, a framed nativity scene. *Wishing you all the Blessings of the Christmas Season and much joy in the New Year.* From, Maeve, Nieve, JJ and Patsy.

Tom felt a tremble in his hand and his heart flutter. Her writing. To him. He turned the card over and on the back, there was a further message. His breath caught in his throat.

Dear Tom
You cannot know what a comfort it is to have you with us. I

worry that Patrick may not always be realistic in his
ventures but I trust your support and advice at this time.
Maeve

She was looking to him. Relying on him. To save them all.
Carefully he returned the card to the envelope his hand still
shaking. He felt the weight of her entreaty and he determined
that he would not fail her.

Tom noticed a change in the Irishman's mood on his return.
He seemed more fractious, prone to impatience, for which he
would not always offer apologies as he might have done in
the past. The cause, Tom could see, was the slow rate of
their progress and Patrick's drive to be working on as many
fronts as possible. In the morning they might continue to
erect the sheep pens but by late afternoon have shifted to
replacing the rotten boards of the verandah.

As the summer temperatures began to soar in the dry heat
the energy of both men was sapped by midday. There was
talk locally of drought. Irrigation was the key to making a
farm like this work. Aside from the reliance on getting all
the watermills operational there were two dams on the
property which had been neglected and virtually dried up, it
was vital that the rains came sooner rather than later in an
area which wasn't known for its abundance.

Tom surmised that the Irishman was being stretched
beyond his means by the level of capital investment needed
in equipment and machinery. The farm had come with the
contents for the good reason that it wouldn't have been
worth the effort to reclaim any of it. Even twenty years back
the set-up had been largely second hand; equipment needed
to be updated or replaced having been left to rot for the
greater part of a decade. The Irishman scoured the local
newspaper for the sale of second-hand tools and trailers and
the like; in the meantime, they did what they could and the
Irishman arranged to lease a tractor to plough up the best
fields for a winter crop. In mid-January the dairy cow took

ill and the vet had to be called in.

As they sat together over supper that evening Tom could see the strain in Patrick's tight set features, felt the heavy weighted silence in the air of unspoken doubts and worries bearing down on his shoulders as he stared down at his empty plate, the gravy wiped clean. Tom wondered if the time had come to confront the Irishman with the true extent of the task ahead, never mind the prospect of subjecting Mrs Glendon and the children to the unavoidable hard times to be endured.

'Boss …' he ventured.

Patrick did not look up.

'Have you thought maybe … the luck's not in it with this spread … not with this drought going on … it'd be a rough trot for any farmer but … you could still come out on top if … while you're still ahead and with the offer from Hobbs –'

'Quit if you want. I'm not stopping you.' The Irishman spoke between gritted teeth.

Tom took in a deep breath, 'It's not a matter of quitting.' His tone softened. 'No one would see it like that, Mr Glendon. It's not a failure to back out where you can't win.'

The Irishman looked at him then and Tom was unnerved by the glint of madness which he saw in his eyes.

'I'm not quitting again and that's an end of it!'

Tom flinched. For a moment he even thought that Patrick would hurl the plate at him.

'You go if you must.' Patrick stood and took his plate to the sink. 'It's little a man asks to be given a chance.' He muttered and Tom felt the words were not for him alone.

That was the beginning of Tom's despair. Which deepened as the days passed. The exhaustion which he felt from the relentless workload tested even his own resolve to stay.

A dry storm blew up in the night, thunder rocking between the hills. The house creaked and groaned under the onslaught. But there was no rain.

In the morning it was clear that some of the strips of

369

corrugated iron on the roof of the shearing shed were dangerously loose. Tom felt his way nervously along the ridge but didn't feel a hundred percent certain that the structure of the shed itself was safe. A dry breeze swept up a fine dust into their eyes, into their mouths, into every crevice, until breathing itself felt like being sanded from the inside.

From the rooftop Tom surveyed the outpost that was Killpool Vale and felt a sickening lurch in his guts. The Irishman could not expect his wife and children to live here. It might be years before the farm would run to a reasonable profit and a decent house be built. He tottered slightly as a strip of the roof shifted underfoot. If either of them was to have an accident it could be catastrophic. Fatal even. Tom paused as he steadied himself. If Patrick were to have an accident—then that surely would put an end to the venture.

ON A PIN

Maeve sat in the busy tea rooms in David Jones department store amongst the Sales shoppers, with Patsy happily picking off the silver ball decorations on the fancy cake and sucking them loudly. A letter had arrived at the Poste Restante in Forest Place. She read it over again, her hands shaking.

After the usual gossipy pleasantries, she arrived at the heart and soul of the letter. Her mother had been considering the future. She was in her early seventies and there was every likelihood that she would live to be ninety or more, the way her own mother and aunts had done; she had everything she needed. The boys were all settled. Sean Og with the business, Kevin and Dominic were at the top of their respective branches of the medical profession and Jerry had his own factory. She was moving to a smaller house and had decided that Maeve should have her rightful portion sooner rather than later; when it might be of some use to herself and Patrick with the new venture underway. An Account had been opened at the central branch of the Allied Irish Bank, a sum deposited in Maeve's name and it was for her to *do with as you will.*

It was an enormous sum. Maeve trembled as the figure leapt off the page and assaulted her eyes. Enough to change all their lives. Enough never to be worried again, if used wisely, if invested and nurtured. Enough to—she dared to allow the thought—buy a passage home and start afresh. A down payment on a snug house in Terenure, enough for the outlay on a small business premises. Enough. Enough. Her thoughts darted this way and that but whichever way they ran they came to one end, Patrick.

Her mind fizzed and boiled and she felt the tears smarting into her eyes.

A waitress passed by clearing tables. 'Aren't you enjoying that?' she remarked in the way that a Dubliner had of meaning the opposite.

'I am enjoying it!' Patsy asserted in her forthright Aussie manner.

And then the waitress noticed the look on Maeve.

'Sad news?' she asked, curious but not unkindly.

Maeve nodded.

'Let me freshen your tea for you.' The girl picked up the empty teapot.

Maeve assented.

She would wait. She would not tell Patrick, not yet. She would think. There would be a way to persuade him. For all his pride. He must see, mustn't he? Their luck was turning. But not if they threw good money after bad. No more desperate throws of the dice. Now there would be plans. Not a future determined by the turn of a card. Proper thought through plans and … and she would make them. Carefully Maeve folded up the thin blue airmail letter.

THE WHEEL OF FORTUNE

The lad was a hard worker and knew a useful thing or two. Patrick liked Tom's quiet ways; he was content to be in his own company and with the dog Spike, only spoke if he had something to say but he was companionable. Patrick was grateful for that; grateful he had offered himself as a hand. Young Tom had leaped at it as though it were the opportunity of a lifetime. Patrick had been surprised, assumed the lad was settled into the ways of Inverness and his undoubted prospects. The young man's desire to join him calmed his own nagging doubts about the venture and emboldened Patrick's resolve. But now, as he stood up on the roof of the shearer's shed replacing the buckled corrugated iron sheets, whose rivets were crumbling with rust, he eyed the lad and felt the undercurrents of the great doubt stirring again.

Tom suggested the luck wasn't in the place. Patrick felt himself unhinged. Was that what swayed the tide of life, only luck? What of the workings of his hands? The sweat of his brow? His will? His purpose? Patrick surveyed the dusty yard below, the crooked house, the dry pastures with the few sheep. He set his jaw. Wherever you would make a go of it, it would be tough.

That was the lesson he had not learned at Killpool Hill. They should have toughed it out, he and Maeve. He had these long years of reflection to work that out. They would have scraped along. Alright, to meet the repayments on the tractor and the new machinery he might have had to go cap in hand to his brother John, or even, getting nothing but an *I told you so* from that quarter, to Maeve's father. Borrowed against the surety of the future. The farm would have prospered, it was good land, no one could doubt that. Maeve

373

would have been the queen of the county by now. He had been a fool, a proud, stubborn fool. He wouldn't make the same mistake again. He'd root out the canker of doubt. He'd make his own luck.

A sheet of corrugated iron shifted underfoot. Patrick felt his boot sliding away from him. He had been so intent on his thoughts that he'd lost his concentration. He was slipping and flailing, grabbing for the ridge. Catching it with the raw tips of one hand. Burning metal. The raised jagged edge of a loose sheet slashing his arm. The other hand grasping. A grunt of shock exploded from his chest. The muscles of his life saving arm snapping taut and straining, tearing. His boots scrabbling and finding nothing for purchase. His wide eyes locked to the boy at the other end of the ridge. Then shut tight against the searing agony.

BEN DOWN AND THE NAME THAT CANNOT BE SPOKEN

It long way, slow. Maali don't want no one see us—away from gunji. Stay outa town, go round farm.

After long walkabout I see my born country. Not many here now, only old people, Aunties and Uncles. Some dead now, can't say the name. They gone, they resting. No good to wake up spirit and call 'em back.

Government been come here. Them make army place. Fence round for military testing, you know. Take too many waterholes 'n sacred place. Our mob can't walk across our country and hunt in the old way.

Maali sick but she don't go to doctor at army base. She angry 'bout wadjela takin' country. Anger inside, eatin' up. Hard for look 'er.

Binni, he sit beside Maali all time. 'im singing. She like songs he learn from old uncles. He got good voice. That fella, good n strong.

THE DEVIL WEARS MANY GUISES

Patrick left early in the morning with first light. He brought his rifle, although the idea of hunting was not paramount. He was under doctor's orders to take it easy whilst the skin knitted and he was to go back in a few days so that the stitches could be removed. It would be an unsightly scar; the cut had been ragged. But nothing broken. That was the main thing, nothing broken.

He conjured the image of his shattered body at the base of the shearing shed and shuddered. If Tom had not been on the roof with him—that was the next thought. He couldn't have held on any longer. His mind had flown to Maeve. The vision of her he always sought out; Maeve standing on the deck of the boat ferrying them out to Skellig Michael, the rock in the Atlantic, two days into their honeymoon, a breeze blowing her hair and the ripple of her laughter catching in his throat and the sparkle of love in her eyes, all for him. Then the lad grabbed him, straddling the ridge hauling him up, yelling at him to take hold. Strong for one so young.

He could sit in the house and fiddle about with the figures in his ledger but that would be sour work. He could stand and direct Tom as he relined the southernmost dam, but no man likes working with someone watching over him, especially when the chap knows what he is about. So, the idea came to explore the hills. In Australia you never knew what you might find. Opals were the thing now. A fellow at the biscuit factory in Sydney had inherited a jet mine from some old uncle, struck lucky. All manner of precious stones you might simply stumble upon. And gold. Of course. Wouldn't that be the biggest joker in the pack, for all the hard work, the sweat and the toil, to be out on a Sunday stroll in the hills and happen upon a gold strike. He chuckled to think of it.

He let his eye roam over the forbidding and jagged terrain, it had a prehistoric beauty. Looking back over his shoulder at the bedraggled borders of his property he thought how quickly the imprint of mankind might be erased in this unforgiving landscape where man so seldom seemed welcome. You could grow to love it. He felt the tug of the soft green rolling pastures of Wicklow slacken and loosen their grip. This red earth pulsed with its own call.

He wandered along the ancient tracks of roos and other game and allowed his mind to wander unfettered. He could imagine walking these tracks in years to come with John John at his heels, teaching him how to use the rifle. Ben had told him that when the men of his people made a kill, they would open a vein and spill a drop or two of blood into the earth by way of making thanks. He could understand that impulse. When he taught John John how to hunt, how to line up the rifle with a steady hand and follow the path of the prey just nudging ahead of its trajectory and squeezing gently he would also teach him to kill with respect. The way a father does with a son. A father who takes care of his son, his body and his soul.

But what if there are two sons and only one can be saved? Patrick shook his head at the unwanted thought, trying to shake it out of his mind. It hung on for a moment or two. How simple it could be to understand what had passed that day if it had been just that choice; you can save one son but not the other. Which son do you love the most?

'All my children!' Patrick shouted into the humming air. 'I love all my children!' A horned lizard eyed him from its perch in the sun. He felt a calm return. The lizard blinked slowly; a sheath pulled over its bulging eyes.

He climbed, rough track and rocky surface. Occasionally he stooped to pick up an unusual looking stone, nothing special he was sure, a streak of copper, iron or nothing at all, he pocketed it anyway. Tom might know. Tom knew a lot of things. Full of surprises. The poetry for one thing. Patrick stumbled on him one evening scribbling in a notebook out

377

on the verandah. Tom flushed like a kid caught with a porno mag and snapped it shut. Patrick held a hand up to indicate he wasn't about to pry.

'Fancy a beero?' Patrick held it out, as cool as the Coolgardie would allow. 'Must get a refrigerator.' He confided 'Soon as the new generator arrives. Maeve can't live without a fridge. Be worth it for the bread and cakes she makes and kids love ice lollies.'

He turned to go away, leave the lad in peace.

'I write a bit of poetry.' Tom explained.

Patrick eyed him. 'I'd say you'd be the sort of poet would have something to say.'

Tom shrugged, 'Had a couple published.'

'G'way?' Patrick saluted him with his bottle.

The lad flicked through his pages, cleared his throat and read a piece about the red-hot earth and the way a man had to sweat and break his back and there was something inspiring in it.

Patrick refrained, '*It's all I have, and mangy sheep* – how did that next bit go again?'

Enough I have and just my keep.
But look, the difference you see,
I enjoy it and here am free.
The hot wind, amid swirling dust and sticky sweat,
Believe you me, is quite a treat,
There's something here a man can't cheat.'

Patrick nodded and repeated, 'There's something here a man can't cheat. That's very true, so it is.'

He topped another hill. It was a cloudless day. Still no rain. The thought made Patrick thirsty and he took a swig from his flagon. No bloody rain. Ben would have had an answer to that. Some ancient God or Ancestor who needed to be placated. For a man who said little he realised he had learned much from Ben. The few words here and there on a smoke-oh. *Walkabout*. Patrick chuckled to himself. That was the message came back to Anderson when Ben took off. *Gone*

Walkabout. Anderson fuming and refusing to pay out the balance of wages to the man who brought the message.

They wanted to take his child, Maeve said; only maybe not his child, a boy that was as blonde as Ben was black. A man couldn't stand by and have his child stolen away. The Australians were good at that, Patrick thought, stealing childhood. Tom, Boswell all those poor boys on every farm around, no mother's love for them. He had heard about these Boy's Towns, Fairbridge and the like. Run by Christian Brothers or protestant empire builders. Children that weren't wanted back home, with all that that implied, *Bastards get a better chance over here!* Ken Duguid had laughed in his harsh way, *Lucky bastards!*

No mother's love though. No father's guiding hand. No brother or sister either. He'd seen a look from under Boswell's shaded eyes, a hunch in his shoulder. Felt a jolt of certainty. *You too,* he'd thought. And there he was. James. His brother James who was now a priest out in some mission station in Africa. Even as Patrick leapt across the boulders fording the iron stained creek; there was James tussling him to the ground as they walked home from the Charity Match, ambling along the banks of the Dodder.

'Did you see that pass from Clancy? Wasn't it a cracker?! But then the way those fellas brought O'Dwyer down!' James, his big open face grinning from ear to ear as he tackled him to the ground, and they rolled in the grass. 'Jaze but he still managed to cross the fecking line! What a Try! Did ya see, ya little bollocks? Did ya see that Try!?'

And then the feeling, the instinct, that suddenly something wasn't right. And seeing that James felt it too but James laughing and pushing Patrick's head down into the grass still damp from the rain of the previous day. Pushing himself up and running on ahead. 'Ya little bollocks!'

No one in the house when they got back. James dishing out a plateful of biscuits with a wink and pouring the thick creamy milk cool from the pantry. 'Get that down your ugly mug, Pat!' Then his brother creasing up with laughter, 'Ugly mug!—just thinking about Bridgie and the hours she's after

379

spending on her face and she's not half as pretty as you Patsy, sure, is she? Sure, you're the looker in this house.'

Patrick disconcerted at the word *pretty*.

'Like a little angel so you are, isn't that right? Butter wouldn't melt in your mouth.'

'I am not.' He asserted tersely.

'Only codding ya.' James punching his shoulder playfully. 'Aren't you getting the big boy now?'

Patrick nodded.

'But still the baby!' James grinned and made a feint.

'Am not!' And they'd sparred around the kitchen table until James tripped over a scuttle and landed on his behind and they both laughed like it was the biggest joke ever.

Then sitting back at the table devouring the biscuits, pink wafer ones you could eat a whole packet and not feel sick.

Patrick stooped by the edge of the creek to fill up his bottle and to splash the metallic water over his face. Scrubbing the sweat off his brow, but James' voice still in his head.

'What is it you like reading these days, Patsy?'

'The Dandy ... Desperate Dan.'

'Come here and we'll go upstairs in a minute, and I'll let you have one of my Biggles books. They're a great read altogether. Peter has his eye on them but isn't he a greedy little tyke.' James winked and Patrick felt chosen and special.

That same evening James returned to the Seminary. Their mother distraught at the dinner table. 'I thought we had him for the whole week!'

His father continuing with his careful boning of the fish. It was a Friday. 'There's a group going to Croagh Patrick, he's a mind to do the penitential walk to the top.'

'His poor bare feet will be cut to ribbons!' Patrick's mother had wailed. 'Such soft feet he has too.'

'I think he's intending to make the climb on his knees.' His father informed and dipped a piece of his trout in the helping of tartare sauce at the side of his plate.

'The lamb.' His mother shook her head and speared a potato. 'He'll be giving it up for the poor starving children of

380

Africa.' Her face was suffused with pride. 'He's his heart set on the missions.'

Patrick stared at the head of the fish on his plate, the dead, lifeless eyes. He knew that if he put anything in his mouth, he would not be able to swallow it. In a voice that was scarcely a whisper he asked to be excused.

His mother looked up, solicitous as ever, 'I hope you haven't caught a chill Pat, you're looking very pale.'

After dinner his father called him to his study.

He motioned for Patrick to join him as he knelt and gripped his rosary. 'I want us to pray for James, Patrick. Sometimes, when God calls us to the greater good, the Devil presents temptation and comes in many guises.'

Patrick closed his eyes and murmured the responses; but all he could see was his father's look of slow horror as he stood in the doorway of James' bedroom, his stiffening lip.

After what seemed an interminable silence, James began to sob, great heaving soundless sobs, spluttering between, 'Tell da it wasn't me, Pat. It wasn't my fault, father!' His hands clasped together in an attitude of prayer.

Patrick was shaking in every part of himself, but he seized his chance and slipped from his brother's orbit. His father stood aside to allow him to take his wordless confusion up to his own small room in the attic.

Patrick lay his hand on the broad flat rock where he sat. Under the hot stillness of the day there was a humming, of insects, of the earth. He stretched back across the burning stone, overcome. He thought of that summer's day long ago when he had lain across his narrow cot in the attic waiting for his father to come up and hold him tight. Tell him that it would all be all right.

But he had not come. Instead a knife had fallen. Patrick had been sacrificed and God had not descended to stay his father's hand as he had with Abraham.

THE GOLDEN YEARS

It was the quiet hours, after an early lunch. When Patsy had her afternoon nap. Before Nieve and John John returned from school with all their clatter and jabber. Maeve had finished writing the letter to Patrick and now she sat at the desk with the shoe box in front of her. The box with all their papers, passports, life insurance and the new bank book which arrived registered mail from the Allied Irish Bank. She took a great breath, emboldening herself. She must gather all the information needed for the shipping office. The hardest part was surely over. Writing the letter. But her hands still trembled. She had said, *No more*. They would go home to Ireland. There was no failure in this. He must be made to see that. Plenty of people went back. They had had their great adventure. Jason and his Argonauts.

He could blame her if he wanted. The Homesickness. Yes. And that was true of course. If he sold Killpool Vale he could hold his head up, they were quids in, ahead of the game. They might do anything back in Dublin. They were young. In their thirties for goodness sakes, all to play for. This is what she had written, labouring over every phrase and sentence. At once pleading with him to come to the decision himself whilst telling him that it was a decision already made.

She riffled through the paperwork. The entry documents. The birth certificates, her own with the spelling mistake, Mave, without the middle 'e'. The vaccination records. And a brown envelope, the sort for paying out wages, on the front in Patrick's hand simply *Killpool Hill*. The flap was loose, the gum had weakened over the years she assumed; inside nothing but seeds.

The wheat.

She spilt a few out onto her palm. Dried up and surely spent.

The thought that Patrick had kept them all this time yanked at her heart. Tears welled and spilled over. Tears she had not realised she was holding back. It came to her again with an irresistible force. That evening when the light had been golden and surged into the dark kitchen at Killpool Hill. Patrick grabbing her at the threshold and swinging her about with his face aglow and his hair aflame and the light in his eyes dazzling her; so handsome, her Burt Lancaster. She shrieking to know the cause with the children laughing and jumping at the sight.

'You'll have it all! Your heart's desire!'

'Patrick, will you ever tell me what's going on?'

'The Buyer. He wants it for the seed. The seed Maeve. That's how good it is!'

That night with the children put to bed they had sat around the kitchen table and plotted their future, Patrick pouring over the details; this and that improvement to the old house, restoring it to its Georgian splendour. A help for Maeve, her own little car. But for Maeve it had been the future itself that beckoned and it held only golden years.

Maeve picked up the letter she had just written and as she read it over, she slowly, but surely, tore it up.

A COAT OF MANY COLOURS

Patrick was following a roo path along the side of an escarpment when he noticed the overhanging shelf. There was a small opening indented into the rock behind, a cave; enough to provide shelter from the searing sun. He would stop and have his sandwich and then think about circling back, maybe even keep an eye out for something for supper, a goat even, since he had the rifle. He began to scramble up the rock face.

His father had been wrong, very wrong.

Patrick could look at it now. All these years later. From every angle. He had never seen James again. It was orchestrated, either by chance or his father's direction, that they were never in the same place. James might have said something to him, an abject apology, the sort of thing you couldn't write down, Patrick acknowledged. The more he thought of it, the more Patrick saw his father's hand. Nothing was to be said. James sent to Croagh Patrick for the penitential climb of the sacred mountain. There was to be an atonement to God. But not to Patrick.

Patrick slipped on the rock and grazed his knee. He paused, catching his breath. He was biting back a rage which he knew could overwhelm him. Had his father thought him complicit? Surely not. But how else to explain that his father had left uncomforted that young Patrick. Burdened him with a sense of wrongdoing, of being unworthy. It had driven the desire to escape, to run away, Patrick was certain of that. Yet, there had always been that deep yearning in him to prove himself the good son, the one who would really make his father proud.

James must have seemed a better prospect. He was going to be a priest. His father betrayed the trust of young Patrick for

384

that. And when his father said, *The devil comes in many guises,* he had branded the six six six on his youngest son's forehead. For the sake of a holy priest in the family; who had himself behaved as a devil possessed. His father had been very wrong, wanting to smother the whole incident in silence, as though it had never happened.

Patrick heaved himself up on to the overhang and crouched there a moment drawing in deep breaths.

There was another angle, he conceded. A notion which was becoming more compelling every time he entertained it. It might satisfy at last the *why* of his father's behaviour. It was not that his father did not love him or that his father blamed him. It was simply that his father loved Patrick's mother above everything, above anyone. James must be a priest and Patrick must be silent. His father thought only of her desires and feared a broken heart that would not have mended at such revelations.

Patrick could see it clearly when he looked back. They had not been an outwardly affectionate family and the times had discouraged displays of emotion, particularly amongst their class, but Patrick could recall the palpable undercurrent between his parents; his father's attentiveness to her. The children's access to their mother always curtailed and Patrick could see now a kind of possessiveness in his father and that his father may only have tolerated his children as a necessary consequence of marriage. His father would naturally keep anything unpleasant or unsavoury from her. To protect and cherish her. Patrick could understand the depth of such love. And perhaps, however misguided his father had been, forgive him.

Patrick stood at the lip of the cave and looked out over the ancient landscape, so ancient it was another world, a time before time. The sun was almost directly above. He turned into the welcoming dark of the cave. His eye was immediately drawn to what looked like markings on the rock face. A shaft of light followed him as he entered and looking closer, he could see faint impressions. Animals, a kangaroo, an echidna but then strange creatures, neither animal nor

385

human, not of this earth. He did not feel them to be malevolent but they exuded a power which he thought might be frightening. He sensed their presence emanating from within the walls of the cave. Their huge round helmet heads, with what might be rays radiating from them. These were beings he had not seen before in the almost comic book literature about the aboriginals. Strange disturbing figures. And suddenly Patrick had the overpowering sense that he was the alien here. That these beings had held sway for hundreds, thousands of years and he was the interloper who had invaded their sacred places.

Had it been fanciful, it struck him now, to imagine that this land could ever be home? Ireland was home. He felt the ripened tang of longing. And heard over and over Maeve's voice calling to him, that day when he had collected her from Sgt. Brookes, *I want to go home Patrick.* His stomach lurched. She was right. She had taken up the refrain again when he made his Christmas visit. Ireland was where they belonged. That was where his children should grow. Where he knew the names of plants and birds and the old stories of the hills.

Patrick had listened only to his own voice, relentlessly urging him ever on, *This time I will succeed. This time I will win.* All in the pursuit and recovery of his broken pride, to mend his broken heart. But at what expense? He would sell to Hobbs. There would be enough to see them home on a boat. Not as a prodigal son but one who wore a coat of many colours, all the colours of love. And then. And then they would start again. He and Maeve, together hand in hand.

The snake began to uncurl. It reminded Patrick of a painting or a drawing he had seen once of a snake consuming its own tail, the alpha and the omega, in the beginning is the end and in the end is the beginning. The snake lifted its head. Patrick carefully raised his rifle and sighted the serpent along the length of the barrel. The snake shimmered a rainbow of colours, Patrick marveled and hesitated, a thing of beauty.

WALKABOUT

John John knew his father was on a Walkabout. His mammie sat them down and tried to explain to them that their da had gone off and not returned. No one knew where he was. No one had heard from him. He had been gone for three months.

He heard Nieve crying like a sissy, 'When's daddy coming home?'

His mammie holding her, saying, 'I don't know. I don't know.'

Then Nieve ventured, 'Is he dead mammie?'

'I don't know, my darling, the police and Tom have searched every bit of the property; they think he may have gone for a trek into the hills. He might have had an accident.'

'Or maybe ...' Nieve snuffled, 'maybe he's just lost.'

But that couldn't be true. Their da had told Nieve that he would never be lost, never, because he could look up at the stars in the sky and always find his way. There was a night he had pointed out The Southern Cross, directing John John's eye to see the patterns amongst the millions of stars. The da said there was a map of the stars and if you had that map, even in your head, you didn't need a map of the ground. The thought of it was so big John John felt his brain might explode and splatter all over his mother's pots of geraniums.

'Yes, maybe, maybe he's just lost.' Their mammie sighed.

That's when John John had his illumination. Their da was on a Walkabout. Because of the stars and because of remembering about the quandongs. The strange red fruit left for them on the picnic table.

'He's here.' The da said when they were in the Bush Park.

It had been the best day ever. Their da sat with them at

breakfast, not rushing to work as he usually did. John John remembered that his mammie's eyes were red and puffy and he worried she might have an ache in them the way he had had an ache in his ears. She was fussing over the porridge on the kookaburra stove and his da declared to them all. 'We're all going on a picnic. How's that?'

His mammie sniffed and kept stirring the pot but they all yelled, 'Yeah!' and Patsy banged her spoon on the table.

The da got up and pulled mammie into his arms, 'Macushla, you're to be our princess, isn't that right, children? And we're going to make all the sandwiches and we'll have a barbecue and mammie isn't going to lift a finger!'

'Yeah!' They all chorused again and at last mammie smiled and pushed him away but in a friendly way, 'Watch now the pan will burn.'

The da took them to the new park where there was a creek which was safe for swimming and picnic tables and a place for making barbecues. Their da organised games and after the sandwiches and the blackened burgers, they splashed about in the water. And the da said, wasn't John John a great swimmer and would he teach his old da one day. John John had swollen with pride and swam even better, better than Nieve, who could only doggy paddle, and he floated on his back to demonstrate to his da how easy it was really. His da gave it a go but splashed about and went under the water and then leaped up spluttering and said he'd rather stay on his own two feet any day. And they laughed and laughed. It was the best day ever.

And then they found the fruit on the picnic table. One for each of them.

'He's here.' The da said and turned about to gaze into the thicket of gums. 'Ben.' He called.

And they listened but there was only the hum of insects and the screech of a cockatoo.

Ben.' His da said reverently and fingered the red fruit. Then grinned and winked. 'He's gone walkabout.'

When John John thought about his father on his Walkabout

he knew that the two were together. His da would be alright because the blackfella would find him; just as he had that day. And Ben knew how to find water when you could see no water, knew how to find honey, knew where to find quandongs. Ben was teaching his da on the Walkabout and every night they would sit around a fire with the cry of the mopoke in the trees and Ben would tell his da a story. The one about the black swans and the wilburroos, the one about the Rainbow Snake. Then his da would tell one of his stories about Coo Cullen and sing about the Shan Van Voct.

Tom arrived at the house in Subiaco. John John slept on a camp bed and they shared the small bedroom with Spike. Nieve was green with envy. Livid. The pungent smell of the dog and the soft snoring from Tom soothed away any lingering doubts which John John may have had that his da would be home soon.

He was sent home early from school the next day because Miss Flynn fainted in the afternoon. Billy said this was because it was her time of the month. John John nodded and stifled his curiosity. The class were dismissed because there was only an hour until the bell. He played football in the park but then he got annoyed with the way Billy had to be boss of everything and decided to go home.

He sidled around to the back of the house where the kitchen door gave out on to the small verandah. Spike was lolling in the afternoon heat and raised his head to acknowledge John John. For the umpteenth time John John wished he had his own dog. On the new farm he surely would.

There were voices coming from within. 'I'm sorry Tom.'

His ears pricked.

'But there's not much point in carrying on hoping is there? You've done everything you could, you don't know how grateful I am to you, and that you were there.' His mammie was saying, 'Thank God you were, I couldn't have faced the police, what with the children and all.'

John John hesitated before the kitchen door. He had a

sudden intuition that if he entered, they would stop talking. Stop talking about the da. Mammie would look surprised and then put on her jolly face and offer him a glass of milk and a biscuit. That was a temptation, but even more than the jammie dodgers in the tin, he wanted to know about his da.

'He may still come back, Mrs Glendon.' Tom was saying and John John felt his heart skip,

Yes! Tom would know. Tom knew things.

'Maeve, you know you can call me Maeve.'

'The sun can do that to a man.' Tom continued. 'Turn his head. Make him go a little crazy. The temperatures out there were going off the scale, Mrs – Maeve.'

John John crept along the verandah to the open kitchen window to be closer.

'Tom, you're trying to help, to be kind, but I don't know how much longer I can ...'

'I'll do whatever—'

'I know. I know ... The Lease here is up in two weeks ...'

John John wondered if his mother was about to cry there was a funny wobble in her voice. If there was one thing he couldn't stand, it was when his mammie cried.

'I can look after you. Look after you all.'

John John nodded, he wanted to shout out to his mammie, Tom would look after them. Until his da got back from the Walkabout.

'The house is a bit rough but it's nearly fixed up, I've been going hell for leather. We can make a go of it.'

There was silence then. John John wished he could see what was happening. But if he poked his head up to the window sill, they might see him.

'Tom. Tom ...'

There was something in his mother's voice which was a bit odd. Why didn't she just say, yes? They could all go to the new farm and there'd be no Boss because they would be the Boss.

'Tom, I can't do *nothing*. All my life I've been sitting back and doing nothing. I have to make a decision. And I have, for better or worse. I've decided to go home.'

'Home?'

John John too wondered what his mammie meant.

'I'm going to have to let you go. The farm was always Patrick's dream, not mine. I know how hard you've worked and I'll pay you every penny from the sale of the livestock if you'll undertake that last favour for me and hopefully that will be enough to see you through to the next job. There's money coming from Ireland.'

'Maeve ...'

John John could feel his tummy jumping up and down. He wanted to be sick. He heard the pain in Tom's voice and he could feel a pain inside himself but an anger too. Why wasn't his mammie listening to Tom! They would go to the new farm and then the da would come back and Ben would be with him and Ben would stay too and there would be a camp fire every night.

He was running, he didn't know why, he didn't know where. Not to the park. He didn't want Billy to see him crying because he knew that might happen any minute, he could feel the burning in his head and the pressure behind his eyes. He would run and not stop running and then he would be lost and his mammie would have to stay to find him. He would make her. He would write her a letter, he had the address off by heart, he would write, *Mammie don't go, I'm lost but you can find me.* And Tom would help her and everything would be alright.

As soon as he had this idea, he knew that it was brilliant. He began to slow down and stopped to catch his breath which was heaving up and down his chest and it was a hot afternoon with the heat bouncing back up off the pavements and he was sweating and thirsty. John John looked around trying to get his bearings. He didn't recognise the street, but up ahead the noise and movement of traffic indicated a busier road at the intersection.

John John trudged along the main thoroughfare passing a petrol station, a Golden Fleece, one like his da used to have, and then there was a waste plot with a broken wire fence and in the corner of the site a cluster of trees held the promise of

391

shelter. John John hopped over the broken wire and headed over the litter strewn ground where the grass was turned to hay and was thick with the monotonous clacking of cicadas.

Under the trees he found the ashes of a fire and a log which served as a bench, surrounded by the debris of cigarette butts and rusting cans. He'd have to keep an eye out for the big boys who probably had it as their den but he could rest for a while. And write the letter. Of course. John John unbuckled his satchel and rummaged about for jotter and pencil. His lunchbox still had an apple in it. He preferred bananas, but he was grateful now that he hadn't eaten the apple at lunchtime because there was a sharp watery juice when he crunched in to it and immediately, he began to feel better and emboldened to his plan.

He was so concentrated on composing the letter that he didn't hear the man approach.

'What y'r writing young fullah?'

'Oh.' John John looked up startled, to find himself being observed by a large black man. With a mass of greying springy hair and a face that had crevices so deep his eyes squinted from sunken holes. He had on a bulky tattered coat and carried a large plastic bag. Thick broken toenails poked through his worn sandals.

'Heh, heh, writing a love letter are you?'

'No.' Instinctively John John covered his text.

'None of my business, hey?

John John shook his head. Should he make a run for it?

'Mind if I sit at your fire, mate?'

John John frowned, the fire was a pile of ashes and a burnt can.

'Know about etiquette do ya?'

John John shook his head. Etiquette, what was that?

'Yeah, well, when a fullah come to another man's fire then he gotta ask permission, can't sit down and make hisself at home, gotta ask permission.'

John John didn't know what to say. 'Oh.'

The big blackfella scratched his neck under the thicket of his hair. 'Like I ses ...'

392

John John nodded. He would pack up in a minute and be on his way anyway.

The blackfella lowered himself stiffly onto the end of the log bench and dropped his bag which made a clanking sound.

'Name's Sam. Sam Kirkwall.'

He didn't offer his hand but rubbed them up and down his legs. His hands were dry and calloused and half of a finger on his left hand was missing.

'I'm John ...' John John paused and didn't repeat the name. If someone came looking for him, they would know immediately that a boy called John John was him.

'On the run, heh?'

John John's eyes widened, how did the blackfella know?

'No worries, won't be me that'll grass you to the gunji.' Sam yawned. 'Tell you what, I take a kip, you clear the ash out that old fire, collect bit of wood and that, nice and dry, and I'll share some tucker. We make a good fire. It get cold later, colder than you'd think.' Sam yawned and slid from the bench onto the ground curling around his plastic bag. 'Course you might be gone time I come around. That be the case, then so long little wudgebulla.'

In minutes Sam Kirkwall was softly snoring.

John John sat and thought. He went for a pee behind a bush. He sat and thought some more. Through the broken wire fence, he could see a straggled line of children in uniform. Nieve would be waiting for him as usual at the gate because they were supposed to walk home together but she always strode ahead until they got to the corner of their street. Hah hah. She'd be wondering where he was and getting annoyed. But then someone would tell her about Miss Flynn. And that would get her even more mad because he'd been let out early and then she'd rush home to see if he'd got any special treats.

That reminded him that he was beginning to feel a little hungry. He took out his lunchbox and fingered up the crumbs. He wished that he'd kept some of the peanut butter sandwich, but how could he have known that this was the day that he would run away. Not forever, of course. Soon his mammie would be looking for him and then she really would cry. But she would get his letter and that would make her realise that she had to stay. They couldn't go to Ireland and leave the da behind.

John John's memories of Ireland were a blur. There was a dog called Flan. And some cows. And a big house with a dark kitchen and stone for the floor. There was a granny who said the rosary beads and gave him a holy medal when they left and there was a granny who smiled and made lovely little apple tarts with cream, one each. He couldn't remember his grandfather really, one of the Johns he was named after, only that he had a prickly moustache when he gave you a hug, but he was dead anyway. That was all. He had lots of memories in Australia. Wasn't this their home?

Sam Kirkwall snorted in his sleep and muttered something. It brought John John back to where he was. What should he do? Should he stay with Sam Kirkwall? Or maybe he could find the caravan site in Como. Nieve used to collect bottles from the caravans and you could get money and then he could buy a burger or a hot dog and coca cola. Maybe that could be a plan for the next day. He wondered what Sam had for his tucker?

John John looked at the ashes. Better do as Sam said and clear it out.

The sparks flew up from the fire as Sam gave it another poke. 'Good fire mate.'

They shared a tin of meatballs and a tin of spaghetti, cooked in the pan Sam Kirkwall took out of his plastic bag. He'd tell his mammie how good it was when he got home. Sam gave John John a bottle of water while he drank something called a Bundy.

'Acquired taste.'

'Mr Kirkwall—are you on a Walkabout?'

Sam eyed him over the lip of his bottle. 'Reckon I am.'

'So's my da.'

'That right, John?'

'He has a friend called Ben.'

'Know a Ben myself.'

'Maybe it's the same one?'

'Yeah.'

'They'll be sitting round a fire right now.'

'Not as good as this one, mate.' Sam Kirkwall chuckled.

'No,' John John grinned. 'You know the story about Wurunna?'

'Wur – what's that?'

'He's like a magician. He changed his brother's into swans.'

'Yeah, yeah, I think I heard that one, and them women fighting, Willburroos, 'nuf to make the sky all red with their blood?'

John John's face lit up. 'That's the one!'

Sam poked the fire again. 'Magicians, heh. Where are they when you need them?'

'Do you know any other stories, Mr Kirkwall?'

'Stories? Not be much of a one for stories ... now Ben, he'd be the fullah for that.'

'Wan the Crow ..?' John John prompted.

'Heh heh, bad bugger. Wan the Crow. Heh, heh. Bad bugger.'

John John could see he wasn't going to get much more out of Sam Kirkwall so he told him the story about the wren and the King of the Birds with more detail and embellishment than his first telling all those months back. Sam Kirkwall laughed and chortled at the denouement.

'Where that story come from?' he asked.

'Ireland.'

'That your born country?'

John John's brow creased for a moment. 'Where I was born? Guess so.'

'Your born country ...' Sam was nodding off.

'Mr Kirkwall ... if you see my da on the Walkabout ... can you tell him it's time to come back.'

'No worries.'

'His name is Patrick Michael Glendon.'

All at once John John felt overwhelmed with exhaustion and all he wanted to do was to curl up in a comfortable bed. As Sam Kirkwall foretold the night was turning cold and he didn't even have a jacket. He could get closer to the fire but the smoke kept getting in his eyes and made them smart. Tomorrow he would figure out a plan. Maye he could sneak home and get some more clothes and a bottle of milk and, yes, he could leave the letter so then he wouldn't have to think about getting a stamp. His eyes were heavy and he couldn't think of a reason to keep them open any longer.

He was curled up by the log bench when the policeman poked him awake.

'Here, wake up kid! You alrighty?'

John John groaned and rubbed his eyes.

He could see that Sam was already being dragged on to his feet, muttering and swearing under his breath.

'He touch you, fella? That old bastard do anything to ya?'

John John blinked, his head spinning and woozy with unfinished sleep. What was the policeman talking about? Was he talking about Sam Kirkwall?

'Mr Kirkwall ...?' John John shook his head and pushed himself into a sitting position.

Sam Kirkwall was lashing out at the tall policeman who was pushing him away from the camp. 'Bugger off! Can't a bloke get any sleep around here?!' He turned to John John. 'Wasn't me grassed you up, mate.'

His heart was sinking and fast. He'd been found and he had not even sent the letter yet. 'Don't forget – if you see my da ...' John John called urgently after the retreating blackfella.

The smaller policeman took him by the shoulder. 'Reckon you should be home in your bed young fella, it's gone midnight. Reckon your ma's having conniptions!'

At the station they gave him a hot cocoa drink and a ham sandwich whilst they waited for an available squad car to take him home.

John John took a step back and glowered at his mother when she flung open the door so she knew not to wrap her arms around him.

'John John!'

'All right then, Mrs Glendon?' The young woman police officer asked.

'Yes, thank you, officer. Thank you, so much.'

'No more running away now Johnnie, y'hear?' The woman nodded and headed back to the police car which had flashing lights but not the siren. She had put the lights on especially for him so she could drive faster down the streets and everyone would think it was an emergency. It almost made up for the fact that he was going home.

John John knew as soon as he stepped into his bedroom; he didn't even have to see the bed which had been stripped, the space on the shelf beside it.

'Tom left this afternoon. He would have liked to say goodbye, but ... he had to go. And then you didn't come home and I was frantic.' His mammie looked tired.

There had been a flash of relief when she opened the door. But now she looked as though the life was draining out of her, pale like a ghost.

'Don't worry mammie; I'll look after you!' he blurted.

She smiled wanly, 'He left you something.'

On the camp bed he could see Tom's old slouched hat.

'Nieve's livid with jealousy.'

They shared a grin then and he let her kiss him goodnight.

THE WICKED WITCH OF THE WEST

Nieve opened her small suitcase on the lower bunk bed. She hadn't even put up a fight when John, just John as he now wanted to be called, shouted, *Bagsy the top bunk!* It was childish anyway, she thought, and John was welcome to it. He had already rushed off to explore the decks, refusing to take Patsy with him. Patsy stomped and whined until her mother suggested they go and find the children's playroom. Nieve was left to herself and that suited her fine.

The SS Roma would be sailing from Freemantle in under two hours. Leaving. Leaving Oz. When her mother told them that they were getting the boat back home, Nieve had been struck dumb. To Italy and then by train across Europe, with the last leg on the ferry to Dublin.

John asked, 'But what about the da? What about Killpool Vale? Is the da back, is he coming with us?'

Nieve knew what the answers were.

'Your da has not been found ....' her mammie said. But what she meant was that the da was never coming back. That much Nieve knew and understood. She didn't know why she understood this and it wasn't the same as knowing for certain that their da was dead, if they knew that then there would be a funeral and they could all cry and be sad together. Instead they were all sad separately.

By the time that the ship's horn gave out a series of forlorn wails and the great bulk juddered and groaned into movement, Nieve decided she would never forgive her mother.

THE WATER OF LIFE

Tom wandered from station to station, never staying long. At one point he was on one of the Patterson farms outside Pinjarra. Whilst he was there, he considered calling in at Fairbridge, but then thought better of it. Those days were long behind him now.

The late sixties found him down near Margaret River. He'd saved up some money, never being one for drinking and too savvy to gamble. He was fed up always working for some boss-man, fed up breaking his back in the searing heat for somebody else's profit. He remembered that first morning alone on Killpool Vale and the thrill of feeling the place his own for however brief a custodianship. So, he took his scrimped savings along to the bank and pressed for a loan with which to buy out a small dairy farm. A Welshman and his wife had had enough of the hassles from the same bank.

The soil wasn't much to boast about but the ocean kept him cooler than up country. And Tom was used to hard work, that much was for sure. The farm was barely above subsistence level but enough to keep his head above water and to employ a blackfella and his missus.

Greg Yamatji, said he had a brother, Danny, worked out Darinup way one time. From what Tom could make out Danny Yamatji had come to a sad end, dying in jail in suspicious circumstances.

'Fixed up proper, mate.'

Greg had a crooked arm, some *bust up long time back,* but it didn't stop him being a grafter and his wife Tana was a decent cook. They rubbed along well enough all three, none of them big on talking, but when they did, they found they had a lot in common. It was Tana who suggested Tom should write one more time.

'Everyone need a mother, that's what they never understand.'

Tana was right of course, they didn't understand. *Forget thee mother,* his grandfather had said. And at Fairbridge the children were discouraged from dwelling on the past, on the motherland, that land where your mother was if you still had one. The future was what counted, you were told at Pinjarra. *Boys To Be Farmers. Girls to be Farmer's Wives.* Held out like some fairytale ending, worth the loss of mother and family.

But you didn't forget a mother, not one like Lily Martin. All those years at Fairbridge, there'd never once been any answer to any of his letters. Later, he wondered if they'd ever been sent. Or maybe that was just preferable to the idea that no one back in Rochdale wanted to hear from him. When he sat down to write this letter, he promised himself it would be the last.

Dear Mr Bradshaw,

I am your grandson Tom. I hope you are in good health. I am writing to you again in the hopes that you will have news for me of my mother and that we may make contact again if she wishes to. I hope she will be glad to hear that I am doing well and have my own farm now ...

He wrote out the address on the envelope hoping they were still at number seventeen Trafalgar Road. Named after a famous battle, he knew that. He licked the stamps and punched them down.

'Want an air mail sticker with that?' The girl behind the post office counter asked.

'Thanks.'

'Dawn.'

He was puzzled for a moment, 'Dawn, right, thanks.'

She waited. There was a twinkle in her eye.

'Tom.'

'I know who you are, Mr Bradshaw, your mail comes

400

through here; everyone's mail comes through here. You ever go swimming?'

'Don't get time.'

'Well you know what they say, all work and no play.'

'Yeah, that's me, a dull boy.'

'Reckon it'll be a nice evening for it down by the old jetty.'

'I'm sure it will.' He was backing out of the post office, almost tripping over an elderly lady. ''Scuse I mam.'

'Seven thirty, don't be late.'

At supper he'd wiped his plate clean of gravy with Tana's flat bread and stared out the window at the golden glow in a clear blue sky.

'Nice evening.'

'Yeah ...' Tana waddled over to the sink. 'Reckon young fella like you should get out 'n enjoy it.'

Tom shook his head.

'Me and Greg do the milking.'

Tom hesitated. What would he be letting himself in for with the big boned girl from the Post Office? Small place like Margaret River you wouldn't want to jump in feet first. There he was racing ahead as usual, expecting complications, trouble. He could keep it simple, casual, just friendly.

'Could take a dip, I reckon?'

'Couple of stubbies on the beach mate.' Greg contributed, to seal the decision.

She was there with a few mates, insurance maybe against disappointment, or was that just his assumption. They were gathering brush and driftwood for a beach fire. Dawn peeled away when she saw him and gave a friendly wave.

'Fancied a dip then?'

Tom caught the amusement in her eye and wondered if there was a double entendre to be inferred or a challenge even. He had to admit he'd never been good at reading

401

women.

'Come, let me show you something.' She headed over towards the old ruined jetty and he followed obediently.

Her eyes scanned the waters for a few minutes and then yelped with excitement and pointed. 'There! See him?!'

He narrowed his eyes and hunted through water fractured by the squinting sunset. Then he saw, 'Whoa!'

'Aint he a beaut?' Dawn grinned with pleasure, like she was offering him a gift. And in a way she was. He had never seen a manta ray before. The sheer size of it took your breath away, the grace as it glided between the rotting stumps of the jetty.

'They come in this close?' he asked with amazement.

'This fella.'

They watched the manta with fascinated wonder until he headed out to sea. 'Safe to swim here?' he enquired.

'If you're prepared to show a little respect.'

'No question.' he blew his cheeks.

'Then you've got nothing to worry about.' She eyed his cooler bag, 'You thinking of cracking one open anytime this century?'

'Sorry.' He reddened and fumbled for the stubbies of beer and proffered one.

Dawn plonked herself down and dug her toes into the sand. 'Nothing like it, sea, sunset and a bottle of beer.'

He settled beside her and they were companionably silent while they enjoyed the glug of cold beer in the last heat of the day. Tom took out his smokes and they both lit up.

As the sun finally set in a glory of orange and purple, they began to exchange small snippets about their lives.

On the third beer he probed, 'You're not married, are you?'

'No. Why? Are you thinking of proposing?' she grinned.

'Just …'

'Aha, I see, married women.'

'Yes, married women.' Tom admitted.

'Snap. Not women of course,' Dawn giggled into her beer, 'men, married men.'

She raised her stubby, 'Here's to being single, foot loose

402

and fancy free.'

They clinked bottles.

'Free to spend all night on the beach if we like.' she added.

Tom looked heavenward. 'Starry night like this …'

The next day a man from the government came to his door asking for a word. At the kitchen table he opened up his briefcase. The WA government had this idea about growing grapes. They reckoned that because of the way the land jutted out into the ocean the climate in the south west area was a lot like Bordeaux. Apparently, some doctors had been experimenting, the man said, and they had a lot of success even in a short time. Over at Forest Hill the Agricultural Department had done some planting that had come good. Viticulture they called it and they were offering a deal for dairy farmers like himself to join the experiment and make the change over.

A lot of the local people thought it was a non-starter, another crazy scheme, but Tom chewed on it and he liked what he tasted. He confided in Dawn. Told her about his father, Massimo Martinelli, and he reckoned the Martinellis knew a thing or two about grapes and maybe it was in him too.

'Sometimes, you've got to take chances, go with your gut.' She encouraged.

Next time he went in to the liquor store he looked along the shelf of wines. There weren't that many but even so it was confusing, riesling, cabernet sauvignon, chablis, chardonnay, merlot, so many exotic names, he didn't know what any of it meant. He bought a couple of bottles, one red, one white. The man behind the counter gave him a queer look.

'Got a special offer on the Tooheys this week, Tom.'

Tom nodded. 'Thought I might like a change.'

'Suit yourself, mate.'

Over the next month he worked his way through the different labels and varieties, taking notes as he went along. The manager cottoned on and ordered more in. Some evenings Tom would take a bottle down to the old jetty. Dawn would have the barbie going and they'd sit on the beach watching the sun go down and taste the wine and talk about what they liked or didn't like.

Dawn ordered a book through the library services. They poured over it. They began to talk about body and depth and tannin, smell the wine first, taking quick sniffs, roll the wine around in the glass examining the colour, take a sip and hold it in the mouth, moving it around, concentrated, then they'd look at each other, grin and swallow.

'Seems a crying shame to spit it out!' was Dawn's opinion.

Dawn encouraged Tom out of his shyness to go and visit the grape growing doctors. He was moved by their enthusiasm and willingness to share their knowledge. By the end of the year he made his decision to sell the cows. That was an exciting time for Tom. He didn't have much in the way of acreage so he couldn't go for volume but he could go for quality. Chardonnay, they decided.

'You might as well grow what you like to drink.' Dawn reasoned.

And a Riesling as an insurance.

Neighbours would drive by and have a good laugh at his sapling vines, 'Growing fences are yer mate?'

They were nervous days, it was all about the right amount of sun and the right amount of rain, at the right time. For a while it seemed like it was coming the wrong way around, too much sun when there should have been rain. Tom was getting twitchy. Government aid only went so far, he was up to his neck with the bank, converting the cow sheds and installing the shiny new equipment for fermenting the grapes on the never never.

Greg stood beside him one day looking out over the young vines. 'What you need—Wandjina.'

'What's that?'

'Wandjina make rain, flood whole damn earth if you like.'

'Yeah, well just an inch or two would do for now.' Tom

dug his toe cap into the powdery dry earth. 'So, can you ask the Wandjina?'

'Not me boss. I was brought up Christian in Mission. Don't know the right way.'

They stood in silence. Greg blowing smoke rings. 'Inanunga.' Greg said a last. 'I heard that was a name of a Wandjina.'

Tom nodded; he exhaled a stream of smoke up into the pale blue sky. 'Great Inanunga, don't know the right words, or the way to say them, but if you could spare a little of your precious rain then I would be truly grateful.'

'Me too boss.' Greg followed looking skyward, and Tom wasn't sure whether the *boss* referred to was himself or Inanunga.

Dusk was approaching as they set off back through the jarrah trees. All of a sudden Greg stopped and frowned. 'Notice something, boss?'

Tom looked around him, puzzled, all was still. 'The birds. No birds.'

Dawn drove over that evening to find Tom and Greg and Tana whooping around on the verandah watching the rain cascade off the roof. As she made the dash from the car to the shelter Tom caught her on the steps and swung her around in his arms.

'What the—!'

'Ain't it beaut!'

'I'm getting wet out here Tom Bradshaw!'

'Inanunga!'

'In a what?'

'Inanunga. That's what we're going to call our wine!'

'Wandjina made rain for Tom.' Greg explained.

Tom set Dawn down on the verandah.

'Come on inside. We're just about to have some tucker.'

'I called over because a letter came for you and …' she paused, 'well I wanted to give it to you myself.'

'Who from? The Government? The bank?'

405

She shook her head and reached into her bag.

It was a pale blue envelope and the address was written in capital letters in a spidery hand.

Tom shook his head and exhaled, 'Whoa.'

'Call me later if you like.' Dawn turned to go.

'No. Don't go. Stay for supper. I'd like you to stay.'

'Sure?'

'Got one of Doc Cullity's riesling's chilling in the fridge.'

'You twisted my arm.'

'And I think I could do with a drink before I open this.'

Tom could feel himself shaking. Dawn laid a hand on his shoulder. And right then and there he knew that whatever else happened, he was not going to let her go, ever.

A LETTER FROM HOME

6th October 1971

My dear grandson,

I hope that this letter will find you even though it is nearly a year since you last wrote to us. I hope that you are well and happy. I have been reading all of your letters for the first time. So many you wrote. They are wet with my tears. It saddens me to think of you waiting all this long time for a reply.

Let me try and explain. Your grandfather Harry has passed away and I have been going through his papers. Harry was not a bad man. I think he always thought that he acted for the best in everything he did. He was a very religious man and sometimes his beliefs might have made him a little harsh. I know this was the case with our Lily, and this has been very hard for me because a wife must support her husband and of course at the time that you were born there was such a disgrace attached to children out of wedlock.

Lily was certain that your father, an American soldier, would return and that they'd be married, so she refused to give you up and that was the first rift with her father. She moved to Manchester and went under the name of Mrs Martin and that must have been tough for her with a young one on her own. For me it was a very distressing time, I had lost my daughter and my grandson. You are my only grandson.

I would love to see you a fine grown man but I am nearly eighty years old now and I don't think I could make such a long voyage even if I could afford it. Times are hard here, and your uncle Frank's worried there'll be a strike at his works. You will always be welcome here. I have told Frank and he is of the same mind. Your uncle Ray takes after his father and would rather the past were left alone but that may be because the grief of Harry's illness, emphysema, and his death is still very close for all of us. But I'm sure if he was to meet you, it would be a different matter.

Now I come to your mother and this is the most difficult thing for me to write. Sadly, our Lily passed away in 1956. She was being treated at The Riversdale Mental Asylum. I was never clear myself what was wrong with her but she had a temper I know. Apparently, part of the treatment was to give her Insulin to make her go into a coma; the psychiatrist explained to Harry later that it's a way to make a patient calmer and it's temporary but, every once in a while, some don't wake up out of it. It broke my heart. But Harry and I were both able to see her at the end. She looked very serene, like a sleeping beauty, so young she still was.

Lily's baby girl was born after you were taken to the Barnardo's Home, that would be in 1952. I don't know if you were aware at the time. Your mother went in to Riversdale and all I learned was that the baby girl was adopted soon after and I suppose we shall never know what's become of her. I only saw her the once, she was quite negro but light eyes, I'd almost say she had your mother's green eyes.

My dear Tom, I hope that you can forgive us what was done, times were different back then. I visit your mother's grave when I can, she's at peace now. I am hoping and praying that you are well and that one day you might come home.

Your loving grandmother,
Phyllis Bradshaw

THE RIGHTFUL HEIR

It was a real pink eye summer. Every so often Jack would tap the thermometer on the verandah to check the damn thing was working, but it was. He took refuge in his office in the darkest corner of the house and reckoned up the accounts. It had been a tough year but he had come out on top, 1972 could only be better. There was a rap at the door. He grunted and Maddy entered, when she didn't speak immediately, he turned to look at her, there was a hesitant, anxious expression on her face.

'Well?'

'There's a man here to see you Jack.'

'Tell whoever it is I don't want any.' He was annoyed at the distraction from his figures.

'He's not that sort of bloke, Jack.' She pushed the door open wider. 'I think you need to see him, it's about Jimmy.'

The news that his son was dead hit Jack like a sky tumbling sideways. He felt like an old man, suddenly he knew he was an old man.

'When will they be flying Jimmy home?' He managed to ask.

The man in uniform shook his head gravely.

Jack wondered in a passing flash if this were a look the man had practiced on others too.

'He was in a helicopter transport. I'm sorry Mr Anderson, the Vietcong blew them right out of the sky. It would have been instantaneous – wouldn't have known what hit them.'

Jack imagined a shower descending from the smoky skies, a shower of crimson petals and flames, what was the expression? His mind groped for the picture, *shot down in flames*, spinning like a Catherine Wheel at a firework show. No, perhaps it was *blasted, blasted to smithereens*; he'd

409

heard that expression somewhere. What were smithereens anyway? His son, Jimmy. His son Jimmy, he was smithereens. He must find the dictionary, they had one somewhere in the house. Maddy had hold of his arm, her fingers pressing into his skin. The man was saying something else.

'... a memorial service.'

A funeral. Without a body would there be a funeral? Without a body could they even be sure Jimmy was dead. For an insane moment Jack imagined Jimmy jumping from the helicopter as the missile struck. He'd have been caught. A prisoner of war.

'...that's what we would advise.' The man was saying.

Jack could see the stain of sweat bleeding from under his armpits. Maddy was suggesting a cup of tea. The man was shaking his head, something about an intrusion. He was shuffling backwards, he gave a salute, or was it a wave, and got into his car. Jack could see the insignia now. Maddy was trying to edge him back indoors but that was not where Jack wanted to be, not hemmed in by walls with the savage groaning of the new washing machine in its final spin ringing in his ears.

In the following week before the Memorial Service, Jack wandered the boundaries of Inverness and all the other blocks and pondered over their future. Would Alex come back, might that be a possibility? No. It would never work and anyway who would there be after Alex? Alex only had daughters too. He had to get his head straight. He was only in his early sixties. There could be another son. It was not too late. He could divorce Maddy. He'd see her right, a generous settlement. He could marry again. That daughter of the Osbornes, the plump one, Nancy, worked over at the new information centre for the Darinup Flora and Fauna Nature Reserve, she seemed to have missed the boat; all right there was thirty years in the difference but men aged better and a girl like that wouldn't turn her nose up at the chance to be mistress of a spread like Inverness.

Jenny flew over from Sydney as soon as she heard the news about her brother. She talked ceaselessly about the old days, teary with memories, took out albums and albums of black and white photos. Jack couldn't stand to be in the same room with her. He knew he should be doing more of the organisation for the event but in the end Maddy took the helm, knew the church people better anyway and the caterers and all the other business of social gatherings.

'You've got enough to cope with, it's the least I can do.' She assured.

Mostly he'd been left alone to his wanderings and had only to contend with the sad eyes of the station hands and their muttered condolences, but they all knew a farm didn't stop, not even for a bereavement of such seismic proportions.

He hadn't been able to dodge the Bodenham newspaperman who wanted to write an article on the local hero, proud member of the 3rd Cavalry Regiment A Squadron, Jimmy Anderson, shot down in the final stages of the evacuation from Nui Dat; he'd have a fitting obituary, Jack was assured. But what was there to say about a twenty-year old boy foolish enough to want to go off fighting in some misbegotten war in some far-off misshapen universe. He was like most young jackaroos who liked fast cars, guns, gadgets of any kind, maybe he'd even had a girl or two. Some blonde eighteen-year old sniffling into her hankie at the back of the Memorial Service thinking she's lost the love of her life. What could Jack say that the whole of Darinup didn't already know? Only that for him, Jimmy Anderson was the most precious thing he ever had in his life, his seed, his son and there weren't any words could convey the tragedy of that kind of loss.

Susan arrived home on the morning of the Service. On the same day a letter arrived from the Bodenham Nursing Home

411

to say that Mr Ashton Croker had passed away peacefully in his sleep at the age of eighty-nine.

Susan had been backpacking in India. She was thin, wore a sequined kaftan type of shirt and her hair was long in a weird assortment of plaits. Jack thought she looked like a daggy hippy but she showered and brushed up and emerged dressed in black and looking respectable enough.

There were a lot of young people at the Memorial and one red headed girl bawling into her hankie and her friends propping her up like she was the young widow. A couple of representatives of the Army attended, polite and reserved. Jenny looked wrung out and didn't seem to have any tears left. The Reverend went on too long about 'young lives cut short' but Jack passed the time notching who had shown up every time he swiveled to scratch his ear or adjust his tie. The Osbornes were there and yes, Nancy was with them, the plumpness turning a little too much to fat he noted.

There were drinks and sandwiches afterwards at the Masonic Hall. After half an hour of condolences and pleasantries Jack felt hot and sticky in his suit and decided to slip out to the back yard to the shade of a bushy yate for a smoke-oh. He gave a cursory wave to a couple of other blokes loitering outside with their cans of beer but they seemed to know to leave him alone.

Then he saw Susan heading towards him. He stubbed the ciggie underfoot.

'So, where you off to next on your travels, missy?'

'I wasn't planning to go anywhere.'

'No?'

'I was hoping to stay right here, dad.' She paused; she was looking him square in the eyes. 'I want to learn how to run Inverness.'

She reminded him of someone; that look, something round the eyes, the strong jawline. Then it came to him, he'd never seen it before because he'd never looked for it, Old Jack.

'You want to run Inverness?'

'It's what I've been thinking about all the way back from India, dad. I realise it's the thing I've most wanted all my

412

life; but well …' Jimmy filled the silence. 'Maybe that's why I went off to India and around, didn't know what I was meant to do with my life. Now everything's changed, hasn't it, dad? And maybe this isn't the right moment but before any other bright ideas come your way; I just needed to tell you that this is what I want and no one, not anyone could want it more than me.'

She took his breath away. His daughter.

Maddy came up then and slipped her arm through his and proffered a scotch, 'Thought you might be needing another one of these, Jack.'

He swung her around to him and kissed her smack on the lips.

'What was that for?'

'You'll never need to know.'

'Better get back to the …' Maddy broke away, a bewildered look on her face.

Jack watched her retreat with a smile.

'Maddy's a good woman.' Susan observed.

'You bet.' He drank the scotch in one gulp. 'There's some new dingo netting going up along the Number Two Rabbit Proof, we should go check it out tomorrow, no knowing what that useless bunch of larrikins are up to, if you're not keeping an eye out.'

'Crack of dawn dad.'

413

MY BROTHER'S KEEPER

John Glendon TD phoned to say that his brother, Father James, had been sent home from Africa and was in a Hospice on the outskirts of Dublin; very ill with some dreadful fever he'd contracted after all these years out in the mission school in Burundi. John felt that Father James should see the children. The underlying message was that he might not have long for this world and he should see Patrick's children before he left entirely.

'It would be a great comfort to him.' Then John added with a note of surprise, 'Bridget pointed out the other day that the last time James had seen Patrick was when he was in the Seminary and Patrick must have been only a boy, twelve or thirteen. Isn't that an odd thing in a family? But Father James has been in Africa a long time and of course he wasn't able to return for our father's funeral. And Patrick always seemed to be away, over in Mount Mellick or at sea, Australia. Still, it would be a comfort to Father James to see you and the children.'

Maeve took the details.

'We don't see enough of you, Maeve.'

'Well, you must be very busy now in the Dail.'

'Yes, politics, politics. I'll get Felicity to ask you over for a lunch and maybe we can rustle up a game of doubles in the afternoon.'

Maeve reckoned Father James must be fifty or thereabouts but he looked more like a man of seventy. His cheeks sucked into sunburnt chasms. And yet she could still make out the Glendon features. It was strange to think that this was the first and probably only time that she would be meeting

Patrick's brother. And what a breadth of the world she too had traveled.

They had lived with her mother when they first returned to Ireland, weary and dispirited after the long journey home, sailing via Singapore and India, through the Suez, up the Italian coastline to Genoa. The exotic places had helped to distract the children. The Tiger Balm Gardens in Singapore, the purple nights of Bombay. Had distracted her from the pain and nausea of her grief.

Over seven years now since she had left Australia behind, but there wasn't a day when Patrick did not enter her thoughts. The pain had eased and the confusion. She had come to accept her state as not quite a widow. Young as she was, still shy of forty, and with any number of interested men, she remained resolutely unavailable.

There were nights when she was haunted by their last parting. The Christmas in Subiaco. The desperation in his face, the plea in his voice.

'If you'll just give it a chance.' he begged. 'We can have whatever you want.'

'I want to go home.' she said.

Well here she was back in Ireland, wasn't this what she wanted? But every mile of the journey that took her further away from the place of Patrick's last sighting jabbed at her heart.

It was terribly sad, they said, so young, a tragedy and to be left with three small children. Behind her back she knew they were saying that the marriage was doomed from the start. She had hitched her star to a feckless man who could never settle and who let a fortune slip through his fingers more than once and now here she was living on the kindness and generosity of her mother.

'You know after seven years you can have Patrick declared dead.' Kevin announced baldly. Kevin was getting a bit of a paunch Maeve noticed, Sinead fed him too well, she was taking a French cookery course, lots of cream in everything.

415

Maeve placed the bag of grapes on top of the small bedside cabinet.

'Father Glendon should wake soon.' The nurse, who was also a nun, assured. It was a well-appointed room. They look after their own, Maeve noted wryly. Father James did not look much like a priest propped up on the plump pillows in his striped pajamas. Patsy stared at him with interest for a minute or two. Now she was scuffing her shoes against the end of the bed and looking longingly out of the window. Maeve should have insisted on the black and white check frock. Patsy looked like a little ragamuffin in her jeans and cardy. She shouldn't have agreed to the short hair-cut either, but it seemed everything Patsy's friend Janey Flanagan did Patsy was sure to be in her wake.

She was just wondering whether a cup of tea were to be had when Bridget entered at the door.

'Oh, Maeve.'

Maeve stood. Patsy paused in her determination to ruin her Clarks sandals.

'Maeve, how lovely that you're here. How kind. And Patsy.' She beamed a smile as she placed a hand on her niece's shoulder. 'You're growing so fast, aren't you Patsy?'

Patsy nodded shyly.

Patrick's sister Bridget, who had no children of her own, had the effect on children that they were suddenly well mannered and demure. She was a well-groomed woman, her hair lacquered in place like a dark helmet. Maeve had always thought her a bit of a snob but Bridget was delighted by the children and seemed to have mellowed with the years.

'Have you spoken yet with Father James?'

Maeve shook her head.

'Well, he does sleep longer these days.'

Maeve indicated the only chair to the older woman.

Bridget stood over her brother. 'He does seem quite fast asleep. It's a blessing I'm sure.'

'I hope Father James isn't in any pain.' Maeve contributed.

416

'The Doctors are doing all they can to ease his suffering.' She patted her brother's loose hand above the coverlet and turned to Maeve and Patsy. 'So, why don't we see if we can't get a cup of tea from the Sisters, there's a little visitor's room with a patio, we could catch up on your news, why don't we? And then we may be in luck when we get back. I hear Nieve will be going to University, to Trinity? You must be very proud.'

Maeve nodded to both. 'Let her get the Leaving Certificate first, she may be top of the class with history and geography but her Irish is on the ropes.'

Bridget opened the door wider for their exit.

Maeve looked to Patsy but she could see the scowl on her daughter's face and guessed the reason, the comic she had bought to entice her on the visit.

'Patsy, would you rather wait here?'

Patsy nodded gladly.

'We won't be long.'

PATSY

There was a smell of disinfectant, but she was sure that underneath that she could smell *piss* as Janey Flanagan called it and even *shite*. Janey Flanagan had pissed on the road once, dropped her knickers and squatted, in front of the boys and all, giving out a great groan of relief. There were no flies on Janey Flanagan. Janey would have said, *Feck Off wit ya, I'm not goin' ta the hospital ta see some old Holy Joe I don't even know!* said that to her mammie, Mrs Flanagan, even. Janey had a lot of older brothers and they were *F_ this and F_ that* all day. Patsy was appalled at first. Now, it just seemed like saying *hell* or *bugger*; not that she did that either. Her mammie wasn't like Mrs Flanagan, all soft and *there, there boys,* you'd never say a rude thing to her own mammie.

Instead Patsy said, 'Mammie, I've arranged to meet up with Janey and Emer to go to the park.'

'Well you can 'un' arrange it.' her mother declared and turned away from any more protestations.

Nieve was studying for exams, her excuse; but Patsy knew she'd be out the door as soon as they were gone. John was away playing a hurling match in Kildare. That left her.

'Father James wants to see the children.' Her mammie explained.

And that left her. But she'd drawn the line at wearing the frock. She wanted at least to be in her jeans so that she could run off to the park as soon as they got back to Terenure.

There was a low gurgling from the bed. Patsy looked up from her copy of *The Dandy*. Patsy knew she was getting a bit old now that she was nearly eleven but she had always liked *Minnie the Minx*. Next September, when she went up to the big school, she would read nothing but about Enid

Blyton's girls in their dormitories at St Claires.

His eyes were a murky blue. There seemed to be a film over them but they were fixed on her.

'Is that you, Patsy? Is that you?' A wheeze followed that might have been an attempt at laughter.

Her eyes widened and she felt her stomach lurch. The old man in the bed knew who she was. He was a priest but he was also her uncle. She nodded in response. What should she say? What should she do? Was she meant to hug him?

'Aren't you the little Devil?'

Why was he saying that, she wondered? Her granny would say just that sometimes when she ate more of the raspberries than she picked for the jam. Had Uncle Priest seen her do something when she thought he was asleep?

'Come to tempt me again, have you, Patsy?'

Then it dropped like the proverbial penny. Of course. He was doolally. That was part of the sickness.

'Come here. Closer, till I see you in the light.'

Patsy grimaced and edged a little towards the neat iron bed. She could see he was only roughly shaven and there was a stain of tea or something else on his dry chapped lips. She hoped very much that she would not be expected to kiss him.

'Would you look at you. The bloom on yer cheek, don't you look like an angel?'

His hand crept over the coverlet, his fingers twitching, signaling her closer in. 'Butter wouldn't melt in your mouth.'

Definitely a looney tune or as Janey would have said, *a feckin' looney tune*.

She shrugged. It seemed the only suitable response.

'What's that you're reading?' he indicated the comic.

'The Dandy.'

The old man wheezed again, 'Desperate Dan! Sure, didn't you always love Desperate Dan and his cow pies.'

'And Minnie the Minx.'

'Come here ...'

Her legs were up against the bed now. There was a little drool of saliva at the edge of his mouth. She hoped he didn't want a kiss on the cheek.

419

'... will I take you to a match?' He heaved up from the pillows. 'Wouldn't you like that Patsy? At Old Belvedere? I hear Clancy's playing.'

He grabbed her hand and was clutching on to it. Patsy felt herself yanked forward and off balance. He was strong for an old man that was sick. The thin strands of hair from the top of his head were hanging over one ear now, a comb over it was called, Janey's brothers were always teasing their da for the one he sported, and he'd retort, *the laugh will be on the other side boys when yous start losing yours!*

Her uncle had a peculiar look in his eye. Wait until she'd tell Janey, *Defo feckin' doolally!* Only it might not be right to laugh about an uncle who was also a priest.

'It'll be our secret ...' he was gibbering.

He was clasping her with both hands now. And one hand drew her in by the waist. Her nose twitched at the sweet sourness of his breathe. 'Our little secret.'

'What secret?' she couldn't help asking.

'Ah, but you're the cute one.' His eyes narrowed. 'What do you want? Sweeties? I can give you sweeties.'

He was rubbing his hand up and down her back and she could see that he did want a kiss after all.

'My little Patsy, ...'

He squeezed her wrist so tight that she dropped the comic. He might be a looney tune but Patsy decided enough was enough. He wanted a kiss and then he'd hopefully let her go. She leaned in and gave him a quick peck on the cheek. There it was done. But he still had her held fast.

'That's hurting, let go now.' she urged.

'You like me, don't ya Patsy?'

'Sure.' She didn't at all like him and next time there was a visit it wouldn't be her turn, for defo.

'It's only a bit of fun, isn't that right?' His hand slipped down her back and clutched her bottom.

She tried to wriggle out of his hold but she was gripped fast. And then his hand was feeling for the waistband of her jeans, they were elasticated at the back so it was easy for him to slip his long bony fingers under.

420

'Only a bit of fun ...'

Patsy knew now for certain that he was crazy, and a dirty old man as well. Should she swivel about and hit him? Even as this thought flashed across her mind, she heard a gasp from behind and the shout from her mother and her mother grabbed his arm away and was hauling her out of reach.

'James ...?' Her aunt's voice seemed almost strangled.

'He's a little liar, you wouldn't believe a word he says.' Her uncle's features crabbed tight. 'Father knows that all right, so he does.' A sharp quivering finger pointed at Aunty Bridget. 'Knows it's Pat's fault, so he does.' A wheezing cough. No, it really was a laugh of sorts. '*The Devil comes in many guises. That's what da told me, The Devil is using Patsy to lead you into the temptations of the flesh. It's the Devil that is in Patsy*—and by God don't I know it!' The old man was collapsing back against the pillows cackling even as he tried to catch his breath.

'James, Father, hush now.' It was her aunt placing a hand on his shoulder.

'Little devils the lot of them! Little black devils—they like their sweeties!'

'Hush now, you don't know what you're saying.'

Patsy could feel her mammie's bosom rising and falling, she held her so tight. 'You know what he's saying, Bridget, you know what he's saying.'

'It's the morphine has him delirious.'

'Did you know? Did you all know?!'

'No! Of course not. Not ... no one ever said a word.' There was a flush across her aunt's cheeks.

Her mammie was squeezing her close and Patsy could feel the weight of the silence hanging over the room.

Father James subsided back onto the pillows and gazed heavenward. 'Bless you all, my children ...' he mumbled, 'In the name of the Father and of the Son and of the Holy Ghost ...'

'I hope he rots.' her mammie whispered. 'God help me but I do.'

Her mammie was still trembling when they got in the car.

'Are you alright mammie?'

'Oh darling, I'm so sorry, if I'd thought for one moment ...'

'It's alright mammie, he didn't get a chance, not really. I'd have belted him, you know, even if he is a priest.'

'Quite right.'

'Janey says there are Perv's everywhere. One grabbed her in Bushy Park one time and she just kicked him in the bollocks.' Realising she had used a rude word; Patsy bit her lip and pulled a guilty face.

'Is that right?' Her mother smiled with a look of satisfaction. 'Good on her.'

Patsy grinned. 'You wouldn't want to mess with Janey Flanagan.'

'Or Patsy Glendon.'

'Mammie, I was thinking when I go to the big school in September, I want to be called Patricia.'

Her mammie nodded. 'You know Patricia, your daddy was a good man and he loved you very much.'

'Sure, I know that.' Patsy thought she would push her luck. 'Could we maybe have a choc ice on the way home?'

Her luck was in.

RINGWAY

The plane skidded down the runway. A fine drizzle. Dawn squeezed his hand. Tom had not known he would have such a fear of flying. Beads of sweat on his brow every time the plane took off and landed, three times he'd been through it now on this journey, a tightness in his throat, his body rigid. But smiling for the sake of the squirming boy in the window seat. Marty straining against the seatbelt to see the ground revealed through the cloud. Their final destination.

Not quite. There would be the trip up to Rochdale in the hire car. The family reunion. His grandmother still indomitable according to Uncle Frank. There would be one of his cousins with her new born. Tom would be a curiosity. A relic from a forgotten time. There would be pleasantries and cakes and the awkward silences which Dawn would help to fill with her full-throated laughter and her way of putting anyone at their ease after all those years in the post office.

But this arrival at Ringway airport, this was the reunion which brought Tom half way round the world. His sister. No, not a 'reunion'; because of course they had never even met. Never been allowed to meet. He had more of the story now, more of the broken threads which made up the weave of his mother's life after he was taken from her.

Lily had been labeled some sort of sexual delinquent. You could be chucked into a nut house for that back in the early fifties. His grandfather had signed the papers. Good old Harry. Tom recalled the meeting at the Barnardo's Home. The smell of his grandfather's damp overcoat. Those words which had reverberated throughout his life. *Best forget about thee mother.* But he hadn't forgotten, never forgotten her quick laughter, the magical stories of far-off lands and the mischief in her green eyes. Lying in his cot in Pinjarra

423

amongst the other lost boys he conjured his mother's smile in his darkest hours and the soothing murmur in her voice as she would lullaby him to sleep. And all that time, as he longed for her to come and rescue him, she also was incarcerated and screaming to be set free until they had at last snuffed the life from her.

His sister had been in the asylum too. There'd been some sort of mother and baby unit, which Tom found hard to credit. The fact that the child was black sealed his mother's fate, confirmed the diagnosis. They'd simply locked her up and thrown away the key.

It seemed at first incomprehensible to Tom. The letter from his grandmother felt like looking into an abyss with no signposts to guide his feelings. Finally, to know that his mother was dead. And the manner of her death. Finally, to know that his mother would never again clasp him to her warmth and call him her little prince. She was dead and how was he to mourn?

For weeks he worked the daylight hours amongst his ripening grapes but as the evening drew in, he found he could not sit still and took to wandering along the beaches, allowing his mind to be sucked blank by the hypnotic swell and ebb of the lapping waves. He would return after midnight exhausted and fall into bed, curling and spooning himself around the curves of Dawn's surprisingly soft body. She was always there waiting for him deep in slumber. He felt the rhythm of her heart penetrate his own and lull him into dreamless sleep. He knew that he must be testing her with the silence of his grief but he could not find the words.

Then one evening Dawn came down to the beach and fell into step beside him. A half-moon shimmered over the waters and cast night shadows in their wake. He could feel a tension rippling through her stride and at last she spoke.

'Look Tom, something's happened and I've got to know now whether I can count on you or not.'

His stomach lurched at these potential unknown calls on his devotion. Could she count on him?

'I'll understand if this is something you don't think you can

424

deal with right now. But I have to.'

He understood then. 'You're going to have a baby.'

She turned to look at him, 'So, are you in or are you out Tom Bradshaw? No part-timers allowed.'

Now at last, eight years later, this was his coming home. The squaring of his circle. His heart pounded and not just from the piercing screech of the brakes. How would they know each other? His sister. After the initial calls there had been a hasty exchange of photos. But would he know her? All the long flights, the stopovers in Singapore, then Amsterdam, there had been a line of a song catching at his memory, playing over and over.

If you see my wild cow baby tell her hurry home because
I had no milk and butter since my wild cow been gone.

So long he had waited for that call. So long. Leaving his address with all the adoption services. The Social Services. The Care Homes.

The seat belt sign clicked off. Marty was already clambouring to be over him. The energy of youth even after thirty-five hours of travelling. Six weeks had been his journey of migration, to return with such unseemly speed made Tom feel the need of a day or two just to allow his thoughts to catch up and rearrange hemisphere. But this moment he had yearned for was waiting and he was filled with dread. He wanted to turn and say to Dawn, *I'm not ready.*

'We'll collect the luggage, Tom. You go ahead.' Dawn nodded urging him to the exit.

She was right. There should be no stalling.

A sea of faces thronged the Arrivals area. Someone called his name.

A young woman, tall, her hair in tight beaded braids. How

425

could he not know her? With those green eyes twinkling down at him.

'Ruth?'

Her eyes said 'yes'.

He held out his hand but even at that moment she was drawing him to her.

'Brother.' she said like a whisper.

Her arms enveloped about him and he held her too. Felt her warmth. Her reality. Held her tight.

'Sister.'

And in her he felt his mother smile on him.

THE FAIRY WIND

Turning thirty gave Nieve an increasing desire to venture beyond occasional jaunts to the Greek Islands or the Balearics. There had always been that restlessness in her. A Round The World Ticket was all the rage and women seemed to be going off on their own in droves. The trip gave her direction, she mused, where there had been so little in her life thus far. She had set out on a steady enough course, studying law at Trinity; but at the end of the first year, over in London for the summer break something in the vibrancy of what was called t*he melting pot* compelled her to stay.

She thought her mother would be distraught but she said, 'Whatever makes you happy.'

Her mammie was always surprising her. After granny died her mammie stopped attending Mass, explaining that she only went out of kindness. She could be stubborn, had set up her own small business even though the uncles deprecated the risk, insisting that with careful investments her future would be more secure and she would not need to work at all.

Her mother began in a small way, hand printed fabrics of her own design. It had been difficult to find custom at first but gradually mammie had been discovered and now interior designers from all across Europe and the US sought her out for their original furnishings. Nieve was glad her mother had found success and a kind of contentment amongst the swatches of colour, the inks and dyes and the painstaking application of the printing blocks.

Nieve envied her mother's natural creative flair and wished she'd inherited even an iota. Wished that she could find her passion. There was a job she enjoyed at a book shop but lost for being more immersed in reading the books than selling them. Then a stint as a barmaid, which didn't really suit her

427

temperament as she wasn't one to suffer fools gladly. However, it allowed her to attend acting classes in the day. She began to pick up work on fringe productions and joined a Theatre in Education company, touring primary schools playing a tree frog in a drama about protecting the environment. There were plenty of resting spells of course but through a friend she picked up occasional admin work with a Young Homeless charity; that gave her the idea that she might train to be a Youth Worker.

First, she would travel. What she couldn't decide was whether she was running away or finding herself. Either seemed possible.

In India, in Ajmer, Nieve shared a dormitory with a young architect, Juliano, who was languishing through a bout of amoebic dysentery. She brought him water, electrolytes and a bowl of packet soup and sat by his bed as he blinked awake from a groaning fitful sleep.

'Uno, Due, Tres, Quatro, Cinque—'

'Parla Italiano?' he asked in surprise.

'Only numbers.' She smiled.

'Useful. Where are you from?' He asked with a soft Edinburgh burr.

'Dublin by way of London.'

'A plastic Paddy?'

'No, I'm the real thing. And what about you? A genuine Guiseppe?'

'Juliano from Morningside. And yes, my parents, who are from Puglia, have a chippy, a very good one.'

'Battered haggis?'

'A speciality.'

Nieve helped him recover enough for them both to move on together to enjoy the colour and enchantment of the Pushkar Fair. By day the camel trading and the horse dealing in a sea of reds and yellow and orange. At night sitting out under the enormous white orb of the moon drinking Bang Lassi and listening to the shrieking peacock who strutted about the grounds of the backpackers' hotel.

After that they'd continued to fall into step with each other.

428

Trekking amongst the hill tribes in the Golden Triangle, sunning themselves in Koh Pi Pi and on down to Singapore. By the time they got to Bali she wondered if she might be in love with her darkly handsome Scots-Italian. It was something she would have time to think about when they got to Australia, where they would part, for a short while.

Nieve left Juliano to a waitering job in Cottesloe at his mother's cousin's restaurant.

'The Irish and the Italians, we get everywhere!' he'd declared.

Left him to his new found cousins, Luigi and Luca, and to a new found passion for surfing.

In truth, she hadn't wanted him with her anyway, this was too private a journey. Nieve splashed out on a hire car in Perth, packed up the tent and the small neat camping stove, which had served them so well since the ashram in Rishikesh, and headed towards Darinup. She knew it was a sentimental journey, what could she possibly hope to find now, twenty years later? Ghosts amongst the gums.

From there she would make the longer trek up north to the farm her father named Killpool Vale. The place where he had last been seen. Could someone simply disappear off the face of the earth? Her mother longed for something, even a body. Her father had been declared dead years past but without a body, without an end, how did you grieve?

The image of her father was vague in Nieve's memory. Sometimes she felt she merely constructed him from the old photos, mainly black and white, pasted into the camel hide albums her mother had bought in Egypt on the way home. But the impression of him loomed large, the great bear hugs, the snatches of stories and songs, the breadth of his smile. Had she ever measured the loss?

Her brother John was convinced that their father would come back. Even now, John had never accepted that he might truly be dead. In the lore which John created, their da had gone away with an aboriginal man called Ben on some kind of walkabout. John was a collector of stories. She supposed that once he finished his PhD, he would opt for a university career and teach anthropology, how else would he scrape along and fund his trips. Nieve thought with pleasure of seeing him again soon in The Solomon Islands, on the next leg. It was funny to reflect how as children they had squabbled over everything and now, she was closer to John than she would ever be to Patricia.

Patricia was the sensible one, about to graduate in medicine and planning to follow in Uncle Kevin's footsteps as a surgeon. It would be tough for a girl, everyone said so, but no one could doubt Patricia's determination and ambition. It seemed that Nieve and John were the *romantics*. What bound them, she supposed, was the shared history with their father. Patricia had been too young to remember him at all, too young to remember Australia. Patricia's life was all mammie and Terenure and Med School and The Mater Hospital. Whereas she and John shared memories which were like the invocations of a secret society.

The proverbial blink and she would have missed Darinup. Had it always been such a small, dusty little place? You couldn't call it a town. A garage, a high street of sorts running up from the highway, a pub, of course, a small caravan park, Nieve didn't remember that. And the railway track, with a station which was more like a bus stop; but along the line were great silos and sheds for the wheat.

In the charity shop, which she thought might once have been the old tea shop, Nieve selected a few old postcards and came across a battered copy of *The Giant of the Bush* which brought a flush of delight. For a moment she wondered if it were her own copy. But there was no large scrawl inside, *This book belongs to Nieve Ann Glendon.* Two elderly sun shriveled women sat by the till, one engrossed in her macramé.

'Hi.' Nieve ventured. 'Nice day.'

'Much as any other.' the one who was unoccupied conceded.

'Used to live here, when I was a child. On the Anderson

430

place.'

The macramé woman shook her head. 'No Anderson's left around here.'

Nieve felt her axis shift. This was news she hadn't anticipated and she found herself suddenly bereft. Anderson was the only surname which had stayed with her from her childhood bank of memories. Perhaps there was no one left who would remember the Glendon family at all.

'Oh.'

There was a lull for a moment.

'Mrs Davidson, she is now.'

'Though we all know who wears the trousers in that pair!' the other woman tittered.

Nieve calculated. 'Susan?'

The woman nodded.

'How would I get to their place?'

'Well dearie, you'll carry on the highway, then on the left-hand side you'll see Anderson Road, keep going and you'll not miss it.'

Nieve paused at the entrance to the station. Inverness. Was that what it was called? Underneath, G and S Davidson. She had a momentary panic. The drive into the station headed straight through vast and parched wheat stubble fields and only in the distance could a blur of trees be distinguished. As she rattled over the grille it felt like trespass. The stony weather beaten faces she had encountered through much of her trip into the Outback didn't offer much encouragement of a friendly welcome. These were not sentimental people. At best they would think her some kind of soft pommy idiot. She felt sure she would be curtly turned about and waved off. She hardly knew herself what she wanted.

As she swung into the main yard, she tried to get her bearings but nothing was familiar. For certain she could not see the old shack with the outside dunny that had been their home. There was a block-built bungalow which looked fairly new and might be its replacement. The huge sheds, she supposed, must have been there in their day. Before the main yard an entrance to a tree lined drive must lead to the main house. There was no one about to ask. Nieve stepped out of the car and looked about. It was coming up for two thirty in the afternoon and out of the air-conditioned car the heat hit you like a sledgehammer. She retrieved her newly purchased Akubra and wondered if she should knock at the new bungalow. As she dithered a woman came out of a shed wiping the grease from her hands.

'G'day?' The woman squinted in the glare.

Nieve recognised Susan immediately, seeing both the girl and the woman all at once. 'Susan.' she exclaimed.

Susan cocked her head, 'Sorry, do I know you?'

Nieve, flustered, garbled an explanation.

'Irish family? Well we had plenty of those. And Dutch and German and Poms. I might not have been about much back then. Anyway, you're welcome to take a look around if that's what you've come for.'

Ten minutes, Nieve thought, a ten-minute squizz about and then I'll skedaddle with my embarrassment tucked firmly under my hat.

'Thanks.' she almost lifted her hat in salute.

Susan turned to go back to the shed but halfway there she paused and called back, 'Little Niv?'

Nieve nodded.

'Little Niv – hey you saved my life once, didn't ya?'

'I'd hardly call it that, all I can remember is holding on to that pony for dear life.'

Susan chuckled. 'I'll be buggered. Where ya staying?'

Nieve shrugged. 'I noticed a motel back in Bodenham.'

'That shit hole, no way, be my guest, plenty of room. Geoff's down in Perth and my boys, Finlay and Little Jack, are over in Sydney on a blow in with Jenny and their cousin, so you've only got me I'm afraid.'

Nieve spent the afternoon exploring Inverness, meandering down to the creek and waterhole which still had the jetty, recently repaired, and a small rubber dinghy, for the boys she supposed. Later she helped Susan to feed the horses in the North Paddock along with a young Jillaroo, Stacy, who was taking a year out of college.

That evening sitting out by the barbie and under a starry night sky she and Susan knocked back the stubbies and shared their life stories, the tragedies, her da, young Jimmy and then the laughs over Susan's rebellious younger self.

'So, plans?' Susan asked.

Nieve sighed deeply, 'What plans? I envy you. You've found your right place, where you belong.'

Susan shook her head. 'All a matter of luck – if you can call it that. If Jimmy hadn't died ...'

'He might not have wanted the farm anyway.'

'Are you kidding! With dad breathing down his neck he wouldn't have had any other choice.'

'Your dad ..?'

'Moved to Mandurah on the coast after the twins were born; think he got the hint it was time to leave me and Geoff to it. Last couple of years he and Maddy got a taste for cruises, the Med, Italy, Greece and what have you, right now they're doing the Caribbean—old bugger might learn a thing or two.'

Susan eyed her up and down. 'You're welcome to stay on you know, couple of months, it'll pay better than the fruit picking. Didn't you want to ride the range or something like that when you were a kid?'

Nieve hesitated. 'Thanks ... I .... could I let you know, in a week or two?'

'Sure, no sweat.'

It was a long haul up to Meekatharra. On the map it looked like a hop, skip and a jump; Australia was like that, Nieve thought. Her mother had deputed her to sell the property. It was something which had somehow been overlooked in the years since Patrick Michael Glendon was officially declared dead; or perhaps postponed as being too final an

433

acknowledgment that there would be no miraculous return.

'I've got a note here.' The solicitor said. 'A bloke name of Hobbs, neighbours the property, wanted to buy the place twenty years back. Might be interested. If he's still out there himself. Got to warn you, state that farm will be in by now won't be worth much.' He handed her the keys.

Killpool Vale. Her father's hand painted sign was still faintly decipherable. Nieve's heart thumped as the car bounced over the grille and she found herself catapulted back in time to a point of fierce emotional connection. Her father had owned this farm. This was the last place where he had been seen. She felt the whole mythology of her father, of her childhood, coalesce as she crossed the threshold with an intensity which took her breath away.

Her hand shook as she worked the stiff lock open and then stepped into the dark musty interior of the house. The few sticks of furniture and linen had been carefully packed up, Tom she supposed and wondered yet again what had become of him. Despite his care the house hadn't entirely evaded the invasion of small creatures, spiders, beetles and insects. But pots and a whistling kettle hung over a stove which might still be functional. On a shelf she found a range of catalogues for farm equipment and the thin browning sheafs of an old newspaper, 1965. There was little that could be described as personal, Nieve supposed that such items must have been sent down to her mother in Perth. What had she expected to find? A world in aspic. The future they might have had. How different her life would have been; she conjectured. She felt the chill of uncertainty. That life could be so random. Its direction turning on a pin or determined by the toss of a coin. As she wandered the farm through the afternoon any residual notion Nieve harboured that she would miraculously find her father where the police and Tom had failed finally evaporated.

That night standing outside her tent Nieve marveled at the panoply of stars overhead in the clear unpolluted night sky.

Stars which she fancifully mused had guided her to this time and location. She had been lost, she realised, and, like her father, might never be found; but this was the starting point for a new beginning.

A breeze was coming down from the hills, something a little more than a breeze, warm and light as it danced around her, ruffling her hair and teasing the hem of her shirt. A Fairy Wind. Nieve shook her head, why had that thought come to her? She smiled at the whimsy. She supposed that once as a child she had believed in fairies and she remembered an old Irish saying her da was fond of quoting, *Any man can lose his hat in a fairy wind.* There was never any knowing what might happen. Or where a mad impulse might take you.

As the warm wind enveloped her Nieve acceded, 'I'll trust to my own luck.'

BEN DOWN AND THE HAPPY MAN

Wadjela think blackfellas look back to old time, think blackfellas live in old time, like. Don't know blackfella way. Ancestors, still nowadays, all one time. Not old time been destroy but nowadays. Too late, maybe, you know. A day come the blackfella have to fight stay alive. Not with burdan, kulata, not gun; but we learn wadjela lingo. That's what I tell our mob.

A year come, big referendum, say we got rights, like wadjela.

'Wadjela words, nothing change.' uncle say.

Binni, he angry fella. Maali gone. Angry I been working on army fences. He angry I make him go school. He don't sit with me at fire. Sit with other uncle, some brother-cuz. He on the grog. Some time I take grog too, Thinkin' 'bout Maali hurt my head, true.

Binni he gone walkabout. Not come back.

One time, red sun going down, we sitting round fire, wilburroos fightin' crazy in the sky. Thinking 'bout Maali, want to beat my head with rock, same muran. Blood 'stead cryin'.

Grog taste good then. Drinkin' grog, telling story 'bout Wan the Crow. Wan hid under big eagle wing, Mullian fly up up top of sky—then Wan leap out and fly up up stars, laughing.

No one been listenenin'.

We see Jeep come. Wadjela boys. Big noise through our camp. Auntie running this way and uncle running other way. Young ones shouting, 'fraid like. Wadjela boys laughing. I look one wadjela boy, know 'im - make big

436

laugh like kookaburra. Gun shot up in sky. Sky is red—
Wilburroos spill lotta blood. Then 'nother shot and 'nother.
Jeep coming for me now. 'Byamee.' I say. Drink up grog.
Hear big noise, laughin', crazy like galahs. I do not run.

Wadjela boy shoutin', 'Shiiiit old man!!'

'Fuck!! Fuck!!' them shout.

Big noise, brakes, tyres and Jeep it turn. Crack. Then red
sky turn black.

Maybe I rather be a big fat moon ...

That woman a stubborn woman *'... a big fat moon.'* Lift
my arm to her but she gone. Byamee angry. Fix me to
ground with his kerl.

'You keep still dad.'

Music playin'. Then it stop.

'Keep still, dad, you're all broke up.'

Binni? It Binni? Boy play didge. Clever fella. Cheeky fella.
Binni?

This a man. A kulamandi. Hair on lip.

'All broke up dad.'

'Binni?'

'I'm here dad. I heard what them boys done. You rest up.'

'Rest up.'

'That's what the doc says—says you're a miracle man, just
some broken bones.'

'Binni ...'

He playin'. Got guitar. Humming. Soft like.

'Got a band now dad.' He say. 'Going to make a record.
Got a deal.'

Then he sing. Sing 'bout our mob. His voice high, it sweet
like honey. About our mob, we been this country thousand
thousand year. We old time and time comin', all one. Telling
stories. One 'bout the emu.

'Where you get em story?' ask him.

'You dad.'

437

Ben Down not my born name, you know. My ngangk say I come out big smile, she call me, Nullandi. Name mean, *Happy Man!* Can't keep that name, you know.

Maybe one day, find 'nother.

ACKNOWLEDGMENTS

There are so many people I would wish to thank on my long journey writing this novel. To all those who have contributed information, stories, feedback or advice, you have my gratitude.

My parents of course, whose own story set this one in motion. I take no credit for the poem *This Red Hot Sand,* that was penned by my late father, Michael, during his time in the outback and expresses something of his complex relationship with the land. I thank my mother, Nora, for sharing memories both joyous and painful. All the colour I owe to them.

My siblings too have played their part. I thank my sister Patricia for her unwavering support and Regina, whose assistance to revise the Ben Down chapters has been invaluable, any errors are my own. My brother Stevie set it all in motion by suggesting that I write a biography of our father—instead of which I chose the easier option of writing this fiction, I think dad might approve as I know how much he always relished a story and the telling of it.

Friends I am blessed with for their encouragement and patience. My go to critic for all my writing is Carole Thomson. Ellen Fox, I thank for her unfailing faith in me. Celeste Joy Engel for the enthusiasm of her response. Other readers at various stages included, Olly James, Ankie Zaat-Visser, my cousin Barbara Partridge, Patricia Cunningham and the members of The South Manchester Writers. I thank Maggie Mackay for all the wonderful dinners she cooked at the house in Loretello whilst I stared at blank pages and tapped out a few words.

My research was extensive; journeys across Australia, including the memorable train ride across the Nullarbor

Plain; visits to Bindoon Boys Town and Fairbridge Pinjarra, kind assistance at the Australian National Maritime Museum in Sydney, and lots of other trips down memory lane.

Some of the literature I read was vital, *Tales From Arnhem Land* by Ann E. Wells; *Aboriginal Myths, Legends & Fables* A.W.Reed: *Rabbit Proof Fence* by Doris Pilkington; *A Beginner's Guide to Australian Aboriginal Words,* by R. Lewis; *A Short History of Australia* by Manning Clark; *Karlwin: A story from Mt Walker* by W. Schmidt; *Orphans of the Empire: The Shocking Story of Child Migration to Australia,* by Alan Gill; *Fairbridge Kid* by John Lane; the writings of Thomas Keneally, Bill Bryson's *Down Under; * Bruce Chatwin's *Songlines; Not On Your Nelly* by Lynne Tinley; *Wild Australia* by Graham, Robert and Allan Edgar; *Giant of the Bush* by John Kiddell; to name a few.

Lastly, I would like to make another dedication:
To the memory of Binni Dirombirong, a life too short.

Lightning Source UK Ltd.
Milton Keynes UK
UKHW010633110521
383527UK00001B/230